ALL THE KING'S MEN

BOUND GUARDIAN ANGEL

Bound Guardian Angel©

All the King's Men, book seven

Published by Phoenix Press

Copyright 2016 Donya Lynne

Cover by Reese Dante - www.reesedante.com

ISBN: 978-1-938991-17-2

ACKNOWLEDGEMENTS

As with every book I've written, this one took a large team to pull off. I want to thank all my wonderful beta readers for your fabulous feedback, and I want to thank Sue and Laura for your invaluable suggestions. You're both more valuable than I can convey. Thank you to Ariel for making my words looks as good as they read, and thank you to Reese for packaging them in such sexy covers.

I want to send a special thanks to Wendi. It was your contribution to this story that created a new, endearing character named Aiden, or little Aidy as her twin brother calls her. I hope she lives up to your expectations and hopes, and I hope you find her as wonderful as I do. She will hold a special place in All the King's Men for as long as the series endures.

Books by Donya Lynne

All the King's Men Series

Rise of the Fallen
Heart of the Warrior
Micah's Calling
Rebel Obsession
Return of the Assassin
All the King's Men - The Beginning

Strong Karma Trilogy

Good Karma
Coming Back to You
Full Circle

Hope Falls Series

Finding Lacey Moon

Stand-Alone M/M Titles

Winter's Fire

Collections and Anthologies

All the King's Men Vol. 1 (books 1-3)
All the King's Men Vol. 2 (books 4-6)
Strong Karma Trilogy Boxed Set
Whispered Beginnings - A Romance Sampler

ALL THE KING'S MEN
BOUND GUARDIAN ANGEL

DONYA LYNNE

"Many individuals have, like uncut diamonds, shining qualities beneath a rough exterior."
-Juvenal

CHAPTER 1

"WAKE UP, FREAK. TIME TO GO."

Trace's head shot up off his outstretched arms at the sound of the guard's gruff voice and the clang of metal on metal. He was tucked in the corner of his cell, on the floor, his forearms stretched over his bent knees. Had he actually fallen asleep?

He wiped his gritty palms down his face and flexed his back, making his spine pop, then squinted and used his hand to shield his eyes against the flashlight the guard aimed at him. "Huh?"

"I said it's time to go. Get up." The guard tossed Trace's clothes at him the way someone might toss a steak toward a starving lion at the zoo. Very carefully and at a distance, making it a point to keep all body parts and appendages out of the cage. "Get dressed. We leave in fifteen minutes." The guard turned off his flashlight, casting Trace into shadow again, then flicked him a wary sideways glance before hurrying off like he couldn't get away fast enough.

A relieved sigh left Trace's lips as he leaned the back of his head against the wall and stared into the dimly lit corridor outside his cell. He'd made it. He'd survived two weeks inside King Bain's dungeon.

His gaze dropped to the well-used razor in his left hand. When Cordray had given him the razor a week ago, it had been shiny and new. Now the blade was dull and dotted with dry blood. His blood. Rows of angry, unhealed cuts lined both arms, as well as his ankles.

But his self-mutilation had worked. He hadn't turned. He hadn't lost control of his power. Yes, he was frayed around the edges. Yes, he'd flirted with sanity's boundaries a time or two. Yes, it felt like ants crawled under his skin and snakes slithered over his body, but he was still a vampire. Still himself. Not some mutant ready to destroy Chicago and everyone he loved.

Cordray's generosity had saved him.

Blech.

Just the thought that Cordray had done something nice to help him left a bad taste in his mouth and made him feel like a traitor.

He didn't want to be grateful to that bitch. He wanted to hate her. She scared him, which was a sentiment he would share with no one, but a truth he couldn't hide from himself. She saw things he didn't want anyone to see. Not even Micah could see into his well-protected mind, but, somehow, Cordray was able to unlock his thoughts. That alone made her terrifying. Because if she could worm her way into his thoughts, what else was she capable of?

Trace had worked hard all his life to shield himself from the pain others could wreak on him. He wasn't talking about physical pain, because, yeah, he dug that shit. He was referring to the mental and emotional pain someone could inflict by discovering his secrets. Truths that shamed him and were best kept private for the agony they could create in the wrong hands.

A small part of him wanted Cordray's hands to be right in so many ways. He wanted to trust her, because as much as he despised her, she was a damn fine piece of female who smelled as good as she looked, but he simply couldn't allow himself to believe she was anything but trouble, which meant avoiding her was a top priority.

Easier said than done, considering she was to be his lord and keeper for the next three months. As long as he could keep his inner beast in check and not lose his Cracker Jacks around her, he stood a chance of making it through his community service without doing her bodily harm. But damn, she'd better not push him. He couldn't make any promises that he wouldn't maim her if she flapped her yap at him the way she usually did.

Pushing forward, his joints crackled as he grabbed his clothes off the soiled floor and unfolded himself into a standing position. His muscles were as taut as an army grunt's bunk and protested angrily as he maneuvered in the tight space. The strain to remain vigilant over his power for two weeks had taken a heavy toll on his body. It hurt just to move.

He readily abandoned the scratchy, filthy prison clothes he'd been forced to wear, discarding them on the archaic cot he'd used as a bed, and pulled on his cargo pants and long-sleeved Henley.

He would pull his own teeth for a shower, not to mention a good beating at Micah's hand. That would put an end to the feverish trembles shuddering through his body like barely contained lightning bolts.

Pacing, he brushed his palms up and down his arms to expel the pent-up energy making his insides feel like a nuclear bomb on the verge of exploding. He was beyond ready to get the fuck out of there.

A few minutes later, the guard returned with three of his buddies and a pair of cuffs big enough to restrain an elephant. Was he *that* scary?

"Really, fellas, this is a bit overkill isn't it?" he said as they manacled him.

The irons were as heavy as they looked, but the strain helped relieve some of the bite from his hovering-just-beneath-the-surface power.

"We're not taking any chances," one of the guards said as they led him through the corridor.

"We've heard what you're capable of," said another.

What he was capable of was certain death. Abrupt, violent, messy, and painful death. He could crush someone's heart with a simple flick of his hand. He could break every bone and rupture every organ inside a person's body simply by making a fist and thinking them dead. He'd done it before. In fact, he'd done it just a couple of weeks ago to that traitor in Bishop's Frankenstein lab in Arizona, where he'd found his father strapped to a lab table with tubes and needles sticking out of his arms, having God knew what done to him.

He'd rescued his father and helped rescue Princess Miriam, earning a shorter prison sentence for his heroics, but he could do nothing to save his own soul. He was still the freak of nature he'd always been. Still as deadly. Still an aberration others were more inclined to run from than embrace.

The guards were right to be cautious. Even wearing the shackles, he could simply focus his mind and snap their necks with a twitch of his index finger. They needn't worry, though. He had no intention of killing anyone tonight. Not unless he unexpectedly transformed into a mutant. Not even these Chewbacca-sized manacles could hold him if that happened. As a mutant, he would be able to break them in half like they were nothing but dry kindling.

At one time, he'd feared turning into a mutant was his inevitable destiny. His power had grown steadily for decades, only forced into submission by pain and humiliation, which was why he'd taken to the life of a submissive.

But a couple of decades ago, he realized he was needing harder and harder punishment as the years wore on. Like bacteria that no longer responded to antibiotics and raged out of control, the monster that resided inside Trace had grown resistant to the beatings and humiliation from his former Doms. Beatings that had once pushed his power into submission for at least two weeks had lost their effect, forcing him to seek punishment more often, eventually to the tune of once every few days.

Now, only one Dom would do. Micah. And he'd found Micah not a moment too soon, given how dire his situation had become in recent years. Micah's hard-handed domination had been Trace's last resort to prolong his life to its very limit before certain mutancy took him.

But now the situation had grown more complicated. Not only had Trace discovered his father was still alive, but Brak was, too. His twin — who had been created to provide balance to his power — lived. Trace was saved. Between Micah and Brak, they would be able to keep his power in check.

As long as he could *find* Brak. Because while he'd rescued his father, he still had no idea where to find his brother. All he knew was that Brak had been there, in his cell. There had been no mistaking Brak's wraithlike essence inside his body, calming him, healing him, doing what Brak had been born to do. Doing what Mother had given him the power to do before they'd even been born.

A shiver of guilt rippled through him as thoughts of his mother touched his mind. His father and Brak were still alive, and he had found his salvation, but his mother was still dead, and it was his fault. All his fault.

He hung his head and trudged up a flight of stone steps as the guards guided him to his freedom. A freedom coated with fresh guilt over what had happened so long ago. Guilt over the death and sorrow he'd brought to his family.

He scoffed silently to himself. He wasn't free. He was still imprisoned by what he'd done, and he always would be. Not even Brak could soothe this torment. If anything, knowing Brak and his father were alive worsened his anguish, because now he had to face the past. He could no longer hide from it. The moment he saw them again, the truth of his actions would detonate inside his mind. God help him and anyone near when that happened, because he had no idea how bad the mental rupture and resulting fallout would be.

Outside, Trace took his first breath of non-stagnant air in over two weeks. God, it smelled good. Fresh. Not like stale sweat and bodily waste.

The guards shoved him into the back of a conversion van outfitted with bars and uncomfortable metal benches on both sides. One of the guards hooked his chains to the floor. Then the doors slammed shut. A few seconds later, the van jerked forward and bounced over what felt like a pothole before pulling out onto smooth pavement.

It was a short drive to the processing and pickup location, which didn't give him much time to dwell on what would happen when he saw his father and brother again. Besides, at the moment, the one thing dominating his thoughts was how he needed Micah to dominate him. Once Micah had beaten his power into submission, there would be more room inside his head to sort out his family issues.

Less than five minutes later, the van slowed, turned off the road, and then came to a stop. The doors opened, he was unhooked, and then guided into a small, white-brick building that looked more like a weigh station than a military outpost for King Bain. Then again, maintaining a low profile was crucial for vampires to remain hidden among humans. A sign declaring the building as an outpost for King Bain would raise eyebrows.

Inside, the guards removed his shackles and secured him inside yet another cell. At least this one had a chair, a small bed that folded away from the wall, and an actual toilet. Five-star accommodations compared to where he'd spent the last fifteen days.

The cell door clanked shut behind him, and all four guards seemed to breathe a collective sigh of relief as they headed away.

"Finally," one said with an air of satisfaction.

"Yeah, man. I'm glad to be rid of that one," said another. "He gave me the willies."

"What a freak," said another.

Freak.

The word struck something deep inside Trace's soul, and he flinched as if he'd been snapped with a wet towel.

The guards' laughter rang out, taunting him, hitting him like a fist.

A painful image launched unbidden from deep within his memory. Flashes of smoke and fire flickered between images of being hit, kicked, punched, and shoved face-first into the dirt.

"No . . . stop." His strangled voice locked inside his throat as he staggered backward, throwing his arms out in front of him as if he could push the memories away. His heel hitched against the toe of his other boot, and he fell, landing hard on his ass. Driving his heels into the floor, he pushed away from the cell door until he hit the wall.

Freak!

The insult from his childhood snapped inside his head as flashes of fists and boots swung toward him.

"No . . . please. Don't." He grimaced and shielded his head with his arms, cowering, tucking his head between his knees and curling into a ball inside the cell.

Look at the little freak! He's scared. Laughter rang through his mind.

He winced and tried to block out the memories of his childhood nemesis, Mason, and his pack of followers as they teased and taunted him. He'd only been twelve years old at the time, his hair as long as Brak's, hanging in dirty strands around his face. Back then, dirt had been a way of life for a young boy who played in the woods and helped his mother dig up roots and herbs for her tinctures. But constantly being covered in dirt hadn't made him popular with the other kids in the small town.

The painful memory sped up, playing out like a fast-forwarded movie as he saw Mason and his friends circle him, shouting, laughing, throwing dirt and pebbles at him. A pebble hit him in the cheek, and Trace flinched, slapping his palm over the side of his face.

Tears squeezed out around his eyelashes. He was that young boy again. The discarded little boy all the other children made fun of, bullied, and ignored.

"No." He ducked and covered his head with his arms again as Mason began slapping him in his memory.

It felt so real, as if he were really being hit, really being kicked.

The memory surged forward, and Trace was on his back, blood gushing from his nose from where Mason had hit him. The others — including Beth, the little strawberry blonde he'd had a crush on — stood around him, laughing. Laughing and pointing. Calling him names. *Lumpish toad. Flogging cully. Freak. Sissy. Crybaby.* The insults echoed in his ears, repeating over and over like he was in a cave where sound carried on forever.

Then Mason knelt and grabbed a rock from Trace's collection. Trace never left home without the small leather pouch his father had made for him. He kept all the rocks he'd collected inside it. He even took the pouch to school. He loved those rocks, collected from his family's nomadic travels. But his favorite was the one he'd found on the shore of the gurgling brook near his home. The one in Mason's hand now. It was white quartz flecked with black obsidian.

Trace rolled and shot forward, on his hands and knees, and reached for the rock. "Give it back!"

Mason jerked it away as he darted toward the pond, laughing.

Pressure mounted inside Trace's body. His muscles tightened. His right hand twitched. Pain lanced his skull, making him wince even as his senses honed to razor sharpness. He could hear the ants skittering across the ground, taste his own humiliation, smell the contempt of his persecutors, and feel the invisible droplets of humidity in the air as they landed on his skin. If not for the tears clouding his vision, the grains of earth at his feet would have seemed like boulders.

Must leave. Must get away.

Something bad was about to happen. He didn't know how he knew, but he did.

"Give it back, Mason!" He unfolded himself and crouched, scurrying to gather the rest of his beloved rocks, so sparkly and beautiful. They were all he had that belonged solely to him. Collected by his own two hands.

As he tried shoving them into the leather pouch, his right hand shook so violently that half the small rocks dropped back onto the ground.

"Where are you going, *Tracy?*" One of Mason's friends shoved him from behind.

He flew face-first into the dirt, scuffing his cheek on a patch of gravel. The scent of his own blood lit inside his nostrils like metallic vapors.

"Let me go." His voice whispered out of him.

"What?"

"S-stop. I need my mother." Mother would know what was happening to him. She could stop this terrifying strangeness.

His whole body trembled, the pressure building, tightening his insides like he was being wound up like a top, spun tighter and tighter.

"Look at the freak!" Mason roared with laughter, pointing at him. *"He needs his mommy!"* He kicked dirt and rocks toward him. "Scrawny little piggy with your silly rocks! Why do you even collect these stupid things?" He eyed the white and black stone in his hand.

"Just give it back!" Trace tried to sit up but couldn't. Whatever was going on inside his body wouldn't let him.

The howls and whoops of the others echoed in his ears, suddenly sounding far away, like he was in a cave.

He clawed, trying to find purchase on anything that would give him leverage to push himself up.

Mason turned the lump of quartz over and over in his hands, sneering. "I think I'll keep this," he said with pompous propriety.

Rage rocketed through Trace's muscles. No! That was *his* rock. *His* prize. He would *protect* it. Mason would *never* take what belonged to him!

Righteous fury ballooned within Trace's soul.

"Better yet . . ." Mason glanced over his shoulder toward the pond. He laughed, and the sound was like acid to Trace's ears.

What happened next played out in slow motion, stretching

through time, even though it only took seconds. Mason fisted the piece of quartz, cocked his arm, and threw the rock as hard as he could toward the center of the pond.

Trace's heart froze. His gaze zoomed in on his prized treasure as it hurtled toward the overcast sky then down, down, down . . .

The moment it broke the water's surface, Trace's right arm shot out almost of its own free will, his fingers splayed.

"NOOOO!"

All the coiled energy inside him blasted from his hand.

The earth tremored as a low boom sounded. The trees shuddered. An instant later, each of the children catapulted away from him as if they'd been snapped back by a puppeteer's string.

Seconds ticked by in the aftermath, but all Trace could do was stare at his hand, his heart racing, his blood roaring in his ears. How had he done that? What sorcery had he inherited from his mother to have such power? Was this the darkness she'd spoken of and warned him about so many times? He'd felt its presence before and often toyed with making small objects move, even though he'd been told not to. But he'd never felt such a powerful force rise inside him with such intensity.

It terrified him.

Six pairs of eyes turned toward him in horrified awe.

They were no longer laughing, too frightened to do anything but gawk.

They were right. He *was* a freak.

"Demon!" Mason's eyes were wide with fear. He scurried to his feet. "You're a demon!" His legs cranked so fast as he tried to flee that his feet went out from under him. He fell, caught himself on his arms, pushed off the ground, and sprinted away as the others did the same, crying and screaming in terror.

Inside his cell, Trace's eyes flew open as the memory came to an abrupt end. He was curled in a fetal position on the floor, his body a shivering heap, his arms hugging his torso as if that could stop the teeth-chattering chills drawing his muscles into tight, spasming masses simply by holding himself.

He'd survived two weeks in King Bain's dungeon without going mutant, yet after five minutes of flashing back to the first time he'd lost control of his power — and the ultimate price his mother had paid for his lack of discipline — he was one breath away from tipping the scales. His vision was sharp enough to see the feathery, microscopic cracks in the ceiling, his hearing keen enough to hear the scratch of a pen on paper out at the desk he'd passed on his way back to his cell. Shit was going critical, and with his voice locking up inside his throat, he could do nothing but wince and curl more tightly into himself, praying Micah would get there soon and bring him back from the brink before he lost control altogether and lost his soul to the beast.

CHAPTER 2

CORDRAY STEPPED OUT OF THE BAR. There went thirty minutes of her life she would never get back. All that mind sweeping, and all she had to show for it was a snippet of thought about an underground fight club named Grudge Match. That and a bad taste in her mouth from watered-down beer.

She checked the time on her black MTM Special Ops Predator watch. Maybe the nine-hundred-dollar watch was a bit overkill, because, really, when was she ever going to chase a bounty six hundred feet underwater? But the watch was boss-ass matte black, durable, cool as shit, and each was individually numbered and shipped in its own watertight tactical case. So top that, Rolex. Anyone who thought she was being a diva over her choice of timepiece could suck it. She liked what she liked, and while she wouldn't be wearing her Predator to any cocktail parties, it made her feel extra badass in the field when she was tracking a bounty, a suspicious dreck, or a wayward vampire who'd jumped to the wrong side of Bain's law.

Tonight, she was on the hunt for information that would help her unravel the truth behind Bishop's operation. Someone had to bring that maniacal asshole down and put a stop to his war-provoking lab experiments on vampires. And since Premier Royce seemed too preoccupied with staring at his own reflection, masturbating to the sound of his own voice, or whatever else he did to turn a blind eye to the destruction a member of his own race was causing, it looked like stopping Bishop was up to her. After all, there was only so much her half-brother, King Bain, could do without risking all-out war.

In the last several months, she and the members of AKM had uncovered a shit storm of dreck activity, and it all pointed back to Bishop. Including this bit of intel about Grudge Match.

From what she'd picked up from the thoughts of the pair of drecks making out in one of the bar's back booths, Grudge Match was a secret fight club where vampires and drecks alike beat the shit out of each other for fun. Not only did this pose a possible peace treaty violation, but it also gave any drecks working for Bishop a prime opportunity to scout and kidnap vampires he could use in his fucked-up experiments.

If only she had more time. This lead looked promising, but duty called. She was due to meet Micah in twenty minutes to sign Trace over to him upon his release, which meant if she didn't leave right now, she would be late. Hell, even if she left this very second, she'd probably be late. She still had to hoof it back to her Range Rover.

Trace, otherwise known as the thorn in her side, was supposed to be released into her custody, but he and Micah apparently needed to flog each other's logs or some shit to get Trace's beast under control before she could put him to work at the ranch, so she'd agreed to sign him over to Micah for twenty-four hours upon his release. Putting a lit fuse like Trace around her kids wasn't going to happen, so she had no problem letting Micah do whatever the hell it was Micah did to tame Trace's itchy hand first, and then she would take him to the ranch when he was nice and docile. Or as docile as a raging, irritatingly virile male like Trace could be.

She took a shaky breath at the thought of being near him. There was just something about Trace that flicked her Bic. All the more reason to make Trace's life as miserable as she could for the next three months so he stayed away from her. She didn't need him touching her and setting off any more waves of physical sensation inside her body. She enjoyed her lack of feeling very much, thank you. As long as Trace and his wicked hand gave her a wide berth for the next three months, nobody would get hurt. He'd already awakened too many of her memories as it was. She didn't want to remember any more.

The wind picked up on her way back to the Range Rover, and a low rumble of thunder sounded in the distance. Looked like the storms were arriving a few hours earlier than expected. Good thing she hadn't listened to the weather forecasters, otherwise she would have ridden her Ducati into the city. And wouldn't that have just put the shit-flavored icing on her roadkill cake if she'd been caught in the storm on her way back?

For the love of God, how hard was it for meteorologists to use all that science at their fingertips to come up with an accurate—

Movement caught her eye out of her peripheral vision, cutting her thoughts off cold.

She stopped abruptly and frowned as her gaze trained upward, toward the Sentinel apartment building and the shadowy figure rappelling down the building's east face. What the hell?

She cocked her head in disbelief as the hooded, black-clad figure lowered halfway down the building then stopped. A moment later, a hand pressed against the glass. She heard a brief, high-pitched sound — kind of like a dog whistle — and a moment later the pane of glass shattered and Mr. Mysterious vanished inside.

At least she assumed the burglar was a Mr. and not a Mrs. The way the figure moved was much too masculine to be female.

But my, my, my, what fun toys he had.

The first drops of rain splattered the sidewalk. One splashed on her nose.

She really needed to go, but her curiosity was piqued. She couldn't just leave like she'd never seen the guy. She had to know what he was up to.

Cursing under her breath, she glanced around to make sure no one was watching then projected herself up to the broken window and into the dark apartment.

She rematerialized inside the living room. A quick inhale confirmed her earlier assumption. The thief was a male. A vampire male, but obviously not a full-blood. A full-blood wouldn't have used rappelling gear to gain access to the apartment. He would have just poofed there the way she just did, which told Cordray she was dealing with a mixed-blood who couldn't dematerialize. Good to know. It meant his exit options were limited.

She glanced around and frowned as she homed in on his trail, which led down a hall to the left.

Wait a minute. There was something familiar about this place. She'd seen it before. Inside Trace's mind.

She sucked in her breath. Holy shit on a plate. This was Micah's apartment. Not that she gave two shits about what happened to that ball sac's digs, but anyone who knew Micah knew not to mess with him. He was AKM's deadliest enforcer with a nasty reputation to match, and he had powerful friends.

Trace came to mind. He could turn a perfectly good body into ground meat with a snap of his fingers.

Which begged the question, why would this guy be fucking around with Micah's shit? Micah's reputation preceded him even in civilian circles, so the burglar had to know how hot the fire would get once Micah learned his apartment had been broken into.

From the high-end rappelling equipment, as well as the fancy toy that shattered the window, the thief was sophisticated. He wasn't the type of cat burglar who didn't do his research. He knew who he was hitting, and he knew him well. And as a vampire himself, he knew the consequences of his actions, both according to Bain's law, as well as Micah's, because Micah tended to operate in the grey area between what was legal and what wasn't. And sure as bears shit in the woods, Micah would go after this guy with everything he had once he found out what had happened.

Then again, maybe that was the allure. Maybe this guy was an adrenaline junkie, and what greater rush than to rob a live wire like Micah and evade him all while breaking royal law?

Cordray knew a thing or two about adrenaline rushes. Without the ability to feel physical sensation, such states of excitement were just about the only pleasurable experiences she enjoyed, which was probably why she got off on the thrill of the chase as much as she did. There was nothing like a shot of biological get-up-and-go to tingle her insides when, on the outside, she felt nothing.

Except with Trace.

For the first time in eight centuries, she had been able to feel again, and it was because of Trace. He'd awakened something she thought she'd lost forever. Physical sensation. And every time he was near her, he awakened it even more.

Quiet rustling from the room down the hall drew Cordray's attention. Dismissing thoughts of Trace and what he could do to her sense of touch, she slinked silently toward what she assumed was the bedroom, hand on her sidearm, eyes sharp in the darkness.

She peered around the doorframe. Yep. Bedroom. Mr. Tall, Dark, and Mysterious was in the closet, rummaging through God knew what. But he was being quiet about it, as if he knew at any moment someone could show up and catch him.

Slipping into the dark room, she watched the beam from his flashlight bob back and forth then go still as if he'd set it on the floor. Tiptoeing closer, she peeked into the closet. He was kneeling in the back corner, facing away from her, slowly spinning the dial on a small, black safe nestled against the wall. He'd pressed an elaborate stethoscope to the metal beside the lock. The scope was hooked up to what looked like a portable computer the size of a small tablet. Numbers flashed on the screen, filling in as he spun the dial left and right.

When the final number filled the third space, he entered the combination, releasing the lock a moment later. After quickly pocketing his equipment, he pulled the door open to extract an intricately carved wooden box. His hood was still up, so she couldn't get a look at his face as he set the box on the floor, pulled out a slim tool with a prong on one end, and inserted the prong into the keyhole. She heard a click. A second later, he flipped open the lid.

Rifling efficiently through the contents, he removed a purple, velvet pouch, loosened the drawstring, reached his black-gloved hand inside, and pulled out a gold artifact that looked like an Egyptian ankh. A ruby filled the space at the top where a loop normally would have been.

Cordray unholstered her gun and raised it, the business end aimed toward his head.

"Whatcha got there?" she said, stepping into the open.

The thief spun around. Under his hood, he wore a skeleton mask that appeared custom made to deliver fear into the hearts of the beholder. The skull face was menacing and marked with scars, and instead of human canines, the mask had fangs. Nice touch for a vampire.

Cordray admired this guy's style. The mask was like the Grim Reaper combined with Charon from Medusa's underworld. Scary as shit and more badass than her watch.

As enviable as his mask was, though, it was his almond-shaped, come-hither eyes that made the most striking impression. They were surrounded by greasepaint, which made his slate irises pop. Not quite gray, not quite blue. Dusky and vivid.

She took a step toward him. "Who are y — "

He thrust his open hand toward her, and the high-pitched shrill of his glass breaker pierced her eardrums. She smacked her free hand over her ear a second before a blast of energy pulsed from the tiny contraption, flinging her back against the solid bedframe hard enough to knock her gun from her hand. She tumbled over herself and slammed onto the floor beside the bed.

Before she could recover, he dashed past her, fleeing down the hall toward the living room.

Motherfucker! Cordray bounced up, retrieved her gun, and gave chase, her ears ringing, her arm heavy as if she'd pulled something. Good thing she couldn't feel pain or this might have been a short chase.

There was nowhere to go in the living room but out the window, and surely this guy wouldn't take that route.

Think again.

He launched himself out the window like he was swan diving off the high platform at the Summer Olympics.

Seriously?

Cordray rushed to the gaping, rectangular hole in the glass in time to see him pull a rip cord at his left shoulder as if he were opening a parachute. But instead of a chute, gossamer wings unfolded like a miniature hang glider from a slim pack on his back, and his outfit turned into a wingsuit.

Damn, this guy was good.

Not to be outdone, Cordray darted back into the living room then sprinted toward the window and leaped into the frenzied wind a split second before dematerializing.

This fucker wasn't getting away that easily. She still had a few tricks up her sleeve.

She rematerialized on his back, landing ingloriously, pitching them into gravity's grip as the burglar fought to regain control of his descent.

"Get off me, bitch!" He tried to reach around and dislodge her, but she ducked and pulled away. "You'll kill us both!"

"Doubtful, mixed-blood!" From the strong, vibrant scent gushing out of him, her earlier assessment that this guy was a major adrenaline junkie was right on target. "Who are you? Why were you in Micah Black's apartment? What's with the ankh?" She had to shout to be heard over the wind rushing past them as they shot between buildings on a steady, haphazard descent toward the ground.

Raindrops pelted her face like tiny bullets, stinging her eyes, making it hard for her to see, but she didn't miss the way he looked over his shoulder at her, or the way the outer corners of his eyes lifted as if he were grinning behind that evil-looking skull mask. And not just grinning, but smiling as if he were having the time of his life.

Then he winked at her. Actually winked.

And disappeared.

Motherfucker!

She pitched into a freefall and barely managed to dematerialize before slamming headfirst into the concrete.

Okay, so maybe the bastard could dematerialize. Maybe he was a full-blood, after all. So much for making assumptions.

Either way, this cocksucker was seriously starting to piss her off.

Skimming just above the sidewalk, she gathered her bearings then rose upward until she detected his vapor trail.

Whoever this guy was, he had his shit together. He'd known who he was hitting, and he'd had a plan for both entry and egress. What else could she expect before this cat-and-mouse game was over?

She didn't have to wait long for an answer as she zipped after him into a dead-end alley and rematerialized . . . only to have a titanium-tipped arrow rip past her, slicing through her jacket. She didn't feel the metal cut into her arm, but she heard the fabric rip and smelled the scent of her blood. Shit. Another article of clothing to mend and another wound to add to her dossier.

Who did this guy think he was? A superhero? The Green Arrow? Were the next words out of his mouth going to be something along the lines of how she'd failed this city?

Well, fuck that shit. If he wanted to play DC Comics' next superhero, she would gladly play his kryptonite.

Another arrow whizzed toward her. She dodged, slapping it away as she beat feet toward him. This asshole was going down.

He nocked another arrow, but she was already on him. Before he could fire, she launched her shoulder into his chest, sending them both to the wet pavement as the rain pounded down harder.

They grappled, fabric tore—hers or his she couldn't tell—and a gloved fist smashed into her lip. She tasted blood, but at least she didn't feel the pain, which allowed her to return the favor, plowing her fist into the side of his face, cracking the cheek of his form-fitted mask.

They rolled, and Cordray briefly gained the upper hand, shoving Skeletor to his back and popping him twice more in the jaw before he fisted her jacket and tossed her over his head.

Her teeth rattled as she slammed into the ground.

"Oomph!" Her vision winked out and back in.

She didn't need to experience physical pain to know when her body would be black-and-blue and look like it had been in a fight with a saliva-flinging rodeo bull.

Briefly disoriented, she blinked through flashing lights.

Her momentary lapse of lucidity gave Skeletor the opportunity he needed. He spun on his heel and leaped onto his waiting crotch rocket. The engine ignited with an angry whine.

"Until next time, sweetheart," he called over his shoulder as she wobbled to a crouch and fought her blurry vision to try and figure out which of the three guys she was looking at had just spoken to her.

Which meant she had a concussion.

Lucky for her she was a vampire and didn't need to worry about the complications head injuries caused humans. Her tissues were already mending themselves back into pristine condition even as she felt the deli sandwich she'd grabbed a couple of hours earlier threaten an encore.

Unfortunately, she wouldn't heal fast enough to catch Skeletor.

But she did catch the shit-eating wink he gave her, as well as his throaty, self-satisfied laugh before he gunned the accelerator. Rubber burned as the fat rear tire spun, sending up white-grey smoke and gravel as the whine of the engine reverberated off the damp brick walls. Then the tire caught the pavement, and he rocketed out of the alley, leaving her in an angry daze.

The buzz of the motorcycle's engine quickly faded, and then the skies opened up in earnest, adding insult to injury. Large, fat drops poured down, soaking her within seconds, plastering any hair not in braids to her cheeks and forehead.

Could tonight get any worse? She hadn't been able to follow up on Grudge Match. She'd been bested by a goddamned cat burglar. She was caught in a monsoon. And now she was late to meet that jizz stain, Micah, and his peckerwood sidekick, Trace.

She checked her watch, thankful for that whole waterproofing feature now that God had scooped up an ocean in a supersized cup and was dumping every last drop of it directly on her.

Shit! Had a whole twenty minutes passed since she'd spied Skeletor scaling the outside of the Sentinel? They say time flies when you're having fun but this was ridiculous. And there was nothing fun about being left sitting in an alley, in a growing puddle of piss-scented water, nursing a concussion, with the taste of blood in her mouth and a fat lip.

Pushing to her feet and wobbling unsteadily for a few seconds, she tried to gather her bearings. Where exactly was she? Better yet, where was her Range Rover? She'd parked it on the side of the road near the Sentinel, but for all her effort, she couldn't cut through the brain fog to calculate what direction that was, given the little stars and birdies still fluttering around her head. What she did know was that she needed to hurry and get to the pickup location before Micah did something to get on her last nerve, such as move Trace without her permission.

Trace was hers for three months. He didn't even get to take a shit without her saying it was okay. But she knew Micah thought Trace belonged to him. And being that Micah was, well . . . Micah . . . and that he was prone to doing whatever the hell he wanted whenever he wanted as if he were the sun and everyone else were just planets caught in his gravitational field, he was bound to do something stupid that would piss her off all the more.

So yeah, she needed to hurry before that skid mark did something above his pay grade. The good news was, if he did and took Trace without her sign off, she would have an outlet where she could take out the night's frustration.

As she staggered toward the mouth of the alley, she considered that maybe Micah *should* take Trace without her permission. Because, yeah, she could use a good fight right about now. One she could win.

CHAPTER 3

MOTHER. DEAD. HIS FAULT. It was his fault.

Trace shivered on the floor of the holding cell. The memories assaulting him had shattered him to within an inch of sanity, and they'd done it in less than sixty minutes. He'd been fine when he arrived at the processing center, but with one casually flung insult— *Freak!*—he was on the verge of crossing the threshold into mutancy.

Curling into a tight ball, his teeth chattered as he fought for control. Where was Micah? He needed Micah.

He barely held on, his mind racing with rampant thoughts from both the near and distant past. He was lucid enough to know where he was, but not by much.

Brak. Father. Dead. No . . . alive. They survived. Would never forgive him. Fire. His fault.

If only he hadn't flicked the razor blade to the floor in his dungeon cell, he could use it now. Maybe that would have been enough to prevent the scales from tipping.

Where the hell was Micah? Trace needed his master, and he needed him now.

Mother's cries. The fire.

Tears broke against the seams of his tightly scrunched eyes, and he cringed through another muscle spasm that ran from the top of his head to the tips of his toes.

Micah, where are you?

He needed his friend and master now more than ever.

MICAH SCOWLED INTO THE POURING RAIN, seething, then checked his watch again.

"She's fifteen minutes late, for fuck's sake." He turned toward the sock puppet dressed in the king's guard uniform behind the industrial desk set up in the small lobby.

The guard lifted his gaze from the screen of his laptop, where he was probably playing Solitaire or some other seemingly useless and nonproductive game.

"The instructions are explicit, Micah. Trace is to be released into Cordray's custody. *Only* Cordray's."

Micah was up the guard's nose in two strides. He slammed the laptop closed and slapped his palms on the cool, rubber-topped desk. "And she's just going to sign him over to me five seconds later, asshole, so we might as well dispense with the middle man." Or woman, as the case may be. Or *it*. Because who the hell really knew with Cordray?

The guard's brow bunched and lowered over his eyes. "You don't hold jurisdiction here. Now, sit your ass down and wait. Or leave. I don't give a shit. Just get out of my face, or you'll be the next one in King Bain's dungeon."

Micah slowly straightened and loomed over the little shit with balls of steel. Or perhaps he thought hiding behind the royal insignia gave him some kind of protection. If only he knew. Micah wasn't beyond doing what was necessary to protect those he cared about. If that meant wiping the floor with this overly confident turd stain so he could get to Trace and get him home, he had no problem with that. After all, Micah believed in acting first and asking forgiveness later. And while the threat of the king's retaliation might send lesser males quaking in their footsies, Micah wasn't so squeamish.

Still, he backed off. He would give Cordray five more minutes. If she didn't arrive by quarter past, he was going in for Trace even if he had to take a bullet to get to him.

He paced toward the door and glared out at the diffuse light from the city reflecting off the torrential rain as he thought back over the conversation he'd had with Sam before leaving AKM thirty minutes ago to come here. He'd been a nervous wreck. Still was. This was Trace, for God's sake. His best friend and the first true submissive he'd taken on in what felt like a lifetime.

"Quit worrying," Sam had said as he let out a heavy, concerned exhale.

"I'm not worried." He had tried to lie to her but she knew him better than that by now.

Sam had made a noise as if she was trying not to laugh, and he imagined she had one of her perfect, loving smiles on her face. "You're like a kid with a shiny new BMX bike on Christmas."

Where did she get these analogies? "Are you saying I'm excited, Mrs. Black?"

"Baby, I thought we'd talked about this. Just because you put a ring on it doesn't mean you can call me Mrs. Black. We still aren't officially hitched." The amusement in her voice made him smile.

"We are *so* hitched. You've no idea."

A moment's silence crossed the line, and he could almost see Sam's cheeks turn rosy as she grinned from ear to ear and stared at the ring he'd given her in February. She'd told him that even though he was a vampire and she was now immortal, she wanted a proper human wedding. She'd been married once before to that abusive asshole, Steve, and Micah suspected she wanted to wipe the slate clean and mark a new beginning by marrying him, even though vampires didn't get married. They mated. Big diff. A marriage could be terminated. A mating couldn't. At least, not without consequences.

Micah knew firsthand how hard losing a mate was. He'd lost his first mate centuries ago and had barely lived to tell the tale.

He shoved his thoughts of the past aside. "If I remember correctly, you told me when I gave you that ring that I could call you Mrs. Black."

"Baby, a woman will say anything when a man gives her that many diamonds."

"I'm no man. All male, baby. Right here. Male." He tapped the tip of his index finger against the center of his chest. He loved teasing her over her constant use of the term man instead of male. Human males were *men*. A vampire male was a *male*. Nothing human or *manly* about him.

She groaned good-naturedly then giggled. "Yes, you are. All male. Down to your pinky finger."

"Don't you forget it." He could live off these playful exchanges. "So, are you saying that you lied?"

"Lied?" She considered it a moment. "What do you mean?"

"When you told me I could call you Mrs. Black?" He tsked. "How quickly you forget."

"Oh, we're back on that." She sighed endearingly. "No, I didn't lie, but my ability to think rationally was severely compromised at the time."

He kicked back in his chair. "I see."

For centuries, his life had been barely more than a shadow, but then Sam had shown up and given purpose to his soul again. She was his life's blood. He was alive because of her.

Well, because of her and Trace.

Trace was his best friend and self-designated guardian angel. He had taken on the role of living shield, caring enough for both of them to watch over Micah when he hadn't given a shit whether he lived or died.

He loved Sam and Trace more than anything in the world, but he loved them each in different ways. There was a part of him that needed something Trace could give him that he refused to take from Sam. The debasement that resided deep in his soul desired a kind of control and submission even Sam, who was one of the strongest females he had ever known, wasn't able to provide. That wasn't the kind of play he engaged in with her, because it was too demanding, too severe, too harrowing, rife with the potential to scar her mind. Only a hardcore submissive could take that kind of treatment.

Trace.

That wasn't to say that Trace's submission was a *requirement* for Micah to have a full life. If Trace hadn't come along, Micah would have been perfectly content to live the rest of his days as Sam's mate without a thought to his BDSM past and the extremes he'd gone to in his dungeon. His life would have *felt* full. But in the way a caterpillar turns into a butterfly, he couldn't go back to the way he had been before sampling a taste of the fulfillment Trace could provide. Trace had given him wings again, and there was no going back from that.

This was why he was like the kid with the new bike on Christmas morning. Because the moment he took possession of Trace, the scene would begin. Trace would need him after two weeks in lockup. And, once more, Micah was ready to don the Master hat to give Trace what he needed. His dungeon was already set up in his basement. Ready and waiting for Trace to fall to his knees in subservience and become Micah's slave.

He and Sam had talked about what would happen once he got Trace home, so she knew the importance of what was about to happen. Trace needed Micah in a way Micah hadn't allowed anyone to need him in a long time. For decades, he had practiced BDSM as a Dom, and a damn good one. Other Doms wanted to be him. Submissives had practically thrown themselves at him. The leather lifestyle had provided an outlet for Micah's tormented side, but also for the long-repressed side of him that had once — almost a thousand years ago — been a strong, trusted leader.

After a while, though, it had become too hard to reconcile himself to reality, and he grew disenchanted. Being a Dom began to lose its luster. Submissives came and went, and humans were too weak to take what he could dish. Vampire submissives were in short supply, and to be honest, he had wanted a more permanent arrangement, not one where the sub only used him to get off on the pain and degradation. Domming a vampire who wasn't his mate had begun to feel like blasphemy, and he eventually backed away from the lifestyle on all fronts, especially after harming a submissive during fireplay. Something he would much rather forget.

Then Sam came along. She rekindled his desire to pull out the proverbial flogger, but even though she could take a lot, she wasn't a true submissive and never would be. She was too strong willed. With her, he enjoyed playing — tying her up, spanking her, even mindfucking her on occasion — but he liked her more hands-on than he would ever allow a true sub to be.

Enter Trace. The perfect solution.

Not only did Trace want to be Micah's submissive, but he also needed Micah's strong hand to keep his mixed-blood superpower shit under control. The fact that Sam approved and had hinted that she wouldn't mind participating gave him a mental hard-on.

And didn't that just make no sense whatsoever. As a mated male, he should be furious at the idea of Sam participating in a scene with him and Trace.

In fact, he should be enraged that Trace even watched him make love to Sam. But his and Sam's relationship with Trace seemed to balk at traditional vampire biomechanics. Trace watched, and Micah got turned on.

So did Sam.

So did Trace.

The three of them formed a bizarre love triangle where voyeuristic and exhibitionist tendencies overruled biology. Trace never touched Sam inappropriately, and she hadn't touched him since the incident at Mistress Diamond's scene party last February.

But Micah had to be honest with himself. He didn't think he'd mind if they did touch each other. But that wasn't what their three-ways were about. Trace never did more than watch, and Sam never did more than perform. And Micah got off on all of it.

"You're excited about picking up Trace," Sam had said to him earlier. "I can tell."

He had responded by telling her he *was* excited. And nervous.

"Why nervous?" she'd asked.

"Because it's been a while since I took on a true sub, and despite society's idea that all Doms are confident control freaks who never doubt themselves, that's not how it really is. There's a lot at stake here. A lot could go wrong." What an understatement.

Vampires didn't live by the same biological rules that humans did. What if Micah got into his dungeon with Trace and Sam, and then suddenly went all mated male batshit crazy out of the blue. It hadn't happened, yet, but that didn't mean it couldn't or wouldn't. Trace could touch her, or she could touch him, and that could ignite a rage that would make human jealousy look like two-year-olds playing in a sandbox. If he hurt Trace, he would never forgive himself. If he hurt Sam, he would kill himself.

But mated-male rage was the least of his worries. What if Trace's mixed-blood powers backfired under the intense working over Micah gave him? None of Trace's previous Doms had been able to do what Micah could, and they both knew it. He had a power over Trace that no one else ever could. He could feel that power every time Trace looked at him. Every time Trace lowered his eyes and called him Master. But what if Trace's powers boomeranged under such a strong hand and tipped Trace into going mutant simply from the overload.

Anything was possible, and Micah had to take great care and patience to explore Trace's boundaries, especially since he couldn't see inside Trace's mind. He couldn't afford to make any mistakes.

Sam had ended the call by telling him she and Trace both had faith in him, and that she would be waiting for him afterward, ready to give him her body the way she knew he would need after the scene with Trace ended.

Damn, he loved that female. She always knew what he needed, because one thing was for damn sure. After he took care of Trace's needs, he would have needs of his own to fulfill. Ones reserved only for Sam.

Lightning flashed, and Micah blinked as he frowned himself out of his thoughts. He brushed back his long black hair and glanced at his watch again.

Twenty past the hour.

Satan's mistress's time was up.

He was taking Trace out of there right now. If Cordray didn't like it, she could kiss his fist. As he slammed it into her mouth, of course. Because, God, he owed that scag for the shit she'd put him and Trace through in the last two weeks.

He swung around and stormed the desk. "I'm done waiting. Go get him. Now!"

A look of irritation crossed the guard's expression as he let out a perturbed sigh and met Micah's gaze frown for frown. "Do we really have to do this again?" The guard sighed. "Only Cordray is allowed to — "

Micah uncrossed his arms and pounded his fists on the desk. "Cordray isn't here, is she, and his sentence ended twenty minutes ago." He made a show of looking at the clock then met the guard's gaze with a healthy dose of heat. "If it was so goddamned important for her to take custody of Trace upon his release, she should have been here the moment his sentence ended. She's not. I am. And right now I think you need to be worrying about me a whole hell of a lot more than you are her, because I'm the one about to knock you into next month if you don't get out of that goddamn chair and get my friend right fucking now."

He wasn't at all fond of Cordray, and just hearing her name did something to his need to draw blood, and not so he could drink it. One day, he and that bitch would swap blows, but right now, his main concern was to get Trace home and taken care of. Trace had to be going ballistic by now.

The guard's hard glare softened as he blinked and reconsidered his stance. "The orders — "

"Fuck your orders!" Micah shot forward and grabbed the guard's shirt at the collar, ready to unload the unholy wrath of Micah if he had to. "He will not stay incarcerated one more minute. If it's so goddamn important for Cordray to be here to sign for his release, where the fuck is she?" Micah let go of the guard's shirt with an abrupt shove. Standing tall, he projected an air of authority the guy had probably only ever felt from the king himself. "Now, you get your ass out of that chair and go get my friend so I can take him home and prevent him from turning mutant. Do you want that on your conscience, asshole? Because if I don't get him out of here right now, that's a distinct possibility. Am I making myself clear?"

The guard didn't seem happy about being bossed around by someone other than his commander or the king, but when Micah mentioned that Trace could turn mutant, his face paled.

"M-mutant?"

Micah backed off a step now that he had the guard's full attention. "Yes. Mutant. You down with that? Because I'm not, especially since we're talking about my friend in there. If I lose him because high-and-mighty Cordray Ass-Fuck isn't here, I will hunt her down after I take off your head and use it as a soccer ball. You feeling me?"

The guard hesitated for only a moment then cursed under his breath as he stood and unfastened his keys from his belt. "Fine,

Micah, but it's your ass if Cordray throws a fit."

"She can *suck* my ass, for all I care." He wasn't especially concerned with making Cordray happy.

Micah waited for the guard to come around the desk, his keys jangling as he flipped his key ring around his index finger and caught the keys in his palm as he led Micah into the back and down a short hallway to a pair of cells, one on either side of the hall. Trace was in the one on the right.

"Shit!" Micah shoved the guard aside as he got an eyeful of his best friend in what could only be described as a state of emergency.

Trace lay on the floor in a shivering heap, his teeth chattering, eyes rolled back in their sockets. His shirt was ripped and shredded as if he'd clawed through the fabric. Dozens of partially healed, razor-thin cuts lined his forearms, as well as several bite marks.

"Oh my God," the guard said as he fumbled with his keys to open the door. "He wasn't this bad when they brought him in. Is he okay? He isn't going mutant, is he?" He turned plaintive eyes on Micah.

Hell to the no! Trace couldn't be going mutant. Micah wouldn't let that happen.

Micah gripped one of the iron bars, impatient for the guard to unlock the cell door. "Just hurry the fuck up and let me in there!"

Terror filled the guard's eyes, and he took a hesitant step back as if he was afraid to open the door. From the thoughts battering Micah in a fearful frenzy, the guard worried Trace was already too far gone and didn't want to let him out. The big pussy. What member of the king's guard worth his weight in salt shriveled in the face of fear?

"Get out of my way." Micah scowled and pushed him aside, reared back, and kicked the cell door. It shuddered on its hinges. He kicked it again, and the metal groaned. He had to get to his friend. He had to get Trace out of there, and waiting for Mighty Mouse with the keys to get over his silly-assed fear so he could unlock the door wasn't cutting it. Mustering all his strength, Micah braced himself against the bars of the opposite cell, lifted his leg one more time, and let out a battle cry as he drove his heel against the metal plate that housed the lock.

The mechanism shattered, and the door flew open. In an instant, Micah had Trace in his arms.

"Trace! I'm here, brother. I've got you. Trace?" Micah hoisted him up, blew past the guard—who shrank away like a coward—and darted for the door. "Give my regards to Cordray!" he shouted back with an air of sarcasm as he kicked open the door to the parking lot and rushed Trace out into the rain to his waiting Audi.

If Cordray's tardy ass had prevented him from getting to Trace in time to save him, he would make it his life's mission to destroy her.

CHAPTER 4

M ICAH ARRIVED HOME IN RECORD TIME, pulled into his garage, hauled Trace's shivering body from the front seat, and shot inside as Sam opened the door.

"My God! What's wrong with him?" Sam darted past him to the door leading to the basement. She opened it and stood aside.

"He's better now than he was ten minutes ago," Micah said. "You should have seen him in his cell."

"*This* is better?" Sam swept her hand toward Trace, eyes wide, mouth gaping.

True, Trace's teeth still chattered, and his body still shuddered with spasms every few seconds, but at least his eyes weren't rolled back in their sockets, anymore. They were simply closed. And he had tried to talk to Micah on the drive over. Not that his words made much sense. Some of them hadn't even sounded English.

"Lock us in," he said, pausing to give her an adoring gaze. "And wait up for me." He leaned in and gave her a hasty kiss.

"I'll be waiting."

He pecked her on the lips again. "You're incredible."

She smiled and brushed her fingers through his hair then palmed Trace's cheek. He relaxed and turned his face into her hand, eyes still closed.

"Welcome home, Trace," she whispered. Then to Micah she said, "Go on. Take care of him. I'm not going anywhere."

"It could be a while." Trace was in bad shape. Who knew how long they would be in the dungeon just to get him back to acceptable.

"Take your time." Sam took a step back and motioned him down the stairs. "Now go."

"I love you." Micah started down.

"I love you, too."

The door latched behind him, and he hurried through the large bedroom to the rustic, arched doorway on the other side that led to his dungeon. The doors were already open. Gentle music played through the speakers, just as he'd asked, and to the side, the massage table and vat of wax were prepared.

Bless Sam's heart. When he had told her two days ago what he wanted to do, she had insisted he teach her how to get things ready so he wouldn't have to worry about it. And then, of course, she had wanted to experiment. She had never engaged in wax play and had looked good covered in his artwork, although the wax he'd used on her hadn't been very hot. Sex afterward had been through the moon. Well worth the practice.

But he didn't need to relive what he and Sam had done with one another right now.

Trace needed a bath. Badly. Micah would have to talk to King Bain about the conditions in his dungeon, because poor Trace smelled like the ass end of a wild boar after it had eaten a skunk.

"Come on, buddy." Micah hoisted Trace more securely in his arms as he side-stepped into the apartment-sized bathroom shared by his dungeon and his bedroom. He set Trace on the marble bench next to the walk-in shower then reached in to turn on the water. It spilled from multiple rainfall showerheads above, as well as from heads in the walls. Taking a shower in here felt like showering in a rainstorm. Or making love in a rainstorm, which he and Sam reaffirmed a couple of times a month.

Once the water was warm enough, Micah turned to find Trace slumped to the side, his head resting against the wall, his arms hugging himself as he blathered unintelligibly.

It was time to get serious. Time to bring Trace back from hell.

SLAP!

The rampant, mind-obliterating thoughts destroying Trace's mind abruptly cut off as his eyes flew open at the sharp sting of pain on his face. He clapped his hand over his cheek. What the fuck? Had someone just hit him? Last mistake that asshole would ever ma—

His gaze met Micah's.

Master.

Devotion surged through his veins, followed by confusion. How had he gotten here? Last thing he remembered was being huddled on the floor in an above-ground cell, fighting back memories of his mother. Now he was in the middle of Micah's bathroom. A giant oval-shaped tub was on his right. A luxurious walk-in shower was on his left. In front of him were his and her basins placed in a stretch of marble with a glasslike shine.

"Sit up!" Micah said as sternly as a Catholic school teacher. "Is this how your other masters allowed you to present yourself?" Micah waved his hand toward Trace as if disgusted.

Trace shook out the cobwebs, coming back into himself, even if only partially. "N-no, sir." He hadn't spoken much in the last two weeks, and his voice sounded like someone had scraped his vocal chords with sandpaper.

"Sir?" Micah pulled back as if affronted. "Did I say it was acceptable to call me sir?"

In a confused daze, Trace looked from Micah's strong, angular face to his own hands, which trembled in his lap. His shirt was torn as if he'd ripped it with his own fingernails. Jesus! His power had almost consumed him. This was the closest he had ever come to completely losing control and falling prey to the mixed-blood gift his mother had given him. But as Micah lorded over him — all alpha dominance and intensity — Trace felt his power shrink and ebb toward the shadows.

Micah stepped between Trace's legs, placed his hand under Trace's scruffy chin, and lifted his face. Micah gazed straight down at him, chin to chest. "You will address me as Master, slave."

The two stared at each other for a heartbeat.

"Say it." Micah squeezed his chin between his thumb and forefinger.

Trace swallowed. This was what he had wanted for months. Years, even. Micah as his Dom. And praise God, the moment was finally, blessedly here. Sure, they'd played with the idea in the weeks before his incarceration, but they had yet to play in his dungeon. "Yes, Master." The two words slid reverently from his mouth.

Micah let go of his chin and stepped back. "And how do you present yourself to your master, slave?"

Trace lowered his gaze to the floor and slowly slid off the bench to his knees. With every second that passed, his power slipped further into the shadows of his mind, leaving him emotionally and mentally naked . . . and what a welcome feeling that was. With just his authoritative voice, Micah freed him at the same time he bound him into submission. This was what being enslaved to a Dom — to Micah — did for him.

He sat back on his heels, head bowed forward, palms on his thighs.

"Good," Micah said, strolling in a circle around him. "This is how you will present yourself to me in my dungeon or whenever you need my services." Micah caressed Trace's peach-fuzzed scalp. "Now rise, slave. And take off your clothes. I won't have you defiling my dungeon with this rankness you brought into my home."

Steam rose from the shower as Trace scooted one foot out from under him and pushed himself to his feet, head still down. As he slipped out of his dirty clothes, Micah paced slowly around him.

"We will discuss our limits later," Micah said. "And rest assured, slave, I have limits even if you don't."

Trace dropped his shredded, filthy shirt to the floor, and Micah swatted his hand. "Is this how you disrobed for your previous Doms? By throwing your clothes so casually on the floor?"

Trace shook his head. "No, s—Master." He would have to get used to Micah's style, but excitement prickled his skin at Micah's harshness. Already, Micah was more than any of his previous Doms had ever been and ever could be. Not just because of his demeanor, but because of the connection between them. Something ethereal—some invisible gossamer thread—linked them to one another in a blissful, spiritual, almost supernatural way. One that uplifted Trace's soul and made his heart sing, even as Micah scowled and used a firm tone.

Micah tapped his booted foot on the floor near his shirt. "Pick it up. Fold it. And set it on the bench behind you."

"Yes, Master." He reached for his shirt, but Micah stopped him.

"On second thought, throw that shirt in the trash. It's ruined. I don't want it here."

He did as he was told then removed his pants, folded them, and placed them on the bench after setting his worn boots neatly underneath it. Then he turned toward Micah and bowed his head, arms behind his back, legs slightly apart as if he stood at military at ease.

Tremors still rippled through his body as his power continued to wane, but for the first time since Cordray had given him the razor in his cell, he felt almost normal.

"Nice," Micah said. "Very good." He hesitated for only a moment. "Now bathe yourself." He opened the glass door to the shower and stood aside.

The water felt like a slice of heaven as he stepped into it, but as much as he wanted to luxuriate, Micah wouldn't let him. The time for soaking would come later. For now, he was in Micah's world. His master's world. And he would do as commanded.

His skin prickled with vibrant anticipation.

"Wash your feet first," Micah said from outside the glass. "Spend no less than fifteen seconds on each foot."

Using a shower loofah, he scrubbed his feet with Sam's lilac-scented shower soap. So what if it made him smell flowery. That was better than smelling like dungeon shit, and the floral scent comforted him. It made him think of Sam, who was almost as calming for his soul as Micah.

Once he finished, Micah said, "Now your ankles and calves. And don't stop washing them until I say you can." After what felt like a minute, Micah said, "Rinse and move up to your thighs."

Trace had never had anyone tell him how to shower before, and he wondered at Micah's reasoning, especially when he jumped from his thighs to his head and began to work his way down. When he rinsed his abdomen, he waited for Micah's next instruction.

"Now your ass," Micah said, just as clinically as before, except there was a hint of sexual undercurrent in his tone. Trace couldn't be sure if that was accidental or intentional, but knowing Micah, Trace would put money on the latter.

"Do you like your ass fondled, slave?" Micah kept his gaze on his watch, but he was clearly trying to get under Trace's skin.

"Yes, Master." Trace worked his soapy fingers and the shower loofah over one cheek, then the other, straining not to look at Micah.

"How many male Doms have you had, slave?"

Trace felt his cheeks flush. "Three, Master."

"And did they all play with your ass?" Micah's gaze never wavered from his watch.

Trace's hands slowed as he continued to wash himself. "Yes, Master."

For several seconds, Micah said nothing, then, "Rinse."

Trace set the loofah down and let the water rinse his hands and backside.

"Now," Micah said. "Wash your cock and balls."

Trace took a shallow breath, picked up the liquid soap, and squirted a generous amount in his palm.

"Did they all fuck you?" Micah said.

Trace nearly dropped the bottle of soap as he lifted it back to the shelf, but he recovered quickly, set the bottle in place, and worked the soap into a slick lather between his hands. "Yes, Master." He hazarded a glance at Micah in time to see one black eyebrow tick upward before settling over his eye again.

"Wash yourself, Trace." Micah's gaze shifted to issue him a warning glance, as if he were reminding Trace not to look at him without permission.

Trace's gaze fell to his semi-hard cock as he worked the lather up and down his length and sac.

"Did you enjoy being fucked by a male?" Micah's voice was softer now, but still stern.

"Yes and no, Master." There was no point in lying. Trace had been fucked by another male, and while it wasn't his ideal sexual encounter, it got the job done, sending him into such humiliation that his power practically evaporated into nothing, allowing him to expend himself sexually when it was impossible to do so at any other time.

"Yes and no?"

"Yes, Master." Even now, the memory of the debasement he had allowed himself to suffer in the name of power control caused his cock to swell, and he struggled not to stroke himself as he continued scrubbing his dick.

Micah didn't push for more and instead dropped his arms to his side and said, "Rinse off, shut off the shower, and dry yourself." Then he turned and walked toward the marble counter, which he leaned against as he watched Trace finish up and do as he was told.

"How do you feel?" Micah said as Trace stepped out of the shower.

His erection tented the towel around his waist like a good little camper. "Good."

Micah sternly arched one eyebrow.

"Good, Master," Trace said, correcting himself.

"That's better." Micah pushed away from the counter, grabbed a can of shaving gel and a razor, and bobbed his head toward the door. "Follow me."

Without another word, Micah turned and walked out.

Trace followed him, his bare feet pattering quietly on the uncarpeted floor. Now the reason for the deliberately slow shower, body part by body part, was clear. His entire body hummed with awareness, fully alive. Every nerve ending tingled as air flowed over his skin and cooled him.

For two weeks, Trace had endured sensory deprivation, held mostly in darkness and shadows, with nothing but a cold floor and a scratchy, dirty cot to lie on. No breeze had flowed within his cell, and aside from Cordray's one and only visit, the only people he had seen were the guards who brought him tasteless food and tended to his waste. He hadn't been allowed to bathe, and he'd had no way of knowing day from night.

Now he was free. At home. At least, this was the only place he'd been in a long time that felt like home. The trailer where he resided had always felt more like a tomb. Lifeless and without joy. That was why he used to spend his downtime at AKM, inside his dorm. Now he spent that time with Micah and Sam.

But this was the first time he had been inside Micah's dungeon, and it didn't disappoint. The space was large and packed with equipment he both recognized and had never laid eyes on before. The St. Andrew's Cross was familiar, but the contraption that looked like a combination ramp and deformed bench wasn't. He wondered what that thing was used for.

One terra-cotta wall was adorned with floggers, and two large, custom-made storage units that looked like dressers stood nearby. In one corner sat an ancient Iron Maiden that looked more decorative than functional, and beside that was a wrought iron bed with enough loops and hooks molded into both the head- and footboards, as well as in the frame and the ceiling overhead, to make for some interesting bondage.

How often had Micah tied Sam to that bed? And would Micah eventually tie him to it, too?

He could hope.

The ceiling reminded him of the Sistine Chapel, only the mosaic in Micah's dungeon included erotic images, not angelic ones. Men and women engaged in all manner of congress stared down at him as he followed Micah to a straight-backed chair in the center of the room. Micah set the shaving gel and razor on a small, nearby table.

"Sit." Micah gestured toward the chair then opened a nearby cabinet and pulled out a plush hand towel.

It wasn't Trace's place to ask what was happening. His job was simply to do, to trust. Not think or doubt.

He sat down as Micah grabbed a deep, silver bowl from a cabinet under the counter. He took the bowl to the bathroom, filled it with water, then returned and set it on the table beside the towel. In the next blink, Micah was behind him, grabbing his arms. Hard.

He almost moaned as Micah bound his wrists to the rear legs of the chair so that they hung straight down past the wooden seat.

The delicious sensation of being bound vibrated through his muscles, and his helpless dick nodded in approval. He always got hard during play sessions. And even though he was only just out of a two-week incarceration, all it had taken was that first slap in the bathroom to awaken his depravity and give his annoying power a kick in the nuts.

Without a word, Micah came back around to the side of the chair, filled his hand with shaving gel, lathered it into thick, musky foam, and slathered it over Trace's head. "If only I had a straight razor," he said thoughtfully as he wiped his hands on the towel. "Oh, the fun I could have with you if I did."

Trace looked up to see the corner of Micah's mouth turn slightly upward, as if he were entertaining a private thought.

"May I speak, Master?" Trace said.

Micah met his gaze and nodded, that half-smile still on his face. The guy looked as content as a nurse in a hospital, right where he belonged. Exactly where he wanted to be. It made Trace feel loved.

Not like sexual love. More like familial love. Brotherly, but not quite . . . a little more heated than that.

Theirs was such a strange relationship.

"Yes. You may speak." Micah lifted the razor and smoothed it down the side of Trace's head. The quiet sound of stubble snapping off against the blade mingled with gentle, synthesized music piped into the room.

"Thank you."

Unfazed, Micah dipped the razor in the bowl of water and went back to shaving his head. "For what?"

Heat spun in the air around Micah, who gave off strength and confidence unlike anything Trace had ever felt. It was why Trace had longed to be his sub. Micah was self-assured, virile, and yes, attractive. He was what Marilyn Manson referred to as one of the beautiful people. Easy on the eyes and hard on the body, with an intensity that measured itself not just on his face, but over every inch of his skin and right down to his bones. Even his clothes—black cargo pants and a long-sleeved, body-hugging Under Armor shirt— seemed alive with his energy.

"For coming to get me."

The razor skimmed another line down his head. "I told you I would . . . that I would take care of you."

"I know, but . . ."

Micah switched sides and continued to strip his scalp of what little hair had grown in over the past couple of weeks. "I wouldn't have left you there," he said quietly, his voice deep and resonant. "I was ready to kill to get you out of that place."

Nothing was said for a while as Micah finished shaving his melon then wiped off his head, grabbed the shaving gel, and collected another palm full of it before smoothing the foam over Trace's jaw, cheeks, chin, and mustache.

"What did you do to your arms?" Micah tugged Trace's cheek with his fingertips and ran the razor up his stubble.

His arms? He began to look down, forgetting that he was bound, but he knew what Micah was referring to. He wanted to know about the cuts and the self-inflicted bites. In his cell, the self-mutilation had been all that had stood between his sanity and full-on mutation.

"Well?" Micah cleared the shaving cream from one side of his face and moved to the opposite side.

"I cut myself. It was how I kept my sanity without you."

Without you. Something Trace never wanted to endure again.

"The cuts aren't healing," Micah said nonchalantly. "When was the last time you fed?" He wasn't talking about food. He was asking about blood.

Trace shrugged. "I don't know. I lost track of the days in there, especially at the end."

"You need blood." Nothing in Micah's tone betrayed what he was thinking, but when he tipped Trace's head back to shave the underside of his chin, he bent down and licked the side of his neck. "You'll feed from me," he whispered against Trace's skin.

Just the thought of taking blood from his master — from Micah — sent warmth into his belly, along with a stab of hunger.

"Micah —"

"I'll hear no protest. It will be my gift to you if you please me in our session. And I know you will please me." Micah's lips caressed his neck as he spoke. "I can replenish myself from Sam later."

The razor made one last pass over his skin, and Micah stood without making eye contact, grabbed the towel, and wiped the remaining shaving cream away.

"How is Sam?" Trace said, his body alive and eager for more as Micah continued to reawaken his senses.

"Ready for you to rejoin us in our play with one another."

In other words, Sam wanted Trace to return to his role of voyeur to her exhibitionist. "And you?"

Micah disappeared behind him, and Trace heard the rustle of his cargo pants as he crouched and released his bound hands. "What are you asking me, Trace?"

Before Trace was sent to King Bain's dungeon, he had admitted to Micah that he was attracted to both him and Sam. How could anyone not be attracted to either of them? They were beautiful. Just look at Micah. Trace's gaze drank in his best friend as he stepped in front of him again. Micah's face was all sharp angles, the perfect balance between handsome and brutally sexy. Black hair hung in lustrous waves past his shoulders, and the black shadow of facial hair lining his jaw made him look more like a god than a sloppy bum. Micah was a sculpture of flesh and bone. A vision. A magnificent work of art worthy of the Louvre.

Trace cleared his throat and rubbed his thumbs over his wrists. "Are *you* eager for me to rejoin you in your play with one another?"

A smile teased the corners of Micah's mouth. "You'll just have to wait and see." He pointed to the floor in front of the chair. "Now, present yourself to me, slave."

The time for talk was over. It was time to revert back to full submission.

Trace dropped to the floor, on his knees, towel still around his waist, head bowed. He placed his hands on his thighs and waited. This was it. His dreams were coming true.

Micah's black Doc Martens entered his field of vision. "Every Dom you've had before me is nothing, slave." He paced to the side. "They could never give you what I can. They never knew you like I do . . . like I *will*. In time, you will submit to me as you've never submitted to anyone." He began walking a slow circle around him. "You think you need pain for your power, but with me, you will come to love it for what it is. You will love it for the pleasure I infuse within it." Micah's palm caressed the top of Trace's freshly shaved head, his hand warm on his damp skin. "You will need it for more than just to keep your power at bay, Trace." His hand trailed down to Trace's neck and shoulder as he stepped around him from behind. "I will bleed your mind more than your body, and then you'll see what true submission is. The Doms you've used before me may have been capable. Some might even have been superior. But no one can give you what I can, Trace. You're mine. You belong to me now. Do you understand?"

A chill raced up and down Trace's spine. "Yes."

"Yes what?"

"Yes, Master."

"Very good. From now on, when we're here, in my dungeon, you will call me Master. Only here. Not at AKM. Not in the rest of my home . . . except if you need me in that way. Do you understand?"

"Yes, Master."

Micah caressed the side of Trace's face, across his forehead, and then rotated his wrist and brushed the backs of his fingers down his cheek as he walked another circle. "Tonight, I will give you just a taste to get you through your needs, and then we'll talk. Since I can't get inside here, yet" — he tapped Trace's head with the tip of his index finger — "you will tell me your limits, if you have any." Micah stopped in front of him, his toes firmly planted directly below Trace's eyes. If Trace lifted his head, he would come face to crotch with Micah. "I will tell you *my* limits now." Micah reached under Trace's chin and urged his head up. As he suspected, Micah's crotch was only an inch away from his face. Micah's expression remained stern. "Despite what you're used to from your previous male masters, I will not fuck you. That part of me is for Sam. Do you understand?"

Trace nodded, and his chin grazed the cotton fabric of Micah's pants as Micah tilted his hips ever so slightly forward, as if he were teasing Trace with what he'd just vowed he would never give him. "Yes, Master."

"Good. And you will not fuck me, because . . ." Micah's right eyebrow ticked upward as his mouth quirked. "Well, because I pitch. I don't catch." He gave a subtle smirk. "But . . ." He slowly lowered himself until he was crouched in front of him. They were eye to eye. Hell, they were almost nose to nose. "Oh, but Trace, I will make you come." He leaned forward and let his scruffy cheek rub against Trace's freshly shaved skin as he whispered in his ear, "I will use what you told me before you went to prison, about your attraction to me, as well as to Sam, and I will use it well."

"Yes, Master."

Micah's lips caressed the lobe of Trace's ear. "You revealed yourself ever so little that day, but ever so much." He ran his lips down Trace's jaw then brought his face around so that he looked Trace squarely in the eyes, their lips so close Trace could feel the warmth from Micah's skin. So close they shared the same breath. "To you, these sessions might be about keeping your power at bay, but to me, they will be equal parts agony and pleasure. Pleasure no other Dom has ever been able to give you like I can."

"Yes," — *gulp* — "Master." Trace's eyelids had grown heavy. He was more aroused from Micah's words than his last mistress had been able to get him by flogging him.

"I will push you, Trace. Not just physically, but emotionally. *Mentally*. But I will never give you more than I think you can handle." He edged closer, and their lips touched, but not in a kiss. "I will earn your trust, and I will break you. And you will never want for another master for the rest of your life."

"I already don't want for another master for the rest of my life," Trace said quietly, his lips moving against Micah's.

Micah grinned, and the tiny lines around his eyes creased, but he didn't pull back. "That's good, slave." He inched backward. "And one more thing."

Trace's gaze locked drunkenly to Micah's as if he were hypnotized, ready to hang on every word Micah uttered. "Yes, Master?"

"You *will* let me in, Trace. You will open your mind to me." He cupped his hand around the back of Trace's head, swiped his palm over his cranium and back down, where he secured his hold against the back of his skull. "I can be so much more effective if you open your mind to me."

Trace blinked, swallowed, and then let his gaze drop away.

Micah abruptly leaned forward and pulled Trace's head to his so their mouths crashed together. Micah growled as he closed his lips over Trace's in a bruising, possessive caress. All Trace could do was relinquish and let it happen.

This wasn't a kiss of passion, nor one of lust. This was a seal of ownership. One that declared Micah as the keeper of Trace's body and soul from here until forever. A promise Trace readily acquiesced to as he opened his lips and gave himself over to the power exchange. He was eager to begin this journey with his new master.

Micah released him and pulled away. "Am I understood, Trace? Do you understand the importance of opening your mind to me?"

"Yes, Master." Trace didn't know how or when, but he knew he would eventually have to knock down the barrier around his thoughts to let Micah see his secrets. Micah was a tenacious fucker. Now that Trace had agreed to let him in, Micah would needle, paw, and—eventually—demand Trace to open his mind.

Just as long as Micah was ready to see everything.

The good, the bad . . . and the regretfully ugly.

CHAPTER 5

I CAN SUCK HIS ASS? REALLY?

Cordray picked up Micah's words from the guard's thoughts as easily as if that SOB were standing right in front of her.

Rainwater still dripped from her hair and clothes, the taste of blood still filled her mouth, her vision wasn't quite back to normal, and from what she could tell, her lip had swelled up like a marshmallow. Even so, what Skeletor had done to her was the least of her worries. Micah had taken Trace without her permission, which shot him to the top of her shit list.

Granted, from the images she'd picked up from the guard's mind, Trace had been one pint shy of overflowing, and the terror streaming off the guard was enough for her to know shit had been critical. Micah busting Trace out had been the right call, especially since she'd been almost an hour late.

Would she ever admit that out loud? Hell no. But she knew if Micah had waited for her to arrive, Trace might not have survived.

The idea that Trace could have died tonight didn't sit well with her. In fact, it chilled her marrow and struck fear into her heart, which only added to her irritation. When had Trace become so important to her?

Okay fine, she'd been drawn to Trace the moment she first saw him two weeks ago, but that didn't mean she cared about him. She was drawn to lots of people. Didn't mean she would cry if they died. So then why did the thought of Trace's demise hit her emotions so hard?

That first day she'd seen him—when she'd found him so magnetically intriguing—he had touched her. He'd grabbed her arm. No biggie for someone else. But for her? Him touching her had been anything but ordinary. Monumental was more like it. Because when he touched her, he lit her world on fire. In an instant, with his hand wrapped around her forearm, life as she'd known it for eight hundred years ceased to exist. Trace could make her feel. Hot, cold, pain . . . *aroused*. Name the physical sensation, and as long as Trace was near, she felt it. But only with Trace. The rest of the time, she felt nothing at all. No pain. No pleasure. Just emptiness.

"Shit," she muttered under her breath as she spun away from the destruction that had been Trace's holding cell and marched up the hall toward the lobby, leaving a trail of rainwater behind her.

Trace aroused her. And not just because she could feel him. He aroused her because he was the most powerful male she'd ever known, and that kind of power turned on any warm-blooded female with a heartbeat. Her especially, because she was one tough bitch who didn't need pussies for lovers. She liked it rough, because rough allowed her to at least *pretend* she could feel. But with Trace, she wouldn't have to pretend. She would be able to feel every heated caress, every bruising thrust, every scratch of his fangs. With Trace, she wouldn't need it rough. Slow and easy would be good enough to send her into orbit.

Just the thought was enough to make her girly parts clench.

But her attraction to him was about more than his power and his ability to awaken physical sensation. About more than his wicked mixed-blood gifts that roused her awareness. Her attraction stemmed from the fact that everything about Trace spoke to every part of her. The low timbre of his voice made her heart flutter. The square set of his jaw beckoned her teeth to take a nibble before tasting his lips. His sultry, pale-green bedroom eyes hinted at carnal mysteries yet to be discovered. And the way he carried himself—all primal power and unbridled aggression—made her want to fall on her back and pull him between her legs.

She hated admitting it, but Trace's soul called to hers in a way she hadn't experienced since her youth. Not since Gideon. But look at how that had turned out. Thanks to the male vampire's traitorous call to mate, she'd lost her sense of touch completely. Until Gideon, she'd felt everything. Cool breezes over her face, warm water on her skin . . . pain, pleasure—all of it. It wasn't until he broke her heart— no, shattered it—that the world became a numb desert she could participate in but never feel.

She hadn't been Gideon's true mate, but she'd fallen in love with him as if she were. Then she'd pretended they'd mated one another anyway. And he'd played along, wishing his body would spark to hers as much as she did.

But . . . oh, snap! That spark had fired for someone else. And when it did, neither her love nor her breaking heart mattered. Gideon was gone. And she'd transformed into an unfeeling, broken, emotional mess, never to feel physical touch again.

Until now.

Trace had crashed into her world and awakened not just her ability to feel, but everything she'd tried for so long to forget.

As she'd done a hundred times in the last two-and-a-half weeks, she mulled over what Trace's influence on her sense of touch could mean as she shoved open the door and marched back out into the pouring rain, leaving the guards and cleanup crew behind to deal with the mess Micah had made.

She couldn't allow Trace in. If she did, and he didn't mate her . . .

Oh, God, she couldn't even bear to think about the repercussions.

She'd fallen for Gideon, and when he didn't bond to her, she lost one of her senses. If she fell for Trace and he didn't bond to her, either, she could lose her life. Because there was only so much hurt and pain one heart could take before it stopped giving a fuck and shut down.

Which was why, no matter how magnetic and exciting Trace was, she couldn't let her guard down and allow him in.

Besides, Trace had Sam and Micah. He didn't need her.

The thought was enough to put a fire under her ass. Maybe Trace didn't need her, and maybe she refused to give in to the way her heart beat a little harder at the idea of feeling all that coiled power inside her as he pinned her to the mattress — or the wall, the floor, the kitchen table, or wherever — and fucked her senseless, but the fact that Micah had taken him without her consent demanded retribution, right decision or not.

At least the excuse sounded good in her head. And she welcomed any excuse to expend some of the frustration coursing through her veins.

Yanking the door of her Range Rover open, she hoisted herself into the driver's seat, which was covered with a pink and blue blanket she'd pulled from a plastic crate in the back to keep it dry, and cranked the engine.

Next stop, Micah's house.

MICAH GAZED DOWN at Trace's back and bare ass. He was lying on the massage table, which was covered with a dark-blue sheet. The dark color would hide the wax stains better, which was more aesthetically pleasing in his dungeon. Another sheet covered the floor. To his right, his specially modified potpourri Crock-Pot was filled with melted wax, and several variously colored wide-based Japanese candles burned, their wells filling with hot wax.

"Have you ever engaged in wax play?" he said quietly, taking a velvet blindfold from the table.

"No, Master." Trace's voice was muffled as he spoke against the thin pillow.

Surprising. All those years as a sub, and Trace had never been waxed.

"Lift your head." He secured the blindfold over Trace's eyes. The velvet-lined mask performed a dual purpose. Not only would it protect Trace's eyes, but it would also heighten his anticipation and sensory response.

Micah retrieved a length of rope from a hook and looped it through a ring on the wall directly in front of the table.

"Lift your arms over your head." Micah knotted the rope around his wrists, pulled out the slack, and anchored the end to the wall so Trace's arms hung parallel to the floor.

"Is that comfortable?" Micah gently caressed the back of Trace's shoulders.

"Yes, Master."

"I'm going to begin soon." Micah set his waxing brush in the pot so the residual wax could melt off the bristles. "I'm going to give you a safeword. One that I know you'll never use unless I've truly gone too far. If you need me to stop, you will say your safeword, and I will stop immediately. Do you understand?"

"Yes, Master."

"Your safeword is . . . Cordray."

Trace tensed.

"Say it so I know you understand."

"Cordray." Trace's voice practically growled the two syllables.

Micah ran the fingers of his left hand along the muscular ridge down the center of Trace's back.

"I chose this safeword because I know how you feel about her, and I know you would never purposely say her name unless I've indeed gone too far. Is my choice of safeword acceptable to you?" He kept his voice quiet, yet stern.

"Yes, Master. Your choice is acceptable."

Micah heard the contemptuous undertones in Trace's voice, indicating he would never willingly say Cordray's name unless he was forced to. Good. Keep that bitch out of their lives.

He lifted the brush from the wax and held it over his own wrist to let a drop fall to his skin. It burned, but it wasn't too hot. He wouldn't hit Trace with heat too high this first time. If Trace tolerated it well, he would make the wax hotter next time.

"I'm going to apply the first coat of wax now." He guided Trace into the scene. After all, anticipation was as much a part of wax play as the application itself.

As the brush touched Trace's shoulder, he hissed, tensed, and then relaxed as Micah painted a strip of red from shoulder to spine. He waited about twenty seconds to let the full force of the heat transfer seep into Trace's skin as the wax hardened, and then he applied another strip of red from his spine to the opposite shoulder. Trace's muscles clenched again, and he moaned softly in his throat. Not so much from pain, and not quite from pleasure. The sound was somewhere in between.

Taking his time and milking the heat application as much as he could, Micah repeated the pattern until he reached the middle of Trace's back. Luckily, Trace had very little body hair other than on his head and face. Otherwise, this could have gotten tricky.

Once he reached the lower half of Trace's back, the reactions became more intense, which wasn't uncommon. Most people were more sensitive in their lower back than their upper. And even more sensitive on the front of their bodies, which was why Micah had wanted to start on Trace's back. Being his first time, this was safer.

Trace might have been an experienced sub, but that didn't mean his reaction to wax play would be in line with how he reacted to flogging, physical torture, or humiliation, which seemed to be what most of his previous Doms had put him through.

With Micah, Trace would experience so much more. Wax play, mindfucks, knife play, fire play, whipping—not to be confused with flogging—and all manner of edge play. Trace had only just touched the surface of Micah's capabilities.

Trace shuddered and groaned as Micah stroked another swath of red wax across the small of his back.

"You're doing well," Micah said. "So good. You should see your back. It's beautiful. Are you still doing okay?"

Trace nodded slowly against the circular pillow.

"Answer me with your voice, Trace. That way I'll know you're lucid."

"Y-yes, Master." Trace's deep voice sounded dreamy, as if he were floating in his happy place. Subspace.

Micah knew the feeling. He was in his happy place, too. He loved seeing his artwork on a sub's back. Micah picked up a black candle.

"I'm going to apply more wax," he said. "This will be hotter."

He tipped the candle and black wax streamed down like black blood over the layer of red. Some splattered onto bare skin while a trail dripped down his side.

Trace no longer reacted except for an almost imperceptible flinch. He was completely absorbed in the heat transferal from the wax to his body, and the pain of the burn seemed to no longer bother him.

After waiting fifteen seconds, Micah dribbled wax from another black candle so that black dots, streaks, and blotches like Rorschach inkblots formed against the red background.

He lost track of time as he continued, checking in with Trace every few minutes. Trace was flying but aware, and that was good. If Trace went so deep that he could no longer respond, playtime would be over.

Once Trace's back was covered in a thick layer of red and black wax that looked like a miniature Jackson Pollock painting, Micah began to close the scene. Trace had lasted longer than he had expected.

He picked up one of his Japanese candles, tipped it over Trace's ass, and let a trail of heat rain down over fresh skin.

Trace shuddered and groaned long, low, and deep as his hips flexed and his glutes tightened.

He grabbed another candle and held it over Trace's other cheek. As a thin stream of black wax trickled over Trace's ass, Micah eased his free hand between Trace's legs. Trace's entire body seemed to pull in on itself as his thighs parted, allowing Micah's fingers to find the heavy sac pulled up tight at his groin. Micah pushed his hand up farther, cupped him, and squeezed as more wax splattered Trace's skin.

Trace grunted as his entire body quivered violently. The muscles not obscured by a layer of wax shuddered and quaked. A moment later, the subtle wave rippled down his legs, all the way to his feet, which twitched then sent the shockwave back up his calves and hamstrings. A split second later, the chains securing Trace's wrists rattled as his arms shivered.

Mmm, so responsive. If only Micah could see inside Trace's mind and share the journey with him—feel what Trace was feeling—the moment would have been so much better. More powerful. More exquisite.

"Lift your hips." He spoke quietly, and his tongue peeked out to wet the seam of his mouth.

Trace did as he was told, raising his hips off the table just enough for Micah to push his hand farther underneath and wrap his fist around the base of Trace's steely cock.

Fuck but his friend was hard. He'd seen Trace aroused before.

He'd seen him hard and straining. He'd seen him come during their twisted love-triangle trysts. But never had he been the one to provide the friction to get Trace off. Sam had assisted doing those honors only once, but Micah had never felt for himself how turgid and thick Trace was. And Trace was very thick, his erection's circumference big enough to hurt someone if he wasn't careful.

He set down the candle and reached up to grip the back of Trace's neck as he began working his other hand up and down the length of Trace's hard-on.

The reaction was instantaneous. Trace's dick swelled even more, and a powerful, intense shudder jolted his entire body. Then his hips jerked forcefully as a harsh, guttural groan vibrated from deep inside his chest. His cock kicked in Micah's hand as the muscles in his ass and thighs convulsed.

"Fuuuuuck." The syllable breathed from Trace's mouth more like a robust exhale than an expletive as his body continued to forcefully contract and release, his cock grinding against both Micah's hand and the blanket covering the massage table. He was coming hard as potent convulsions pulsed through his body in time with every vigorous kick of his dick.

For at least thirty seconds, Micah massaged the base of Trace's cock through his orgasm, which seemed reluctant to end and was one of the most erotic episodes of sexual release Micah had ever witnessed from one of his subs.

Then Trace's body went limp. He didn't even seem to care that he was lying on his own spunk.

Micah gently drew his hand from between Trace's legs, caressed his smooth, wax-speckled ass, and took a few long moments to compose himself as Trace's body rose and fell as he breathed through the aftereffects of his orgasm. The only thing that would have made the experience better was if Micah could have connected with Trace's thoughts the way he did with Sam's when she came. There was nothing like riding out her orgasms with her. He had a feeling sharing Trace's would be just as good, if not better. Well, maybe not better, but certainly different.

In time. One day, Trace would open to him, and he would have what he wanted. Micah refused to accept this was as close as he would ever get to his friend. His submissive. His *last* submissive. He already knew he would never take another if Trace ever ceased to be his. From now on, they were linked at least in that respect. But Micah wanted more. He wanted all of Trace. Not just body and soul, but mind, too.

Micah took a deep breath and gathered himself then placed his hand on the back of Trace's head. Trace purred low and deep within his chest with every exhale.

"Time to clean you up, buddy," Micah said quietly. Without taking his hand off Trace's head, he turned and blew out the candles then shut off his small Crock-Pot before unplugging it. "You were amazing, Trace. You did such a good job." He removed the blindfold and stroked his friend's head, beginning his aftercare, which was his favorite part of a scene. The tending and caring that came after a session completed the circle and always sparked the deepest emotional response inside him. The love he felt before and during a scene magnified in the crucial steps afterward, when he released his sub, wiped him down, bathed him, held him, and ensured his mental well-being and safety. Any worthy Dom always provided this crucial coming-down phase to ensure his submissive didn't free fall into darkness and feelings of incompleteness and confusion.

Moving quietly, he stepped in front of the table, untied Trace's wrists, then gently laid his arms alongside his body.

"You were perfect." He caressed Trace's shoulder and arm as he moved back to his bench. "I couldn't be more pleased with your performance."

He picked up the knife Sam had set out for him. It was one of his favorites. Not his Bowie, but one made of black steel, with a charcoal-colored handle.

Turning back toward Trace, he said, "I'm going to remove the wax now. Just lie still and relax."

Carefully, so as not to cut skin or break the wax canvas, Micah slowly peeled back the thick, hardened sheet. As Micah gently pulled it away, Trace's mochaccino skin stuck to it, so Micah had to work slowly. He didn't want to cause Trace any discomfort. Not when he was so relaxed and gliding over invisible clouds.

Once the last corner pulled free, Micah set the entire rectangular sheet on the floor in one glorious piece.

"How you doin', big guy?" Micah gently brushed his palm over the red skin on Trace's back as he set the knife down then grabbed the dry shower loofah from the table. "You hanging in there?"

"Yes, Master." Trace's voice was barely a whisper.

Micah grinned wickedly to himself. Who said you had to get flogged bloody to have a deep submissive experience. See what a good waxing at the hands of a patient master could do?

Trace groaned and purred again as Micah lightly brushed the

loofah up and down his back and bottom, using circular motions to clear away any remaining wax.

Once he was satisfied Trace was clean and clear, he took a damp cloth, walked around to the other side of the table, rolled Trace toward him so Trace's back was propped against his torso, and carefully wiped away his semen.

Trace's cock was still hard, and as Micah wiped the damp cloth down the shaft, Trace came again. Out of nowhere, Trace's body convulsed and a creamy stream shot out onto the dark-blue sheet, followed by several smaller spurts. Trace groaned through each one until his body calmed once more and he took a heavy, cleansing breath.

"Look at you, champ." Micah glanced up to find Trace's pale-green eyes watching him. "Twice and I barely even had to try."

Trace blinked heavily, and the corners of his mouth curled weakly. "You da man."

Only Trace could crack a joke at a time like this.

Micah chuckled softly then shook his head. "No, buddy. You are." He stroked his palm over Trace's hip. "Now, come on. Let's finish cleaning you up and get you to bed." Trace had to be tired after not only the scene, but everything else he'd endured over the past two weeks.

Micah tucked his left arm around Trace's shoulders and his right arm under his knees. Then he lifted Trace off the table. He could clean up the wax-covered sheets tomorrow. Right now, he just wanted to take care of his friend.

CORDRAY GLARED through the rain-splattered windshield at Micah's house. Lightning streaked the sky as she shot the Range Rover into his driveway. Before the engine completely shut off, she was storming up the walkway toward the front door as thunder rolled.

She pounded and rang the bell as the clouds continued to empty their contents on her. When no one opened the door within two seconds, she pounded her fist on it again then hit the bell three more times.

"Micah, you son of a bitch!" she stepped back and yelled. "Open this goddamn door!"

Racing over here, she'd had time to discard the voice of reason that had told her taking Trace without her there had been the right thing to do. Now, the fact that Micah had broken protocol just pissed her off. Check that. It infuriated her.

She lifted her fist and was about to go Thor's hammer on the heavy wooden door again when she heard a system of locks disengage inside, and then the door swung open.

"Who the hell . . .?" A striking blonde with boy-short hair and green eyes gathered a peach, floral print robe around her neck as a gust of wind blew across the lawn.

Cordray was briefly taken aback. Samantha was lovelier and taller in person than she had been in Micah's thoughts during those times when Cordray poked around inside his head.

"You must be Sam," she said.

"Good guess. Who the hell are you?" Sam glared at her.

Oh, Cordray liked this one. She was feisty. "I'm Cordray. I'm sure you've heard my name once or twice."

From the way Sam's eyes narrowed and one brow lifted defensively, it was obvious Micah and Trace had no doubt blasphemed her name to hell and back, and she didn't need to go mind-probe to prove it.

"Do you mind?" Cordray lifted her hands to her sides, catching the rain as she tilted her face skyward and squinted. "Getting wet here."

Sam stepped aside and waved her in, but those green eyes never faltered and held Cordray with an air of wary contempt. "Why are you here?" she said after shutting the door and relocking it.

Cordray glanced around the entryway that led into an impressive open floorplan. Dining room, kitchen, and living room all shared one massive, elegantly appointed space, separated only by changes in flooring and furniture. The windows were covered by blinds, as well as cream and gold opaque curtains.

"Nice home." Cordray took off her dripping leather coat and held it out to Sam.

"Hang it up yourself." Sam huffed with exasperation and walked away from her into the kitchen, then stopped and looked back at her. "Well? Are you coming? The mud room's back here."

With a catty smile, Cordray followed her into a wide room with an eight-foot rack dotted with heavy-duty hooks on one wall. A low shelf held two pairs of boots and a pair of gym shoes. Sam gestured impatiently toward one of the hooks, spun on her bare foot, and walked out.

"I can see why Micah likes you," she said after hanging her coat and joining Sam in the kitchen.

Sam regarded her with a perturbed expression. "Why's that?"

Cordray plopped down on one of the barstools. Water sloshed under her ass. Her hair and pants were soaked, but if she could make a quick in and out with her bounty, she could handle it. "Because you've got moxie."

"Moxie?" Sam crossed her arms and leaned against the opposite counter, next to the fridge.

Cordray nodded and spun herself around on the rotating seat of the stool as if it were a merry-go-round. "Uh-huh. Moxie. Woman balls." She grabbed the edge of the counter to stop spinning, her gaze trained on Sam.

"Something you seem to know a lot about." Sam sucked her teeth, flashed her green peepers with a bob of her deceptively delicate eyebrows, and turned for the stove. "I'll ask again. Why are you here, Cordray?" She grabbed the teapot and carried it to the sink.

"Micah didn't tell you?"

"Should he have?" Sam switched on the faucet and began filling the pot.

Cordray drummed her fingers on the granite counter. "Oh, I don't know. I suppose the fact he took Trace without my permission and could get arrested for that might have slipped his mind." She had no intention of turning Micah over to her brother for what he'd done, but Sam didn't need to know that.

Sam slammed the metal teapot back on the stove and spun around, hands on her hips so that her robe parted to show off a patch of perfect, unblemished skin below her neck. "If you're here to arrest Micah, you'll have to go through me. I won't let you touch him *or* Trace." Sam wagged her finger at her. "Trace needs Micah right now. He was in bad shape when Micah brought him home, and—"

"Ooooooo, you *are* feisty, aren't you? I like that in a woman." Cordray let her gaze rake Sam up and down as she smiled and tilted her head suggestively to the side.

Cordray had been known to take females to bed as much as males, and Sam was exactly her type. Tall, blonde, and all spitfire. Might as well show Sam a little appreciation while she was here.

Sam sucked in a quick breath, swayed backward, and frowned as she secured her robe more tightly around her.

"Don't worry, honey," Cordray said with a coy grin. "I don't bite." She winked as her gaze took a little vacay down Sam's toned calves. "Although . . . for you, I might make an exception."

"Excuse me?"

She winked then spun herself around again as she flashed a catty smile. "Just get Trace for me, and I'll be out of your way."

"He's unavailable." Sam switched on the burner.

The tension in the kitchen was thick enough to bitch-slap.

"What do you mean, he's unavailable?"

Scowling at her, Sam nabbed a cup and saucer from the cabinet.

Just one cup. Either she wasn't going to have tea herself or she was about to be a bad hostess.

Sam set the cup and saucer on the counter. "Why should I tell you anything?"

"Because I said please."

"No you didn't."

Cordray slid off the bar stool, strolled around the counter, and drew near Micah's lovely mate. "Please," she said seductively, slinking up beside her.

SAM PULLED BACK.

What was Cordray's story? The woman — female, whatever — had a barrier of barbed wire around her so thick it cut Sam's thoughts just to think about trying to get through it. It was as if Cordray wanted to keep the entire planet at arm's length, if you could consider the length of a football field arm's length.

Sam was more than familiar with such behavior. Hadn't she done the same thing after what she'd endured with Steve? He'd beaten her. He'd mentally and emotionally abused her. After leaving him and fleeing as far away as she could, hadn't she erected a similar barrier around herself? Until she met Micah, she'd left as small a footprint as possible, never allowing anyone to get close, always keeping a layer of pushback between her and everyone around her.

Cordray reminded Sam of herself. A lot. Except Cordray seemed ten times worse. Not only did she push people off with her flippant attitude and mouthy jabs, but even her black, extreme attire and the tattoos that coated her neck and arms seemed to scream "Keep away!"

And what was up with her face? She looked like she'd recently been on the losing end of a fistfight with Sasquatch. Scuffs marred her cheek, and she had a gash on her swollen bottom lip that looked like it had been a profuse bleeder not too long ago.

In every way, Cordray was a walking billboard for the socially dysfunctional. And, the way Sam had done after leaving Steve, she would bet Cordray was using her abrasive behavior to protect herself from some pretty nasty demons.

Sam regarded her out of the corner of her eye.

"Please?" Cordray said again, slinking closer, no doubt in an effort to intimidate her.

Sam sighed and gestured to Cordray's drenched hair and wet pants. "You're dripping water all over my floor." She shook her head and sidestepped in the direction of the laundry room. "Let me get you a towel and a change of clothes. I have a feeling you're going to be here a while."

Before she could turn away, she noticed Cordray's perfectly curved, black eyebrows twist into a subtle frown as if she hadn't expected Sam's hospitality.

All the more evidence that Cordray was not what she tried to portray herself as. She wasn't used to kindness, and it was becoming more and more obvious she had a lot of skeletons in her closet. Skeletons that only a heaping serving of unconditional love could exorcise.

In the laundry room, she found a folded pair of pale-pink sweats, a white baby-doll tee with faded-red, Greek lettering across the chest, and a towel. When she returned to the kitchen, Cordray was still standing where she'd left her, looking a little dumbfounded . . . and maybe a tad wary.

"Here." Sam held the folded clothes toward her. "You can change in the bathroom." She pointed toward the hall. "It's the first door on the left."

Cordray cautiously took the stack of clothes, flipped through them, and then curled her upper lip. "Pink? You want me to wear pink?"

Sam cleared her throat to prevent herself from laughing, and then crossed her arms as she leaned her hip against the counter. "It's all I've got, honey. Take it or leave it."

"Honey?" Cordray arched one eyebrow. "You do have moxie."

Sam uncrossed her arms and held them out as if presenting the obvious. "I live with Micah. Moxie comes with the territory, babe."

Cordray eyed her suspiciously. With a resigned frown, she carried the dry clothes out of the kitchen toward the hall bathroom. "This doesn't make us friends, Sammy."

Grinning, Sam turned toward the cabinet and grabbed a second teacup. "I didn't think it did."

"Just so that's clear."

"Crystal clear."

"Okay then."

"Fine."

Cordray disappeared into the hall, and a moment later, Sam heard the bathroom door click shut.

Micah would probably throw a fit, because he had ranted ad nauseam about Cordray for over two weeks. How she was a bitch. How she had been the one to put Trace in prison. How she was so far up King Bain's ass there was nothing Micah and Trace could do to retaliate against her without fear of repercussions. And sure, Sam had bought into his animosity. When she had opened the door less than ten minutes ago to find a regal, beautiful woman—female— with sapphire eyes, long, crazy braids, a swatch of two-toned blue hair framing the left side of her face, and tattoos from here to Sunday standing on her porch, she had known in an instant who she was and had reacted defensively.

But now that she'd met Cordray, the phrase *there are always two sides to every story* came to mind. She felt Micah—and even Trace— had gotten her all wrong. After all, they were big, stupid men—males, whatever. They were warriors who thought first with their fists, second with their penises, and only when their first two thinking mechanisms were depleted did they turn to their brains for help.

Sam's gut told her Cordray was simply misunderstood. *Very* misunderstood.

Not that Sam needed to be Cordray's savior, but being that Cordray reminded her so much of herself, her heartstrings tugged a little for the woman—female.

She really needed to stop thinking in human terminology. Vampires were male and female. Humans were men and women. Maybe by the end of the decade she'd get with the lingo.

As she grabbed a box of herbal tea from the cabinet, she pondered what kind of trauma could make a tough-assed vampire like Cordray become so abrasive. Or maybe she'd donned the tough-as-nails persona because of some traumatic emotional wound, and she was really a sweetheart deep down.

Sweetheart. There was a word she couldn't see anyone associating with that fireball changing into pink sweatpants in the hall bathroom. But if the past had shaped Cordray into living barbed wire, that meant whatever had happened had been harsh, cruel, and likely the equivalent of an emotional tsunami.

Sam thought back at her own life. She'd made a major misstep marrying Steve before she really knew him, and she still bore a scar on her abdomen to remind her of the abuse she'd suffered at his hand. But thanks to her upbringing, she'd been strong enough to break free. True, before she met Micah she'd lived every day in fear of Steve catching up to her and dragging her back home, where he would have made her a prisoner, but she'd had the strength to get away. That alone was a step most abused women were too frightened to take.

Fear made for a treacherous ally. It kept you in bad situations when what you really needed was to find the courage to strike out and make a new reality for yourself. She had let fear rule her decisions far too long, even though she'd broken from Steve within a couple of years. But those two years had affected her terribly. Even now, within the safety of Micah's protection and knowing he had wiped Steve's memory clean of her, she still looked over her shoulder when she went out in public. She still feared giving her real name anywhere she went. Using the credit cards Micah had given her still gave her anxiety. Paying with cash had become such a way of life to protect herself from being found that using a credit card even now made her nerves quake. Part of her was still terrified Steve would remember her and use the credit cards to track her down. Yes, the name on the accounts was Micah's, but the name on the cards was hers.

If just a couple of years with Steve could fill her with that much insecurity and dread, what would it be like for an immortal vampire to endure abuse or at least some devastating emotional blow for decades or even centuries?

What would it be like for Cordray, for example?

She'd had a lot more time to suffer. Longer for the pain to seep into her soul and alter not just her outlook, but her behavior, as well.

She was making a huge assumption about Cordray's past, but Sam would bet a million dollars that Cordray had been severely hurt at some point. The question was when, how, and why? And how had that damage manifested into the woman—female— Cordray was today?

She poured hot water into the teacups and dropped a bag of herbal tea into each. Maybe what Cordray needed was a friend. Not that Sam necessarily wanted to volunteer for the job, but a friend might be able to help Cordray sift through the shit.

One thing was certain, though. She couldn't let Cordray think she felt sorry for her. If Cordray thought that, the thorny atmosphere around her would just get thicker and draw more blood. Cordray was one female who clearly didn't take well to compassion or sympathy, so Sam wouldn't give it to her. But she didn't have to show compassion and sympathy to feel it, and feel it she did.

She took a careful sip of her tea and gazed down the hall toward the bathroom. Hopefully, Micah would understand.

CORDRAY STARED AT HER REFLECTION in the full-length mirror. Pink? Really? Pink sweatpants? And pale pink at that? As if white had bitch-slapped red into submission then ejaculated a bucketful of semen on it.

And then there was the shirt.

Young.

Cutesy.

Feminine.

And one hundred percent *not* her. It didn't even fit. Not really. It fit everywhere but around her boobs, which pressed against the fabric and stretched the red, Greek lettering into distorted, geometric shapes.

In the movie *Nightmare on Elm Street*, there was a scene where Freddie Krueger pushed his face against what was supposed to be a sheet but looked like a layer of latex. It stretched over his face, smashing his features until he used his knife-fingers to slice himself free.

That's what her boobs reminded her of in this shirt.

She was so not taking a selfie with this getup on. And no one else would, either, if they valued their ability to pass waste without a colostomy bag.

With a perturbed sigh, she hung her wet clothes over the shower curtain rod, set her combat boots to the side, and grabbed the towel, draped it over her shoulders, and began unraveling her braids. Her hair would dry faster if unbraided, but damn, she hated undoing Aiden's impressive work. That two-year-old mixed-blood had mad skills when it came to hair.

Five minutes later, a small pile of elastic bands sat on the bathroom counter, and her wavy, black-and-blue hair spilled over her shoulders and hid her breasts. That was better.

She dabbed the tip of her index finger against the scuff marks on her cheek then poked at the laceration just to the inside of her lip ring, which constricted her swollen bottom lip like a belt that was two sizes too small. Her injuries appeared better than they had an hour ago, though, and seemed to be healing nicely. Her vision was even back to normal. By nightfall, her face would look good as new, thanks to her vampire heritage.

Granted, she was only half vampire. She was also half human. Her human half allowed her to go out in the sun. Full-bloods couldn't do that. But vampire genes trumped all others, so while she was granted certain gifts from her mortal side, her immortal side ensured she was more vampire than human. So much so, she was classified as a vampire. A mixed-blood, but a vampire nonetheless. She still had fangs and still had to feed off blood. Furthermore, those high-octane vampire genes she'd inherited from her royal father, along with regular feedings, kept her healing powers in tip-top shape.

When she returned to the kitchen, Sam was leaning against the counter, sipping her tea. Cordray noticed a second cup awaiting her where she had been sitting earlier.

Well, lookie there. Sam had decided to play nice hostess after all.

Without saying a word, she sat down and lifted her cup. Chamomile. Not her usual poison, but it would do. She took a sip, her gaze meeting Sam's.

Neither spoke for a long time. It wasn't in Cordray's nature to accept charity, nor was it in her nature to say thank you when such charity was given. If Sam couldn't deal with that, tough shit.

After a few more tense moments, Sam set her cup and saucer on the counter. "How does everything fit?"

She smirked, set her own cup down, and stood, pulling back her hair. "Like my boobs are pregnant."

Laughter burst from Sam's mouth. She quickly bit it back. "I'm sorry. Um . . ." She turned away and tried to wipe the smile off her face.

"You're punishing me for being such a bitch earlier, aren't you?" Cordray let her hair fall over her chest again and sat back down.

"No, I . . . uh . . ." Sam poured herself another cup of tea and offered the teapot in Cordray's direction.

She waved it off. "It's okay, you can admit it. I was a bitch. I deserve it." She lifted her cup and blew over the tea's surface.

Sam set the teapot back on the stove. "Well, maybe I'm punishing you just a little."

"I thought so." Cordray grinned and caressed the rim of her teacup with her fingertips as she set it back in the saucer.

The two eyed each other for a moment, and then Sam burst out laughing again, almost spilling her tea as she haphazardly set the cup on the counter. "*'Like my boobs are pregnant'*?"

Cordray glanced down and chuckled, unable to hold back any longer. "Well, yeah. I mean, look at this." She lifted her hair and glanced down at her chest. "Don't you have *any* cleavage, Sam? I mean, my *God!* I'm like two basketballs trying to fit inside a Pringles can." She flipped her hair over her shoulders and patted her palms over her breasts, which made Sam laugh harder.

And just like that, she and Sam went from being mortal enemies to tentative friends, laughing and bridging the gap between them. Sam wasn't the bad guy here. She was just mated to one. Cordray couldn't hold Micah's and Trace's misgivings against her.

And, honestly, she liked Sam. That woman had big lady balls, but in a good way. Don't mess with her, because she wouldn't just sit back and be walked on. Sam was a fighter. She'd taken on drecks to save Micah's life, and she'd almost died from Apostle's venom before Micah gave her his and made her his davala. The transformation had to have been painful as hell, maybe even excruciating, and now Sam was taking her new body and the strange new world of vampires, drecks, and the supernatural in stride. The woman was a fortress of mental strength and fortitude.

Cordray had to admire a chick like that. Hell, after what she'd been through in her own past, maybe she could learn a thing or two from Sam, because she certainly hadn't taken change half as well as Samantha had. It was enough to make her question who the stronger female in the room really was.

"I wasn't blessed with busty genes." Sam dabbed the knuckle of her index finger under one eye then the other to clear away tears of laughter.

"Then maybe you should give me one of Micah's shirts." Cordray groped herself one last time then shook her head as she disengaged her hands from her breasts and picked up her cup.

"Hey," Sam said, giggling and pretending to be offended. "Are you saying my man has big tits?"

It was Cordray's turn to laugh. "You tell me, girl. He's *your* mate."

The two chuckled, and Sam joined Cordray at the counter. "I'd give you one of his shirts, but—no offense—he would probably make me burn the thing after you left."

"No offense taken. I know how he feels about me." Everyone else felt the same way about her as Micah did. She eyed Sam over the rim of her cup. Well, not everyone. She and Sam seemed to have found an accord. "But I guess that answers that question."

"What question is that?"

"Whether or not Micah has told you about me."

Sam smiled at her. "Yes, I've heard all about you."

"All good, I'm sure," she said sarcastically.

With a roll of her eyes, Sam laughed. "Micah is ultra-competitive . . .

and ultra-protective. And he's a man." She rolled her eyes again then caught herself. "I mean, I love him and all, but you know how thick men can be."

Cordray swirled her tea and nodded. "I do." All too well. Males were ruled by their biology. The primal urges in their balls tended to overrule their hearts and brains.

Her past threatened to strike her with sadness again, but she shook it off, took a deep breath, and saluted Sam with her teacup. "Sam, of all the times I've seen you in Micah's thoughts, I'd never have taken you for a cynic."

Sam tilted her head in acknowledgement. "Well, from all the bitching Micah has done about you, I'd never have taken you for someone with such a great sense of humor."

Cordray set down her cup and held her fist toward Sam. "Hell yeah, girl. Give me some." She nodded toward her fist.

Sam grinned and fist-bumped her. "Here's to cynics and bitches with senses of humor."

"Amen." Cordray killed her tea and settled the empty cup in the saucer.

"More?" Sam got up.

"Sure. I'll have one more cup." In the right company, she enjoyed a good cup of tea as much as a shot of Jack. And Sam was swiftly becoming the right kind of company for both.

As Sam fetched the teapot from the stove, Cordray's gaze swept the room. "So, how bad a shape was Trace in when Micah brought him home?" She tried to sound disinterested. No sense making Sam think she was more concerned than she was, even if she couldn't quite convince herself of that.

Sam poured water in her cup. "I figured you would have poked inside my head by now to see for yourself. Micah says you're as bad as he is about seeing inside people's thoughts."

"I'm being nice," she said with an air of false modesty.

One of Sam's eyebrows shot up. "Ooohh? How did I warrant such special treatment?" She returned the pot to the stove.

Cordray stirred the water around her used tea bag. "It's true, I do have talents in unlocking mental barriers, but I *can* restrain myself."

"Micah told me you can see inside Trace's thoughts. Is that true?" She lifted her cup to her lips and blew over the hot liquid.

Cordray cleared her throat and shifted on the bar stool. "Yes, I can unlock Trace's mind."

"Really?" Sam swept around the counter and sat down beside her.

"What's going on with him? Is he okay? Is—"

Cordray held up her hand. "I can't answer that."

Sam sighed and sat back, appearing ashamed for even asking. "I'm sorry. I shouldn't have asked. It's just that Micah and I care about him so much, and it would really be helpful if Micah could get inside his thoughts."

Something in her chest fluttered at hearing Sam talk about Trace. Kind of like she had heartburn, but good heartburn. As if she *wanted* it to feel like it was a bad thing when it really wasn't.

Still, she felt she owed Sam a morsel for being so nice to her. "I'll tell you this much. Trace thinks the world of you and Micah. You're always first and foremost in his thoughts. I'm almost jeal—" She cut herself off, frowning as she caught her Freudian slip and attempted to cover it. "I mean . . . as much as I can't stand the guy, Trace is lucky to have friends like you."

When she met Sam's gaze again, it was clear her slip hadn't gone unnoticed. Sam's acutely aware green eyes were laser-locked on hers, studying her. "We all need friends like that, don't we?" she said as if probing for information.

Cordray pursed her lips and looked away with a shrug. "I wouldn't know."

She liked Sam, but she wasn't going to reveal her history after one good booby joke. One shared laugh did not a bonded friendship make, and she wanted to get herself out of the spotlight before this conversation went any further and shed light on her personal feelings.

"So how was he? Trace, I mean? How bad was he when Micah got him here?" Getting them back to the original question was a good plan, even if she had to work to keep the personal inflection from her tone.

"He was pretty bad." Sam's voice held a suspicious undercurrent, and a shrewd twinkle lit in her eyes as a subtle, knowing grin turned up the corners of her mouth. "I'm taking it as a good sign they've been downstairs for so long. Hopefully, that means Trace is better now."

Cordray checked the gold-faced clock on the wall. It was well past sunrise, but she never would have known with the blinds and drapes blocking out the daylight.

"Yeah, hopefully." She spun her cup in its saucer, suddenly uneasy under Sam's scrutiny. All edgy and shit.

Trace was in the basement with Micah. The two of them were doing God knew what to each other. And, well . . . it kind of pissed her off. Part of her felt she should be the one giving Trace what he needed while the other part of her protested that belief.

But by giving Trace what he needed, maybe she would get what she needed, as well. It had been so very long since she'd felt that kind of pleasure. The breathtaking, quivering release of her muscles. The feel of a warm, moist mouth as it consumed her tender flesh. The delicious brutality of rough hands kneading her breasts.

All she had left of such sensations were gossamer memories so old and ethereal she almost couldn't remember how being made love to felt. She knew it felt good. She remembered crying out as her body let go, remembered enjoying Gideon's mouth and hands on her skin, but she couldn't remember exactly how it felt.

She wanted to know that feeling again. With Trace, she could. If only she could get past her own fears and his utter disdain of her.

"So, what are you going to do with Trace for the next three months?"

"*Do* with him?" She turned toward Sam, her heart skipping a beat. What she *wanted* to do with him was a wholly different answer than what she *would* do with him.

Sam's eyes narrowed as she angled her head to the side, almost as if she'd seen the incriminating thoughts Cordray had just entertained. "Yes, while he's on parole, or whatever you call it in the vampire legal system. Micah said he's to be in your custody. What are your plans for him?"

Working harder at keeping her game face on so Sam wouldn't become any more suspicious than she already was, Cordray sipped her tea. "I run a shelter of sorts. It's more of an orphanage, but we have a school there, too." She swept her hand in a half circle as if to encompass the whole gamut of possibilities. "It's a place for pre-transitional and newly transitioned vampires, mostly mixed-bloods. It's easier for mixed-bloods to get lost in the human system than full-bloods. I find them, take them in, give them a home. Asylum is a place that gives such kids an anchor in a world that would otherwise overwhelm or even consume them." Talking about Asylum and her kids gave her a welcome reprieve from thinking about Trace.

Sam's eyebrows shot up like this was the last thing she'd expected to hear. "You take care of them?"

Cordray tucked her still-damp hair behind her ear and glanced into her half-empty cup. "You sound surprised."

"Oh, I . . . it's just that . . . from what Micah's told me . . ." Her cheeks flushed and she fidgeted with her teacup.

"In other words, what's a bristly witch like me doing caring about anybody other than myself, right?"

Sam's shoulders fell as she looked down, abashed. "No, that's not—"

"Don't worry about it." Cordray set her cup in its saucer a little more heavily than necessary, her back stiffening. "I know what people think of me. I know what Micah and Trace say about me and that I'm not the most popular bitch in Chicago. But I do have a heart. I do care. Maybe I don't always show it, but I do." In fact, she cared a great deal. Probably more than most. When you've suffered great pain, you tend to feel equally great compassion, even if you don't wear that compassion on your sleeve.

She faced the counter again as she recalled taking the razor to Trace in Bain's dungeon. She'd known Trace was struggling to keep his power under control, and it had pained her to see him suffer. She wanted to believe that the only reason she'd provided him a means to keep his inner demons under control was because, being in the dungeon, he was close to Bain's royal residence. But the truth was, she hated seeing him in so much agony.

Maybe she and Trace didn't get along. Maybe they even detested one another—or at least pretended to detest one another in her case. But even an injured wasp deserved mercy. After all, it was still a living, breathing creature that toiled and struggled to survive just like the rest of God's creations.

"A shelter is a noble endeavor," Sam said, recovering from her social hiccup. "Definitely not for the faint of heart. Are you planning to have Trace help you there?"

"Yes."

"That'll be interesting." Sam lifted her cup to her lips.

"Why? Do you think I need to worry about how he'll behave around the kids?"

Sam's eyes met hers. "Your guess is as good as mine. I've never seen him with kids. But he's a gentle soul. I think he'll be okay."

"Gentle? Did you say he's a *gentle* soul?"

Sam issued a short laugh. "Okay, let me qualify that by saying that he's gentle around here. I know he can be a terror to others with that hand of his, and I know you and he have a few bumps to work through before you'll agree with me—"

"Just a few." As in, she didn't think she would ever be able to call Trace gentle. At least not from what she'd seen of him.

Sam shrugged. "Yeah well, he's a good male. He won't hurt your kids." An awkward, somewhat chagrined smile twisted her mouth. Then she sighed and brightened as if she'd forced away a sad thought.

"So, what kind of things are you going to have him do at the shelter?"

"Manual labor. Heavy work. I've got a lot of land, and now that it's spring, there's a lot of mowing, tilling, and landscaping that needs to be done, as well as a lot of cleanup."

"At least you'll be keeping him busy. I have a feeling he's going to need that."

"Why do you think that?"

"Gut feeling. AKM was sort of his life before he was arrested. Now he's got to find a way to fill all that time." She looked away and chuckled quietly. "Do you realize that I don't even know where he lives? I've known him since January and have never seen his home."

Cordray dropped her gaze into her teacup. "Look around, Sam."

Sam frowned then said, "What do you mean?"

An empty ache dove into her stomach as she faced Sam again. "Look around." She gestured toward the house. "*This* is Trace's home."

Those four words bothered her more than anything she'd said, heard, or done all morning. And she knew why, even if she refused to admit it.

Deep down, in a place she struggled more and more to suppress, she wanted Trace's home to be with her.

CHAPTER 6

TRACE LUXURIATED IN BOTH THE BATH Micah had drawn, as well as Micah's presence, which enveloped him like a warm blanket. Just being near Micah soothed him. Feeling his hands scoop warm water over his chest, arms, neck, and head was enough to bliss him out even more than he already was.

Micah took his time bathing him, but as the water grew tepid and Trace's fingertips shriveled into clam-like nodules, Micah opened the drain and helped Trace from the tub.

Trace couldn't even speak. He was too relaxed. Too lost in the tranquility that only came after a scene. Only this time it was much deeper. Micah had taken him further than anyone ever had, and he didn't want to talk, move, or even breathe for fear of losing this treasured, euphoric feeling.

Micah seemed to sense his mental state, because he remained quiet, and he moved with unobtrusive restraint. As if he knew how precious and fragile the moment was.

Micah guided him to the marble bench near the shower, retrieved a towel from the precisely stacked linens organized by color and thickness, then knelt in front of Trace as he wrapped the plush softness around his shoulders. He gently scrubbed the towel up and down his arms, over his head, across his back, down his torso and legs, slowly lifting each foot to dry his soles.

All Trace could do was watch. And feel. And indulge his placid senses.

"How do you feel?" Micah asked, his voice low and sedate.

"Good." Trace's voice sounded deeper than usual. Not having to guard against his inner beast made even his vocal chords relax. "I'm calm."

Micah smiled. "We live to breathe another day then."

Trace's lips curved into a lazy grin. "Thanks to you."

Micah wrapped his forearm behind Trace's head and pulled him forward until their foreheads touched. "I'm here for you. I'll always be here for you. I won't ever let anything happen to you, Trace."

Trace closed his eyes and breathed in the warmth pouring out of Micah's body. This was his friend, his master, his confidante. His savior. Without the hope becoming Micah's friend had given him, Trace wasn't sure he would still be alive today. It was that hope — that Micah would agree to be his master — that had kept Trace going.

The wait had been worth every second. He'd just experienced the most incredible scene in his memory.

The hot wax, the tightening of his skin, the controlled care and dominance Micah had exercised, the way he'd been bound at the wrists so he couldn't move and had to relinquish trust in himself and pass it to Micah . . . all of it had led to the most astonishing and glorious trip through subspace he'd ever taken, culminated by the most intense orgasm any of his masters or mistresses had ever given him.

The release itself had been something beyond reality. He'd been floating, sailing along inside his head, and then Micah's fingers had grazed his balls. The electric pulse of arousal had awakened every nerve ending in his body, tossing him into a furious spiral. He'd felt like a new star being born, drawing every fragment of cosmic dust into his body as Micah's palm wrapped around his erection and began pumping. Within seconds, dark matter exploded, sending heat into the universe, expelling light in all directions.

When he drifted back into consciousness and found himself still on Micah's table, his whole body had hummed with electricity. He'd known then that he had another orgasm inside him, on the verge of erupting. One that a simple, subtle caress would release. A caress Micah had given him as he began his aftercare.

Trace had never come twice like that. So hard, so completely.

He wanted for nothing.

Nothing, that was, except a mate of his own who could do to him all that Micah had just done without requiring his submission to achieve it.

Don't get him wrong, he relished this. He enjoyed flying through subspace at Micah's hands. The pleasure experienced as Micah's submissive was beyond compare, but he didn't always want to rely on being taken to another place mentally to experience pleasure. He didn't want to always be subjected to pain, degradation, and being bound to find arousal. He dreamed of being the master. Of being an active participant rather than the object of someone else's stimulation.

A true mate — one he bonded to and experienced a calling with — would allow him that. At least, he assumed she would. And in his mind, his true mate *was* a female. A dynamic, spunky, spitfire of a female who could take as well as give. That's what he wanted. That's what he dreamed of. Where could he find such a female?

Cordray.

His eyes flashed open as Cordray's name whipped unbidden through his thoughts, as if she were the answer to his question. Hell no. Cordray was the last female he needed. The last who could give him all that he desired.

Wasn't she?

His brow tightened as he recalled how his body responded every time she was around. Not one time had he walked away from her without an erection. She heated him inside and out with her smart mouth and verbal jabs. Even now, just thinking about their aggressive exchanges made him want to find her just so they could argue and toss insults at each other. The only time he felt as alive as Cordray made him feel was when he was with Micah. But with Cordray, he didn't have to go submissive. He could get in her face, verbally spar with her, and still feel his power bow out and recede into the shadows.

Maybe that wasn't the same as being dominant, but it sure as hell wasn't falling into submission, either.

Was it possible that Cordray could be . . .?

He couldn't even think that question to its conclusion. Cordray couldn't be his mate. She simply couldn't be.

He mentally shook off the possibility. In his dreams, the female he imagined he would mate didn't have tattoos all over her body and didn't come prepackaged with the attitude of a Tyrannosaurus Rex.

Still, Cordray was a fine piece of female. She had all the right curves in all the right places. He didn't have to like her to appreciate the package she came in.

"Come on, buddy," Micah said, pulling him from his thoughts, "let's get you to bed so you can rest."

He let Micah help him up then followed him into the master bedroom, where Micah pulled a pair of boxers and a T-shirt from his bureau.

"Here." Micah tossed the clothes at him. "You can wear these."

Trace held up his hand and motioned toward the doorway leading to the stairs. "I've got my own bedroom, Micah." He stayed at the house enough that he'd all but moved in. "I can go up and get my own clo—"

Micah softly slapped his cheek. "No arguing with me. Wear mine and get into bed." Micah snapped his fingers and pointed to the massive, custom-made bed he normally shared with Sam.

"But—"

"Do I have to dress you myself and strap you down?" Micah grinned, crossed his arms, and propped his hip against the dresser. "Don't think I won't."

"You're impossible." Trace dropped the T-shirt on the bed and unfolded the boxers.

"Sam says I'm incorrigible."

"Same thing."

"I know." Micah chucked his chin toward the boxers. "Now, get dressed."

"Shit, but you're bossy." He smirked and pulled the shorts on and snapped the elastic waistband around his waist.

"Yep. But that's why you're here, isn't it?"

Trace's grin stretched even wider as he met Micah's gaze. "Yeah, that's why I'm here." He picked up the T-shirt. "But this is your bed. Where are you going to sleep?"

Micah's eyes flicked upward, indicating upstairs. "Sam set us up in one of the spare rooms." The tone of his voice, as well as the erection straining his cargo pants, suggested that while Trace's fun was winding down, Micah's was only beginning.

"Gotcha." Trace tugged the shirt over his torso. "Wish I could join you."

Micah pushed away from the dresser and closed the distance between them. "Yeah, me too. I'd have invited you, but you need about a week of sleep, so . . ."

"Next time."

"Absolutely." Micah swiped his palm over Trace's head. "We've missed you, but we can wait a couple more days."

He'd missed their threesomes, too. Missed watching the two most beautiful people in the world make love to each other. He got a semi-boner just thinking about it, but Micah was right. He was exhausted. Hell, he was beyond exhausted. Totally depleted was more like it.

The comforter, blankets, and sheets were already pulled back, and Micah ushered him to lie down then pulled the blankets over him.

"I'll be right back." Micah disappeared inside the bathroom again as Trace sank into the warm, soft bed.

He hadn't even had a pillow in King Bain's dungeon. How thankful he was to finally be free, back where he belonged, with creature comforts like soft sheets, a pillow-top mattress, and indoor plumbing.

Within seconds, sleep encroached, and his eyelids grew heavy.

Micah returned holding a glass of water. "Drink this."

He helped Trace sit up and held the glass for him. Trace downed every drop. He hadn't even realized how thirsty he was.

"You need more?"

Trace shook his head. "I'm good." Even to himself, he sounded seriously out of it.

"You want to talk about what happened in there?" Micah bobbed his head toward the dungeon as he crawled onto the bed and lay down next to him. He propped himself on one elbow and gently stroked Trace's bald head with his fingers.

Trace closed his eyes at the gentle touch. "It was . . . unexpected."

"Good unexpected?" Micah said.

"Very good."

"You liked it then?"

Trace nodded lazily.

"I thought you would." Micah shifted, and Trace peeked out the corner of his eye to see that Micah was fully reclined on his side beside him, staring at him. "I loved seeing your reactions as I applied each coat of wax. The more I put on, the more relaxed you became. The deeper you fell into subspace."

Trace rolled his head on the pillow and held Micah's gaze for a long time. The longer they stared at one another, the louder the unspoken messages between them became.

He was grateful. So damn grateful. Micah didn't have to take him in. He didn't have to give Trace such a large part of himself and take his time away from Sam, but he had, and he did. And he seemed ready to continue doing so.

Frowning through his gratitude so that he didn't actually shed tears, Trace turned his body into Micah's and buried his face against his friend's chest. "Thank you." He had never felt as accepted by anyone as he did with Micah—not even with his own family—and never would have allowed anyone but Micah to see him like this. With Micah, he was vulnerable, even afraid, and that was okay. He could save his scary, tough face for the rest of the world.

He could save it for Cordray.

Micah wrapped him in his arms and rocked him. "You're safe now," he said softly. "You're back home and you're safe. You're in my care now, Trace, and it's my turn to look out for you for a change."

Trace gripped him tightly and nodded against his chest, trying to contain the immense gratitude welling inside his chest.

"No more prison," Micah said. "No more being away from Sam and me. We're a family again, and you were so good tonight. So damn good. You made me feel like a true master."

"And you made me feel . . ." What? What was the word to describe how Micah made him feel. "Normal." Normal wasn't something Trace had felt in a long time, if ever. He'd always been different.

Freak!

Until Micah and Sam had welcomed him into their lives, he had never truly felt normal. With them, he wasn't a freak. He wasn't a demon or a walking natural disaster. He was just . . . Trace.

And that was the greatest gift Micah could have given him.

MICAH HELD HIS NEAREST AND DEAREST FRIEND like his life depended on it.

Trace made him feel powerful. He gave himself entirely to the process and sacrificed every ounce of control so that Micah could take it. A responsibility Micah didn't take for granted. One slip with a candle — one mistake — and the tiny bubble of trust that had formed between them would shatter.

The enormous power exchange Trace had granted him was enough to send Micah on a head trip of his own, so aftercare was as much for him as it was for Trace. He needed this time of bonding and cooling off as much as Trace did.

Trace's hold on him finally weakened, and Micah gently rolled him to his back and fluffed the pillow around his head. "Are you comfortable? Too warm? Too cold?"

Trace blinked drowsily. "I'm perfect."

Micah rolled up his sleeve, revealing his wrist. "I made you a promise earlier."

Hunger stirred in Trace's pale-green irises as his eyes opened wider and met his.

Lifting his wrist toward Trace's mouth, he shifted closer. "Take my blood."

Trace licked his lips almost nervously but hesitated.

"I told you before we started I would give you my blood if you pleased me." He held Trace's gaze for several seconds then nodded before pressing his wrist to Trace's lips and lowering his voice. "You pleased me. Very much."

That was all it took, and Trace's mouth opened to expose his fangs, so like Maddox's. One set of uppers and one set of lowers. Tonight, after they'd all gotten some much-needed rest, he and Trace would talk about Maddox and Brak. They needed to figure out what to do about the situation, and Trace needed to see his father and brother. But right now Trace needed rest above all else.

Fangs pierced his wrist, and an instant later venom euphoria took him. Under the onslaught of sensual overload, Micah lazed back on the bed, loose and flying high, moaning as thick arousal stabbed at the heart of him. Sam had better be ready for him, because he needed her. God, how he needed her. She would provide the rest of his aftercare, because after spending more than two hours with Trace, waxing him, cleaning him, and now feeding him, Micah was in a state unlike anything he had felt since his calling.

It seemed like five minutes before Trace released his arm, but Micah knew better than that. There was no way he had fed for five minutes. One or two, yes, but not five.

"Your blood is" —Trace licked his lips and rolled toward him— "strong."

Micah didn't push him away, still lost to euphoria. He welcomed Trace's arm as it curled over him almost protectively. But wasn't that at the heart of their relationship? Protection?

More than once, Trace had put himself at risk to keep Micah safe. Such as when Sam almost died after he changed her into his davala. And again two weeks ago, when Micah had made that insane outburst during Trace's trial and the king's guards jumped him. Trace refused to let anyone hurt him, and he became severely protective if Micah appeared to be in danger.

What they had was devotion. They were both unconditionally committed to one another. Trace had proven himself back in January, when he had helped Micah save Sam. Now, Micah couldn't imagine his life without Trace, and he could sense Trace felt the same way. They were bonded more tightly than brothers, even when it came to Sam, because Trace was the only male on the planet Micah could even fathom letting participate in his intimate time with her.

Micah sank into Trace's sheltering embrace and breathed. As with Sam, when he was with Trace, he could breathe so damn easily. "You make me feel safe," he said softly, almost a murmur, as the euphoria finally began to dissipate.

"Ditto." Trace's cheek pressed against the back of Micah's shoulder, and then he rolled away.

Micah rolled with him so they faced each other again, and he took hold of Trace's wrist. The lacerations that had lined his forearm earlier were already healing now that Trace had fed, but a few of the particularly bad cuts lingered.

"Let me help you with these." He pulled himself up and straddled Trace's hips over the covers, lifting Trace's arm to his lips.

The glands in his mouth released their venom as he held Trace's expectant gaze, and then he languidly drew his tongue across one of the cuts. Trace's eyes closed, and he sighed. Again, Micah positioned Trace's arm and swirled the breadth of his tongue over another wound. He continued treating each remaining lesion until the last one silently vanished. Then he laid Trace's arm carefully over his stomach.

"All better." He bent forward so they were nose to nose and eye to eye when Trace opened his eyes again.

The two simply stared at each other, caught in the intimacy of the moment. Micah knew Trace could feel his erection, but he said nothing and gave no indication he did.

After several seconds, Micah leaned down and brushed his lips over Trace's. "Welcome home." Micah held his gaze for another long moment then slid off the bed and straightened the covers over Trace's body, tucking him in. "I'll stay with you until you fall asleep."

Trace didn't say a word, just nodded once and blinked as if he were coming out of a dream. Micah pulled the chair in the corner toward the bed and sat down, sprawled his legs to give his erection space, and got comfortable as Trace maintained eye contact with him from across the room.

Unspoken love and allegiance passed between them, but nothing more was said. In less than five minutes, Trace's eyelids grew too heavy to stay open. He blinked wearily once . . . twice . . . and on the third, his eyes stayed closed. Within minutes, his breathing evened out, grew fuller, and his lips parted as he quickly fell into a deep sleep.

The weeks of incarceration, stress, and now his first session with Micah, had caught up to him.

Micah grinned, quietly got up, set out a change of clothes for when Trace woke this evening, and shut off the main light so that only the dim illumination from the night-light in the bathroom lit the room. Then he tiptoed up the stairs, unlocked and opened the door, and noiselessly shut it behind him.

Now, to Sam.

He started toward the kitchen, ready to dart upstairs and sink himself into Sam's waiting heat, needing to feel her fire and —

He stutter-stepped to a halt as he caught the scent of a visitor. His upper lip curled. He knew that smell. As he entered the kitchen, he saw Cordray on the couch next to Sam, looking as cozy as a hyena robbing the lion of its prey, teacup in her hand, a smile on her face.

What was that bitch doing in his home? And why was Sam acting like her presence was no big thing?

CHAPTER 7

CORDRAY HAD BEEN LISTENING TO SAM tell her about the night she met Micah and how she'd shot Apostle when the door to the basement opened. She and Sam both turned toward the kitchen, and a moment later, Micah appeared, looking and smelling as ready for sex as a two-cent whore.

Then his eyes met hers, and the mood instantly shifted.

"What the fuck are you doing here?" he said, his thick, black brows knitting together over the bridge of his nose.

Not to be intimidated, she set down her tea, stood, and crossed her arms. "You took Trace without my permission. I'm here to retrieve him."

Sam bristled as she stood beside her, but not as if she were angry. More like she was concerned that World War III was about to go postal in her living room.

"Everybody just calm down," Sam said, holding her hands up.

Micah ignored her and barged forward, getting in Cordray's face. "Oh, so now you want to put Trace on your priority list, is that it? Where were you three hours ago?" He jabbed his finger toward her. "You were late, and my buddy needed me, so if you don't like that I took him without your goddamn approval—"

"I can suck your ass," Cordray finished for him. "Yeah, I got the message from the guard on duty. Now, if you and Trace are done swapping cock snot, I'd like to take him and get the hell out of here."

Even as she said it, she knew moving Trace right now wouldn't happen. She wasn't so clueless that she didn't understand how badly Trace needed to rest after his stay in her brother's dungeon. But damn it, she should have been there on time. She should have been the one responsible for making sure he got out of that nasty place and safely into Micah's hands to receive the care he needed. It hurt her heart that she had failed at something so important. Something that *felt* important.

"Damn straight, you can suck my ass." Aggression blazed in his navy blue eyes as he took a menacing step forward.

"Stop!" Sam jumped between them. "Micah, back off. Cordray, let me handle this."

Sam had no fear, jumping between two tigers about to shred each other.

Cordray took a deep breath and stepped back before turning away and squeezing her eyes closed. She'd seen inside Micah's mind. She knew what he and Trace had done to one another. Or rather, what Micah had done to Trace. He'd made Trace come. He'd kissed him. They'd held each other like lovers in a bed the size of Chicago.

And knowing that hurt.

She didn't want it to hurt. She didn't want what Micah and Trace had done together to carve out her insides like she was a Thanksgiving turkey. But that didn't stop the ache from gnawing at the inside of her chest.

Something about Trace threw everything inside her into upheaval, and tears stung her eyes at the idea that he and Micah were so close they could be as intimate as lovers.

And then there was Sam. She and Micah were so in tune with one another. Cordray stole a glance over her shoulder. Sam had pulled Micah aside, her fingers massaging the pulse point in his neck, their foreheads touching as she spoke soft, coaxing words to calm him.

At one time, she had had that. A long time ago, with Gideon, before she had lost her sense of feeling, she had loved and been loved that deeply. And then it had all been stolen from her.

She turned away again, breathing through the emptiness, hugging herself as she willed her tears not to fall. Forever had passed since she'd last cried, which had been over losing Gideon.

Now she was crying over Trace. Damn him!

She cleared her throat and dropped her arms to her sides. "Go get him," she said without turning around, forcing iron resolve into her voice. "Bring him to me now."

"Trace is resting," Micah said between clenched teeth. "And he will remain resting until he decides he wants to get up."

"Well, I'm not leaving without him." Cordray faced him and crossed her arms, doing her best to put on a steadfast front. She was good at putting on tough façades. After all, she'd been doing so for eight hundred years. Another five minutes shouldn't be too hard.

"Then I hope you're ready to get good and comfortable." Micah took Sam's hand and ushered her toward the stairs. "Because he stays until I say he's ready to leave."

"Fine." Cordray jutted out her chin and squared her shoulders. "I'll wait then."

Sam held her tongue, although Cordray sensed she wanted to speak. Perhaps she remained quiet because she wanted to hurry Micah away before another outburst occurred.

"Don't go downstairs," Micah warned, pointing his finger at her as Sam tugged his arm. "I swear to God, Cordray, if you go near him and fuck with his head, I'll beat your ass into next year. I don't care how tight you are with King Bain. You've caused Trace enough problems. You don't need to cause him any more, so just park your ass on the couch and don't fucking move."

Cordray threw eye daggers at him. If only Micah knew her true relationship to King Bain, he might not be so arrogant about threatening her.

Issuing a mock salute, Cordray stepped toward the couch and plopped down, keeping her gaze locked to Micah's as Sam pulled him up the stairs. Only when he disappeared from view did Cordray allow herself to exhale. Her entire body slumped forward as she dropped her head into her hands. Her long hair hung over her face, the ends sweeping the floor.

For the past eight hundred years, she had prevented anyone from getting close enough to hurt her the way Gideon had, but now Trace threatened to do just that.

Part of her wanted nothing more than to let that happen.

Another part of her simply wanted to run the way she'd run away from the cabin in the woods when she found Gideon with another female.

Her whole life ceased to exist that night. Now Trace threatened to resurrect her heart. She was stuck between fight or flight. Should she fight for what she wanted, or should she flee before he could destroy her completely?

She didn't need a Magic 8 Ball to tell her the outlook wasn't good.

Sam sighed irritably as Micah closed the door to the upstairs bedroom. A small, dim lamp on the nightstand served as the only light. The blackout blinds and curtains were secured over the windows, shutting out the sun.

"How long has she been here?" Micah said quietly, almost as if he were hissing.

Sam brushed her hands over both sides of his neck, massaging his pulse points in a continual effort to keep him calm. "About an hour. Maybe a little longer."

Micah purred and leaned his head into her right hand before turning and kissing her palm. "I'm sorry I left you with her."

"She wasn't so bad. I, uh . . . I actually kind of—"

Micah's eyes shot open, and his gaze spun toward hers before she could get the words out. Obviously, he had seen in her thoughts what she was about to say. "You like her?"

She still wasn't used to having her mind read twenty-four seven, but she was beyond chastising him for it. It wouldn't do any good, anyway.

Sam huffed and crossed her arms as she took a step back. "Yes, I like her. Have you got a problem with that, Mr. Bossy Pants?"

He raked his fingers through his hair as he let out a frustrated growl and looked away. "Whose side are you on here, Sam?"

Now it was her turn to get frustrated. "I'm on my *own* side. Look, I know you and Trace don't like her, but I think it's because you're both too close to the situation. I—" Micah began to pace away, but she grabbed his arm. "Don't you walk away from me when I'm talking to you."

His gaze burned into hers. "I can't believe you would take her side over ours."

She bopped him V-8 style on the side of the head. "You aren't listening to me."

He blew out an irritated breath. "Fine. I'm listening."

She took a step toward him and caressed his cheek, which was covered with black stubble. She loved how he looked when he hadn't shaved for a couple of days. "Hear me out." He rolled his eyes, but some of the steam had left his chimney. "You and Trace are looking at Cordray all wrong."

"And how would you suggest we look at her?" Then, under his breath, he added, "Especially when neither of us wants to look at her at all."

She fought back a grin at his flippant tone. Micah was so damn stubborn, but part of her loved that about him. "You're the genius, Micah. You're the one who can see all, remember?" She tapped the side of his head.

"Yeah, but I can't see inside *her* mind. She's got a wall up, same as Trace. You know that. I've told you that before."

"You are such a man."

He narrowed his eyes as he slinked closer and placed his hands seductively on her hips. "I'll remind you again, I'm not a man. I'm a male. All male, baby."

"And don't I know it?" She trailed her index finger down his jaw to his neck. "But right now, you're being a total *man*. Because men can be total douche bags when it comes to *females*."

"Okay, fine, baby. What's your point?" His hands slid up the sides of her hips, and then inward to the robe's sash tied around her waist.

"My point is, if you can't see inside her mind, then open your damn eyes. Think. Use your common sense." She leaned in and kissed the side of his neck as the robe fell open and his hands slipped inside. "Baby, your mind probe abilities are your greatest strength, but they're also your biggest weakness. You depend on them too much to tell you what you can easily see for yourself if you just look."

"Mmm, what are you telling me, baby?" He nuzzled the side of her neck. "That you've figured Cordray out in less than an hour, and I haven't because I'm too hung up on being pissed off at her . . . and because I can't see her thoughts."

She nodded. "Something like that."

He backed her toward the bed and eased her down. "Look who's the smarty-pants now." He crawled over her as she lay back against the pillows.

"Damn straight, Skippy."

He chuckled and nibbled her collar bone. "Okay, I'll bite."

She giggled at his double entendre and pushed her fingers into his long hair. "I hope so."

His fangs teased the side of her neck. "So, what have you figured out about Cordray that I haven't?"

She wrapped her legs around his hips as he slid the thin strap of her nightgown off her shoulder. "That she's seriously misunderstood."

"Okay?" Micah licked her shoulder. "And . . .?"

"That she's been hurt before and has a wall up to protect herself from getting hurt again."

Micah pushed himself to a sitting position and tugged her onto his lap. "What makes you say that?"

"Women's intuition." She straddled his hips and brushed her palms over his shoulders as he nipped the side of her neck. "She reminds me of the way I was after I left Steve." Micah tensed at hearing Steve's name and pulled away to look in her eyes as she continued. "Until I met you, I pushed everyone away when all I wanted was to pull them closer. I was so alone. I desperately wanted a friend, but I couldn't risk letting anyone get too close for fear of Steve finding out."

Micah caressed her cheek, his gaze intensely protective. "You don't have to worry about that asshole anymore, baby."

"Thanks to you, but I still feel the effects of what he did to me. I still fear letting anyone get close."

"You let *me* get close."

She smiled and ran the backs of her fingers down the side of his face. "You're different."

"Damn straight I am." He reached around and patted her on the rump. "But what's this got to do with Cordray?"

"I think she's been through the same thing. Or at least something similar. Which is why she's so abrasive."

Micah's eyes narrowed as his brow furrowed. Sam had seen that look before. He was processing Sam's logic and running through everything he knew about Cordray to validate what Sam had just told him. A moment later, he pursed his lips and raised one eyebrow as he sighed. "Okay, I'll concede you might be on to something."

"So, do you think you and Trace can cut her some slack?"

Micah grinned. "Not a chance." He dove in and sucked a mouthful of skin at the top of her breast into his mouth, causing her to shriek and fall into uncontrollable giggles.

"Micah! Stop it! I'm trying to be serious here."

He released her and lapped his tongue over the place he'd just given a love bite. "So am I." A lusty growl broke inside his throat. "God, I need you so badly right now." He lifted his face and hit her with a gaze fiery enough to burn down Chicago.

"I take it things went well with Trace." She tugged his shirt over his head and tossed it aside.

"Mmmm, yes. Very well." His fingers hooked the other strap of her gown and drew it down her arm. "So no more talk about Cordray. She's killing the mood."

With that, he claimed her mouth with enough steam to push all thought of anything but him from her mind.

The atmosphere in the room grew thick with arousal. Heavy waves of it pulsed from his body like ocean surf as he continued to undress her. His fingers trembled with such force as he unfastened his belt that the metal prong vibrated against the buckle, and the more time that passed, the more urgent he became.

Whatever had gone on in the dungeon had definitely worked Micah's sex drive into a frenzy. She hadn't felt such heady surges of energy from him since his calling.

When he finally entered her, he held her wrists over her head with both hands as he devoured her body with his, until finally he sank his fangs into her shoulder and shuddered through the most earthshaking, mind-blowing climax he'd spent on her in months, sending her body into the stratosphere as she blew apart beneath him.

IN THE AFTERGLOW of what had been the strongest orgasm he'd had since his calling, Micah held Sam against his body, drowsy, lazily caressing her arm with his fingertips. He wasn't finished. Sexual need still vibrated up and down his spine, the lust-filled tide already rising again. He would have his mate once more before falling asleep. Maybe even twice.

Sam kissed his chest, and he could feel her eagerness for more as her hand traveled south along his abdomen.

"One more thing about Cordray," she said softly against his chest, somewhat distracted.

He didn't want to talk about Cordray. Maybe Sam was right and Cord was hiding some awful, painful past that turned her into a bitch with devil horns to keep people away from her, but he didn't care about that right now. At this moment, he only cared about the female in his arms — his perfect, sexy mate — and Trace.

Undeterred by his silence, Sam continued. "I think she likes Trace."

Micah's eyes shot open, and he sat up, pushing Sam up with him. "What?"

Sam frowned. "Oh come on, you can't tell me the thought hasn't crossed your mind." She stared at him then gaped. "Oh God, it hasn't." She straightened and crossed her legs so that her knee rested on his thigh. "It's so obvious, Micah. I can't believe you didn't see it."

"No. I . . . how . . . no way." His brain rejected the possibility that Satan's mistress had set her sights on his bestie.

"Think about it." Sam pushed to her knees then straddled his lap, hanging her forearms over his shoulders.

"I don't want to think about it," he said under his breath, cupping her ass in both hands. "Cordray with Trace makes my stomach turn."

Sam laughed. "Will you grow up for two seconds. You're not Trace's father. You can't prevent women from being attracted to him."

"Cordray is *not* a woman." He voiced the sentiment with a little more bite than was necessary.

"Fine. Female. Whatever." Sam rotated her hips, teasing his erection.

He relaxed and gripped her hips, churning her more forcefully against him. "I was thinking she was more like an ogre."

She rolled her eyes and giggled, grinding against him again. "My point is, if she likes him, you can't *force* her not to. Not everything in this world must bend to your whim, you know."

Micah yanked her against him, thrusting to strengthen the friction between them. "Why would you think she likes him? She does nothing but insult him and give him grief."

Sam's eyelids fell erotically to half-mast, and she smiled. "How does a grade-school boy show a little girl he thinks she's cute?"

Micah frowned then smirked. "I haven't been a grade-school boy in a while, so I wouldn't know."

"He pulls her pigtails and teases her, silly," Sam said coyly. "Don't you see? Cordray is pulling Trace's pigtails and teasing him . . . all to get his attention."

Micah refused to believe that, because Trace went after Cordray as much as she went after him. The two were like bickering children on a playground.

Bickering children.

His heart stopped. Oh God. Sam was right. More right than she knew. Because not only was Cordray pulling Trace's pigtails, he was pulling hers.

"No," he said aloud, pulling Sam closer, as if by wielding his possession over her, he could do the same with Trace.

"Yes." Sam nipped his neck and clung to his shoulders. "Face it, baby, Cordray likes Trace."

He set his jaw and shook his head.

Sam threw her head back and giggled. "Cordray and Trace, sitting in a tree. K-i-s-s-i-n-g." She pecked him on the lips. "First comes love" — peck — "second comes marriage —"

Micah placed his hand over Sam's mouth before she could say the last line of the song he'd heard kids sing from playgrounds for decades. "No more talk about Cordray, or Trace, or how they're k-i-s-s-i-n-g in a tree." He flipped Sam to her stomach, and she arched her back so that her hips raised to meet his as he fell in behind her and forced her legs apart with his knees. "We really need to work on your pillow talk, baby." He smoothed his palm over the cheeks of her ass then gave her a swat. Her supple flesh rippled and bounced back.

She squeaked then sighed, her body drawing in as if she were preparing for him. "Why?" She moaned as he positioned himself, using his fingers to spread her slick labia. "I think we have some of our best conversations when we're fucking."

He thrust into her, making her gasp and fall forward.

"No more talking."

She nodded, mewling for more. "Okay. No more talking. Fine. Just" — she moaned — "don't stop."

This time as he took her, he not only claimed his mate, but willed himself to claim Trace, as well. Sam was his surrogate to connect him in the most intimate way possible to his best friend.

He couldn't lose the most incredible submissive — a piece as vital to his soul as Sam — when he had only just found him. In just a few hours tonight, Trace had become critical to Micah's survival, and hormonal heat suffused the air around him as he poured his mind and heart into keeping this new element of his life intact while pouring his body and soul into his beautiful, exquisite female.

He wouldn't lose Trace. Not to Cordray. Not to anyone. As he shattered into another mind-numbing orgasm more powerful than the first, Micah forced into the universe his will to keep Cordray away from his best friend. As much as Sam was his, so was Trace. Trace belonged to him. Beware all who tried to take him away.

CHAPTER 8

BRAK STOOD ON THE BACK PATIO of the house Micah had set him up in, gazing at the sliver of crescent moon hovering over the dusky western horizon.

God, he had missed this. Watching the sun set. Feeling the cool breeze on his face. Hearing the birds sing at twilight. All of it.

He still wasn't fully recovered from the events of the last week and should have been resting, but he couldn't bring himself to stay in bed. Not when there was so much to see and experience now that he was free.

His body protested, though. His muscles were achy and weak. He always suffered after using his power, especially to kill, which wasn't what his mother had intended for his gift.

In the past week, he had exhausted his abilities and, as a consequence, his body. Not only had he saved a life—Gina—by bringing her back from death after pulling deadly poison out of her, but he'd also killed two drecks and the two vampires who'd held him and his father prisoner for almost two hundred years. He needed about a month in bed, but he refused to remain indoors just because he was tired and ached from head to toe. He'd spent two centuries locked in a basement cell. The last thing he wanted was to remain inside, especially when the weather was so benevolent. Unlike this morning, when cold rain had forced him back into the house while he'd been lounging, tea in-hand, in the patio chair with a blanket over his lap. Even so, he'd stood at the patio door and watched the lightning streak the sky and the wind whip the tops of the trees to and fro.

While his body cried for recovery, his spirit needed healing, too. Watching the storm this morning, and now feeling the refreshing breeze lift his long hair away from his face as the birds sang their good-bye to another day, was like a balm to his soul.

Closing his eyes, he lifted his face skyward, letting the long-forgotten sounds of nature provide the soundtrack for his evening.

A few minutes later, the sliding door behind him opened. "Brak?"

He glanced over his shoulder to find his friend, Cynthia, standing on the shallow concrete step just outside the door. She'd been the one to care for him while he'd been imprisoned. She'd sat by his side and cleaned him up after he returned from his godforsaken killing missions and vomited all over himself. She'd been the one to lift a glass of cool water to his lips so he could drink, to cook soup for him once he could eat again, to help him bathe, dress, and even walk when he was too weak to do those things for himself.

Cynthia was also the one who'd helped him learn about the new world. She'd shown him how to use the Internet, how to invest online, how to use computers to create his music, how to surf the Net and learn how the world had changed.

But even though he'd seen pictures of cities, cars, and storms, nothing could compare to the real thing. The exhilaration of seeing a storm with his own eyes, of feeling its energy, of riding in a car for the first time, and of standing in the heart of Chicago, where he could feel the pulse of every living entity in the city beat against his skin, was beyond compare to a two-dimensional image.

He was no longer an observer of life. Once more, he was a participant, and he had a lot of ground to make up before he was comfortable with the changes the world had undergone without him.

"Can you hear that?" he said, facing the trees again.

Cynthia quietly joined him and wrapped her arm around his reassuringly. "What? What do you hear?"

He breathed in as if he could inhale twilight's essence. "The wind. The way it rustles the young leaves on the trees and bids the sun farewell until tomorrow morning."

Her arm squeezed his. "I've taken for granted so many things." She sighed. "Spending the last few days with you and watching you discover the world again has made me realize that."

He slid his hand around hers. "You've seen all this every day." He waved his other arm as if to encompass the backyard and beyond. "For me, it's a novelty." A slow smile blossomed on his face as he drank in the ochre colors of the western sky. "It's been two hundred years since I experienced any of this."

"You're like a newborn opening his eyes for the first time." Cynthia's fingers embraced his as she leaned into him and rested her temple against his shoulder.

He towered over her, but she had enormous strength for a human. Not just physical strength, but mental fortitude. Without her courage and conviction, he wouldn't be free right now. She'd been the one who allowed him to find Jacob and Haslet and kill them, thus freeing himself and all the others they'd held as slaves in one way or another.

"Come on," Cynthia said, "let's go inside. It's getting cold out here, and dinner's almost ready." She shivered against him as she gave his hand a light tug.

Brak didn't mind the cold. It made him feel alive. Not the way he had in that environmentally controlled basement he'd been kept in like a lab rat.

Not the way Trace must have felt in that dungeon Brak had found him in a week ago.

He let Cynthia lead him inside as his thoughts turned to his brother. Micah had told him Trace had been due to be released last night. Early this morning, to be exact. Before the sun came up. Which meant Trace was free now. Like him. They were both free.

"Has Micah called?" he asked as Cynthia slid the glass door shut behind them.

"No."

He sighed and lowered his gaze. Micah was supposed to contact him after he'd talked to Trace. Micah had thought it would be better if he broke the news Brak was in Chicago, simply because he hadn't known the condition Trace would be in upon his release.

Brak was eager to see his twin. To talk to him. Ask him where he'd been all this time? To tell him why he'd never searched for him. That he'd been taking care of their father then locked into servitude by the opportunists who'd altered the entire course of his life.

From the brief glimpse Brak had gotten inside Trace's head a week ago, he had seen the torment Trace had put himself through — both mentally and physically — over their mother's death. That he blamed himself. That the guilt he carried burdened him as if he were carrying the weight of a hundred suns on his shoulders.

"He needs to know it's not his fault," he said quietly.

Cynthia turned off the stove. "Who? Trace?" She ladled his favorite soup — a combination of chicken, spinach, and artichokes stewed in a brothy cream — from a large stock pot into a bright-yellow bowl.

He met her gaze and nodded as she turned and placed the bowl in front of him. "He blames himself for the death of our mother, and I need to let him know it wasn't his fault."

Cynthia's eyebrows turned up at the inside corners as she caressed his arm reassuringly. "I'm sure Micah will call soon."

He nodded again, as if he were convincing himself she was right, but until he saw Trace with his own eyes and heard his voice with his own ears, he wouldn't be satisfied.

Cynthia ladled up another serving of soup for herself, and then they ventured to the living room to eat while they watched a movie.

Twenty minutes later, with their soup bowls abandoned on the coffee table, he settled into the oversized couch, his arm around Cynthia's shoulders as she nestled against him. She'd always snuggled him during his recovery, so he didn't think anything of the gesture.

Tonight felt different, though.

She was quieter than usual. Not just less talkative. Her energy was quieter, too. Yet it was also thicker. More electric. As if *she* were a storm like the one that hit this morning. Except she was still building. The buzz around her was tight, focused, spiraling toward some destination he could neither see nor predict, and it was affecting him, as well.

A strange sensation thrummed through his veins. A charged current that wasn't necessarily unpleasant, but it wasn't comforting, either. His nerves bristled as if reaching for something palpable that wasn't there.

He'd never felt anything like this before, and Cynthia seemed to be the source. Whatever this was, it was coming from her, wrapping around him, stirring his senses, bringing his body to life.

"Brak?" The way she spoke his name, so soft, so husky . . . made him draw in a steadying breath.

He blinked several times, his brow tightening as he looked away, trying to figure out what this sensation was. Why was his pulse racing? Why were his muscles tensing? Why did his flesh stir between his legs, tingling in such a provocative way, all from the way she'd lilted her voice when she said his name and caressed his chest as she snuggled a little closer?

"Hm?" he acknowledged quietly, absently tilting his nose into her soft hair.

Like him, Cynthia came from parents of different races. Her father was Caucasian while her mother was African American. Cynthia was the perfect blend of both. Fair, mocha skin. Dark-brown, silky soft hair with tight, wavy curls framing her face. Effervescent irises the color of cognac, with just a hint of amber and flecks of green around the edges.

For all her beauty, Brak had never thought them more than friends. Two people burdened by the same fate, held prisoner by those without scruples.

Cynthia had been born into servitude to Jacob and Haslet, taking over her mother's duties to tend to him when she was eighteen, when her mother became too ill to do so. That had been almost five years ago, and in all that time, Brak had never considered Cynthia could be attracted to him.

But now . . .

Cynthia's tentative palm slid over his chest. Then she slowly pulled away and turned to meet his gaze. "You're free now." Her long lashes fluttered as she shyly cast her eyes downward. "No one's watching you, anymore. We're finally alone. Just the two of us." She nibbled her plump bottom lip, and her gaze darted to his again, searching his eyes. "We can be together now." Her hand trailed boldly down his stomach, but her expression remained reserved. "If you want to."

Her fingers grazed the head of his swollen penis through his linen pants.

He sucked in his breath, and every muscle in his body gently contracted as a sensation akin to pain but more like pleasure lit inside his blood. Even as his body reacted, he couldn't speak. All he could do was stare at her, awed by how she'd changed so rapidly. Ten minutes ago, they'd been only friends. Now, his body seemed to be calling him to be more. To kiss her as the men in the movies kissed their women. To touch her and look upon her naked flesh as she looked upon his.

He'd never lain with a woman, and the realization began to dawn on him that Cynthia was seducing him to do just that.

She leaned in again, bringing her face to the crook of his neck as her palm caressed his hard penis more firmly. She sighed, and her breath warmed his skin. He closed his eyes, relishing the heated wash of air followed by the soft, supple touch of her lips under his ear.

"Do you want us to be together?" she said, her voice hushed and breathy. Her body slid against the side of his as she bent one leg over his thighs and kissed his neck again.

Tiny eruptions quaked under his skin, in his blood, over his nerve endings, sending fiery warmth down his spine to settle between his legs as he grew even harder. He became faintly aware that he was nodding.

He'd never known he wanted this, but now that he was faced with the possibility of discovering all that went on between a male and a female, there was nothing he wanted more.

"Yes." His voice, normally so tranquil and benign, sounded foreign to his own ears. Even though he spoke softly, his voice was deep, gruff, full of a kind of desire he'd never experienced.

A moment later, her entire body seemed to melt against his as a gentle, satisfied moan stirred in her throat. Her arm encircled his torso, and she pulled herself onto his lap as he sank more deeply into the cushions and gazed up at her.

She pulled her fuzzy, baby-blue sweater over her head, revealing an expanse of pristine skin. A light-blue, satin bra covered her breasts, but only briefly, because she reached around, unfastened it, then tossed it onto the couch beside her sweater.

Brak had never seen bared breasts before. At least not in person. Only in movies. But as with everything else he'd seen in pictures — the city, cars, thunderstorms — no image seen on a TV screen or online compared to the three-dimensional reality poised in front of him.

Cynthia's breasts were small but perky, tipped with light-brown nipples that tightened into pert nubs as he stared at them. But his amazement and utter awe were about so much more than what he could see with his eyes. He could feel her. Feel her warmth. And when he tentatively raised his hands to her breasts and let his fingertips slowly sweep around the supple swells of flesh, he absorbed her frenetic energy. It poured out of her, engulfing his senses, making him breathless and needy for more.

Reaching down, she gripped the hem of his shirt and pulled it up. He lifted his arms, and the fabric swished over his head.

Then her mouth was on his chest, his neck, and her hands worked the fastenings of her jeans before untying the drawstring of his pants. A vortex of energy threatened to consume him as it wound more tightly, bunching, pulling them closer to one another. With feverish adeptness, she freed them both of their remaining clothes. And then there was nothing between them. No barrier to impede desire's demands. Her thighs straddled his. Her lips sought his. Her heat engulfed him as she took him inside her.

He'd never felt anything like this. The ache that demanded release. The painfully pleasurable way his body lifted, sang, searching. But searching for what?

He knew the way of male vampires. How their bodies sought to link with a mate.

Was Cynthia his mate? Had she been under his nose the whole time, and he hadn't known? He'd been too young when Mother died and Father fell into a healing sleep to learn much beyond the basics of how things worked among his kind, but he knew of mated males and of male callings. And he knew enough to understand the rite of passage having sex with Cynthia granted him.

But was having sex enough? Did this mean they were mated?

Barely a minute into the act, his body seized. A moment later, he fell into convulsions. And then all he could do was hold on tight as pure, white-hot pleasure lanced his soul. His fangs punched out, and his gaze sharpened on the vein in her neck even as his body fell into uncontrollable shudders.

"Feed from me," she said on a gasp, fisting the hair on the back of his head and yanking him forward so that his mouth pressed against her skin.

He could smell her blood. He could practically taste it, having fed from her before. But this was different. Hormones poured through her veins alongside her blood. Pure, unadulterated adrenaline. If desire had a scent, this would be it.

Without hesitation, he sank his fangs into her flesh and drank in long, drunken pulls as his body fell into bliss again. Above him, Cynthia gasped then trembled, and he felt her inner muscles quiver against him as she found the same pleasure he'd found only moments before. The air was thick with it.

An hour later, the scent of lust permeated every molecule inside the house as Cynthia rolled to her back on the bed and took Brak with her.

Brak's thirst for this newfound worldly pleasure was insatiable. He'd had a taste, and now he wanted more. But as his body released yet again, he wondered once more if Cynthia was his mate. This time, a voice in the back of his mind responded.

No.

There was no denying the truth. Cynthia was not his mate. He knew with the certainty of the rising sun that there was another meant for him. That another female existed somewhere, out there, in a place he'd yet to discover. And once he found her, what he was feeling now would pale in comparison to the craving, devotion, and pleasure his true mate would awaken in his heart.

But that didn't mean he couldn't enjoy the gift Cynthia was willing to give him now. That he didn't appreciate her physical generosity. Knowing another awaited him elsewhere didn't mean that what he felt with Cynthia wasn't real. And it didn't mean he didn't love her. He did. He loved her very much. But loving wasn't the same as mating, and he knew enough to know the difference.

He only hoped Cynthia did, too.

CHAPTER 9

WHEN TRACE AWOKE NINE HOURS LATER, he felt as loose as a slack rubber band.

Last night had been unreal. He had never sunk so deeply into subspace. Micah truly was all he'd hoped for and more.

Until now, submitting himself hadn't been about pleasure so much as it had been about battling his crippling power. But under Micah's firm hand, and steeped within his domination, Trace had found pleasure. Pure, genuine pleasure.

He had come during scenes before. In fact, he couldn't remember a time when a session hadn't led him to orgasm, but always because the pain had allowed him to feel something other than the presence that otherwise invaded his mind and body twenty-four seven. Last night, there had been very little pain. Just the slow burn of hot wax on his skin. In combination with Micah's presence, that had been enough to send him to a whole new place both mentally and physically.

Micah was at once demanding and loving, stern yet compassionate. Everything he did and said held a duality. He was the kind of Dom you wanted to obey and please, not because he demanded it, but because he earned it. Trace had never felt such love and devotion from another master, and he grinned as he stretched and remembered the way Micah had tended to him after their session.

Breathing hadn't come so easily in a long time, and Trace just wanted to lie there and feel the oxygen fill his lungs with every breath. For ten minutes, that's all he did as he luxuriated in Micah's and Sam's bed. Then his full bladder got the better of him, so he sat up, swung his feet around, and made his way to the bathroom.

After tending to business, he stood over the sink and stared at himself in the mirror. He was where he needed to be. Where he wanted to be. He belonged here.

But something was still missing. No . . . some*one*. Even though his relationship with Micah and Sam was damn near perfect, neither belonged to him. Neither was his mate. With them, he would always be the fifth wheel. The guy who tagged along but never had anyone of his own.

Part of him wanted to believe that Micah and Sam were enough, but he knew deep down they weren't. Until he found the one female put on this earth expressly for him, the void in his heart would remain. The void only his mate could fill.

At least he no longer had to worry about the holes left by the deaths of his father and brother. They hadn't died, after all. He'd found his father, and he'd felt Brak's presence during his incarceration, which was proof enough that his twin lived. Shocking, yes, but true.

A myriad of emotions stirred inside him. Excitement, happiness, relief, but also fear. Also regret, worry, and doubt. While he was happy to know they hadn't died, an unsettled anxiety had latched onto him, and its grip tightened every day. Old memories had awakened. Old pain. Things he hadn't thought about in a long time and didn't want to, but which he could no longer avoid now that his dad and brother were back.

He splashed water on his face to clear his mind then took a quick shower to wash away the cobwebs still lingering from last night's trip down the rabbit hole.

With a towel wrapped around his waist, he returned to the bedroom. A pair of black sweats and a light-grey T-shirt were folded on the dresser as if they had been set there for him, so he put them on and headed upstairs. He was famished and needed to raid the kitchen ASAFP.

As he opened the door at the top of the stairs, he heard kitchen cabinets open and close. Good. Sam was already up. He couldn't wait to see her, hug her, smell the lilac scent of her hair.

"Hey, beautiful, what's for breakfa—" He came to a dead stop as Cordray spun around, blue eyes wide, her black and bright-blue hair flowing in long, lustrous waves over her shoulders and down her back, all the way to her ass.

As if frozen in a pose from a Halloween snow globe—because, really, could Cordray be associated with any other holiday than Halloween?—the two stared at each other. Then she sniffed dismissively and shoved her hair behind her ears as she turned away and bent to look inside another cabinet.

Wow, um . . . okay, he'd never really noticed her ass before, but those pink sweats hugged her in all the right—wait a second. Pink? On Cordray? He had never seen her wear anything but witch black.

"Don't just stand there waiting for an invitation," she said, rifling through the cabinet.

His eyebrows shot up. An invitation? To what? Smack her ass? Because he was having a hard time keeping himself from reaching out to see if that thing was as firm as it looked. Amazing what her usual leather attire hid that a layer of pink cotton put a spotlight on.

She stopped and looked over her shoulder at him. "Are you going to help me find the coffee or what?"

Oh. Oops. His mind had gone in a totally different direction than she'd intended.

But at least she'd confirmed he wasn't in another dimension where a nice Cordray who wore pastels and said please and thank you existed. She barked out her commands the way she always did. No please. No thank you. No good morning. No nicey-niceness. This was the real Cordray, not a figment of his imagination. If he painted her red and gave her a pitchfork, she would be the devil.

Trace stayed rooted in place and crossed his arms. "What are you doing here?"

Devil horns and bad manners aside, Cordray looked different. All girly and shit. He'd never seen her with her hair down, without her black leather, and without all that Gothic-style makeup she usually wore. But those wicked tattoos on her arms weren't going anywhere anytime soon, and for once he was able to admire them without all the peripheral bullshit to distract him. That was some crazy-cool ink right there.

She sighed heavily, stood back up, and settled her fists on her hips. "I'm looking for coffee, jackass. I thought I'd just made that clear. Did you suddenly forget how to speak English since I last saw you? Now, are you going to help me or stand there like a paperweight for floors?"

Maybe she looked different, but she still had the same smart-assed mouth. Score one for continuity and lack of progress.

He refused to let her spoil his good mood. Micah had left him flying, and he would enjoy the sensation for as long as he could.

Nudging her aside, he opened the cabinet in front of her and reached over her shoulder for the can of Folgers as she pointedly leaned away from him as if he were covered in porcupine spines. She nearly tripped over her own feet as she took an abrupt step to the side.

"Here." He handed her the canister, reached back in for the filters, tossed them on the counter by the coffee maker, and then turned for the fridge. "And I meant, what are you doing *here* . . . as in, in general? In this house? Or is English your second language, too?" He pulled out the milk then retrieved the Peanut Butter Cap'n Crunch from the pantry.

"Cute," she snapped, popping the top off the Folgers.

He tucked the cereal box under his arm. "Shouldn't you be polishing your pitchfork or stealing babies or something?"

She didn't say anything for a moment, and Trace flicked his gaze over his shoulder to find her staring at him as if he were some kind of horror movie monster.

"Well?" he prompted. "Why are you here, Cordray?" He shut the pantry door a little harder than he intended. "And don't tell me it's out of some newfound concern for me, because while I could use a good laugh, I'm not interested in wading through your bullshit right now." He grabbed a bowl from the cabinet.

Her chin jutted out, and her eyes narrowed. "I came to get you," she said as she dropped the open Folgers canister on the counter. Then she spun around, grabbed the carafe, and flipped on the faucet, avoiding eye contact. "Micah took you without my permission, and you're supposed to be—"

"Chill out, sweetheart. You'll *get* me soon enough."

She jerked her head around and scowled at him. "You're supposed—"

"Give it a rest, Queen Succubus. I'm not going to bail on my community service. You've got me by my short and curlies for the next three months. I know, I know. Jesus. I don't have to like the situation I'm in to accept it, for God's sake, because God knows I'd rather be anywhere but in *your* service." The last he said with a roll of his eyes as he plopped onto a barstool, spoon in hand, ready to get cozy with his Peanut Butter Crunch—the food of the gods.

"Nice breakfast," she said sarcastically with a nod at the Captain as he poured a heaping bowlful.

He scowled at her and pointedly poured more into his bowl just to piss her off.

"Aren't you supposed to be making coffee?" He slammed the box on the counter beside him. "How about you focus on *that* and quit playing nutritionist. You might be my—*ahem*—boss for the next three months—and I use that term loosely, by the way—but I'm pretty sure I'm still allowed to eat whatever the fuck I want."

She frowned and turned away, sweeping that intensely long hair over her shoulder. Trace's eyes dropped to her ass again. He'd never noticed her heart-shaped ass behind all that Gothic clothing she usually wore, and now he couldn't take his eyes off it. As he admired the perfection of her curves, his head absently tilted to one side as he held the milk carton at a shallow angle over his bowl, briefly forgotten, his gaze following her backside as she busied herself making coffee. Okay, so Cordray's ass was nice. Real nice. Hypnotically nice. The kind of nice that makes a male think not-nice thoughts.

Thoughts he did *not* need to have about her.

He tore his gaze away. "What's with the clothes?" He finally tipped the carton far enough to pour milk into his bowl. A few nuggets of peanut butter gold splashed over the edge, which he picked up and tossed back in. "Did your cave troll take the day off and forget to leave out your pointy hat and broom?"

Cordray shifted her weight from one leg to the other, making those glorious globes of flesh plump, one then the other. "Gee, that's a good one, Trace. Did your ass give you that one, or are you just especially clever now that you've swapped spit with Micah?"

He chuckled and shoveled a spoonful of cereal into his mouth.

Cordray looked over her shoulder and frowned. "You think that's funny?"

Trace shrugged one shoulder and scooped up another heap of cereal. Something about Cordray was different. Softer maybe. But she still held an edge. A rusty, gnarled, jagged edge. But instead of being an axe, she was more like a chisel. It was as if her leather and usually extreme appearance acted as an energy source for her foul temperament and smart-assed mouth. But in real-people clothes, she wasn't so tough.

Well, far be it for him not to take advantage of a gift from God. Maybe now he could gain the upper hand on this bitch. "I just think you sound like a jealous girlfriend." He sneered and winked at her.

He got the exact reaction he wanted. Her perfectly arched eyebrows drew together, and her mouth fell open.

"Not so tough without your armor, are you, sweetheart?" He spooned more of the Captain's finest into his mouth, stared her down, chewed, swallowed, and grinned like the devil on Judgment Day. "Although . . ." His gaze pointedly dropped to her breasts, which were testing the tensile strength of Sam's shirt. "Parts of you *are* a bit more appealing now than they usually are."

Looked like her ass wasn't the only thing her normal clothes played down. Cordray had enough up top to sprain his tongue if he were ever so inclined to poison himself by sucking her nipples.

Not that Cordray would ever let him get away with something like that, but the unbidden thought of shoving his face between her breasts sent an unexpected jolt of lust-filled electricity down his spine. What the fuck? He shook off the unusual sensation.

"You bastard." Cordray hastily adjusted her hair to cover her chest as she turned away.

Thoughts of motorboating her boobs aside, this was fun. Finally, he had found Cordray's weakness. Trace's evening just got better and better. "How about you hurry up with that coffee, honey. I could use a cup myself."

Something that looked like pain crossed Cordray's features as she turned and headed out of the kitchen. "Make it yourself." She disappeared down the hall and into the bathroom, where she slammed the door.

Good riddance.

Even so, it felt like some of the air had left the room with her. Her presence added a sense of exhilaration he could easily become addicted to. He frowned and lowered his head as he ate with a little less joy. He ended up throwing out the last few bites of his cereal before setting his empty bowl in the sink.

He eyed the Folgers and the carafe full of water. An uncomfortable sensation that resembled guilt settled over him. He had no reason to feel guilty over how he'd treated her. After all, this was Cordray. The goddess of the underworld. The bane of his existence.

"Fuck her," he muttered as he turned to leave the kitchen.

He got two steps then stopped, shoulders rolling forward as he bowed his head and rubbed his palm over the back of his neck. Blowing out an exasperated breath, he turned and scowled at the abandoned coffee maker.

Fine. He could be nice. After all, everyone needed their coffee just after waking up. Even a witch like Cordray.

He crossed the kitchen, poured the water into the coffee maker, dumped three scoops of french roast into the filter, put everything in place, turned it on, and waited.

A few minutes later, he poured a cup, carried it down the hall, and knocked quietly on the bathroom door.

No reply.

He knocked again and huffed, shifting his weight to one foot and looking down at the floor.

"I made the coffee," he said.

Still nothing.

How humiliating. He was actually trying to play nice with the spawn of Satan. Who would have thought he would ever stoop this low?

"Cordray?"

The door flew open, and Trace jerked his head up as he took a step back. Cordray had changed into her normal clothes, and she had braided and tied back her hair. Before Trace knew what was happening, she snatched the coffee, poured it down the drain, slammed the empty mug on the counter, and shoved her way past him.

"Fuck you and your coffee! I'd rather drink a cup of monkey piss." She marched toward the mud room.

Old Cordray was back. Yippee.

"I'm not sure I could get you any monkey piss, but . . ." Trace followed her, pointing toward the back door. "After last night's rain, I'm sure I can find a puddle in the backyard and bring you back a mug of muddy water. Ungrateful hag." He wasn't ready to give up his earlier advantage just because she was back in her black leather armor. "I might even be able to find a couple of earthworms to make you feel like you're drinking tequila."

She snatched her coat off a hook and spun around. "You shouldn't even be here! You should be—"

Trace threw his arms in the air. "I know, I know! God, you're like a fucking broken record. Nag, nag, nag. Bitch, bitch, bitch." He flapped his hand as if it were inside a puppet. "Always thinking about what *you* want. What *you* need."

"Oh, I see. And that's why I'm *here*, isn't it?" She swung her arm around to indicate Micah's house then got in his face and jabbed him in the chest with her index finger. "I'm here because of what *I* needed, right? Because there was nowhere else *I* wanted to be all day but inside this fucking house with fucking you and fucking Micah. Look in the mirror, asshole. I'm here right now because of what *you* needed. Because of what *you* wanted. So don't you get all holier-than-thou with me, motherfucker." Fire sparked inside her eyes as she snarled and got chest to chest with him. "*You* needed Micah to fuck you up. *You* needed to play whack-a-mo to keep your power from going all"—she raised her arms and wiggled her hands dramatically—"crazy shit on you. That was all you, pal. Not me." She shoved past him and marched back through the kitchen. "I would be within my rights to take both you *and* Micah in and throw you in Bain's dungeon for what you did."

He wasn't one to hit a girl, but right now, Cordray was pushing it. He followed her back into the living room. "You frigid cock blocker. You're damn right I came here for me. Would you rather I go mutant on your ass? Huh? How would you like that? That would sure taint your image in the king's eyes, wouldn't it? His prized" — he looked her up and down, wrinkling his nose — "whatever you are. Little Miss Can-Do-No-Wrong-In-The-Eyes-Of-The-King lets a prisoner go mutant because she's too far up her own ass to see he needs something she can't give. How would the king like you then, honey?" He pushed himself farther into her personal space, but damn if she didn't hold her ground, even though he could feel her wanting to retreat. "So how about you get out of my face and go get laid or something? Maybe then you'll calm down. You need a good fuck like no one I've ever known!"

Her hand shot out and slapped him so hard he felt like his body wouldn't catch up to his head for a week.

Damn!

And . . . *wow!*

Every thought in his head vanished.

He spun back around, eyes wide, mouth agape, with the most incredible burn of arousal he had ever felt tearing through his body.

She seemed to realize she had unleashed a demon and went deathly still except for her heavy breathing.

He was breathing hard, too, but for entirely different reasons. His gaze locked to hers, and he slowly ran his tongue over the seam of his mouth.

All he wanted was for her to hit him again. To feel her palm flash against his cheek and leave sacred, delicious pain in its wake. For her to shove him against the wall with enough force to bruise his back as she scratched her nails down his chest with enough viciousness to draw blood as she sank to her knees in front of him. What would that mouth — her *teeth* — feel like on his — ?

"What the fuck is going on down here?"

Trace jerked away from Cordray and shot his head around to find Micah charging down the stairs with Sam on his heels, both of them haphazardly dressed. Micah was wearing the same pants he'd worn last night, with the button unfastened at his waist. He wasn't wearing a shirt. Sam had on flannel pajamas, which she had clearly just put on, since she was still buttoning the top.

Still somewhat dazed by what had just happened between him and Cordray, Trace's mouth flapped open then shut. His voice had retreated into oblivion.

Micah jumped between them, shoving them apart. "You two could wake the dead."

Trace's voice finally returned, but as soon as he spoke, he wished he'd stayed mute. "She started it." Yeah, like that was a mature response.

He looked away, but not before he caught the wary glance Sam exchanged with Micah.

"Seriously, Trace?" Micah said. "She started it? Are we in grade school here?"

Trace met Micah's gaze and saw a shade of concern—and maybe worry—pass over his features.

"And you!" Micah turned toward Cordray, who looked as dazed as Trace felt. "I thought I told you to leave him alone."

She snapped awake, and her eyes fired in Micah's direction. "Fuck you, Micah. I *did* leave him alone. Get your goddamn facts straight before you pin your one-sided bullshit on me."

"I *would* get my facts straight if I could see inside either one of your heads!" Every muscle in Micah's body seemed to strain against his skin. "But both of you have such fucking thick walls up, I can't—"

"Damn straight I've got my walls up around you, asshole!" Cordray's face flamed red as she yelled at him. "Those are my memories, not yours!"

Sam stepped forward and tugged on Micah's arm. "Baby, don't. Come on, leave her alone."

Micah took a deep breath then glanced over his shoulder at Sam. The look they exchanged made it appear they'd already talked about this. Whatever *this* was.

What gave here? What was Trace missing that everyone else seemed to be in on? He looked from Sam to Cordray to Micah and back to Sam, who smiled awkwardly at him and blinked several times before she let go of Micah's arm and hustled toward the kitchen.

"Thank God," she said. "Someone made coffee. How about we all come in and have breakfast. I can make waffles." Good ol' Sam, always trying to diffuse the tension.

Now that the magic from Cordray's slap had dissipated, Trace scowled at his female nemesis. "I already ate."

Cordray raised her chin and glared at him. "And I'm not hungry."

Micah crossed his arms over his sculpted chest. "Quit being idiots." He lifted his chin and called into the kitchen. "Waffles sound fan-fucking-tastic, baby. I'm starved."

Gathering herself, Cordray whipped her coat from the crook of her arm, punched her arms through the sleeves, and whipped the collar in place before crossing her arms over her breasts and tapping her foot. "I'm done waiting. Trace comes with me now, or I'll have you both arrested for breaking the terms of his release."

Trace started forward. "You bi—"

Micah planted his palm in the center of Trace's chest before he could body slam Cordray into next month. "Cool it." Micah's voice betrayed his irritation, but he seemed to be exercising an enormous amount of patience as he turned toward Cordray. "Let's calm down here. I need more time with him. He and I need to talk. There are" — his eyebrows bit into his eyelids — "*things* he and I need to discuss."

The way Micah said *things*, Trace wasn't sure if this was good news or bad.

Cordray's eyes brightened as a measured smile spread over her mouth. "Aaaahhh, I see." Her gaze bounced from Micah to Trace and back again. "This is about Brak."

Fear jolted Trace's heart. "Brak? What about him?" If something had happened to his brother now that he'd just learned he was still alive, Trace would lose it. "Is he okay? Is he safe?" Maybe a better question was how Micah even knew about Brak, seeing that Trace had never talked about him and Micah couldn't see inside his head to find out about him on his own.

Micah gripped Trace's arms. "Just . . . calm down, Trace." To Cordray he said, "And you. Get. Out. Of my head."

Trace resisted Micah's hold and turned toward Cordray with a lot of you'd-better-not-be-behind-this and don't-fuck-with-me pouring from his glare. After all, Cordray had made threats against Brak when she visited Trace's cell a week ago. When she saw inside Trace's thoughts and learned that Brak's ethereal form had been there.

"If you did anything to my brother," he snarled at her, "I swear to God, I'll—"

"Simmer down, buttercup." She uncrossed her arms and leaned her hip against the back of a chair. "I haven't touched your precious brother."

Trace's frown deepened, and he turned toward Micah. "What's going on?" Irrational fear stabbed his gut as the memories he'd forced away barely forty-five minutes ago in the downstairs bathroom resurfaced.

Cordray slid back out of her coat. "Yes, Micah. Why don't you share the good news with Trace?" She gave them both a sickly sweet smile then breezed by them in the direction of the kitchen. "You know, Sammy, I think I'll be staying, after all." She flipped her long braid aside as she threw a self-satisfied glance over her shoulder at him. "After all, I love waffles."

Trace turned toward Micah, feeling helpless and agitated. "What's going on?"

Micah blew out a heavy breath, his expression serious. "Come on. Let's go to the kitchen. Have some breakfast. Then we can talk." He tipped his head toward the sound of an iron skillet being set on the stove.

"No, not until you tell me what's going on with my brother. How did you even find out about him? Did *she* tell you?" He scowled and gestured aggressively in the direction Cordray had gone. "What has she done? Did she hunt him down?" He was giving Cordray a lot of credit if he thought she'd been able to do in one week what he hadn't been able to do in two hundred years, which should have been a clue he was thinking irrationally. "I swear if she's done anything to hurt Brak—"

"Cool it, Trace." Micah braced his arms, giving him a little shake to jar him back to reality. "Cordray hasn't done anything to Brak. He's fine." Micah's grip eased as he let go and took a step back.

"What do you mean, he's fine? Have you seen him?"

Micah nodded reluctantly. "Brak's here, buddy. He's in Chicago."

The world spun for a second, and Trace staggered backward until his butt met the back of the same chair Cordray had used as a hip support a moment ago. Brak was here? How . . .? Why . . .?

His dismay must have shown on his face as he wordlessly glanced back up at Micah, because Micah stepped forward and planted his palm reassuringly on Trace's shoulder.

"Your brother came here looking for you," he said. "He's been here about a week. He's desperate to see you."

Trace nodded numbly. He was desperate to see Brak, too, but since feeling Brak's presence in King Bain's dungeon, the sewage he'd stored away in the catacombs of his mind had begun to seep into the forefront of his gray matter. What would happen when Trace actually *saw* Brak? Maybe a face to face wasn't such a good idea right now.

He'd thought he'd lost his entire family two centuries ago. That not only had his mother died, but his father and Brak, too, even though his gut had told him they'd lived.

Now, nothing was as it seemed. He was glad for that, but knowing his father and brother had survived did little to ease his guilt, and everything to bring the events of the past back to his thoughts. Memories he'd kept tucked away for decades were resurfacing. He was even remembering the details he'd long forgotten. The acrid smell of smoke, the roaring, crackling sounds of wood popping against the intense heat, the scent of burning flesh.

Trace slammed his eyes shut as his mother's tormented face, shrouded by smoke and soot, reached from beyond the grave and slammed into his mind front and center. She was screaming, the fire consuming her.

It was his fault. All his fault. He'd done this to her. To all of them. His arrogance and carelessness had caused them all so much pain. So much sorrow. Dizziness overtook him, and it felt like his soul was lifting from his body as he spun downward.

"Trace?" Micah's voice cut through the sudden turmoil. "Shit! Trace? Are you okay? Open your eyes, buddy. I've got you. Just open your eyes."

He blinked several times, wincing against the light, until finally he peered up at Micah's concerned face.

He was on the floor. As in, he'd passed out or had some seizure-like episode and fallen flat-backed onto the carpet.

Micah gazed down at him, wide-eyed, his expression both confused and concerned.

"Are you okay?" Micah pressed closer, examining him.

Sam stood behind Micah, the fingers of one hand over her mouth, the fingers of the other pressed worriedly against the back of Micah's shoulder.

"Is he okay?" she asked.

Cordray stood to the side, her slender, black brows bunched over her eyes. Even she appeared concerned. Maybe he rated higher than amoeba piss with her, after all.

"I'm fine." He tore his gaze away from Cordray's and clapped his hand into Micah's outstretched one.

A moment later, he was on his feet again, dazed, his hands trembling. He rubbed them together, trying to hide the physical effects of what had just happened. But when his gaze met Cordray's again, he knew she'd seen everything.

She had been inside his head and borne witness to how he'd killed his own mother.

CHAPTER 10

No one said a word as they congregated in the kitchen.

Sam plucked the bacon and sausage from the skillet and set it on a serving platter, working mechanically, as if she were trying not to stir up the tension still lacing the air. Beside her, Micah removed a waffle from the waffle iron and added it to the stack on an oversized plate as he cast Trace yet another wary glance, as if he feared at any moment Trace would fall back into whatever hellish episode he'd experienced a few minutes ago.

Several feet away, Cordray sipped a cup of coffee.

Everyone was keeping their distance.

Just like when he was a kid. Everyone had thought him a freak then, too, giving him a wide berth.

His gaze flicked cautiously toward Cordray without meeting her eyes. In his periphery, he could see her rubbing her hand up and down her arm as if she were soothing a rash.

Maybe Cordray was treating him like a leper, but God bless her little black heart, she hadn't uttered a peep about what she'd seen in his thoughts. If anything, she almost seemed compassionate. Or maybe understanding was a better word, because compassion wasn't something Trace associated with Cordray. Either way, it felt like they'd made a connection. A bizarre, twisted, fucked-up connection, but a connection nonetheless. One where a silent promise had been made that she wouldn't reveal what she'd seen, and he would show his gratitude by not baiting her further.

Not that he needed her pity, but since she didn't seem eager to expose his secret, maybe he could cut her some slack. She was normally so eager to use his thoughts against him, so if she was willing to scratch his back on this, he could scratch hers. Because anyone who knew his deepest and darkest and still kept his or her mouth shut at least deserved a chance.

"So," Micah said, eyeing him as he set the plate of waffles on the breakfast bar, "let's try this again." He retrieved the platter of sausage and bacon and set it down beside the waffles. Despite eating a bowl of cereal barely thirty minutes ago, Trace's stomach growled as he glanced at the sausage links. "Brak wants to see you. Today if poss—"

The cordless phone on the kitchen counter rang, cutting him off.

Micah cursed. "Goddamn if we can't get this shit out on the table without some kind of interruption." He snatched the phone and briefly frowned at the caller ID before pressing the phone to his ear. "Micah Black."

Trace stole a sausage link and bit it in half, wondering if seeing Brak was such a good idea, given the nosedive he'd taken a few minutes ago as thoughts of his brother awoke memories of his mother's death.

He was still contemplating the idea when Micah's expression froze and pure rage rose in his eyes.

"What?" The word shot from Micah's throat like a bullet. "Someone broke into my apartment! How? When?"

Sam nearly dropped the pitcher of warm syrup she was carrying to the breakfast bar. She rushed forward. "What? Broke in?"

Trace swallowed the bite of sausage before he'd barely had a chance to chew it.

Cordray shifted beside him and uttered a curse under her breath. When Trace turned toward her, she bowed her head into her hand, covering half her face. She peeked sideways at him. From her guilty expression, it was clear she'd known about the break-in and had forgotten to tell Micah.

Looked like he'd be scratching her back sooner than expected if Micah tried to kill her in the next five minutes.

Micah paced to the end of the counter with the barely bridled aggression of a bull preparing to charge. His neck was as rigid as a two-by-four, his gaze intense. His free hand curled into a fist.

Trace glanced at Cordray again. "Did you know about this?" he said quietly.

She sighed then nodded once. "I was there. It's where I got this." She pointed to a small, nicely healed cut on her lip.

"Why didn't you say anything?" Micah's apartment had been burgled, and Cordray hadn't even thought to let them know?

She dropped her hand to her lap. "Honestly, I didn't even think about it. I was more concerned—"

"With me. You were more worried about how Micah broke your precious code of conduct and took me without your permission, right?"

"No, I—"

"Nice, C." He scowled at her and let out a perturbed sigh as he shook his head then looked away. Shit, but scratching her back was going to be damn hard to do when she was always pissing him off. "Why am I not surprised?"

"It was an honest mistake."

"Mistake my ass."

Micah stopped pacing and slammed his palm against the counter. "This happened this morning, and you're just now calling me?" He paused and scowled as if he didn't like what he was hearing. Then he reached into his back pocket and pulled out his cell phone and looked at the black screen. "My mobile was off."

Of course he would have turned off his mobile. The last thing Micah would have wanted was for his phone to ring and interrupt him while he was working him over in his dungeon.

Micah hit the power button and waited. Trace pressed forward and peered at the screen. When it came to life, it lit with several missed-call notifications.

Shit. This was bad.

"I'll be there in thirty minutes," Micah said. Then he disconnected and tossed the phone on the counter.

"What happened?" Sam stepped forward as Micah made a break for the stairs.

He barely slowed down as he replied, "Someone broke into my apartment."

Sam called after him, "Did they take anything?"

Trace's gaze shot toward Cordray. "Did they?"

CORDRAY'S HEART JOLTED AS ALL EYES TURNED TOWARD HER.

Micah froze in his tracks. "Wait . . . what?" He looked between her and Trace and back again as he took a menacing step toward her. "Why is Trace asking *you* if the thief took anything?"

Trace warily rose from his barstool as if preparing to make like a barricade. "She was there."

The tension in the room grew tighter than a virgin's vagina as Micah's gaze scorched hers. "You were there?"

She'd been in enough fights to know that if she so much as flinched, Micah would pounce. Keeping her movements slow and controlled, she glanced at Trace and Sam then back at Micah.

"Yes." She jutted out her chin, owning her guilt even though she felt bad about not telling him sooner. She should have, but her mind had been elsewhere.

She glanced at Trace again. He was totally fucking up her ability to function.

Micah's eyes burned with aggression. "You were there. You knew someone had broken into my apartment, and yet you said *nothing*?" As the word snapped from between his clenched teeth, he pressed ominously forward.

She took a measured step back, not wanting to provoke him. "Yes. I'm sorry." God, this was humiliating. Her face felt ten degrees hotter than the rest of her body, and thanks to Trace's proximity, she was keenly aware of how it felt when blood filled her cheeks. She would have rather remained ignorant to the physical sensations of embarrassment.

Micah shook his head in disgust. "You're sorry?" He turned toward Trace and Sam. "She's sorry. Can you believe that shit?" He faced her again. "You fucking hypocrite. You knew someone had broken into my apartment and said nothing, and yet you come here . . . to *my* house . . . and have the goddamn nads to harass me about taking Trace out of that hellhole without your goddamn consent? You've got some nerve."

His anger was justified, but it was too late to go back to the moment Micah walked around the corner as she sat with Sam on the couch sipping tea to say, "Hey, by the way, your apartment was burgled."

Besides, it had been daytime. The sun had been out. It wasn't like he could have left. So, really, by forgetting about the break-in, she'd spared him and everyone else unnecessary stress.

"How many times do you want me to say I'm sorry, Micah."

"Maybe if you said it like you meant it I might believe you."

Insufferable bastard.

She set her jaw and locked gazes with him for a long, tense moment. "I said I was sorry. I meant it." Apologies felt all wrong on her tongue, but they felt even worse on her conscience. As someone who knew what it felt like to be let down, she didn't like putting others in a similar position. Having to apologize meant she'd done just that.

Micah began to turn away as he started for the stairs again. "Yeah, well, your apology is for shit, Cordray."

She glared at his back. She deserved his ire, but that didn't mean she had to like it. "I forgot, okay? It's done. You know about it now."

Micah whipped back around and jabbed his index finger toward her. "I could have known about it ten hours ago."

"And done what? It's not like you could have gone anywhere ten hours ago!" She flung her arm toward the curtained windows. "The sun was out!"

"I could have sent someone over from AKM."

"Please." Cordray scoffed, bobbing her head to the side as she glanced at Sam. "Would Micah really have been content to send someone else to his apartment when he would have been stuck here?"

Sam's gaze danced between her and Micah. "Ummm . . ."

"Leave her out of this," Micah said, blasting forward. "You don't get to use my mate against me, not when you're the one who fucked up."

"She does make a good point, though," Sam said cautiously.

Micah scowled at her then turned his aggression back on Cordray. "You should have told me. End of story."

She refused to back down. "I did you and everyone else here a favor by *not* telling you."

"How do you figure?"

She gestured toward him as if the answer should be obvious. "You would have driven us all insane if I had. Look at you. You're about to blow out of your skin as it is. If I'd told you ten hours ago, you would have been cooped up inside, unable to leave because of the sun, storming around here like a pissed off rhino. You wouldn't have slept, nobody else would have slept, and you sure as hell wouldn't have been able to fuck Sam to delirium for three hours."

Sam blushed and ducked her head.

"Yeah, I heard the two of you!" Had she ever! Listening to Micah and Sam go at it had been torture, given how much she'd thought about doing the same thing to Trace over the past couple of weeks. "My point is, you would have been fucked up, and you would have fucked up the rest of us, and we would all be a lot more sleep deprived right now, so how about you cool off so we can get to your place and figure out who this asshole is?"

Micah glared at her. "What's this *we* shit?" He turned away as if dismissing her and started for the stairs again. "I don't want you anywhere near me."

"Have it your way, asshole, but I saw the guy. I fought with him. I know what happened." Micah was still walking away from her, so she decided to pull out the show stopper. "I know what he took."

Micah halted on the first stair and flashed her a vicious glance. "What? What did he take?"

"You want to know?" She crossed her arms and gave him a moment to reconsider. "Then I go with you." For her, finding Skeletor was personal. He'd bested her in a fight, and that was hard to do. She wanted in on the hunt to find him so she could wash the bad taste of defeat out of her mouth by kicking his ass.

Micah's jaw clenched as he glared back at her. "You're pushing your luck, female."

"Get used to it." She turned toward Trace. "You, too, because afterward, you're coming with me."

Strained silence gripped the air for several seconds.

Then Trace pushed away from the counter as he folded a pair of sausage links inside half a waffle. "Fine. I'll get my things."

Micah started to protest. "No, Trace. You—"

Trace held up his hand and stopped him. "She's not going to let up until I go, so let's just do it."

"But, you're not ready."

Trace stuffed half the waffle taco into his mouth as he clapped Micah on the shoulder reassuringly and started up the stairs. "I'll be fine," he said around a mouthful of food.

Micah watched him go then turned his gaze on Cordray. "If anything happens to him—"

"He'll be fine, Micah. I'll take good care of him for you. Now get dressed so we can get going."

Cordray was ready to get back to the ranch and her kids, and the sooner they left Micah's house and did recon on his apartment, the sooner she could get home.

Shaking his head and still fuming, Micah darted up the stairs and disappeared, leaving Cordray alone with Sam.

The two stared at each other for a moment, then Sam began putting food away and cleaning up the kitchen.

"You really should have told me about the apartment," Sam said quietly, unplugging the waffle iron.

"I know. I'm sorry." There was that damn word again.

"Why didn't you?"

She had no excuse. At least none she wanted to share. This morning, she'd been so consumed with her conflicted feelings for Trace that everything else had slipped her mind. All her mental energy had been devoted to tamping down her emotions and a kind of desire she hadn't felt in eight centuries.

She sat on the barstool Trace had vacated. She could still feel the tingle of his presence. "I forgot." She lowered her eyes and smoothed her hands over the edge of the counter just to have something to do.

Sam sighed then flipped on the faucet.

This morning, Sam had almost felt like a friend. They'd chattered and laughed over tea and told stories to one another. Now, a sense of loss compounded the tormented thoughts already ping-ponging inside her mind. Loss of newfound friendship and the hope that went along with it that maybe, just maybe, she could lead a semi-normal life.

"You like him, don't you?"

Startled, Cordray lifted her head to find Sam standing in front of her. She hadn't even heard her approach.

She frowned. "What do you mean? Like who?"

The corners of Sam's mouth ticked upward. "Trace." She said his name as if her attraction to him was as obvious as ice at the North Pole.

Cordray's heart skipped a beat, and she sucked in her breath as her shoulders stiffened.

Sam's clover-colored irises brightened as she smiled and scooped the silverware she'd laid out for breakfast into her palm. "Thought so."

Cordray gaped at Sam's back as she dropped the silverware into a drawer then began loading dishes into the dishwasher. Sam knew. Somehow Sam had figured out what she'd tried so hard to hide.

Clever female.

She only hoped that Micah and Trace weren't as perceptive as Sam, and that Sam knew how to keep her mouth shut.

CHAPTER 11

GLASS CRUNCHED UNDER MICAH'S FEET as he surveyed his apartment's living room. The place was packed with CPD detectives, police officers, members of building management, and one guy from security. They were making enough noise for an army and may as well have been scratching their balls for all the good they were doing.

Cordray could feel the frustrated, helpless aggression rolling off Micah, and for once, she kept herself out of his thoughts. She didn't need to see inside his head to know what he was thinking, and she didn't want to risk setting him off again. He was already pissed, and right now they had more important things to worry about than fighting each other. Such as finding out Skeletor's identity.

"Trace," Micah said, tilting his head toward his sidekick.

"Yeah?"

"Get these people out of here."

Using his tongue to slide a matchstick from one side of his mouth to the other, Trace acknowledged Micah's request with a quick nod then turned toward the humans still milling around the apartment. Barely lifting his hand, he captured every one of them under compulsion. Instant silence replaced the nonstop chatter.

She'd only seen Trace use his freakshow influence once before. Inside Bain's courtroom, when he'd held the guards under his control to protect Micah. God help her, but seeing him wield his power again turned her on as much now as it had then.

As the humans began moving robotically toward the door, waves of energy wafted around her like ribbons of silk. They circled her, caressed her, and lit her senses on fire.

She drew in a long, trembling breath as his energy touched every part of her. Her pulse hitched. Her nipples tightened. Her core clenched. If just the energy he put off was enough to make her feel this way, how would it feel to actually have him against her body, inside her, licking her nipples with his tongue instead of his aura?

It was suddenly too hot inside the apartment. Too sultry. Too so-help-me-God-but-I-need-to-come. She shrugged out of her coat and pressed her fingers to her brow as she fought the arousal building inside her like the impending eruption of a volcano. She hadn't had an orgasm since Gideon, and she didn't want her first one since to be in front of Micah and Trace while they were supposed to be investigating a crime scene.

She sat down in a side chair and pressed her legs together, but that didn't help. Trace's energy was invading her like a Viking hoard, pillaging her body indiscriminately, and all she could do was pray he would get those humans out of there in the next ten seconds before she humiliated herself.

"Jesus, can't you hurry it up already?" she barked.

The door slammed shut as the last human exited the apartment.

Trace lowered his hand, and the unbearably pleasurable sensations shut off. Thank God! She'd only been seconds away from the most incredible cataclysmic orgasm she'd ever had. Not that she wouldn't mind that kind of pleasure, just not in front of an audience. Not in front of *him*.

Trace turned toward her and plucked the matchstick from between his sensual lips. "What's your problem?" His strong brow scrunched over his heavily lidded eyes.

Why did his eyes always make him look like he was seducing someone? Trace rocked bedroom eyes like no one she'd ever met.

She gathered herself against the fading sensations as they released her nerves then stood, brushing her hands down the front of her black shirt. "Nothing. You just move like molasses. You'd think with all that fancy power you could get the job done a little faster."

Any faster, and she might actually have splintered into a million euphoric pieces.

Trace's sexy mouth twisted into a knowing smirk. "Sometimes slower is better, baby."

Bastard! Had he used his energy on her on purpose?

"You son of a —"

"Stop it, both of you," Micah said, turning away from the heavily tarped window to face them.

Cordray squared her shoulders and set her jaw. If Trace thought that little stunt had been cute, she had news for him. Just wait until they got to her ranch. She would make him pay for his repugnant antics.

"Cordray," Micah said sternly, snapping her attention back to him. "Spill. Now. I want to know what happened here."

With human ears no longer invading the space, they could finally talk openly.

She glared at Trace then paced away from them, more to get out of his circle of influence than anything. "I don't know who he was or why he targeted you, but one thing was clear. He gets off on the thrill of the chase. He's an adrenaline junkie. The greater the risk, the more interested he is."

"Good." Micah toed a shard of glass. His eyes were narrow, angry slits.

"Good?" she asked.

His malevolent gaze shot toward her as if he wanted to use her as a replacement for the real thief and expend his aggression on her. "Yeah, good. Is something wrong with your hearing?"

She wasn't above taking her lumps for forgetting to tell him about the burglary the moment she saw him, but she'd be damned if she was going to continue letting him treat her like a verbal punching bag. "How about you cool out? I'm not the bad guy here."

"Could have fooled me."

"Fuck you, Micah."

Micah was in her face in two seconds flat. "I don't like you. The only reason you're here is so you can tell me everything you know about who broke into my apartment and why, and then you're outta here. Got that? So talk before I lose the last thread of my patience and throw you out that window." He jacked his thumb over his shoulder to the blue plastic tarp billowing in the wind.

She met his gaze glare-for-glare. "I'm shaking."

"You should be."

"We're getting nowhere," Trace said flatly as he stepped between them.

How about that? For once, the voice of reason came from Trace.

Micah's expression hardened briefly then lost its rough edges as he took a step back. Cordray held her ground, not ready to give in. Then again, she'd conditioned herself for eight hundred years to be a tough-assed bitch who refused to give an inch. It was the only way she'd survived.

Strained silence stretched between them.

"Fine," Micah said a moment later. "Truce . . . *for now.* Let's just get through this."

Cordray scrutinized him and Trace for a moment. "Agreed."

"All right then." Micah toed a shard of glass and let out a perturbed breath. "So, tell me what happened here."

She told him about how she'd spotted Skeletor scaling the side of the building, the high-tech gadget he'd used to shatter the window, and how she'd decided to investigate, only to realize after she got there that this was his apartment. "That's why I was late last night," she said. "I was here, trying to ascertain exactly what this asshole wanted."

"So what did you find out?"

She sighed and turned toward the hall leading to the master bedroom. "Not as much as I would have liked, but my gut says this guy knows you."

"Why would you think that?" Trace asked, chewing on his wooden matchstick as if it were a toothpick.

She looked from him to Micah. "Women's intuition and centuries of bounty hunting." She let that sink in for a moment then added, "That, and he seemed to know right where to look."

"Look for what?"

"You tell me." She led them into the bedroom. "I found him in here. He didn't go anywhere else. Passed right by all the priceless art in the living room — the antique sword on the wall. He went straight for the safe."

Micah flipped on the light, entered the closet, then knelt in front of the wooden box still sitting on the floor in front of the open safe. With a frustrated sigh, he plucked the empty purple pouch off the floor. "He took the ankh?" His voice held a stab of concern. He stuffed his hand inside, even though the pouch was obviously empty.

"That's what it looked like to me."

Trace brushed past her, sending up her sensory hackles, and lowered to his haunches to peer inside the box. Cordray could see from where she stood that it was filled with gemstones, antique gold jewelry, and dozens of small, priceless trinkets.

"All this, and the only thing he took was an ankh?" Trace said. "That must be some ankh."

Cordray brushed her hand up and down her arm where he'd touched her as he passed. "That's what I thought."

"Why did he take it?" Trace looked at Micah. "And why didn't he take any of this?" He gestured toward what had to be at least a quarter-of-a-million dollars' worth of precious gemstones and gold in the box. "What's so important about an ankh when he had all this to choose from?"

Micah shook his head. "I don't know. My father gave me the ankh right before he died."

Both Cordray and Trace bobbed backward, eyebrows shooting high in their foreheads. Hearing Micah mention his father was like hearing Satan talk about *his* dad. You just didn't associate a paternal connection with someone like Micah, who seemed to have been conceived from the same midi-chlorians responsible for Anakin Skywalker's birth in *Star Wars*.

"What was it for?" Cordray asked, exchanging glances with Trace.

Micah's eyebrows furrowed harshly. "He never had a chance to tell me. But it felt important, so I kept it. I figured someday I would learn why he wanted me to have it."

Cordray searched her memory for anything she might have missed. Anything that could provide some clue as to the importance of an Egyptian ankh. She recalled reading something a long time ago in one of Bain's historical texts about ankhs, but she couldn't recall specifics.

"Did your father say anything that might hint at its purpose?"

Micah shot her an angry glare. "If he had, don't you think I would have told you?"

She took a deep breath and bit back her usual, snarky reply. Now wasn't the time to add insult to injury. "I'm just trying to help, Micah. I thought maybe I could help you remember something he might have said or —"

"He said it was important that I keep it safe. That the ankh couldn't fall into the wrong hands. That's all he had time to tell me. Our village was under attack by a dreck raiding party. Then he and my mother died, and he never got the chance to tell me the full story. You happy now?" He flung the purple pouch into the box, pushed himself to his feet, and paced past her into the room as he combed his fingers through his hair. "Is that what you wanted to hear? That he never got to finish telling me the ankh's purpose because he was murdered?"

"Of course not." Cordray's heart hurt for him. No one should lose someone they loved like that.

Micah spun and scowled into the closet at the open safe. "Yeah well, I figured if I waited long enough, I'd eventually find someone who could fill in the blanks my dad never had the chance to."

Trace stood. "Looks like you did."

"Yeah," Cordray said, "and I bet Skeletor's hands are exactly what your dad referred to as the wrong ones."

"He's going to be lucky to *have* hands after I get through with him," Micah said, marching into the hall.

She and Trace exchanged concerned but wary glances then

followed him.

Their investigation had uncovered more questions than answers, but what Cordray wanted to know more than anything else was, who was Skeletor, and what did he know about that ankh they didn't?

CHAPTER 12

After investigating the apartment and not learning much about the thief who'd taken Micah's ankh, Cordray took them to the location where she and Skeletor had fought.

Trace tried to follow Skeletor's trail, but it was practically nonexistent then went completely cold the moment he exited the alley and turned in the direction the thief had gone. It was almost as if the guy hadn't been there at all.

Perplexing. Trace could follow just about any trail as long as it was less than forty-eight hours old, sometimes even older. But Skeletor had fallen off the face of the planet the moment he left the alley. It didn't make sense.

They scoured the area for hours, searching for any trace of Mr. Sticky Fingers, but the only clue they found that he'd even existed was his discarded mask. Just north of the river, near the Trump Tower, they found it in a dumpster in a small parking lot between buildings. The left cheek and jaw were smashed from where Cordray had struck it.

"Do you think he left it to mock us?" Cordray said, eyeing the mask with a look of vengeance.

Trace sniffed the inside, picking up Skeletor's scent for the first time since the alleyway. He shrugged and tossed it toward her. "Who knows?"

She caught it and took a whiff, probably locking in his scent the same as he had before handing it over to Micah so he could do the same.

"He won't stay hidden forever." Trace swept his gaze around the surrounding buildings and along the Riverwalk. "We'll find him eventually."

And when they did, Trace would have a little fun with the fucker. After all, Skeletor had messed with his best friend. His keeper. His master. No one fucked with Micah without fucking with him, too.

"Cool that shit, Trace," Cordray said, obviously inside his head.

How the hell did she do that without him feeling her?

She shrugged one shoulder almost coquettishly then turned away. "It's a gift."

"Yeah well, stop gifting me with your gift." He didn't like his thoughts invaded, but ever since the incident back at Micah's, when she'd seen his memories about his mother and hadn't peeped a word about them, some of his animosity toward her mind-stripping habits had fizzled.

"What are you two talking about?" Micah said, tossing the mask back in the dumpster.

"Trace wants to take a crack at Skeletor's nog for making you a target," Cordray said.

"Good for him." Micah began scouring the rest of the parking lot for clues. "It's nice that someone has my back."

"Not good," Cordray said before Trace could second Micah's sentiment.

Micah stopped scanning the pavement and frowned at her. "Why the hell not?"

"Don't you get it? That's what this guy wants." Cordray waved her hand toward the surrounding skyscrapers. "For all we know, he's watching us right now, listening to everything we say. And he's probably getting a Skeletor boner at the idea that Trace wants to turn his brains into worm food. Remember, this guy is an adrenaline junkie. He loves the risk for the simple fact that it raises the stakes and gives him something real to play for. And what's more real than his own life?"

"You don't know that for sure," Micah said.

"No, but I've chased enough bounties to know the type. He fits the profile." She let out a derisive breath. "Hell, he exceeds the profile."

"So, what do you propose?" Trace said. "That we invite him for tea and cupcakes?"

"I'm not big into cupcakes," Micah added with a smirk as he knelt to investigate what appeared to be burnout from a motorcycle tire. "I vote for Trace's plan."

"Worm food it is," Trace said. "Sorry, C. You're outvoted."

Cordray sighed and shook her head. "Males," she muttered. "Always thinking with your fists or your dicks, but never with your brains." She joined Micah and nodded toward the black skid mark on the pavement. "That's from his bike. It had a fat rear tire like that. I bet he left it as a calling card to let us know he was here. He knew we'd find the mask. Cocky bastard. He's playing with us."

Trace studied her as she stood next to Micah, her long braid draped over her shoulder, her eyes sharp as she took in the surroundings. Under all that makeup she usually wore, he'd never noticed how pristine her skin was. How smooth and flawless. Without a smoky layer of eyeliner shaping her eyes and dark-red lipstick coating her lips, she appeared youthful, even innocent, and he liked the natural, pink shade of her lips. It made them appear dewy and lush . . . beckoning.

For the first time, he noticed her rounded, high cheekbones and gently upturned nose, like a bunny's. It was a kissable nose, if a nose could be considered kissable. Hell, her whole face was kissable. Even her elegantly arched eyebrows, which perfectly framed her almond-shaped eyes, begged to be tasted.

"What are you staring at?" she said, frowning.

Trace snapped out of his thoughts and blinked, realizing she was glaring at him. "Nothing. Just realized this was the first time I've seen you without your mask on."

"My mask?" Her eyebrows cut more sharply toward the bridge of her nose.

"Yeah. All that Gothic shit you wear on your face." He waved his hand in her general direction and shrugged indifferently. "You might actually be able to pass for a female now instead of an ogre."

"Aw," Cordray tilted her head sarcastically. "Such sweet words. I'm not sure what's better, a compliment from you or coming down with Ebola."

"Would you two stop bickering," Micah said, standing. "I thought we'd called a truce."

Trace kept his gaze locked on Cordray's. Something was different about her. Or maybe he was just beginning to feel differently *toward* her. Either way, something between them had changed in the past eight hours. And, to be honest, he kind of liked how it felt.

His gaze slid to Micah's. "Sorry. Couldn't help myself." He glanced back toward Cordray, who was looking at him as if she didn't know what to make of his behavior.

Something about Cordray made it impossible not to insult her, but only because he wanted her to insult him back. He actually enjoyed the verbal sparring. It was like they were competing to see who could one-up the other. To see who could throw the greatest insult. But this competition had no play clock, no final whistle. Life was the playing field, and any time they were near each other, it was game on.

The eastern sky was beginning to turn from inky black to midnight blue. Dawn wasn't far behind. "It's getting late," Micah said. "The sun's going to be up soon. I'll talk to Io about hacking into the city's security cameras to see if I can uncover anything else."

They began making their way out of the parking lot.

"Good idea," Cordray said. "While you're doing that, I'll look through Bain's records to see if I can find out anything about that ankh. I seem to remember reading something about ankhs somewhere in his archives."

"How do you get away with calling him Bain instead of King Bain?" Trace said as they hit the sidewalk. "Are you special or something?"

Without missing a beat, Cordray said, "We're hunting down a cat burglar who broke into your pal's apartment, stole what I'm assuming is a priceless artifact, and we have no clue as to his identity or why he did this, and you're concerned with how I refer to our race's sovereign?"

"I can multitask." And so the game continued.

"So can I, but my relationship to Bain is none of your business."

"So, you have a relationship with him, huh?"

"It's a figure of speech, Trace. You know what a figure of speech is, right?"

"I'm familiar with the term, but since you're always so damn literal, I—"

"Jesus, you two," Micah said. "Give it a rest. You're giving me a headache, for Chrissakes."

The constant jabs had given Trace something much better than a headache. His balls actually tingled. He might even be able to get off just arguing with Cordray. How was that for foreplay?

"Okay, so," he said, meeting Cordray stride for stride as she picked up the pace. "You're going to do research, Micah's going to investigate security footage . . . what am I going to do?"

Cordray shot him an amused glance as one eyebrow whipped into a humored arch. "Oh, don't worry. I've got a whole list of things you'll be doing. You won't have time to think about our friend Skeletor or what his intentions for your bufu buddy are."

"Bufu?"

"Butt fuck," Micah said flatly. "Butt fuck buddy."

"If only she knew." Trace smirked and met Micah's gaze out of the corner of his eye.

After last night's scene, it was clear from Micah's limits he would never do that to Trace, nor would he allow Trace to do it to him. Fine by him, especially if Micah continued taking him on head trips like he had last night. But Cordray didn't need to know the truth. If she wanted to think he and Micah fucked each other ten ways to Sunday, let her.

"I don't want to know." Cordray's pace picked up steam.

Trace and Micah laughed.

Once they made it back to where they'd parked, Trace grabbed his duffel from the trunk of Micah's Audi and tossed it in the back of Cordray's Range Rover.

"Tell Sam I'm looking forward to a bowl of her famous chili," Trace said, clasping hands with Micah in a one-armed hug.

"Sure thing." Micah released him. "And don't forget, Brak's waiting to see you."

Trace glanced toward Cordray, who hovered near the driver's side of the Rover, watching him. "Yeah, tell him . . ." What? He had no idea what to say to Brak. Hell, he wasn't even sure seeing him was a good idea right now, given how he'd melted down at Micah's house. "Just tell him I'll see him as soon as Satan's mistress gives me a reprieve from purgatory."

Cordray crossed her arms irritably and huffed, but she kept whatever retort she wanted to sling at him to herself.

That didn't last long, though. Once he was in the passenger seat and they were heading off to her lair, she wasted no time starting in on him.

"You know, after how I kept my mouth shut about what went through your mind when you blacked out or seized — or whatever happened to you — the least you could do is show a little gratitude."

"I'm grateful." He turned toward her. "But that doesn't mean we're friends."

"You can say that again." She cut the turn at a stoplight short, and the rear tires jumped the curb.

Trace bounced and grabbed the oh-shit bar above the door. "Where the fuck did you get your driver's license? A Cracker Jack box?"

She shot him an icy glare then frowned as her gaze dropped to his mouth. "Why do you chew on those damn matchsticks?" she snapped, ignoring his Cracker Jack jab as she returned her gaze to the road.

He pulled the wooden stick from his mouth and looked at it. Chewing on matchsticks had been a habit for so long, he couldn't remember when he'd started. But he definitely remembered why. Matchsticks were a reminder of his past. For a long time after his mother's death, he hadn't been able to start a fire. He'd been too afraid. Even striking a match caused his heart rate to hitch. So rather than light them, he chewed them to remind himself of how dangerous fire could be. That it should never be taken for granted, or bad things would happen.

He slipped the match back into his mouth. "None of your business."

"Well, keep your nasty habit away from my kids."

His head whipped toward her. "Your kids?"

That's when he noticed the car seat behind her. He leaned around, looked behind him, and found another one. Car seats. Two of them. As in, for toddlers.

Toddlers?

Cordray had kids?

When had that happened?

He leaned back in his seat and stared at her profile. He'd never even considered Cordray could be mated. He wasn't sure how he felt about that possibility. Who could the father be?

Maybe King Bain—

"Jesus Christ," she said. "I'm not doing it with Bain." She shuddered as if she'd just taken a sip of two-dollar wine. "Just the thought of that . . . just . . . *ew*."

He slammed his mental door on her, kicking her out of his head. "Then whose kids are they?"

Her blue eyes darted toward him then back at the road. "They're mine, dumbass."

"You're . . . you've . . ." He swallowed, not liking the ache setting up shop inside his chest. "Who in their right mind would fuck you?"

Honestly, the job of being her baby daddy sounded more appealing than he wanted it to.

She briefly appeared wounded before hardening her expression. "Considering you were just thinking the king and I were making babies together, I'm not sure if you're insulting me or the king."

"Just tell me who the father is." For some reason, this really bothered him.

"They're not *biologically* mine, idiot. They're kids in my shelter. I take care of them. But for all intents and purposes, they're mine. I think of them as my own."

Unexpected relief swept through him.

"You? A mother?" Who would have thought Cordray had a single maternal bone in her body? Her entire sexy, perfect, desirable body.

"Can you at least try to talk in complete sentences?" she quipped, turning onto the ramp for the interstate.

He bit back a grin. "Gee, I don't know. Could you at least try to talk to me like I have a brain?"

"Do you?"

And here came his tingling balls again.

"I can add two and two."

"And get what? Ten?"

He almost chuckled. Almost.

"No, eight."

He felt her look at him from across the console. He met her gaze out of the corners of his eyes. The air went deathly still.

Then Cordray laughed.

She actually laughed.

And the sound did something to the inside of his chest. Something warm and wonderful. Light and airy. Something that made him feel alive. More alive than he'd ever felt outside the playroom. Alive enough that he couldn't stop his own laughter when it bubbled up inside his throat and made a break for freedom.

This was the sound of tension breaking. Of enemies meeting each other in the middle and realizing how much fun they were having giving each other hell, even if neither was willing to admit it.

"You're a world-class asshole, Trace," she said, her laughter subsiding. But she still wore an effervescent smile.

"And you're a world-class bitch, Cordray." He cleared his throat as another chuckle bounced around inside his chest.

"I've been called worse."

"By better people, too, right?"

She dipped her head thoughtfully to one side. "Given my present company, that would be a yes."

"Thought so." He turned his gaze out the window as downtown grew farther behind them by the ninety-mile-per-hour second. Cordray had one hell of a lead foot.

After a couple of minutes of silence, he shifted in his roomy, leather seat and got more comfortable. "So where is this shelter with all these Cordray-influenced rugrats running around? I assume that's where we're going?"

She drummed her long fingers on the steering wheel. "It's in McHenry."

McHenry was a bit of a hike from Chicago, but the way Cordray was driving, they'd be there in no time.

"You'll be working off your community service there," she said.

"Doing what? Teaching them the way of the Force?" He lifted his right hand.

She shot him a semi-amused glance. "I don't think they're ready for that just yet, but don't worry. I've got plenty to keep you busy." She smirked like she was enjoying having him under her thumb a little too much. "I own twenty acres of land. Lots of trees, lots of grass, a massive garden, and horses. You're going to be very busy."

"Got any pigs?"

"No, why?"

He shrugged and propped the heel of his boot on the dash. "Just wondering where you keep your relatives."

"Ha ha," she said flatly. "You should be a comedian."

"Maybe in my next life."

"Do you mind?" She reached across the console and knocked his foot off the dash.

He lowered it to the floor. "My boots are clean."

"That's not the point." She huffed. "Just . . . sit there like an adult."

He rolled his eyes and looked out the side window, muttering, "Gee, are you sure I can?"

She ignored him, and nothing was said for a while as they flew at Mach 1 along the interstate. The eastbound lanes heading toward the city were getting busier, but nothing like how congested they would be during rush hour.

"So," Cordray said a couple minutes later, "do I need to worry about having you around my kids?"

"Why? Do you think I might taint them with my *disease*?"

She sighed irritably. "What I meant was, after what happened to you last night—your seizure or whatever that was. Are you sure it's safe for you to be around children?"

And there it was.

Fear.

Of him.

The story of his life.

Trace frowned and averted his gaze back out the passenger window. He'd been an outcast all his life. Teased by the other kids when he was younger, made fun of and bullied by Mason and his cronies, and then avoided as if he'd carried leprosy when the strangeness within him began to show itself. Back when he couldn't control it. Back when it scared the living shit out of him as much as it did everyone else.

Everywhere he went, he left destruction in his wake. It was inevitable. Sooner or later, his power got away from him, just as it had when he thought he'd killed Apostle, as well as when he found his father in Bishop's lab. In both instances, his power had risen like it wasn't even a part of him, as if it were a separate entity merely using his body as a vessel. And he'd unleashed it. He'd let it do as it pleased, killing Deacon and his dreck friends and turning that traitorous vampire working for Bishop into splattered protein residue.

But such occurrences were rare. For the most part, he'd learned how to control the beast.

"I'm not a danger to your kids," he said.

"Are you sure?"

"Yes." The word left his lips on an irritated hiss as his frustration over being such a freak of nature simmered just under his skin.

"I'm just being careful, Trace. These kids are everything to me. They're why I get up every day and do what I do to make this world a better place. When you've got nothing else to live for, you—" She sucked in her breath and snapped her mouth shut as if she'd said too much. Then she sniffed proudly and lifted her chin. "But then you probably wouldn't know anything about needing something to live for, would you?" Contempt dripped from every syllable.

Was she jealous? Of him?

"You'd be surprised." For over a century, the only thing that had kept him going was the smallest shard of hope that one day his life would hold meaning. That he would meet his mate and find his place in the world.

Then he'd met Micah. But even though Micah and Sam had filled a gaping vacancy in his soul, there was still a void neither could permeate. An emptiness only a mate could fill.

He glanced sideways at Cordray. She was more than enough female for twenty normal males, but just enough for him. Strong and fearless. Bold. Rough. Not too soft, not too hard, but just right in a way that made his dick stand up and take notice every time she was near. And now that he'd seen her without all that makeup she normally wore, he realized she was strikingly beautiful. Everything he'd always wanted in a female. The longer he was around her, the more he wanted to let his fingers do the walking all over her ample curves.

The only problem was, if he touched her that way, she'd probably cut off his hand. Or castrate him. Since he would rather not part with his dick over a novelty, it was better to pretend he hated her than actually admit he found her attractive.

Too bad, because he wouldn't mind seeing what sex without submission felt like. He never got hard outside the playroom, but around Cordray, he was hard all the time. Maybe not fully erect, but it wouldn't take much to get him there.

"Yeah, well," Cordray said, "just make sure you don't lose your juice around my kids." Resolve tightened her jaw. "My ranch is a haven for young vampires who get caught up in the human system. It's for our orphans. Those who have no one else and have lost their parents and everyone they've come to know as family. They need stability. They need to know the world is safe. I give them that. I become their family, and I won't let anyone hurt them. Not even you, Power Ranger."

"How maternal of you." He tried to sound unimpressed, but the fact that she looked out for the abandoned children among their kind touched his heart.

At one time, he'd been young and alone. Terrified and unsure. Abandoned. If not for those who'd taken him in, looked after him, and helped him understand and control his power, he might not have survived beyond his transition.

The work Cordray did was a noble endeavor. One he wanted to support.

He turned his attention to the stretch of interstate in front of them. "So, how many kids do you have?"

"Right now? Only seven. But I'm equipped for at least thirty. I've taken care of as many as twenty at one time, so seven is pretty manageable." She held up her index finger. "But don't take manageable to mean easy. They're a handful. Each one has his or her own problems to deal with. Their own needs to fulfill. I currently employ two full-timers who help shoulder the load, and I have several volunteers who tend to the grounds and do other small tasks."

"With all that help, it sounds like you don't even need me."

"Oh, there's plenty for you to do, trust me. Our annual fundraiser is coming up in a couple of months, and it's all hands on deck. We'll be lucky to get everything done, so you'll have your hands full. There will be gift bags to fill, party favors to wrap, phone calls to make, and about a thousand errands to run, and not nearly enough volunteers to do it all *and* keep up with the day-to-day operations. You'll be helping out and picking up where everyone else has had to drop the ball."

Trace glanced down at his large hands. Those babies weren't made for wrapping party favors and filling frilly-cutesy gift bags. "Great. Lucky me," he muttered.

Ten minutes later, Cordray took the McHenry exit and headed west. Shortly thereafter, she slowed and turned off onto a long, white-gravel driveway that led to a house twice the size of Micah's that sat in front of two smaller buildings: A barn that looked like an Old West general store and a structure that looked like a small apartment building or dormitory.

The Range Rover rocked as the left tires rolled through a shallow pothole. Water from yesterday's heavy rain sloshed out to the side.

"I'm having a fresh load of gravel brought in for the driveway this week," Cordray said. "The winter took a toll on it, so it needs repairing before the spring rains make it even worse."

"Let me guess. That's going to be my job."

She gave him the wink and a finger-gun. "Bingo."

"Why don't you just have it paved?"

"And ruin all my fun watching you toil over it? No way."

Trace rolled his eyes. So this was what hell looked like? On the surface, the place was nice. Deceptively innocent. Homey even. But once you passed through the gate, purgatory began. Hellish, burdensome, backbreaking purgatory.

The next three months were going to be a nightmare. He could just tell.

She pulled into the attached, four-car garage and parked next to a white Yukon Denali with the word *Asylum* painted in black and navy blue letters on the doors. The *A* formed the roof over a small house.

"Asylum?" he asked.

She shut off the engine and pulled the key from the ignition, palming her key ring as she opened her door. "It's the name of the shelter."

"Fitting." He pushed open the passenger door and pulled himself out of the seat.

Cordray opened the back hatch and grabbed her duffel. "What's that supposed to mean?"

He reached in and grabbed his own bag. "Just that asylums are normally associated with the insane."

She rolled her eyes and gave him a sour look as she shut the hatch. "You're like someone searching for the end of a circle, you know that?"

"How so?" He spied a sick-ass Ducati in the last bay and leaned to the left to get a better look.

"You never stop."

Taking her jab in stride, he nodded toward the motorcycle. "Whose wheels?"

She cast a quick glance over her shoulder then turned toward the open bay door. "Mine."

Trace's steps stuttered as he took a second glance at the tricked-out Ducati. Nice ride for a wicked female. "I guess it's better than your usual broomstick, huh?"

Other than a tolerant sigh, she gave no sign that his comment bothered her as she continued around to the back of the house. "Much better."

Cordray rode a Ducati. Nice. He wouldn't mind pretending to be a Ducati if she ever wanted to straddle him and take a ride.

"I feel sorry for it," he said, following her.

"What? My Ducati?"

"Yeah."

"Why?"

"Because I can't imagine a more vile place to be than between your legs."

She stopped and spun around, her expression one of utter irritation. "For God's sake, don't you ever turn off?"

Not when I'm having so much fun. "Nope."

"Well, how about you tone it down a notch?"

Before he could respond, a loud clang sounded behind him. He jumped instinctively and lifted his right hand as he spun around. Cordray slapped it down before he could send a charge at whoever had startled him.

"Cool it, twitchy fingers," she said as two toddlers burst from the back door of the house and charged onto the deck.

"Coco!" The children tumbled down the steps, blond curls flying as they rushed toward Cordray. "Coco! Coco!" Their tiny arms flew out, their stubby, unsteady legs kicking as they ran.

Cordray dropped her duffel and knelt, arms outstretched, then scooped the little girl up and tossed her in the air as she screeched with laughter.

"Me! Me, too!" The little boy hopped up and down as he reached for Cordray.

Trace stood back, unable to do anything but stare, curious how Cordray could be so welcoming to these two small children yet so callous and gruff toward him and everyone else. Surprising even himself, he realized he actually enjoyed seeing this side of her.

She set the little girl down and lifted the boy, who laughed as she spun him around. It was as if she'd forgotten Trace was even there. The little boy shrieked and laughed, begging for more.

"Did you two miss me?" Cordray said, still pirouetting the boy while the little girl danced and skipped a circle at her feet.

Their bubbling laughter sang infectiously through the morning air, warming his insides as the sun's first light heated the back of his neck.

Trace wasn't even aware he was smiling until the little girl caught sight of him and stopped. She sucked in her breath, her plump cheeks bright pink, and stared up at him. Her light-blue eyes popped open wide, and her tiny pink lips formed an *O* before she slid behind Cordray and grabbed her leg.

"Hi," Trace said to her, trying to sound friendly. He wasn't known for his warm fuzzies, though. More often than not, people shied away from him because of his scary disposition, so he had no idea how a two-year-old would react to him.

He sure hoped this went well.

Cordray looked down at the little girl, then up at Trace. "Don't worry, Aiden. He won't hurt you." Cordray issued him a stern, warning glance to drive her point home. "This is Trace. Trace, that's Aiden." She nodded toward the little girl. "And this little guy" — she set the boy down as if presenting him — "is her brother, Nelek, but we all call him Null. They're fraternal twins." She knelt between the two children and wrapped her arms around their tiny waists. "Aiden? Null? Trace is . . ." Cordray caught Trace's eye, clenched her jaw, and then continued. "Trace is a friend of mine."

That must have been hard for her to say, because it was extremely hard for him to hear without laughing. Her friend?

Was hell freezing over right now?

Biting back the urge to laugh, Trace knelt in front of them. "Hi, Aiden." The little girl ducked against Cordray's shoulder, hands shyly covering her face. He turned his attention toward the little boy. Maybe he'd have better luck there. "Hi . . . Null, is it?"

The little boy nodded and grinned, cheeks flushed, but he didn't shy away like his sister. "Hi," he said softly. His blue-eyed gaze landed on Trace's head, and he took a cautious step forward. "What happened to your hair?" His voice was soft, gentle, the *r* lilting a bit like a *w* so that hair sounded like haiow.

Null took another tentative step, his eyes fixed in fascination on Trace's head as he lifted his small hand. Trace could have fit five of Null's hands into one of his.

Out of the corner of his eye, Trace saw Aiden's luminous blue eyes peek curiously out from between her fingers.

Trace grinned. "I shaved it off." He leaned forward. "Wanna feel it?"

Null drew in an enthralled breath, and his eyes, which so perfectly matched Aiden's, grew wide as saucers. "Why did you shave it off? Did you have lice? This kid I knew once. He got lice. His mommy shaved his head, too."

Cordray choked back a laugh. No doubt she had an insult sitting on the tip of her tongue she was dying to let rip.

"Nooo," Trace said, drawing the word out. "I didn't have lice." He raised an eyebrow at Cordray to warn her not to bring this up later, but he doubted she would heed it.

Aiden blinked her big peepers at him and took a tiny step his direction. "Do you have cancer?" Her expression turned sad as she dropped her hands from her face.

Who were these kids? How did they know about things like lice and cancer at such a young age?

"How do you know about cancer?" Trace said.

Aiden glanced down at her feet and spoke quietly. "Mommy had it. She died."

Cordray gave him a look that made it clear she would tell him more about Aiden and Null later.

"I don't have cancer," Trace said, turning a gentle smile toward Aiden. "I just don't like hair. Never have. The less the better, so I shaved mine off."

Null shuffled closer and patted his small hands on the sides of Trace's head. *Tap-tap-tap.* His palms made quiet slapping noises against Trace's skull. "Then why do you like Coco?" He kept patting as he glanced curiously between him and Cordray, his blond eyebrows scrunched over his nose. "She's got *lots* of haiow."

Trace's voice caught in his throat as he looked at Cordray. With her kneeling as she was, the tip of her long black braid brushed the ground. "Uh . . ." He frowned, not sure what to say.

"The things that come out of the mouths of babes, right?" Cordray said with an air of dismay as she averted her gaze. "And if you haven't figured it out, yet, they call me Coco. Cordray was a bit too much for their young mouths to handle."

"Um, yeah. I kind of got that." Trace locked eyes with her for an instant before glancing back at Null. "And you ask too many questions, little man." He tapped Null's tiny nose with the tip of his index finger.

"Nuh-uh." Null jutted out his bottom lip as he fought not to smile.

"Uh-huh." Trace poked him in the stomach, making him giggle and grab his tummy like the Pillsbury Dough Boy.

"Nuh-uh!" Null stepped forward almost daringly and poked Trace in the chest, then jumped back, giggling.

"Uh-huh!" Trace grabbed the little boy and shot to his feet, lifting him into the air.

Null squealed in laughter as Trace plopped him on his shoulders. His little arms flung around Trace's head, halfway over his eyes, and his sneakered feet hooked under his armpits.

Trace trotted in a small circle, giving Null a pony ride as he secured his tiny legs in his grip so he didn't fall. Null screeched and let out another peal of bubbly laughter.

Cordray lifted Aiden and set her on her hip and shook her head at Trace. "You'd better be careful. He's not yet—"

"Uh-oh." Null stopped laughing, and Trace felt wet warmth trickle down the back of his neck and shoulders.

Trace froze. Uh-oh was right.

Cordray started laughing. "As I was about to say, he's not yet got full control of his bladder."

"I'm sowwy," Null said.

Trace lifted him off his shoulders. Null hung his head and tears welled in his eyes as Trace set him down and knelt in front of him.

Poor little guy looked like he was about to cry.

Trace ruffled his hair. "Don't sweat it, little man. I won't melt."

Null didn't look convinced.

Trace lightly pinched his button nose between his thumb and forefinger, trying to get him to smile. "It takes a lot more than a little pee to upset me." He grinned as Null cracked a smile. "If it makes you feel better, I'll pee my pants, too, and then we can make Coco clean it all up. What do you think of that?"

Null scrunched his face and giggled like he'd just been told an incriminating secret.

"Um, no," Cordray said. "How about no one pees their pants anymore today and Coco won't have to kick Trace's butt any more than she's already going to kick it?"

Null and Aiden giggled, but the look Cordray gave Trace was laced with a silent warning. He smirked wickedly at her, knowing she wouldn't do or say anything foul in front of the kids.

The back door opened, and a female with long, sandy-blond hair, wearing jeans and a peach-colored, oversized tunic, stepped outside, bringing the scent of pancakes, bacon, and hot maple syrup with her. She smiled at Cordray. "You made it just in time for breakfast." The female's gaze met Trace's, and she acknowledged him with a wary nod. "Hi. Are you joining us?"

"Trace, this is Brenna," Cordray said. "Brenna, Trace. He's going to be working here for the next few months."

Brenna's eyes narrowed as her gaze shot from Cordray to him. "I see. Well, you'd better eat before you get started." Her words were welcoming enough, but her gaze was still guarded.

Apparently, Brenna wasn't the type to trust easily. Good for her. That was a good skill to carry in this world where it was sometimes hard to tell who your enemies were.

Cordray set Aiden down and gave her rump a pat. "Go on in with Brenna and get ready for school." Aiden glanced at Trace, waved shyly good-bye, and then awkwardly darted up the steps to the door—almost tripping on the top step—and disappeared inside with Brenna.

Cordray took Null's hand. "You come with me. We'll get you into a fresh change of clothes."

She motioned for Trace to follow her as she headed toward the building behind the main house that looked like a cross between a dorm and an apartment building. Her gaze flitted to his soiled T-shirt. "You can change while I take care of Null. Then I'll give you the thirty-second tour and have Brenna toss your shirt in with the laundry before she starts class."

"Class?"

She took the prefabricated concrete steps up to the small porch and twisted the door handle. "Yes, class. She's one of the teachers I have on staff." She pushed the door open and led him inside.

They entered what appeared to be a large community room. The space was filled with beanbag chairs, a couch, a couple of desks, a table, two recliners, and bins for toys. On the far wall hung a large flat-screen TV with a boss gaming console on the entertainment unit underneath. These kids lived in style.

He followed her past the room toward a set of stairs. Null toddled along beside her.

"This is where the kids go to school." She waved her arm as if to encompass the entire first floor. "There are six small classrooms, even though we only use two of them right now." She started up the stairs. "The kids' rooms are up here. Brenna and Mya sleep up here, too." She let go of Null's hand and patted his rump. "Go up to your room and grab a clean change of clothes, okay? Hurry up."

His tiny feet pounded on the stairs as he darted ahead of them.

"Mya? Who's Mya?" His gaze was level with her firm, round ass, and his eyelids slid like silk over his eyes as he grinned at the thought of giving her a little hello squeeze.

"Mya's the other female who helps me out full time around here. Asylum relies on volunteers for most of the labor, but Mya and

Brenna are always here. They take care of the kids when I'm gone, and they run the school."

At the top of the stairs, she directed him into the bathroom, where she wet a washcloth and grabbed a towel out of the linen closet. "You can change in here. Meet me back downstairs when you're finished." She briefly eyed his chest then turned and hurried down the hall. A few seconds later, he heard her say, "Okay, little man, let's get you out of those clothes and clean you up."

Trace shut the bathroom door and set his duffel on the counter before peeling his soiled shirt over his head.

He grabbed a washcloth of his own from the closet, wet it, and brushed it over the back of his neck and shoulders as he blindly stared at his reflection in the mirror. But it wasn't his adult self he saw. It was the child he'd once been.

Scared, hungry, and cowering in the dark, cold forest. His mother was dead. He'd thought his father and brother were dead, too. Like the kids Cordray looked after, he'd been alone. An orphan.

Luckily, a tribe of Choctaw Indians had found him on their way west to Oklahoma. The tribe's prophet, an elder named Holahta, said it was a great honor to save him. That he would grow to be powerful and do good deeds for mankind. For a short time, Trace had found a place with the tribe and hadn't felt like a complete freak, even though many in the tribe kept their distance.

But his time with the Choctaw, while comforting and educational, had been short-lived. On his twenty-sixth birthday, fully transitioned into his adult vampire body, Holahta passed away, and the tribe's chief told him it was time for him to make his own way. That his path didn't lie with the Choctaw. And so he was cast from the nest.

That had been nearly one hundred eighty years ago. He'd headed north, eventually finding his way to Chicago and AKM. Then he'd found Micah, and Sam by extension.

With Micah and Sam, he was no longer a lonely freak. For the first time in his life, he fit in. He was accepted and loved.

And yet, it still wasn't enough. He wanted more. He wanted a mate of his own. He didn't want to have to always borrow Micah's during their trysts.

He desperately longed to form the kind of attachment to his own mate the way Micah had with Sam. The way Sev had with Ari, Malek had with Gina, and Io—the resident playboy—had with Princess Miriam. Hell, if Io could find a mate, surely he could.

But he hadn't. Not yet. Maybe he never would.

Everyone around him was taking a mate, and, once more, he found himself on the outside looking in. Left behind. With a family of vampires all around him, and yet utterly alone in the one way that mattered most in his heart.

He shut off the faucet and tossed the washcloth aside before drying himself and pulling on a clean shirt. Then he zipped up his duffel, snagged his dirty shirt, and made his way back downstairs, where Cordray was waiting alone, arms crossed, ass planted on the arm of the couch.

"Where's little man?" he said, looking around for Null.

She pushed to her feet and dropped her arms to her sides as she opened the door. "He went up to the house for breakfast." She stepped outside. "What the hell took you so long up there? I was beginning to think you were jacking off or something."

He scowled and sauntered down the porch steps. "Maybe I *was* jacking off."

She shut the door behind them. "What you do in your own time is your business, but I won't have that kind of shit around my kids."

He held a palm toward her. "Christ, talk about chasing the end of a circle." He huffed. "I was kidding."

"Good."

"What have you got against a little self-gratification, anyway?"

"Nothing, it's just—"

"It's not like beating off is a sin or anything. Unless you're a bible thumper. Did you suddenly go all bible-thumper-crazy-Christian lady on me? Because you're going to be no fun at all if you did." He adjusted the strap of his bag over his shoulder and smirked, enjoying giving her shit. "I mean, I'd have to stop calling you Satan's mistress. That would suck."

"Would you just shut up and let me give you the rundown?"

"Rundown away, church lady."

She sighed and shook her head then pointed to the barn. From here, he could see there was a chicken coop behind it, surrounded by a fence made of chicken wire. "That's the stable. We have two horses right now, but the kids want more, so . . . we'll see." She ushered him toward a pair of wooden boxes situated along the side of the building. She tipped the tops open and peered inside. He leaned over her shoulder and did the same. Both were empty. "Damn," she said. "These are our cat houses. I was hoping to find a new mother in one of them." She closed the tops.

"New mother?"

"We have a pair of females who are about to have kittens."

"Oh." Another thing his hands weren't made for. Holding kittens.

As they made their way to the large deck, she quickly pointed out the open fire pit behind a wall of shrubs that needed trimming, the tennis court in the distance that had ivy growing up the surrounding chain-link fence, and the horse ring overgrown with grass now that spring was in the air and all the vegetation was coming back to life.

Then she pointed to the wing on the back of the house. "That's the pool room."

"Pool room?" Asylum had an indoor pool? He looked closer. Sure enough, through the large windows, he could see the pool's decking and tiled walls, as well as a winding water slide.

"We have two swimming pools. A larger one for the older kids, and a smaller kiddie pool for the younger ones. We have pool parties once a month. The kids love them." She gestured toward the windows as she continued on toward the house. "The windows open outward, and the ceiling retracts, too, which the kids love in the summer."

Trace's gaze traveled down her curves as she took the stairs to the deck. He wouldn't mind seeing her in a bikini. A black leather bikini that showed off her tattoos. Nope, he wouldn't mind that one bit.

"I guess you in a bathing suit is one way to scare off would-be suitors," he said, catching the mouth-watering scent of butter and bacon as she opened the back door.

She stopped and glared over her shoulder at him. "Is it even possible for you to behave?"

"Behaving's not in my genome, sweetheart." He winked as he passed in front of her and stepped inside what appeared to be the mud room.

Her eyes narrowed. "Don't call me sweetheart."

He sneered. "Queen Bitch?"

The way blue flames lit inside her eyes made the jab worth any aggravation she'd put him through later. "Try again."

"Coco?"

"Only if you're a two-year-old." She gasped in mock surprise. "Oh, that's right. You *are* a two-year-old."

"What can I say? I'm a kid at heart." He inhaled her dark, edgy scent as she let the door slam behind her and shrugged out of her coat. As much as he didn't want to admit it, she smelled sexy. Like feminine perspiration, oranges, and musk.

"How about you try growing up for a change?" She hung her coat on a hook.

"And spoil all the fun? Never." He wanted to grab her hair and pull her back around to face him, just so he could get a look at all that blue fire in her eyes.

"I'm not amused."

"Ah, now you're just hurting my feelings, Coco."

"Don't call me Coco."

"But you said—"

"It's Cordray to you, Cro-Magnon man. Or C. Those are your choices." She crossed her arms, pushing her breasts into tantalizing mounds.

He looked her up and down. "I can think of a few c-words I'd like to call you right about now."

"I bet you can."

"I kind of like Coco myself." He hung his jacket on the hook beside Cordray's. "Makes me think of chocolate and marshmallows served up in a cozy mug. Something you clearly aren't, by the way. Just sayin'."

She sighed. Was that the hint of a smile he saw biting at the corners of her mouth? "Are you finished?"

"I don't know. Are you?" He glanced toward the sound of children chattering farther inside the house and, for the first time since arriving, felt a tremor of fear vibrate inside his heart. How would the kids react to him? Would they shy away like everyone else in his life did? Would they be scared of him?

She huffed and turned for the doorway leading into a short hallway. "You can leave your bag in here for now. I'll give you the tour of the house after breakfast." She brushed by him and left the room as if she didn't care whether he followed her or not. On the way out, she muttered, "I hope you don't need a drop cloth when you eat."

He set his bag beside a bay of lockers, two of which on the bottom row had Aiden's and Null's names on them. "Naw, I follow the five-second rule," he called after her.

"Of course you do," she called back.

He followed her into the kitchen, where Brenna was scooping four golden pancakes from a griddle. Another female—presumably Mya—was taking up bacon and sausage from a large iron skillet. Her hair was dark brown, almost black, and it was pulled into a ponytail, which swished and bobbed as she glanced over her shoulder and smiled. Her catlike eyes gave him a swift once-over. When she turned and set the platter of meat on the counter, he read the front of her T-shirt. *I'm what Willis was talkin' 'bout* was written in bright-orange block letters.

"You must be Trace." She set down her tongs and extended her hand.

He took it and nodded. His pulse quickened as his nerves danced up a notch. Social situations weren't his thing. After shaking his hand, Mya went back to helping Brenna finish breakfast.

He wasn't used to being around so many people, and he didn't have the best track record when meeting this many new faces. Tightness and panic fluttered through his chest.

Beside him, Cordray perked up as if she'd felt his fear.

"Are you okay?" she whispered. Concern edged her voice. "You're not . . . you know . . ." Her gaze flicked quickly to his hands.

His eyes darted to hers as he took several small, rapid breaths.

She touched his arm, and in a blink, his heart rate calmed. His breathing returned to normal.

What the hell? He glanced down at where her hand delicately curled around his forearm. Never had anyone calmed him with such a gentle caress. Always in the past, when his beast pushed forward or fear gripped his throat, it had taken the heavy-handed pain that he now received from Micah to pull himself back from the brink. Cordray had barely touched him, but it had been enough to tame his demon.

"I'm fine." He reluctantly pulled his arm from her loose grasp. "Just . . ." Admitting that he wasn't good in social situations sat about as well on his stomach as food poisoning. "I'm not a people person."

"No shit," she whispered. Then, more calmly, "You sure you're okay?" Her tone and expression were surprisingly compassionate. Then worry crept over her face as she dropped her gaze to his right hand again as if she feared it would blast her into the next decade any second. "I can't have you losing control in here, Trace. I need to make sure my kids are safe around you."

"They are." He frowned and took a step away from her. "I won't hurt them."

Maybe he was a Cretan, and maybe he was the Hand of God who could crush his enemies' innards into pulp, but he wouldn't hurt Cordray's kids. Of that much he was certain.

Kids were his one and only soft spot. Especially orphans who reminded him of his own lonely childhood. He would lay down his life to make sure Cordray's children remained safe.

"Everything okay here?" Brenna said.

He glanced up to find her and Mya staring at him like he had a bomb strapped to his chest.

Cordray stepped forward. "Everything's fine. Let's eat. The bus will be here soon."

With one more glance at him and Cordray, Brenna and Mya carried their platters of food out of the kitchen and into the dining room. The sound of chattering kids intensified as they dug into their breakfast.

"You seem . . .off," Cordray said, stepping closer, invading his nostrils with that dark scent of hers. "If this is too much . . ."

He didn't need her closer, because it made him want to do things to her. Naughty things. The kind of things he shouldn't do with kids in the next room.

Frowning, he took a step away. "I told you, I'm fine. I'm not losing control or anything, so don't worry you're pretty little head."

Her head cocked to the side as she swayed backward. "Pretty little head? Now I know something's wrong with you."

"It's a figure of speech. You know, kind of like the one you used earlier. Don't read anything into it." But he'd fucked up. When he'd said she was pretty, it hadn't been just a figure of speech in his mind. He'd really meant pretty little head. Because in that moment, that's exactly how he saw her. She was pretty.

Beautiful really.

Desirable.

In the past twelve hours, he'd come to realize she was a stunning female. Especially here. Her guard was completely down around the kids. A different light shone around her, casting her into his awareness in a new way. One that made his heart beat a little harder and blood rush to his groin.

"Fine. Whatever." She exhaled heavily and headed toward the dining room, fatigue sagging her shoulders. "Let's just eat so you can get to work and get out of my hair."

The dining room was alive with activity and chatter, and somewhere upstairs, a dog barked. A moment later, a tabby cat tore through the dining room, a small dog on its tail.

Cordray snapped her fingers. "Roxy. Out."

The dog halted, turned, and trotted back into the living room, where it dropped onto a small dog bed beside a dark-green recliner.

The place was a study in controlled chaos, but when he stepped into the dining room behind her, everyone quieted. Forks suspended over plates, halfway to mouths, as nine sets of eyes turned toward him, including those of Aiden, Null, Brenna, and Mya.

"Who's that?" said an older boy who looked a year or two away from his transition.

"Leon, this is Trace," Cordray said. "He'll be helping out around here for a few months."

Leon's expression hardened. He was the oldest boy there, almost a full-grown male. No doubt he took it upon himself to be the man of the house and didn't like a strange male invading his space.

Cordray took a seat at the head of the table and heaped a stack of pancakes and sausage on her plate.

Null wiggled, waved, and motioned him over. "Sit next to me, Twace." He beamed proudly from his booster seat, as if knowing who Trace was pushed him into a higher social standing among the others.

Trace made his way around the table, the stares of the other kids like ice sliding down his back. It made his skin prickle and reminded him of when he was a kid.

In school, the other kids had never talked to him. They had just stared and whispered to each other about what a freak he was. They hadn't known he could hear them, but he could. It was just one of the oddities about him that had isolated him from everyone else.

Freak.

A dark shadow had seemed to hover over him everywhere he went as a child. The other kids had ignored and avoided him as though he were a demon. He scared them. He scared everyone. He still did.

Unlike Brak, who had been everyone's friend. No one had been afraid of Brak.

But then Mother had given his twin the gift of white light, hadn't she? She'd given Trace darkness. Wasn't that what she'd told them when they were about Null and Aiden's age?

"While I carried you inside me, I gave each of you powerful gifts," she'd said. "To you, Brak, I gave the light. The gift to heal. To create. To mend." She'd brushed her hand lovingly over Brak's hair. "And to you, Trace, I gave the gift of darkness. The power to destroy, to hide, to protect." There had been no loving caress through his hair. Just a hardness in her expression, with the barest hint of compassion in her eyes. As if he'd brought the darkness on himself rather than received it from her.

He blinked away the memory as sadness tugged at his heart, even as the kids around the table recovered from his introduction and began eating.

Null reached toward him and wrapped his tiny fingers around one of his. The moment he did, all sadness vanished from his mind as if blown away on a breeze. Calm and peace swept over him, and he turned his gaze toward the little boy.

Null smiled up at him, his blue eyes shimmering, his irises shifting as if they were tiny oceans. Then they shifted back to normal.

"Bettew?" Null said.

Trace nodded weakly, not sure what to make of those eyes, then glanced at Cordray, who was watching them. The curiosity must have shown on his face, because she raised her fingers as if to tell him she would explain what had just happened later.

He certainly hoped so, because he felt like he was in an episode of *The Twilight Zone*. Asylum sure was living up to its name.

CHAPTER 13

"WHAT HAVE YOU GOT?" Micah stood behind Io at the massive computer console that looked like something out of the movie, *The Matrix*. Six monitors displayed frozen images from various security cameras around or near the Sentinel.

Io swiveled in his chair to face him, pulling a cherry Tootsie Pop from his mouth with a slurp. "You owe me for this."

Io normally didn't stay at AKM during daylight hours, especially not since he'd mated King Bain's daughter, but Micah had implored him to stick around after his shift to help hack into the city's security cameras.

"Yeah, yeah, I'll buy you a fruitcake for Christmas. Now, what have you got." He crossed his arms and glanced from one screen to the next, trying to figure out what he was looking at.

With a snort, Io spun his chair to face the monitors as he shoved the Tootsie Pop back in his mouth and tucked it against his cheek. "I hate fruitcake." The hard candy knocked against his teeth as he tapped a couple of keys on his keyboard. The top left monitor sprang to life. Io slurped the lollipop as he pulled it out of his mouth again and used it to point to the screen. "Okay, here's our boy at your place, playing Spiderman."

Micah watched as Skeletor's dark image glided down the side of the building, placed his hand on the window of his apartment, and then a moment later, the glass shattered.

"What did he use to break the window?"

Io tapped another sequence of keys and brought up the image of a small device that looked like one of those hand buzzers people pranked their friends with back in the fifties, only this was larger, flatter, and matte black. It had what appeared to be a small speaker in the center. The contraption looked military grade.

"My guess is that he's using one of these."

"And this would be . . .?"

"It's called an oscillator. I found this one on the Dark Net."

The Dark Net. The black market. Where society's criminal element did their online holiday shopping.

Io brought up several more images as he continued explaining. "The idea is, you hold one of these babies up to a pane of glass, activate it so it gives off a sound at the right frequency, and"—he popped his fingers open as if mimicking an explosion—"Boom! Broken window." Io crossed his arms. "But ones this small and this powerful ain't cheap. Your guy is well funded."

Great. Just what Micah needed. A rich cat burglar with nothing better to do with his time than to break into his apartment and steal ancient artifacts.

He should have put the ankh in one of the two seventeen-thousand-dollar Fort Knox safes in his home in the burbs. That's really where the damn thing belonged, not in the small, easily cracked safe in his apartment. But through centuries of despair after losing Kat, he'd lost his ability to give a fuck and had tucked everything into the small safe without much care over what happened to it. When he mated Sam in January and finally bobbed back to the surface to breathe again, he'd all but forgotten about the safe. Besides, he'd grown complacent with the idea that if no one had stolen his priceless heirlooms in nearly a thousand years no one ever would.

He'd been so wrong, and now he was paying the price.

But hindsight was twenty-twenty. Once he got his father's ankh back—and he *would* get it back—he would rectify his mistake and put it where it should have been in the first place.

But first, he had to get the damn thing back.

"Okay, so what else have you got?"

Io grinned, leaned forward, and typed out another command. Another monitor came to life. "Okay, here's your boy in the alley fighting that drag queen, Cordray."

Micah smirked. "Drag queen. You're funny."

"Thought you'd like that." Another monitor unfroze as Io continued typing and sucking on his Tootsie Pop. "And this is the shot from the alley. See, there he goes." The thief gunned his motorcycle and raced away from where he'd left Cordray sitting on her ass in the rain. "And this"—Io pointed to another monitor—"is the parking lot where you found the abandoned mask. Watch."

Micah leaned forward and rested his hand on the desk beside the keyboard. A moment later, Skeletor rolled into the parking lot. His back was to the camera, and he was hunched over as if he knew it was there and wanted to hide his face. He reached under his hood. A moment later, he tossed the mask in the dumpster. Then he gunned the throttle, spun the rear tire around, and sped away, keeping his head down.

Yep, Skeletor knew the camera was there.

But Micah caught the flash of skin around his jaw. "Stop. Rewind."

Io did as instructed.

"Now, go forward. Slowly."

The image began to scroll.

"There. Stop."

Micah leaned closer and narrowed his eyes. Looked like Skeletor had a square jaw and black, close-shaved stubble. It wasn't much to go on, but it was something. Add that to what Cordray had said about Skeletor having vivid, grey-blue eyes, and they at least had the start of a suspect's sketch. Slowly but surely, they were building a face to go with the mask.

Io squinted and leaned toward the monitor. "Is he laughing?"

Micah pushed off the desk and stood tall as he peered at the frozen image. "Yeah, he's laughing. Little fucker. He knew the camera was there. He knew we'd use it to track him."

"Which means . . .?"

"That he's toying with us. He obviously knows who I am, and he obviously knows I have resources to hunt his ass down." Which put Micah behind the eight ball, because he knew exactly squat about Skeletor. Eye and hair color, and a square jawline with black stubble weren't a lot to go on.

"And he's using those resources to taunt you." Io turned his attention back to his screens. The hard cherry shell of his Tootsie Pop knocked against his teeth as he tongued it to the other side of his mouth. "Ballsy little fucker."

"You're telling me." And when he found this sonofabitch with balls the size of an elephant's, he'd teach him a thing or two about respect the Micah Black way. Which involved fists and maybe a pair of steel-toed boots.

"So," Io said, "if he knew we would tap into the city's cameras to track him, what good is all this footage I found? He probably staged his entire egress for maximum exposure to ensure you'd follow him."

"Exactly." Micah leaned forward again, placing his hand on the back of Io's chair as he scanned the monitors. "Which means he's got an ego. And you of all people know how egos are. They sometimes get in the way of smart decisions."

Io had been known to make some pretty boneheaded decisions in his past, all because he thought he was the bee's knees. In fact, one of those decisions — going after Princess Miriam — had almost gotten him killed a few weeks ago. It had also been the reason Trace had spent two weeks in King Bain's dungeon, Tristan was still on house arrest, and Micah was in charge of the team now. So yeah, it was safe to say Io knew the trouble an inflated ego could cause, even if all had ended well when Miriam turned out to be his mate.

A knowing grin spread across Io's face. "Hey, I resemble that remark." He chuckled. "But you're right. If we're patient, our boy will eventually screw up."

"And we'll be there when he does." Micah would personally lead the welcome party when Skeletor — or whoever he really was — made his first wrong move and walked straight into Micah's waiting fist. "Show me the rest."

The next screen came to life. "I followed him through the city to this location."

"That's the Millennium Park parking garage."

"Yeah, and guess what?"

"What?"

"Less than five minutes after he pulled in on his motorcycle, he came back out on foot." Io sped up the playback and stopped as a black-clad figure exited the garage, headed north on Michigan Avenue, crossed the intersection at Randolph Street, and disappeared inside the Heritage building.

"That's a residential building," Micah said, frowning. "Do you think he lives there?"

Io shrugged. "Hard telling."

Micah straightened. It seemed too easy. If Skeletor knew Micah would tap into Chicago's street cameras, why would he lead him to where he lived?

"Did he come back out?"

Io shook his head. "Nope, and I've scanned all the footage. He went into the Heritage and stayed there."

"Doubtful." Micah's instincts told him he was missing something.

"Maybe he *wants* you to find him."

"Why? So I can kill him?" Because killing the guy was right near the top of his to-do list. Right under stuffing his foot up the guy's ass.

"Maybe that's the game he's playing. Maybe this was all just an elaborate ploy to get your attention, and he wants something from you."

"Oh, he's got my attention all right." Micah considered his options then pulled out his phone. He hit Severin's speed dial. As he waited for Sev to pick up, he said to Io, "I want you to do background checks on everyone who lives at the Heritage."

"That'll take some time."

"I don't care. Do it. I want this asshole." He started for the door.

"On it." Io turned back to his console just as Sev picked up.

"It had better be burning, bleeding, or in the middle of an apocalypse for you to interrupt me right now, Micah." Sev sounded out of breath.

Micah heard Ari moan in the background. Those two fucked more than he did, and that was saying something, because his favorite pastime was exploring Sam's body as often as he could.

"Don't you two ever quit?" he said.

Sev let out an irritated sigh. "Either tell me why you called, Micah, or I'm hanging up."

Micah grinned. He respected Sev's style. "I need you. Now."

Sev cleared his throat, and Micah heard a rustling noise that sounded as if Sev's head was planted firmly in a pillow. "Um, not only am I in the middle of something right now, but you're gonna make Ari jealous saying shit like that to me."

"Like what?" Ari said in the background.

It sounded like Sev put his hand over the phone, but Micah still heard him say, "Nothing, I'll tell you later."

Micah chuckled softly. "Fuck your mate, Sev, but make it a quickie. Then get over to the Millennium parking garage." Micah marched down the hall toward his office.

"The Millennium garage? Why?"

"Just hurry and fuck your mate and get going. I'll e-mail you the details." Micah disconnected.

He needed a day walker for this task, and since Trace was cooped up with Medusa's daughter, that left Severin.

Sometimes, being a full-blooded vampire pissed him off. Mixed-bloods had all the fun. They could go out in the sun, came with a variety of nifty powers, and had a lot more flexibility, in general.

No more than ten seconds after he e-mailed the video and all the pertinents to Sev, Micah's mobile rang.

He answered without checking the caller ID. "Micah Black."

"Micah." It was Brak.

Shit, he'd forgotten to call him.

"Brak, hey. I'm sorry I haven't called about Trace. It's been . . ." He thought back over the last twenty-four hours. "Crazy. Very crazy." Understatement.

"Oh, okay." Brak sounded disappointed.

Micah felt like a cad for dropping the ball. "He knows you're here, Brak. He knows you want to see him. But things got a little out of hand, and there's been some personal shit going on . . . and the bitch—I'm sorry, female—who was supposed to sign for his release has got a hair up her ass and—"

"When can I see him? It's important I see him, Micah."

"I know. I'm sorry. I'll make sure to set something up soon."

"And our father. Is he doing better?"

Maddox had been moved to the new underground facility a few days ago. He'd been too much of a loose cannon to keep here, where they couldn't secure him without strapping him to a hospital bed about a foot too short to hold his massive form. And Micah wasn't going to have any of that shit. The new facility had Plexiglas hospital rooms for these exact situations. Maddox could remain safely tucked away until his mental synapses began regularly firing to the tune of less violent outbursts. Right now, his mood blew with the wind, sometimes creating a tidal wave and sometimes a refreshing ripple. And sometimes he was a tsunami, like he'd been the day he redecorated his hospital room by breaking just about everything not bolted down and putting a few holes in the walls for good measure.

"Your father's safe. He's behaving erratically, so we thought it best to keep him—"

His desk phone blared, then the incoming speaker turned on. "Micah! We need you in the trauma unit! NOW!" Urgency shot through Dr. Snow's voice as something crashed in the background.

Trauma was where the victims of Bishop's lab had been taken, and a couple of them had been in pretty bad shape. This couldn't be good.

"Brak, I'm sorry, but I've got to go. There's an emergency." He was already racing out of his office. "I'll call you back."

He disconnected before Brak could say anything more.

Trevor strolled around the corner up ahead, wearing nylon shorts and a sweat-drenched T-shirt. His face was turned downward as he read something on his phone. Micah was glad Trevor had chosen to stick around for a while now that his friend, Gina, was settling in as Malek's new mate. The guy came in handy in tight situations at a time when they were badly shorthanded. Like now.

"Trev! I need you."

Trevor glanced up then immediately stuffed his phone in his pocket and snapped to attention. "What's going on?"

"Trauma unit. We've got a problem."

Trevor fell into stride alongside him as they ran down the hall. "Any idea what?"

"Something that requires some muscle if they called me." So the more muscle he could take with him, the better.

They cranked around a corner and almost ran into Stryker, who jumped out of the way.

"Where's the fire?" Stryker quickly recovered and joined them.

"Trauma unit," Trevor said.

A few seconds later, the three of them plowed into the medical ward and were greeted by angry shrieks coming from behind the double doors where Bishop's victims had been taken.

Holy hell! That shit sounded more mutant than vampire.

God help them if one of Bishop's vics had turned.

Micah busted through the double doors to find the staff scurrying every which direction, some with hypodermics, others simply trying to get out of harm's way. One ducked as a flesh-colored upchuck tray flew through the air.

"What's going on?" He and the others rushed into the fray.

One of the nurses pointed toward the second room on the right. She was out of breath and bleeding from a gash over her eye. Fear blasted from her gaze. "It's Kieran. He's melting down."

Melting down. Hopefully that wasn't the medical term for a patient who was going mutant.

The commotion from inside the room intensified. Machines buzzed, and metal crashed against metal as someone yelled for help.

"Help them!" Micah said to Trevor, pointing to the nurses rifling through medical supplies. Then he snapped his fingers at Stryker, who looked like a howitzer in a T-shirt. "You're with me. Now!"

He and Stryker rushed into the small room just as Kieran picked up a nurse and tossed her as if she weighed nothing more than air. She slammed into the wall and crumpled to the floor.

"Get her out of here!" Micah shouted at the other nurses.

Dr. Snow struggled to get close enough to inject Kieran with what Micah assumed was a sedative.

Shit better be strong enough to knock out a brontosaurus. Kieran was severely out of control.

"Micah!" She caught his eye. "I need you to hold him down."

Just how was he supposed to do that? By asking nicely? Not gonna happen. He and Stryker would have to do their best cement truck impersonation if they had any hope of restraining this guy.

One of the other nurses shouted, "Grab him! Don't let him go!"

Kieran strained for the door. The muscles and tendons of his neck were strung tight, his fangs exposed, black eyes full of fear, panic, and something else. Evil. Pure evil.

Fear, panic, and evil. There was a Hallmark moment if he ever saw one.

Kieran spotted Micah, and evil took the lead as his eyes narrowed into malicious slits. "You're dead." He sounded more like a gorilla trying to speak English. The black mass of tattoos covering his arms, chest, and torso shifted and slithered over his skin.

Okay, that was fucking bizarre. Who was this Kieran character, and how the hell did he have tattoos that moved?

"Jesus, he's . . ." Trevor stood in the doorway, his mouth hanging open as he stared at Kieran.

Micah dashed a glance at Trevor. "He's what?" But he didn't have to hear Trevor's answer. He could see it in his mind.

"Beautiful." Trevor breathed the word more than said it.

"Yeah, well, he seems about ready to tip to the dark side, so put your tongue back in your mouth and give us a hand."

Trev hurried into the room. "I'm there. Just . . . damn!"

Great. Trevor had a hard-on for the Antichrist.

"You're all dead!" Kieran seethed violence. "I'll kill you all for doing this to me!" He flung off one of the nurses trying to contain him. She tripped over her own feet and fell ass-first to the floor in her haste to get away from him.

Micah jumped over her and shot around him, wrenching Kieran's phantasm-covered arms behind his back before he could take another step. Shit, Kieran was strong.

Kieran growled and thrashed, tugging against Micah's hold. Then one of the wispy, black markings lifted off Kieran's skin and began to curl around Micah's wrist.

And freaked Micah the fuck out!

Are you shitting me?

"Stryker! Trevor! Get over here! Take his other arm."

Whatever those tattoos were, they weren't ink.

Within seconds, he, Stryker, and Trevor had Kieran in a stronghold and dragged him to his knees. The black tendril left a trail of ice as it continued winding its way up Micah's arm. What the hell was it doing to him?

"Doc! You'd better hurry up if you're going to get that needle in him!" Micah clenched his jaw and pulled on his reserves, his muscles straining.

Dr. Snow rushed forward and stabbed the hypodermic into Kieran's shoulder, plunging the contents into his arm.

Kieran screeched, and Micah winced as the sound split his eardrums. But the black-tattoo-ghostly-devil-mark thing released Micah's arm and snapped back onto Kieran's skin.

Thank God.

Within seconds, Kieran's body sagged, but he wasn't unconscious. Just super chilled.

"Please, God," Kieran said, voice ragged, "just kill me and get it over with. I can't live like this anymore." Desperation, sorrow, and fatigue wrapped around Kieran's words, and he sounded as if he were surrendering, but to whom? Then a weak but malevolent chuckle rose unexpectedly from inside Kieran's chest. "God can't help you, and I'll never let you die." This voice was different than the one Kieran had just used to beg for death. It sounded as if someone — or some*thing* — else had taken up residence inside his body and was using Kieran's voice to talk to him. Talk about your split personalities.

Micah eyed the freakish tattoos as he let Kieran go and hastily backed away. The farther he got away from that devil paint, the better. Given the conversation Kieran had just had with himself, Micah was starting to think there was a lot more to Kieran than met the eye, and he would bet those living tattoos weren't ink, but something worse. Much worse.

Kieran's drugged gaze wobbled to his. "Who are you?" He was back to voice number one. The normal voice. The one Micah guessed was Kieran's true voice.

"Name's Micah." He raked his hair off his face, breathing hard. "How about you help me out, Kieran, and stay calm so we can get you back into bed so that nobody else gets hurt?"

Kieran's face relaxed further, and his lips parted. For a moment, he didn't say anything, just sat there on his knees in the middle of the floor as he looked around. "Where am I? What is this place?"

"You're in Chicago. At AKM. We rescued you from Bishop's lab."

A shallow frown crossed Kieran's brow, and Micah sensed the pain of cobalt withdrawal assaulting him. "It hurts." Kieran tried to pull out of Trevor's and Stryker's hold, but the sedative Dr. Snow had given him was doing its job, making him docile. Manageable.

The nurses shrank away as Micah warily stepped forward, eyeing those wicked black markings, and lowered onto his haunches. "You're in withdrawal. Bishop drugged you. He was giving you cobalt. We've been detoxing you, but it's not going to be easy. It's going to hurt. But that's a sign it's working and the shit's getting out of your system."

Kieran's face contorted painfully as he tried to free himself again. "It HURTS!" Kieran threw back his head and shrieked toward the ceiling. The nurses cringed and skittered from the room. He doubled over and groaned, his tattoos breaking through their outlines and bleeding black into the surrounding skin.

Micah frowned as the images rolling through Kieran's mind began splintering into fractured shards, as if Kieran's brain was running into interference and could no longer process rational thought.

Then Kieran's body went deathly still. His demeanor changed so suddenly that it felt like a wizard had slammed his magical staff against the floor and sent a shockwave of silence through the room. An instant later, Kieran's head snapped up. His eyes glowed red.

Ummm, okay . . .

"Let me go." They were back to voice number two. The one that belonged to someone—some*thing*—else.

Kieran tore himself out of Trevor's and Stryker's grip and lurched to his feet, knocking Micah over. The fist he took to the jaw sent his brains into next year. The one that landed on his abdomen a split-second later nearly made him lose his breakfast.

That was going to leave a bruise. On his stomach.

In a blink, Kieran leaped off him and shot toward the door. Micah scrambled to all fours, coughing through the pain in his diaphragm, and looked up as Stryker blocked the exit like a concrete wall. Trevor staggered to his feet then gave chase. Moving with the speed and grace of a leopard, Trevor caught Kieran's arm, kicked his feet out from under him, spun him around, and locked him in a choke hold as he drove him to his knees again.

Go, Trevor! Micah hadn't known he had it in him.

"Calm the fuck down, buddy," Trev said. "You're not going anywhere right now."

Kieran resisted, growling and spitting as he tried to reach around and pull free of Trevor's hold. But Trevor had him, and he had him good and tight. His biceps and the muscles in his forearms and shoulders flexed impressively as if he were tapping into every last reserve of strength he possessed to keep Kieran down.

Micah jumped to his feet and reached for the hypodermic Dr.

Snow had just picked up. "Give it to me!"

Pale-faced, she handed it over.

He spun back around. "Hold him still," he told Trevor.

"I've got him." Trevor's voice strained. "Just hurry up. He's stronger than he looks."

"No shit." He knew firsthand exactly how strong Kieran was. What he didn't know was whether it was the cobalt withdrawal, that freakish black shit crawling over his skin, or the unknown entity squatting in Kieran's body making him that strong. Two out of three? All of the above?

Micah drove the needle into Kieran's neck and plunged the contents into his body as Kieran's red eyes lasered fury at him.

"I'll kill you!" Kieran strained but began to relax almost immediately as the sedative went to work.

"Yeah? Well, you'll have to get in line behind everybody else." Micah pulled the needle out and carefully handed it back to the doctor.

Hopefully, this dose would top off the first and knock Kieran out for good.

Within seconds, Kieran melted into a mass of lax flesh in Trevor's arms.

Thank God. Micah collapsed into a nearby plastic chair and rubbed his bruised stomach.

"You okay?" Dr. Snow touched his shoulder.

He combed his hair off his face. "I'll be fine." He looked around the disheveled room. It appeared the drama was over, but the cleanup would take a while. "What the hell happened in here?"

One of the nurses poked her head into the room as Trevor lifted Kieran and carried him toward the bed.

Dr. Snow motioned her to enter then turned her attention back to Micah. "We were pulling him out of his induced coma today. Everything was going well, and then he just went crazy."

"Obviously." Micah scanned the mess of broken equipment littering the floor. "Maybe you should transfer him to the new facility, where they can keep him under observation in one of the Plexiglas rooms."

"Once we stabilize him, I'll consider it, but he's obviously too strung out on cobalt withdrawal to move right now."

Kieran's head lolled back over Trevor's arm, exposing his neck, to which Trevor sucked in an audible breath.

"You doing okay there, Trev?" Micah said.

Trevor nodded hypnotically without looking at him. "I'm good."

Micah could almost see the little hearts with cupid wings fluttering around Trevor's head. Looked like the Antichrist had an admirer. Micah only hoped Trevor knew what he was getting into with Kieran. Falling for this guy couldn't be good for anyone's health.

Dr. Snow addressed the nurse. "Keep him heavily sedated and start pumping him full of fresh blood. And up his dosage of buprenorphine."

Micah had heard of bupe, as it was called on the street. It was an opioid used to counteract human opioid addiction. How about that for fighting fire with fire?

"You're using bupe on him?" he said.

The doctor nodded. "Yes. We've found it's as effective in vampires against cobalt as it is in humans against opioids."

"But not as effective as Io's all-natural approach."

"No, but much more palatable."

From what Micah knew of Io's anti-cobalt tonic, which was used inside AKM for the most extreme overdoses, it wasn't the tastiest of concoctions, but it sure got the job done. It had helped Miriam beat her own cobalt addiction in record time, keeping her indiscretions out of the public eye. Something King Bain was extremely grateful for. The last thing he needed was bad press on the royal family.

The nurse helped Trevor get Kieran settled back into bed. Then Trevor gently pulled the sheet over him as if he were tucking a fragile Fabergé egg into a velvet pillow. From the awestruck expression on Trevor's face, as well as the way he pushed back Kieran's shaggy, dark-brown hair then brushed the backs of his fingers down his cheek, he clearly wasn't going anywhere soon.

Stryker helped clean up the room. Broken equipment was hauled out as limping orderlies brought in new monitors and an IV.

Dr. Snow lightly touched his arm. "There's something else I need to talk to you about." She bobbed her head toward the door as she stepped toward it.

Micah regarded Trevor. "Hey, Trev. You gonna be okay in here while I talk to the doc?"

Trev looked up, his gaze glossy, as if he were having a special moment with demon boy. "Yeah. Fine. I'm fine."

As Micah passed Stryker on the way out of the room, he said, "Could you stick around for a few and help Trevor keep an eye on that guy."

Stryker gave him a single, tight nod. "I don't need to be anywhere right now. I'll hang here for a while."

"Thanks."

Micah followed Dr. Snow to the other side of the circular nurse's station. Everyone was busy putting the pieces back together, picking up dropped supplies, and straightening strewn paperwork, so no one paid them any attention.

"What's wrong?" he asked.

"It's about Savill."

Savill was the young male Bishop had turned into a dissection tutorial in his lab. Thankfully, they'd been able to rescue the kid before he died. Hopefully, that hadn't changed since the last time Micah had checked in on him, because the doctor's expression was pretty grim.

Micah snapped to attention, his sore abdomen and jaw forgotten. "Is he okay?"

Dr. Snow paused. "We found his parents."

Based on her tone, this wasn't a good thing. "And . . .?"

She sighed and brushed back her hair. "Micah, they're human."

That sound splatting in Micah's ears was the proverbial shit hitting the fan.

"Human? How is that possible?"

"They adopted Savill when he was just an infant. They didn't know."

As if Savill's situation wasn't bad enough. Surviving and coming through this ordeal alive had just become the least of his worries, because with human parents, odds were damn good that Savill had no idea he was a vampire. And since he was still young — barely twenty years old, if that — he probably hadn't yet experienced any significant physical changes to raise concerns.

And yet Bishop had still been able to identify him as a vampire. Poor kid probably had no idea why he'd been taken or what was happening to him.

"What's the status? Have the parents been handled?" he said.

"Yes, a team from AMD was sent to fix the situation."

The Adjustment and Manipulation Department — AMD — was responsible for handling such cases. All the King's Men had protocols in place to handle situations like this, where efficiency, delicacy, and attention to detail were required. Pictures were faked, false stories were concocted, and any and all bases were covered. No doubt AMD had already supplied the CPD with a file detailing Savill's "abduction." Or maybe they had told the parents Savill had been killed in some tragic accident. Micah had no idea how the AMD did its job. He just knew they did it and covered the vampire race's collective ass.

"What about Savill? Has he been told?"

Dr. Snow shook her head. "He's still in an induced coma, one I'm inclined to prolong under these new circumstances."

"I agree. Hearing he's a vampire could blow a fuse bigger than the incision down his abdomen." He dragged his palm down his face then stood akimbo, head bowed. "Jesus, this is a mess."

The doc let out a heavy sigh. "You don't know the half of it."

He raised his head. "Why? What haven't you told me?"

She cursed and looked away, her expression grim. "We've taken some blood."

"And . . .?"

"There are some anomalies."

"What kind of anomalies?" A sinking feeling dipped into his gut.

Worry filled her eyes. "Micah, he's not half-human."

"But I thought . . ." Micah frowned past her shoulder to the prone form of the young male in the room behind her. "Isn't he a mixed-blood?"

"Yes, but he's not a vampire-human mix."

Something in Dr. Snow's tone made dread shimmy down his spine. "Then what is he?"

"Micah, Savill is half lycan."

Well, how about that? A vampire and a lycan had gotten together and made a love child. There went the neighborhood. This had to be the third time today hell had frozen over.

"Are you sure?"

She gave a single nod. "I personally ran the results myself. Three times. I'm positive."

"Fuck me." Micah rubbed his palms up and down his face.

No one in the vampire community would want to take in a young that was half lycan. It was too risky.

This was a double dose of shit news. Savill needed someone to help him acclimate to his new world, but no one would lift a finger to help a young, pre-trans lycan, even one that was only a half-blood.

It wasn't that vampires and lycans didn't get along. The two races got along fine, or as fine as they could. They weren't besties by a long shot, but for the most part, they coexisted peacefully with one another, if not a bit tensely at times, given their history. The problem was that when it came to lycans, no vampire wanted to risk getting in the way of a mouthful of juvenile lycan fangs, and who knew whether Savill would lean toward vampire or lycan once he reached maturity? It was a toss-up. There wasn't a lot of precedent to provide an informed hypothesis about how a vampire-lycan mix would mature, and lycan genes were the only ones on earth strong enough to compete with those of a vampire.

He could contact Memnon and Rameses for help. They were the leaders of the lycans. But they would probably disown Savill rather than take him in or offer assistance. After all, in their eyes, Savill was a genetically inferior orphan. Hell, they might even kill him. Lycans were a lot stricter on mixing bloodlines than vampires, so it was a wonder Savill had been conceived at all. Some lycan had risked an awful lot—including his place in the lycan hierarchy—to mate with a vampire. Micah wasn't sure if that was incredibly courageous or insanely stupid.

Either way, he was in a tight spot. No way would he hand Savill over to Memnon and Rameses if there was even a chance they would kill him, but who could he convince in the vampire community to take Savill in? And how would he convince them when there was no way to know which genes would dominate Savill's blood once he matured?

He needed to do some research to see if something like this had ever happened in the past and how it had turned out.

"Goddamn it." He glanced back inside Savill's room. "This is shit ugly news."

Dr. Snow followed his gaze. "Tell me about it. He's going to need constant monitoring once he comes out of this."

If he came out of it, because they still didn't know if Savill would survive the damage Bishop had done to him.

"Any ideas how to handle that? Given what we now know about his lineage?" Because no way could they release Savill into someone's care without providing full disclosure.

The doc shook her head. "Not yet, but he's going to need someone to take him in and teach him about his new life. We can't just toss him back out on the street. He'll never survive. He's going to need a lot of care and counseling, Micah, and I can tell by your reaction that you already know how hard that's going to be to find under these circumstances."

"Damn near impossible." Micah shook his head, feeling about as helpless as a peanut.

The electronic ringtone of his mobile phone snagged his attention. Damn, couldn't he get just five minutes to think?

He pulled the phone from his pocket. Sev.

"I've got to take this," he said to the doctor. "But I'll do some checking and get back to you about Savill."

She nodded and turned her attention back to Kieran's room as Micah started out of the trauma ward.

"Sev, hey. You at the Millennium garage?"

"Yeah. Found your guy's motorcycle, too."

"How do you know it's his?" Micah pushed through the double doors leading back into the outer hall.

"Because he left you a note."

Micah came to an abrupt stop. "He what?"

"It's actually a poem, but it's definitely for you."

Something in Sev's wary tone rankled Micah's nerves. This was going to leave a bad taste in his mouth, wasn't it?

"What's it say?"

Sev awkwardly cleared his throat. "It says" — Sev let out a heavy exhale — "why don't I just send you a picture?"

"Do that."

He disconnected, and a moment later, his phone vibrated with a text. He opened the attachment. The poem had been handwritten in neat, block print.

> *Oh, mighty Micah*
> *You aren't as tough*
> *As I've been led to believe.*
> *You're just a pussy*
> *A great big wussy.*
> *You make me want to heave.*
> *You think you're good*
> *You think you're great*
> *But I do so make this oath.*
> *I stole the key*
> *It's now with me*
> *And good luck finding both.*

Rage boiled inside Micah's blood as he hit Sev's speed dial. That little prick.

"Our guy's a real Shakespeare, isn't he?" Sev said.

"Shakespeare's dead, just like he's going to be when I find him. Get over to the Heritage hotel. I'll call you back in five." Micah disconnected, already storming toward the surveillance room, where Io was hopefully making headway on his background checks. Micah refused to rest until this cocky little fucker went down, and everybody had better be with him on that or they'd get his booted foot up their asses, too.

"Tell me you've found something," Micah said as he burst through the door.

Io had just stuffed half a Snickers bar in his mouth and turned toward the door, eyes wide. He glanced at his screen then gave Micah a helpless I-just-got-started-so-how-could-I-have-found-something look as he started chewing.

Micah leaned over Io's shoulder, scanning the screens, unable to make sense of anything Io was working on.

Io chewed as fast as he could then swallowed. "Jesus, Micah, I've only been at it for thirty minutes. Do you know how many people live in the Heritage?"

"No." He hit Severin's speed dial and cranked his phone to his ear.

Io's fingers began flying over his keyboard. "Well, it's a lot. There's a lot of people to check."

Sev picked up. "Micah, hey, I'm at the Heritage."

"Find anything?"

"Define anything."

Micah could already tell he wasn't going to like what Sev had to tell him. "What did you find?"

"You're not gonna like it."

Hopefully it wasn't another in-your-face poem, or Io's console might be in danger of suffering a natural disaster at the hands of Hurricane Micah.

"Tell me."

Sev let out a heavy breath. "You know how Chicago has an underground pedway?"

The pedway consisted of five miles of underground tunnels pedestrians could use to travel around the heart of Chicago without exposing themselves to the elements.

The bad feeling in Micah's gut intensified. "Yeah? What about it?"

"The Heritage has access to it."

"Motherfucker! I knew you were going to say that." Micah snapped his fingers in the direction of Io's keyboard. "Bring up a map of the pedway."

Io made a few keystrokes, and the map popped up on his center screen.

Just as Micah thought. The Heritage was smack in the middle, with branches of underground walkways extending in all directions. "Damn it." He slammed his palm on the desk. Skeletor could be anywhere.

"Your guy could have gone anywhere," Sev said, as if reading Micah's mind.

Io's shoulders drooped as he sat back in his chair. "Let me guess, our guy doesn't live at the Heritage. He only used it as part of his escape route."

"That's what it looks like," Micah said.

"So the trail's gone cold?" Io shoved the other half of his Snickers bar in his mouth. The room smelled like chocolate and peanuts. Just how many of those things had Io eaten since killing his Tootsie Pop?

"Yeah," Micah said. "Stone cold unless Sev can pick up any clues." To Sev he said, "See if you can find anything. This guy likes to play with us. Maybe he left something for us to find."

Or maybe he made a mistake. That would be even better. Given Severin's history as special forces in the human military, if Skeletor had left anything behind, Sev would find it.

"I'll see what I can dig up." Sev disconnected.

Micah raked his fingers through his hair and began pacing. *Think, Micah, think.* Who could he have pissed off who would want to seek retribution against him? Well, shit, that was a pretty long list. But who of that list had this kind of verve? This kind of intelligence and cunning? These resources?

He couldn't think of a single suspect.

"What the . . .?" Io said behind him.

Micah turned around. "What is it?" But he could already see what had Io frowning and holding his fingers several inches off his keyboard as if it had grown snake scales.

The monitors flashed then blacked out. Small squares blinked randomly over the screen.

Then a message began typing out in large letters.

> *You're a day late and a dollar short*
> *But oh so fun to watch*
> *As you chase, toil, and try to keep up*
> *While I knock you down a notch.*
> *The key is mine, with me it stays*
> *No more of your concern*
> *Because I'm better, a real go-getter*
> *So fuck you, Micah. Crash and BURN.*

This prick wanted a war? Well, he just got one.

CHAPTER 14

CORDRAY RUBBED HER SANDPAPERY EYES as she leaned back in her desk chair. In the three hours since breakfast, she'd accomplished a lot.

First, she'd searched the Dark Net for references to Grudge Match. That seemed like the easiest task to tackle first, and her search paid off. Not only had she found information about where the underground fight club met, but how to join. She'd even filled out the interest form. Supposedly, she would receive a text within twenty-four hours with more information.

Next, she had logged into Bain's personal archives and searched for anything related to ankhs. And what do you know? She struck gold. Turned out that ankhs had been used by the lycans in the time of the pre-dynastic Egyptian pharaohs to open the gateways between dimensions. It had been how they'd traveled between their world and Earth, but sometime soon after the pyramids were built, the gateways had allegedly been sealed. At least as sealed as they could be, with the lycans securing the ankhs and hiding them away.

Vampires had discovered these gateways, too, coming from their planet in some kind of teleportational accident a few decades after the first lycans arrived. Call it a gateway glitch, but when the lycans opened one of the portals during a ceremonial rite, a whole bunch of vampires poured through. Apparently, their planet had been in the right place at the right time and they'd been sucked into the worm hole that brought them here.

But at least now she knew why vampires couldn't tolerate the earth's sun. According to the translated history, they'd come from an earthlike planet whose sun was a dim but powerful white dwarf. It churned out a lot of warmth, but not a lot of light, so when they came through the portal, the earth's brighter sun caused an illness they called sun sickness, which led to a large number of deaths in the early vampires, forcing them to become night dwellers. The only vampires capable of surviving the sun were those born from a union between a vampire and a human . . . or with a lycan. But lycans hadn't been keen on seeing their kind mix with vampires, so there weren't a lot of half vampires-half lycans walking around, if any.

Scouring the background material had made for an interesting history lesson, but the part about the ankhs was what had interested her most. Ankhs were keys. Each opened a different portal or set of portals to a different dimension or to a different location in one dimension. From the crude map she'd pulled up, if she read it right, it looked like some dimensions had multiple doorways, all marked by pyramids or obelisks. The bigger the structure, the bigger the gate, and the more supernatural entities could enter or exit through it.

That must have been quite a site on the Giza Plateau—seeing hundreds, if not thousands, of beings appear out of nowhere or vanish without a trace—given that there were three massive pyramids on site. And back in pre-dynastic times, who knew what other structures had been there to enhance the effect?

It was all very confusing and hard to understand, but one thing was clear. Each ankh had a protector to keep it from falling into the wrong hands, with one master ankh that belonged to Memnon, the alpha of the lycan race, which opened all gates. Obtain the master, and you could unleash hell on Earth, but from what Cordray had read about Memnon, good luck prying the master ankh from his powerful lycan fist. Ole Memnon had a nasty reputation and an even nastier disposition, at least according to the picture the archives painted of him.

So, the question was, why did Micah have an ankh? Furthermore, how did he have a key that opened a doorway to another dimension and not even know its purpose?

No sense dwelling on that question, though, or she'd just give herself a migraine.

With Grudge Match and ankh research off her list, she turned her attention to learning more about Skeletor. It was a good bet he was aware of the ankh's purpose, or he wouldn't have stolen it. Maybe he was linked to the lycans and knew about the ankh that way, but that would mean the lycans had given Micah's father the ankh or had at least known about it. Cordray wasn't sure of either option's plausibility. Maybe Skeletor had hacked into Bain's archives to learn of the ankhs' importance, but that didn't explain how he'd known Micah possessed one or where to find it. Skeletor had known right where to look.

There were dozens of possible answers to every question Cordray came up with.

She checked the time. Surely, Micah would have come up with something by now. She logged in to the AKM mainframe and piggybacked into the data from Tristan's team. She wasn't exactly hacking, but then again, she was. Her actions fell into a grey area.

Almost immediately, videos from the night Skeletor broke into Micah's apartment popped up, along with a map of Chicago's pedway. She quickly scanned the videos and realized why the pedway was of interest when she saw Skeletor enter the Heritage building.

Smart little fucker. He'd known he was being watched, so he'd ducked into one of the buildings with direct access to the pedway so he could slip away unseen.

Clever.

She closed her eyes and stretched, yawning. God, she was tired. Spending over eight hours in Trace's proximity had taken it out of her. Who would have thought experiencing physical sensation could be so exhausting.

She was about to head upstairs and go to bed when her screen flashed then went dark. What the hell? An array of tiny squares danced around the screen.

All semblance of exhaustion evaporated as letters began appearing at the top of the screen.

Well, hello, little mouse. Following the crumbs, are you?

The green cursor dropped to the next line then blinked off and on, off and on, as if waiting for her to respond.

Fine, she'd play along.

Who are you? she typed.

Tsk-tsk. It's not going to be that easy, Cordray Buveau.

Her blood ran cold. He knew her. How did he know her?

I'll ask again, who the fuck are you?

She waited several seconds before he began typing again. *I think you refer to me as Skeletor. I like that. Let's stick with that.*

Bastard! How . . .?

Letters began stringing into place on her screen before she could reply.

And yes, I got quite the Skeletor boner watching you three stooges bumble around as if you'd found something of consequence in that little parking lot. It was very entertaining.

She'd known he was watching.

She could almost hear his laughter. And wherever he was, he *was* laughing. At her. At them. He was playing a sick, twisted game, and he was getting off on it.

Taking a deep breath, she decided to take a different tack.

What's your interest in Micah Black?

Seconds ticked by. A minute. Two.

Just when she thought he wasn't going to answer, the letters began falling into place again.

We all have our secrets, Miss Buveau. Including you, it would seem.

She bobbed backward. What secret was he referring to?

I'm an open book, she typed. *Maybe you should be, too.*

Are you now? I wonder . . . how many people know you and King Bain are brother and sister?

Her heart swan-dived into her intestines. Oh, God. He knew. How did Skeletor know about her and Bain? She was going to throw up. Who the hell was this guy?

Her fingers shook as she slowly typed, *We're not brother and sister.*

Oh, that's right. He's only your half-brother, isn't he? Tell me, how does it feel to be excluded from the royal family? To be forced to keep your secret even though it means you will never share the same wealth and status as your dear brother? To be shunned by those who worship your own flesh and blood as if he were a god while ignoring your existence as if you're just another face in the crowd? A nameless faceless nobody?

Cordray frowned. Okay, what was up with all that? She didn't like that Mr. Sticky Fingers knew who she was, but she didn't resent Bain or her relegation into virtual anonymity. Skeletor's last message came off a lot more aggressive than the others, which had been more playful. It was as if he was taking his anger out on her. But anger over what?

I don't know how you know about Bain and me, but gee, Skeletor, you seem to be taking the news a lot more personally than I am. Is this some kind of identity crisis you're having, or is something else at work here you aren't telling me?

She waited for a reply.

And waited.

Five minutes passed.

Skeletor? Did I lose you?

Nothing.

Radio silence.

A few seconds later, her screen flashed and recovered, taking her back to the map of the pedway she'd pulled from Io's search data.

Skeletor was gone.

Interesting.

Maybe she'd hit a nerve when she asked if he was having an

identity crisis. Or maybe . . . hmmm . . . maybe Skeletor had just made his first mistake. Maybe he hadn't intended to say what he'd said. Not that it made any sense to her, but if he slipped up once, he could do it again.

The least she could do was begin a backtrace to see if he'd left a trail by hacking her. She doubted it would turn up anything, but it was worth a shot.

She started the tracking program then turned off the lamp, pushed her chair under the desk, and went to the kitchen for a snack before heading off to bed.

Grabbing a banana, she turned to leave but stopped as she glanced out the window and saw Trace working on the fence around the horse ring, which was really more like a horse rectangle. In the summer, the older kids enjoyed setting up jumps in there and running the course with the horses, but the harsh winter had snapped a few of the fence rails. Trace was replacing them.

A full-blood never would have been able to work in the sun, but Trace was like her. Half human, half vampire. And like the mixed-blood vampires from Egyptian times, the human blood that ran through his veins protected him from the harmful effects of sunlight. *Sun sickness.*

He stopped hammering the rail he was working on and slipped off his sunglasses. He wiped his brow as he squinted skyward. Then he slid his sunglasses back on and knelt beside Null, who had his orange, blue, and neon-green Little Tikes hammer in his hand. He was tapping it against the wood, imitating Trace.

She couldn't hear what Trace said, but Null beamed and nodded before resuming his pint-sized hammering. Trace smiled and ruffled his hair.

"You like him, don't you?"

Cordray jumped and almost dropped her banana as she spun to find Mya entering the kitchen.

The dark-haired female laughed as she opened the fridge and grabbed a can of Pepsi Vanilla. "Well, if there'd been any doubt before, there's none now. You're hot for the help."

"How can you drink that stuff?" She gestured toward the can of soda. "It tastes like cologne."

"It does not." Mya popped the tab and pressed it back. "And quit changing the subject. You like him. I can tell."

"You're imagining things."

"Am I?" Mya took a sip of her soda as she parked her hip against the side of the counter. "I saw how you kept looking at him during breakfast."

Cordray shut her eyes and sighed. The last thing she needed was for Mya and Brenna to begin hassling her about Trace. "Oh? And how was I looking at him?"

Mya set her drink down and moved to the cupboard, where she started pulling out items to make lunch. "Like your biological clock was ticking."

Cordray began peeling her banana. "Vampires don't have biological clocks."

"Maybe not, but that's how you were looking at him." Mya winked and shot her a cockeyed grin over her shoulder. "Like you were ready to have his hot little mixed-blood babies." She shut the cabinet and set two large cartons of chicken broth on the counter. "Don't get me wrong. You could do a lot worse. And he's terrific with Null. I've never seen that kid open up so much. He already adores Trace, and he only just met him."

True. Null usually kept to himself, but with Trace, he'd been a chatterbug. Throughout breakfast, he had grilled Trace with questions, regaled him with stories about life on the ranch, how he'd found a really cool rock behind the barn a few weeks ago, who his favorite superhero was — Thor, because how cool was it that he could create a tornado with his hammer? — and how he had dreamed about goblins kidnapping him a couple of nights ago.

Trace had told Null he would never let Goblins take him and that maybe he didn't have Thor's hammer, but he could still create a tornado to keep any nasty people away. Null had laughed at that, probably because he hadn't thought Trace was telling the truth. If only Null knew. Trace really could create a tornado, as well as about a dozen other natural disasters, all with just a thought and his hand.

A part of her anatomy melted at the idea of all that power being unleashed on her body.

"Where did you find him?" Mya said, sliding up beside her as she glanced out the window at the male who was currently rocking Cordray's world in ways it hadn't been rocked in a long, long time.

"Huh?"

Mya snorted in amusement. "I asked where you found him. How did you get that stud to volunteer to work here?"

Cordray discarded the banana peel and tore off a piece. "He broke one of the king's laws."

Mya's eyebrows shot up as if she were impressed. "Ooo, a criminal.

Nice, C." She smirked as she turned for another cabinet and grabbed a large soup pan. "What a great influence on the children."

"He's an AKM enforcer. He just bent the rules a little too far and overstepped Bain's law, that's all." Two weeks ago, she had testified against him. Now she was defending him. She didn't need anyone pointing out the significance of such an abrupt about-face. Trace's effect on her was making her change her mind about a lot of things. She stuffed another piece of banana in her mouth as she glanced back out the window. "I wouldn't have brought him here if I thought he was dangerous or could hurt the kids."

"So, why did you bring him here?" Mya waggled her eyebrows as Cordray turned away from the window. "Trying to keep him close?"

"I thought you were the jaded one." Cordray ate another bite of banana and eyed Mya suspiciously.

"I am, but even I have eyes, C. I mean, look at him." She gestured toward Trace. "What female wouldn't want to spend a night with *that* inside her?"

Rolling her shoulders, Cordray ignored the green-eyed shockwave rippling down her spine as she forced herself not to stare at Trace's sculpted physique and the way his jeans tightened over his ass as he bent to pick up another rail.

"I guess if you're into that sort of thing," she said. "Which I'm not, of course. And I think you know why."

Mya froze, and the humor drained from her expression. "Oh God, C. I'm sorry. I didn't mean . . . I totally spaced it." Mya hung her head. "I know you can't feel—"

"Forget it." She swallowed the last bite of banana. "Look, I'm exhausted. I'm going to head upstairs, take a shower, and go to bed. I've got things to do in the city tonight." She dusted her hands together. "Save me some of whatever you're making for lunch, though, okay? I'll eat before I leave."

"Yeah, sure. Of course."

Cordray left the kitchen, sensing Mya's awkward discomfort and guilt, and headed upstairs to her bedroom, stripped, took a shower, then changed into a loose, dark-grey tank top with a bedazzled image of a black widow spider on the front. Then she tugged on a pair of black, wide-legged yoga pants that felt like melted butter on her legs.

She was about to shut the blinds and turn in, but the moment her gaze landed on Trace in the backyard, she stopped, hand on the drawstring.

Sunlight rained down from blue skies, and the thermometer

outside her window read seventy-four degrees. For the first week of May in Chicago, that was warm.

Trace had taken off his shirt. Sweat glistened on his skin. She sure hoped someone had given him sunscreen. He might be a daywalker, but that didn't mean he wouldn't get a sunburn. Just that he'd heal from it faster than a human would.

Aiden sat nearby in the grass, wearing a lightweight, pink jacket, playing with her dolls and braiding their hair, but Null remained at Trace's side, stuck to him like Velcro, helping him position the rail and hold it in place while Trace hammered in a nail.

The muscles in Trace's back bunched and flexed, rippling with each impact of the hammer. The supple vibrations reminded her of the way the muscles in a thoroughbred undulated as it ran. Pure, unbridled power.

Sexy as hell on a male.

Trace stopped, plucked the ever-present matchstick from between his lips, and bent to inspect something Null held up in his hand. Probably another rock. Null loved his rocks and had a whole box of them in the room down the hall where he and Aiden often took afternoon naps while the older kids were in class.

Trace smiled and smudged dirt on Null's button nose, making the little boy squeal and swipe at Trace's hand. Trace laughed as he stood, slipped the matchstick back into his mouth, and returned to work. Little Null joined him and *tap-tap-tapped* his plastic hammer alongside Trace's sturdier one, gazing up at Trace with awe and pride.

They were like a living family portrait. Love, warmth, and a sense of belonging blossomed around them. If only she could be a part of the picture, but that kind of happiness wasn't in her cards.

After staring for at least ten minutes, Cordray turned and came face to face with Mya, who stood a few feet away, holding a basket of folded towels. The air smelled of corn chowder.

"You don't like him, huh?" Mya smiled compassionately then bobbed her head toward the door. "Your door was open."

"How long have you been standing there?" Cordray looked away.

"Long enough."

"For what?" She glanced back to see Mya purse her lips as she set the laundry basket on a chair.

"Long enough to see that look on your face again. You were undressing him with your eyes."

Cordray chuffed. "Please. I was so not looking at him that way." She let the blinds drop then left Mya at the window so she could pull back the covers on the bed.

Mya faced her and crossed her arms. "Why don't you just fess up and admit you're attracted to him. Then maybe we can get past all the bullshit."

"What does it matter? It's not like anything's going to happen between us, anyway."

"And why's that?"

"It just won't work, that's why."

"Because of Gideon?"

Cordray's head snapped up, her gaze locking on Mya's.

"That's it, isn't it? You're pushing him away because of what Gideon did to you."

"Leave him out of this."

"C, you're being an ass. Did you ever stop to think that Gideon never mated you because you were supposed to mate someone else? Hmm?"

Truthfully, she hadn't. Gideon had been *it* for her. Her one and only chance at happiness. And he had spurned her. He had taken another. "Drop it, Mya." She picked up her pillow and fluffed it like she was punching a dreck in the nose.

"You're such a chickenshit."

Cordray spun on her. "You don't know what I've been through. You don't know what I go through now. I've given up so much to make sure these kids — of which you *were* one, if you recall — have a better life than I ever had. To make sure they're taken care of, loved, wanted, and — "

"And you've left yourself behind in the process!" Mya got in her face. "You give all these kids every ounce of love in your heart. You show them every time you're here how wanted they are. But when it comes to you, C, you leave nothing in the bank. You don't stop to give yourself any love. You don't allow yourself to want for anyone, because you're afraid that nobody will want you back."

Cordray tried to push Mya out of the way so she could shut herself into her bathroom. Screw this. She didn't need to hear this shit.

Mya blocked Cordray's retreat.

"No, C. You're going to hear me out for once. You pulled me from the brink of hell, and you instilled in me a sense of self-worth I'll forever be grateful for, and now it's my turn to return the favor." She squared Cordray up in her sights. "Gideon wasn't the one for you."

Cordray closed her eyes and cringed. "You don't know — "

Mya shook her. "He wasn't! It's been long enough. You need to let him go and let someone else in. Let *him* in." She pointed toward the window. "Maybe he's the reason why you and Gideon never mated. Maybe *he's* your mate. And even if he's not, what harm could it do to let him in? Huh? To let someone love you again. To let him love you."

"He doesn't want me!" Cordray flung Mya's hands off. "Don't you get it? He hates me."

Mya took a step back and let Cordray pass. "How do you know?"

"I just do." She slipped into the bathroom and grabbed her toothbrush. She'd already brushed her teeth once, but with nothing else to keep her hands busy, brushing them again was all she could do.

"Maybe you're wrong." Mya shrugged.

"And maybe I'm right."

"Have you asked him?"

Cordray flipped on the faucet and stuffed the brush in her mouth.

Mya leaned through the doorway. "Have you?"

Jesus, Mya couldn't take a hint.

She spit out the mint-flavored paste and spun around. "No! Now drop it!" She quickly rinsed and slapped off the faucet.

"No." Mya followed her back into the bedroom. "Not until you tell me why."

"This is my life, Mya. Why do you care so much?"

Mya looked at her as if she hadn't a clue about anything, frowning and tilting her head. "How can you even ask me that? You're like a mother to me, C. A mother, a sister, a best friend. Believe me, I care."

Cordray slumped onto the edge of the bed, eyes closed, the wind draining from her sails. Her still-damp hair hung over her face.

The bed dipped as Mya gingerly sat down beside her.

For several long moments, neither said anything. Then Mya took Cordray's hand in both of hers. The only way Cordray knew she had was that she felt her arm being lifted away from her leg. She couldn't feel Mya's hand on hers, or whether her hand was warm or cold. Just a shifting of weight.

She opened her eyes and stared at Mya's long, elegant fingers wrapped around hers. If only she could feel.

But then, she could, couldn't she? With Trace.

"I can feel him," she said quietly.

"Who?"

She sighed and lifted her gaze to Mya's. "Trace. When he touches me, I feel it."

Mya pulled in a gentle gasp. "That's good, isn't it?"

She frowned. "How is that good?"

Confusion tore at Mya's expression. "Because . . . you can feel him." She spoke slowly, as if she thought it should be obvious that this was good news, not a death sentence. "You can't feel anybody, so yeah, this sounds like a good thing to me."

"Didn't you hear me? Don't you get it? He doesn't want me. He hates me. If I give in to this, he's just going to hurt me." She shook her head, eyes closed. "I barely survived Gideon. If I allow Trace in, it will kill me when he rejects me. And he *will* reject me. It's inevitable."

"You don't know that."

"Yes, I do. I'm the reason he got arrested. I'm the one who got him thrown into Bain's dungeon. Which means he's not my number one fan, and I'm not his."

"But if he's as attracted to you as you seem to be to him, all that shit's water under the bridge."

The day Trace let what she'd done to him become water under the bridge would be the day no water remained anywhere on the planet.

"I doubt that's the case."

Mya let go of her hand. "Maybe you're just too chicken to find out."

To hell with that. "I'm anything but a chicken, Mya. You know that."

Mya shrugged. "If the shoe fits." She pushed off the bed, grabbed the laundry basket, and headed toward the hallway.

"Just drop it, Mya."

"Fine." Mya stopped in the doorway and looked over her shoulder. "But you like him. You can't deny that." Mya turned on her heel, stepped into the hall, and shut the door behind her.

Cordray glared at the door for at least a minute.

Mya was a dear friend, but that didn't mean she knew everything, or that she had the right to get in Cordray's face about things that didn't concern her.

Still, she was right. She did like Trace.

And didn't admitting that sit like angry lizards on her gut?

Cordray reluctantly stood and walked toward the window, where she slipped her fingers between two faux wooden slats and split them so she could peek outside. Trace picked Null up and placed him in the wheelbarrow. Aiden was already in it. Then Trace got behind the handles, lifted them, and pushed them farther down the fence to where another rail needed to be replaced.

He was good with Null and Aiden. Better than she thought he would be.

But he was awakening parts of her she thought had died a long time ago.

She felt as if she had never moved on. That she was still the young, innocent, and terribly naïve pre-transitional girl she'd been with Gideon. For all her bravado—for all her toughness and blustery rough talk—she was just another insecure kid. One who'd been required to divide her father's time with another family, who had been abandoned by love, and had lost every aspect of life that made it worth living.

Cordray smiled as Trace hoisted Null out of the wheelbarrow and spun him around. She heard Null's peals of laughter as he spread his arms and legs in midair. Aiden bounded toward them, her arms outstretched. Trace set Null down before picking up Aiden and spinning her, too.

Yes, Trace was fucking up everything. He was opening her heart again. He was making her smile, giving her a false sense of hope that there was more to life than this self-imposed loneliness she had surrounded herself with. He was allowing her to think she could have it all.

But that was a pipe dream. What she'd had with Gideon hadn't been real. If it had been, he wouldn't have mated someone else. And now, here came Trace, like a knight in shining armor, to drag her from the tower prison as if she were Rapunzel or Cinderella or whatever sissy-faced fairy-tale maiden had allowed herself to be treated like shit and captured by evil forces.

Cordray wasn't a damsel in distress. And Trace wasn't Prince Valiant. And life wasn't a fairy tale. In real life, the prince saved the princess and then left her after falling in love with someone else. That's how it was, and that was why she couldn't let Trace rescue her now.

But he was damn good with the children.

Too damn good.

Spinning, laughing, and tossing their little bodies in the air and catching them as they screeched for "More!" and "Higher!"

He would make a wonderful father.

A heartwarming mate.

She let the blinds flap shut then climbed into bed, pulling the blankets halfway up her body as she settled her head on her pillow.

She did like Trace. She liked him a lot.

And she wanted to feel the pleasure he could give her.

Maybe she could feel it now.

Slipping her hand under the covers and inside the waist of her pants, she closed her eyes and tried to imagine Trace touching her.

Tried to feel . . . something. Anything.

But her long-dormant sex drive refused to budge. Without Trace doing the honors, she was a frigid, dried-up desert. No physical sensation whatsoever. Just . . . nothing. Not even numbness. Her libido was like a massive void. No spark.

She stopped trying.

Just let her fingers go lax against her mound.

Then she broke down in pathetic sobs.

She was that heartbroken, unfeeling, lonely girl she'd been that night in the woods.

The night Gideon shattered her heart and stole her sense of touch forever.

CHAPTER 15

TRACE TOSSED THE LAST BROKEN RAIL into the wheelbarrow and stuffed the hammer through the loop in the tool belt he'd found in the barn. Null and Aiden were busying themselves poking sticks in a shallow mound of muddy dirt.

His stomach rumbled, and he pulled out his phone to check the time. It was almost eleven thirty. What time did they eat lunch around here?

"Twace! Twace! Look what I found!" Null darted toward him, holding a flat, brownish rock in his tiny hand.

"What's that, little man?" He knelt and held his hand out, palm up.

Null placed his small treasure in his palm and beamed as if he'd found a lump of gold. "It's an awwowhead."

"So it is." Trace rolled the arrowhead between his fingers, admiring it, reminded of his time with the Choctaw. "Do you know what kind of stone the Indians used to make arrowheads like this?" He held it out so Null could take it back.

"No." The little boy squinted up at him.

Trace tapped the tip of his index finger on the arrowhead. "They used flint, or even a type of rock called obsidian, or another called chert, which contains fossils. Do you know what fossils are?"

"Like dinosaur bones?" Aiden said, joining them.

"Something like that, but the kinds of fossils in chert are smaller. Like seashells and bird bones."

Null eyed his arrowhead as if searching for evidence of fossils. "Is this chewt?" He lifted his gaze questioningly to Trace's again. It was adorable how his tiny mouth couldn't handle the letter R, but someday he would grow out of that.

"I don't think so. I think this is flint."

Null examined the arrowhead again then looked up, beaming. "Wanna see my wock cowwection?" It seemed R wasn't the only letter he had trouble with.

Before Trace could answer, Null grabbed his thumb and tugged him toward the main house as Aiden brought up the rear, never letting her brother get too far away from her.

The smell of corn chowder and garlic bread assaulted his nose as he followed Null inside. Mya was in the kitchen tending to the stove.

She turned, and her gaze swiftly inspected them as if she were in the habit of making sure no one tracked dirt inside. "What's going on? Is everything okay?"

Null hardly slowed as he galloped through the kitchen. "Twace wants to see my wock cowwection."

He shrugged helplessly as Aiden took his free hand and pulled him along.

Who could resist these two?

Mya grinned at him, shaking her head. "You've gone and done it now."

"Done what?"

"Made two new best friends." Her eyes sparkled as she suppressed a smile.

"Yeah, looks that way." He nodded toward the soup pot. "Smells good." He'd have to see if he could get the recipe.

Null stopped and faced him, tugging harder on his hand. "Come on, Twace!"

Mya held her finger over her mouth. "Sssshhh. You need to be quiet. Cordray's sleeping."

The beast actually slept?

Null hung his head. "Sowwy."

Mya went back to stirring the soup. "Remember, quiet feet on the stairs. And only whispers." She stepped back and checked inside the oven. "And don't be too long. Lunch will be ready in a few minutes. So get washed up and hurry back."

Lunch. Thank God. Trace's stomach had been rumbling for the past hour.

Null yanked his hand again, pulled him through the dining room, the living room, and upstairs to a room outfitted with two small beds.

"Is this your room?" he said, feeling like Gandalf in Bilbo Baggins' hobbit hole. Everything was so tiny.

Aiden opened a toy box under the window and pulled out a stuffed Pooh Bear as Null dropped to his knees and dragged a small plastic storage bin from under his bed.

"No. My woom is in the school." Null gestured toward the backyard without looking up. "But Aidy and I take naps and play in hewe sometimes." He popped the blue lid off the box and dropped it on the wooden floor.

"Sshh." Trace placed his hand on the lid, quieting it. "Remember, Coco's sleeping."

Null's wide eyes peered toward the door. "Sowwy." Then his little hands dove into the box of rocks.

What an impressive collection. He had all kinds and sizes.

"This is my favowite." Null held up what appeared to be an unremarkable, jagged rock, but when he turned it over, sparkles of fool's gold covered the other side.

Trace reached inside the box and pulled out a small, shiny piece of what looked like rose quartz. "Where did you find this one?"

"In the gawden."

"You know," Trace said, sifting through the pile. "When I was a kid, I collected rocks, too."

"You did?"

"Yep. I didn't have as many as you do, though. I kept them in a leather pouch my father made for me."

He smiled at the memory. His parents hadn't been overtly compassionate, but they'd loved him. He knew that now, and remembering the small things his father did for him made him see things in a different light than he had at eight or ten or even twelve years old.

He should visit him, but he just wasn't ready, especially now that he knew Brak was here. In time, though. He would visit them both when he felt ready.

Facing them wouldn't be easy. He'd fucked things up. He was responsible for Mother's death. He'd be lucky if his father hadn't disowned him.

His eyes lit on a rock in the corner of Null's box, half buried by the rest of his collection. He frowned. The rock looked familiar.

Slowly reaching in, he rolled the other rocks away and pulled out the one that looked similar to the one from his own childhood collection. His favorite. The one that Mason had tossed into the pond two centuries ago. The white quartz with the black flecks.

It wasn't the same rock, but it easily could have come from the same place. That's how similar Null's was to his own.

"Where did you find this?"

Null lifted onto his knees and glanced into his palm. "Um, I think I found that one in the woods by the stweam."

Aiden hopped to his side and stared at the rock. She nodded. "Uh-huh. It was by the stream. I remember."

"Yeah." Null nodded with his sister. "On the bank." He rubbed his fingers back and forth over the rock's surface.

"Were there more like this one?" Trace brushed his thumb over a concentration of tiny black specks.

Maybe he would never get his own rock back, but if he could at least replace it with one that was similar . . .

"Want me to take you thewe? We can look." Null's big blue eyes shone as he grinned up at him.

He closed his fist around the rock and nodded. "I'd like that, but we'll probably need Coco's permission first, huh? She runs a pretty tight ship."

Aiden tilted her head and frowned. "What's a tight ship?"

He had to remember he was talking to two-year-olds who weren't yet familiar with such phrases. "Running a tight ship just means she likes order. That she likes everyone to be where they're supposed to be and doing what they're supposed to be doing. And if you're going to do something else, you need to let her know."

The frown lifted from Aiden's face, and she nodded. "Uh-huh. Coco likes a tight ship."

He chuckled. "I thought so." He placed the rock back in Null's box and bobbed his head toward the door. "So, are you two as hungry as I am?" He rubbed his belly.

Both nodded.

"Okay, then let's go get cleaned up for lunch. I'm starved."

Null and Aiden hopped up and darted for the door.

"You can sit next to me," Null said. "I'll save you a chaiow."

"Sounds like a plan, little man." He high-fived Null, and then the two kids skittered into the hall. A moment later, he heard their clumsy footsteps tumble down the stairs.

He might as well get cleaned up himself. Then after lunch, he'd get some sleep. He'd been up all night and was starting to feel it, especially after the time in King Bain's dungeon had taken so much out of him.

His room had a private bathroom, so he hopped in the shower, quickly lathered up and rinsed, driven by his growling stomach to hurry the hell up and get back downstairs. A few minutes later, he changed into a fresh pair of jeans and a clean T-shirt then left his room and started down the hall toward the stairs.

As he passed Cordray's closed bedroom door, he slowed and inhaled. Her citrusy, midnight scent wafted into the hall.

God, if only he could bottle that shit, he could rub it all over his skin and get high on it anytime he needed a pick-me-up. Closing his eyes, he took several deep breaths. What was it about Cordray's scent that was so intoxicating? It wasn't like she smelled any different than other females, and yet . . . she did. Hundreds of women carried the sweet but citrus scent of oranges, but with Cordray, it was darker, lustier, more exciting.

He felt himself drift toward her door, and when he opened his eyes again, his hand was on the doorknob . . . and he was turning it. A force deep within him compelled him onward. He needed to get closer to her scent. To wrap it around him. To bathe in it. To revel in the way it washed through his senses and absorbed into skin.

As the latch released, warmth blossomed inside his chest, and tingles shimmied through his fingers.

He had no idea what this feeling was, but he liked it.

Once he'd opened the door, he stared transfixed at the tattooed female in the center of the bed, surrounded by a sea of red satin.

Cordray lay on her side, facing the door. Her black hair with its multihued blue streak covered half her face and spilled over the pillow.

Of course she would sleep on a blood-red bed. She probably fantasized that her sheets were her victims' blood. After all, this was Cordray.

Lovely . . . breathtaking . . . exhilarating Cordray.

In sleep, she looked as peaceful as a napping kitten, her prickly armor shed, leaving only tranquility. All that serenity enveloped Trace like a cozy blanket made of rabbit's fur. Soft and warm. Magnetic.

As if in a trance, he crossed the space between the door and the bed and knelt beside her. He placed his forearm on the mattress and rested his chin on it as he gingerly reached out with his other hand and caressed just the tips of her hair with his fingers.

Her hair was cool and felt like strands of silk.

Quiet calm wrapped around him. And something else. Something primal and urgent that ran starkly opposite from the calm energy taming his beast. Something that awakened his blood in such a pleasant, exciting way.

Her chest rose and fell evenly as she breathed. Then she shifted and murmured as if talking in her sleep.

Her lips parted, and a breathy moan that sounded almost sexual broke the stillness.

Whatever she was dreaming about, it sounded good.

She twisted and rolled so that she was partially on her back.

"Don't stop," she whispered sleepily, followed instantly by another moan. "Yesss." The word trailed off on a drowsy sigh.

Her breathing deepened and intensified as subtle waves of hormonal heat pulsed from her body.

Trace's cock stiffened, and he lifted his head off his arm, staring. Just staring.

In that moment, she was the sexiest thing he'd ever seen, and he wanted more. Needed more. Would die if he didn't get more.

Before he could stop himself, his mind penetrated hers, snapping in an instant to the image of him on top of her. She was dreaming about him. Him! And he was fucking her. Hard. And she liked it. She wanted it.

And then he was in his dream self, buried inside her.

For the love of God, this was more than just a wet dream. This was like an out of body experience, where his soul and hers had met up for a little nocturnal emissioning with one another.

Her scent invaded his senses. Her arms gripped him to her. Her legs locked his hammering hips in place.

"More, please more!"

And he wanted to give her more. He wanted to expend himself and fall into her body forever. God, she felt good. Hot, wet, tight.

She came again, digging her nails into the back of his shoulders as pleasure shredded her vocal chords.

Then shit got crazy.

As in crazy hot, crazy good, and crazy holy fuck!

Her fingers clawed at his bare back, her cries coming hard and fast as she fell into delirious spasms beneath his body, coming again and again, unable to stop. Cordray was a nympho. A wired-up bundle of unleashed orgasms he wanted to keep tapping into.

He thrust into her, shoving her legs apart with his knees, grabbing her arms and holding them against the bed, demanding with his clenching thrusts that she give him more. That she give him all of her. He would bleed every ounce of pleasure from her body. He would own her, possess her, claim her! She belonged to him!

As she blew apart yet again, his own climax crested, sweeping him away on a lava flow of molten delirium.

God, he'd never come so hard. So long. With such incredible intensity. He closed his eyes to savor the explosion happening between his legs and hers. Jesus, she was good. No. *They* were. They were good *together*. He was fire, and she was gasoline, and as she came again, another orgasm rocketed through his scrotum.

This was what he'd spent his whole life looking for. The one female who could put the smack down on his beast and keep it chained like she was a dragon tamer and it was a pussycat. A female who could arouse him in a way that no other female — or male — ever had.

Just . . . wham, bam, and holy-hell-oh-my-God-and-hallelujah thank you ma'am!

Cordray was the shit in bed!

He could get used to dreams like this. Fuck yeah.

Then the mood shifted. The atmosphere changed and it no longer felt like a dream.

"What the . . .?" Cordray's sexed-up, sleep-infused voice reached him as if from a cave. "What the fuck?"

He peeled his eyes open. Something was way off here. She was awake. And under him. He had climbed on top of her.

Oh. Shit.

On a stick.

Her eyes opened wide, and she stared up at him like he was the Grim Reaper come to claim her soul.

His hips were between her thighs.

He was rocking himself against her, and she was doing the same to him.

And his cock was throbbing in his jeans.

And, oh fuck, he'd come. He'd fucking come for real, not just in her dream.

Jesus, this was bad.

Oil-spill-in-the-Gulf bad.

He stared down at her, his mind blank.

She stared up at him, mouth open, breathing hard. Then her stare turned into a glare. Then into invisible poisonous daggers.

"What the *hell* are you *doing*?" She shoved him off and jumped out of the bed, brushing her hands over her body as if she were covered in spiders. "How dare you! I can't believe . . ." Her expression morphed into one of fear. "Oh my God, did we . . .? Did you . . .?" She stared in horror at the bed then looked down at her body as if to ensure she was still wearing clothes. Then her gaze hardened as it met his. "You'd better hope we didn't actually fuck" — she gestured toward the bed — "or I'll rip off your dick, asshole!"

Shock and awe sent shivers down his spine. "We're both still dressed, for God's sake. How could we fuck when we're both dressed?" He scampered off the bed and toward the door, bile rising in his throat. What had he done? How could he have enjoyed *that*? With her? Cordray? Satan's mistress? He must have lost his mind.

"Get out. Out!" She pointed at the door. "You're supposed to be working, not in here molesting me."

"Molesting you? Are you kidding? Don't fucking flatter yourself. You're not my type."

Her mouth fell open. "And yet you were on top of me, dry humping me in my own bed."

"Believe me, honey, there was nothing *dry* about it." The words flew from his mouth before he could stop them, and he instantly regretted it. The last thing he wanted was for her to know he'd gotten off. Way off. Because the thick and sticky mess in his Calvin Kleins was one of the biggest loads he'd ever shot, if not the biggest. Damn shit had to be seeping down his thighs.

She gasped. "I should throw you back in Bain's dungeon for that."

He blew out a derisive breath. "For what? Coming without a license?"

If looks could kill, he wouldn't just be dead. He'd already be worm shit. "No, for—"

"Besides, I didn't hear you complaining," he said defensively before she could get out another word. "You were getting off as much as I was, sweetheart. Or do you always come a dozen times when you dream about me?"

Her eyes flew wide. "This is your fault. You made me think I was dreaming, when actually you planted that scenario—"

Trace frowned and held up his hand. "Hold up, Maleficent. *You* were dreaming about *me*. I didn't plant *anything* in your head. I simply looked inside—big fucking mistake, by the way—and there I was. Surprise, surprise. So if anyone should be crying foul, it should be me."

"Whatever. If that's the way it really happened, the last I heard, dreaming of having sex with someone isn't a crime. But you *were* physically on top of me when I woke up." She slapped her palm on her chest then shivered as if recalling the way she'd come undone beneath him.

He made sure to stay across the room from her, even though every bone in his body, including the one still straining for more between his legs, wanted nothing more than for him to storm her, toss her on the bed, and bury himself inside her for real for a week.

"We didn't have sex! Jesus!" He swiped his palm over his scalp. "Get over yourself."

She crossed her arms over her chest and practically cowered away from him.

God, he wasn't that bad, was he? Surely, she could think of someone worse to fuck than him. Even though, technically, they hadn't fucked. After all, dreaming about fucking wasn't the same as actually fucking.

But, man, it had sure felt real.

After a few long, tense moments passed, she seemed to calm from a rapid boil to a simmer. "Okay, okay. Fine. Whatever. Let's just . . . this never happened, okay?"

Like hell it never happened! His dick was still letting him know that, yes, it had happened. And that it should happen again. Sooner rather than later. Christ! His dick was in heaven. Wow. That had been unbelievably hot!

But he nodded, anyway. "Whatever you say, chief." He slashed his hand horizontally through the air like he was karate chopping a slab of plywood and wiping the proverbial slate clean. "Never happened." It was better to pretend than to acknowledge that major fireworks had gone off inside his balls and that they wanted an encore. "I'm heading down to eat lunch, and then I'm going to bed." Right after he changed his clothes again.

At this rate, he'd go through every piece of clothing he'd brought with him in less than twenty-four hours.

In his room, he shut the door and plopped his ass onto the edge of the bed and lowered his head into his hands. For the first time in five minutes, he was able to take a deep enough breath to fill his lungs.

Jesus, that female was something. A sexy, infuriating, scorching, aggravating, remarkable, offensive, blood-pumping-in-a-good-and-bad-way something.

CHAPTER 16

CORDRAY SANK ONTO HER BED and collapsed forward, her palm pressed to her forehead.

Her body still hummed from the orgasms Trace had given her, both in her dream and in real life. What they'd done had been incredible. Mind-numbing, body-blasting incredible. But as the seconds ticked by now that he was gone, her sense of touch gradually faded, leaving her in an unfeeling void again.

How would she survive three months with him? She'd barely survived the first twelve hours. All she wanted to do was march down the hall, throw open the door to his bedroom, throw him on the bed, and demand that he fuck her until she saw stars, passed out, or both.

Taking a deep breath, she folded herself back into her sheets and clutched a pillow to the front of her body. Maybe if she closed her eyes and fantasized hard enough, she could pretend the pillow was Trace. Except she still wouldn't be able to feel anything. If the pillow really were Trace, she'd be in sensory overload.

Waking up to find him on top of her, pouring warmth and pleasure into her body, had both thrilled and terrified her. His weight had felt so right pressing down on her, and yet inexplicably horrifying.

For thirty minutes, she fought to go back to sleep. Just when she thought she wouldn't be able to, she finally drifted off.

Four hours later, with the smell of fried chicken and homemade dinner rolls drifting up from the kitchen, she awoke.

Thankfully, she'd had no more dreams about Trace, sexual or otherwise.

After taking a quick shower, she slipped into black pencil pants that laced from her outer thighs to the insides of her knees and cinched snugly around her ankles. A jacquard skull pattern stretched up the front of her thighs. Over her black-lace bra, she pulled on a black, short-sleeved top decorated with the image of a giant white skull covered in rhinestones.

As she brushed her hair and pulled it into a ponytail, her mind drifted back to what had happened with Trace. She would have to face him tonight. He would be at dinner, and she would have to look at him. Would he see in her face how much she'd enjoyed what he'd done to her?

She flipped off the bathroom light and returned to her bedroom, where she sat on the edge of the bed and pulled on her boots.

What if she had wrapped her arms around him instead of pushed him away? What if she'd allowed herself to feel him . . . hold him . . . God forbid, kiss him? What would have happened? Where would their dream-induced interlude have led?

She closed her eyes, letting herself float among the possibilities. These moments were precious. So incredibly rare. If only she didn't need Trace to be near for her to actually feel.

Her phone chimed on her nightstand, and her eyes popped open. She swiped the phone into her palm and checked the screen.

She had one new e-mail.

We're pleased to invite you to audition for membership to Grudge Match. Auditions are performed by running the gauntlet, where you will face some of our toughest members. If you pass, you're in. If you don't, membership will be denied.

You're scheduled to run the gauntlet tonight at 9:00 p.m. If you are unable to audition at this time, please reply to this text and request another audition. We'll do our best to accommodate you. Attached are the rules for the gauntlet, as well as the address where your audition will take place. We hope to see you this evening.

Cordray raised her eyebrows. This wasn't the kind of message she'd expected from an underground fight club. She'd assumed her correspondence with the coordinators of Grudge Match would consist of monosyllabic words and a lot of Neanderthal grunting. This message was polite and spoke to a level of refinement more appropriate for royalty than someone in charge of an army of UFC fighters.

She scanned the attachment and plotted the location on her map app. Hopefully, this meant she was one step closer to gathering much-needed evidence against Premier Royce. Bain needed proof that the drecks' leader was, in fact, conspiring against him and violating the truce that had existed between their two races for centuries. Once they had proof, Bain's monthly meetings with Royce could take a decidedly different course, because until now, Bain had been required to play nice with that bastard. And she knew playing nice with Royce had just about tapped out Bain's patience, especially when Royce was obviously hiding incriminating evidence.

Standing, she tucked her phone into her pocket and made her way into the hall. Nine o'clock was still hours away, but if she was going to have the energy to fight, she needed to pack in a good dinner.

Downstairs, she stopped at her office and checked the backtrace she'd run on Skeletor. Just as she'd suspected, it had come up empty. She still had nothing to go on to discover his identity or where he was hiding. He wouldn't remain hidden for long. In her experience as a bounty hunter, the bad guys always turned up. Maybe it would take a while, and maybe he'd run her in circles, but eventually, Skeletor would fall into her path. When he did, she would be ready for him.

She shut off her computer and headed toward the chatter coming from the dining room. Trace was already seated at the table between Aiden and Null. Now that the school day was over, the other kids seemed as fascinated with him as the twins. He was the center of attention.

"Where are you from?"

"All over, but I live in Chicago now."

"What do you do?"

"I'm an AKM enforcer."

"Do you have a gun?"

"A couple."

"Cordray has a gun."

"Oh?"

"Are you Cordray's boyfriend?"

"Um…"

Cordray stepped in. "Okay kids, that's enough of the twenty questions. Let's let Trace out of the hot seat and get ready to eat. Books off the table." She pointed at the random textbooks beside the plates, and then called into the living room to Leon and Riley, who were too busy crushing on one another to pay Trace much attention. "Leon? Riley? Come on, you two. Time for dinner."

Leon and Riley thought she wasn't aware of just how strong their puppy love was, but they didn't know she saw all, knew all. Neither had developed the awareness to sense when she was digging through their minds.

Their infatuation with one another was endearing, but also

troubling. They were in young love. For humans, young love could easily turn into something more permanent, but for vampires, young love often ended badly. Very, very badly. And didn't Cordray know how true that was?

Sighing inwardly, she turned her attention back to the table as the others settled into their seats. There was no need to think about her past right now — or the pain that went with it. She tried not to dwell on those old memories, but they still filtered through on occasion. And now that Trace was around, those memories seemed to be filtering in more and more, as if he were an antenna tugging at her brain waves to pull her most painful memories to the forefront.

As Mya and Brenna carried platters and bowls of food to the table, she took an accounting of the kids. "Where's Gavin?"

Gavin, the resident loner. The resident firebug. He'd grown unusually fascinated with fire in the last year, and she was struggling to figure out how to put a stop to his pyromaniac tendencies. She, Mya, and Brenna had to keep a close eye on him at all times to ensure he didn't burn the whole place down.

Brenna set down a large serving dish of green beans and looked around then glanced in the direction of the back door. "He was just here."

"I'd better go look for him." As she stepped out on the deck, she was thankful to have something to do to keep her away from Trace a little bit longer.

Lifting her nose, she inhaled, locating Gavin's scent, as well as the telltale sulfuric odor of matches and smoke, coming from behind the dorm.

"Gavin!" She leaped off the deck and sprinted toward the smell.

She'd told him countless times not to play with fire, and yet, there he was, doing it anyway. Again. For about the tenth time in four weeks.

How the hell was he getting to the matches? Hadn't they all been put up where he couldn't reach them? They must have missed a stash somewhere.

She rushed around the corner in time to see him lift a lit match to the corner of a piece of paper.

"GAVIN!"

He jumped and dropped the burning paper in the grass.

Cordray darted forward and stamped her boot on it, putting out the flames. "I've told you a thousand times to stop playing with fire, Gavin." She snatched the box of wooden matches from his hand.

"Where did you get these?"

Tears welled in his eyes as he lowered his head, his bottom lip trembling. He didn't answer her.

"Where, Gavin? Where did you find these?" She shook the box of matches.

Then it dawned on her. These were Trace's matches.

She took a deep breath and calmed herself as she tucked the box into the cup of her bra. Then she gave Gavin's hand a light tug. "Never mind, it's time for dinner. We'll talk about this later." But first, she and Trace needed to have a little chat about leaving his matches where Gavin could find them and feed his fire addiction. "Come on."

Gavin sniffled, stood, and fell in step beside her as she led him back to the house.

He was so quiet, hardly ever speaking, hardly looking anyone in the eye. But the poor kid had watched both his parents fall into cobalt's grip and die tragic deaths when he'd only been five years old. The trauma had been enough to shut him inside himself.

But you could only shutter the pain from the past for so long before it seeped through, making itself known. And the longer you bottled up the past, the more destructive it became when it broke free from its bonds.

She looked toward the back of the house, thinking about Trace. She'd seen his fear. She'd seen what had happened to his mom and that he'd never talked to anyone about it. He'd held that shit inside him for two hundred years. Sooner or later, it was going to come out. Maybe it already was. Perhaps that's what caused his seizure at Micah's house.

Like Gavin, maybe Trace's pain was beginning to ooze out and take on a mind of its own, too. For Gavin, it meant addiction to fire. For Trace, who knew? Given how powerful he was, it was hard telling how explosive the snap would be once his rubber band broke.

Back inside, she waited in the hall while Gavin washed up in the downstairs bathroom, and then the two of them returned to the dining room.

She had barely sat down when sixteen-year-old Panya shoved a bowl of mashed potatoes into her hands.

"Thank you." She took the bowl and spooned some potatoes onto her plate then passed the bowl along to Leon on her right.

Silverware clinked on ceramic as everyone loaded up their plates and dug in.

The din was comforting. Seven kids and four adults made a lot of noise around the trough, which was so much better than the clinical silence that greeted her at the table at her city mansion. That place was more of a giant closet for her shoes than anything, but Bain had insisted on buying it for her, so she occasionally used it. Specifically when she sought companionship. She never brought her few-and-far-between sexual partners—which were mostly one-night stands meant more for feeding than sex—around Asylum.

Not that she got much out of her liaisons, but when she fed, she enjoyed giving pleasure to another even though she could no longer take pleasure for herself.

In that respect, the mansion came in handy.

But Asylum and its noisy familiarity always comforted her. Giving a home to those who were unwanted was her life's mission. She knew what it was like to be discarded. Left with a broken heart because the life she thought she would have was no longer attainable.

If only Trace knew how similar they were to one another. He'd been abandoned. So had she. They both carried such heavy burdens from their pasts.

He sat three seats away, bookended by Aiden and Null. His attention was split between them as he helped fill their plates. They giggled as he spilled corn on the tablecloth and tried to hide it under his plate. That's when he looked up and found her watching him. His cheeks briefly shaded deep pink.

"And here you said you didn't need a drop cloth," she said.

He grinned sheepishly and held the dish toward her. "Corn?" His eyes pinched uncomfortably as he met her gaze. Clearly, he was remembering their rendezvous from earlier.

She reached past Panya and Aiden and took the bowl as she gave him a warning glare. "Sure."

His eyes held hers for a lingering moment then broke away as Aiden giggled and shoved a buttered roll in his hand. He smiled at the mangled handful of bread. Giant, pale-yellow globs of butter clung unevenly to what barely even resembled a dinner roll and looked more like something a baby had torn apart and slapped around in its high chair. But Trace accepted it with a gracious thank you before tearing off one of the doughy appendages and stuffing it in his mouth.

Cordray had to admit that Trace behaved himself better than she'd expected around the kids, even if he couldn't control himself anywhere else. But the children were what counted. Nothing was more important than the children.

Of course, later, when the kids were dismissed to the dormitory and she and Trace were alone in the main house, she was certain the insults would fly again and the charade of politeness would be forgotten. Especially after the day's events.

As they ate, Cordray scouted the minds of the kids around the table. Leon and Riley were thinking about taking their courtship to the next level. *Sigh.* It had been destined to happen sooner or later. The combination of young love and young hormones were second only to a true mating when it came to the power of attraction and the need to copulate.

At twenty and nineteen, Leon and Riley were long past the age of cooties and were entering the earliest stage of their transition into adult vampires. She'd had "the talk" with them years ago, and they knew what to expect as adults, but despite all her warnings to the contrary, both were certain they would mate one another when they came of age. Nothing Cordray said to warn them otherwise got through. They were already naming their children, for God's sake.

Even now, Leon struggled not to stare at Riley, who blushed as she ate like a proper young lady, which was an improvement over the ill-mannered child who had eaten with her hands and flung food at the other kids when she'd been brought to Asylum eight years ago.

Cordray continued around the table, checking the minds of the others. Panya already had a crush on Trace. Great. Not even a full day there, and Trace was already stirring up the young females. As well as the older ones, if she counted herself.

Eight-year-old Faith was too busy writing poetry and short stories in her head to think of anything else. To her, Trace was inspiration for her writing and nothing more. She planned on becoming a world-famous author or songwriter someday and had already declared that she would never get married. Little Faith was too young to understand what she was, yet, or that if a male mated her, she wouldn't have much choice but to mate him back. The laws were very explicit about protecting mated male vampires that way.

But it wasn't as if Faith would abstain, or that she would always feel this way about "boys," as she called them. Maturity and hormones had a way of changing a person's mind — vampire, human, or other — into being more receptive to the opposite sex.

Riley and Leon were the perfect example of how powerful hormones were in that respect. Not even three years ago, Leon had been dead set on staying single his entire life, and then . . . snap! Something changed. Maybe it was that Riley's body had finally developed. Or maybe it was simply his adult hormones kicking in, and Riley was the only female at Asylum close enough to his age to catch his eye. Whatever the reason, seemingly overnight, Leon had fallen head over heels for Riley. They'd been together ever since.

That left eleven-year-old Gavin, the loner and fire lover. Gavin was struggling with math and was nervous about heading off to human school next year. He'd recently finished the curriculum she'd put in place to prepare the young for their vampire lives, and he now understood what he was. Today, Brenna had broken the news that next year he'd be sent to public school.

A scary step.

Maybe that was why he'd been playing with Trace's matches. Stress and anxiety were his triggers.

Chatter hummed around the table as silverware clanged on plates, and for the first time in days, the tension in Cordray's shoulders melted away. These were her children. They may not have been her flesh and blood, but they were still hers. She would have legally adopted every single one of them if it were required for her to provide such care, but Bain kept the human authorities away and kept the money flowing into her coffers so she never had to worry.

They held an annual fundraiser and charity ball, but that was more to keep Asylum and its children in the minds of their people than to collect funds.

After dinner, all the kids but Aiden and Null filed out to the dorm with Brenna while Mya started in on the dishes.

"I'll get those," Cordray said, setting the last of the plates on the overloaded counter.

"You sure?" Mya rinsed her hands.

"Yep." Actually, Cordray planned on having Trace clean the kitchen. Might as well put him to good use while she had him. "You go on out to the dorm with the kids. Help Gavin with his math. He's struggling. And watch Leon and Riley. They're thinking about sneaking into each other's rooms after everyone goes to bed."

"Good to know." Mya dried her hands on the towel hanging from the oven handle and looked up as Trace entered the kitchen with the last of the dishes and set them on the counter. "Good night, Trace." She glanced from him to Cordray, her eyes narrowing into knowing slits.

Cordray shot her a venomous glare. "Good night, Mya."

"Night-night. Don't do anything I wouldn't do." With that, Mya exited the back door and crossed the yard to the dorm.

That left her and Trace alone. Aiden and Null were playing in the living room.

On second thought, maybe she shouldn't have been so quick to dismiss Mya.

For a long moment, she just stared at him. He stared back. With all the commotion and diversions suddenly gone, as well as the protective shields that came with them, she felt stripped bare and hung out like an offering to the gods.

Unbidden, her gaze drifted down his body. After their dream-induced liaison today, she knew firsthand how solid he was. How hard. How warm.

A dark rumble rolled deep within his throat. When she pulled her gaze back to his face, he wore an amused smirk.

"Do you like what you see?"

She frowned and took a step back. "You wish." She spun for the dishes, grabbed the first one she saw, and began scraping the scraps into the trash.

He joined her, standing close enough as he wiped food off another plate that his body heat warmed her side.

"I'll do this," she said quickly. "You can . . ." She looked around the kitchen. "Just put all that away." She gestured toward a batch of condiments, butter, and sauces on the counter.

He muttered a disdainful response she couldn't make out then set the plate down, wiped his hands on a paper towel, and began clearing the counter. He opened the fridge and put the container of butter on the middle shelf.

She set aside the plate she was scraping and stepped forward. "The butter doesn't go there. It goes here." She opened the plastic drawer and slammed the butter inside with a huff.

"Well, *excuse* me for not knowing the butter had a permanent residence."

"Look," she said, "there are a lot of people here and a lot of food. Everything has its place. Got it? You just don't start throwing things in the fridge willy-nilly, or it won't all fit."

It felt good to get back to being mean to him. Being mean kept her out of trouble. Kept her from thinking about how incredible he had felt between her legs.

Trace rolled his eyes. "Look at you. The butter police. How fortunate for your condiments."

He started to put the ketchup away, but she snagged the bottle from his hand. "And that goes here, not there." She dropped the ketchup on one of the shelves in the door.

"Jesus H." He took a step back. "Are you always so goddamn controlling? I'll make sure to memorize where everything goes for the test I'm sure you'll give me later." He rolled his eyes. "You told me to put this shit away. I'm putting it away."

She huffed and waved him off. "Fine. Go scrape the dishes then, and I'll put all this away." She picked up bottles of pickles, olives, mustard, and salad dressing.

"Gee, I don't know. Are you sure I can handle it?" He grabbed one of the plates and pushed the scraps into the trash with a fork.

"Don't test me, Trace. I'm already pissed at you."

"Me? For what? Making you come this afternoon?"

Flames shot up her back, and she dropped the jar of mayonnaise so it fell over on the shelf. She floundered to pick it up then stood and glared around the door at him. "How dare you!" She shoved everything into the fridge, slammed the door, and heard one of the bottles fall over in the back. "And keep your voice down."

"Look in the mirror, sweetheart." He waved the dirty plate he'd just scraped toward the fridge. "And you'd better fix that. Wouldn't want to crowd the lettuce."

"Don't call me sweetheart." She scowled at him then yanked open the refrigerator door, righted the jar of spaghetti sauce that had tumbled over, and shut the door more gingerly this time. "And I'm talking about these." She pulled the box of matches from inside her bra and tossed them at him.

He snatched the box of matches in midair then frowned at them before glancing back at her. "You've lost me. You're pissed at me because I chew on matches? You already knew that." He tucked the box into his back pocket.

She pushed past him to get to the sink and turned on the water to let it heat. "I found Gavin with those before dinner. He was behind the dorm lighting paper on fire. I thought I told you to keep those things away from the kids."

"Here's an idea." He set another scraped plate on the counter and slid it toward her. "Maybe Gavin got into my things, and you should be lecturing him on how he shouldn't go snooping around in other people's stuff instead of jumping down my ass for leaving them out where he could find them, because these, sweetheart" — he pulled the matches out of his pocket and waved them in front of her face, making the small wooden sticks rattle inside — "have either been in my pocket or in my bag upstairs in my room the entire time I've been here. So get your own house in order before you go barking at me about mine."

Cordray leaned away from him, because just having him near was setting her nerve endings on fire. "I told you not to call me sweetheart."

Trace pressed toward her, and the sensation of his shoulder touching hers caused tingles to shower down her arm. It took all her strength not to close her eyes and relish the sensual response.

"How about I just call you the Wicked Witch of the West. It's fitting, don't you think?"

She drew away and glared at him. "How about you grow up and call me Cordray? Do you think your tiny brain can handle that?"

He tossed more scraps in the trash. "Can yours?"

"Fuck you, Trace."

"You're too frigid to know what to do with me if you fucked me."

The retort came out of nowhere and caught Cordray completely off guard. For a moment, all she could do was gape at him in disbelief as his words stung her heart. "How dare you."

"If the shoe fits." He pressed seductively against her, as if he were trying to intimidate her. Or perhaps challenge her. "Whaddya say? Do you really think you could handle me?" His gaze blazed into hers as he let out a quiet snort. "I dare you to prove it."

She could hardly breathe as her gaze fell to his full lips. Was he trying rekindle the fire he'd sparked in her bedroom earlier? If so, it was working. Her fire was definitely rekindled. But what if he was only toying with her? What if this was some sick game where he pulled away and laughed in her face the moment she showed interest in taking another trip with him into the land of the erotic? She would be so humiliated.

Forcing her shoulders back, she raised her chin. "I've fucked plenty, Trace. I'm just not interested in fucking freaks of nature who are masochists and criminals."

His gaze hardened as his mouth pressed into a thin line, and his eyebrows pressed downward as if she'd caused him pain. Clearly, her insult had hurt him. But his had hurt her, so eye for an eye.

He let out a derisive puff of breath and pushed away from her. "You're a real piece of work, you know that? You can't even apologize. You were wrong about the matches. You know it. I know it. And rather than say you're sorry, you harass me. Then you insult me."

"Hey, jackass, you insulted me first." She reached behind her and slammed off the faucet. "I'll admit, you behave admirably around the kids. I appreciate that. And yes, I'm sorry for blaming you for the matches. But let me make it clear. I own your ass for the next three months. Got it? You're mine. You do as I say. And if you want to go back to your precious AKM job and beat off with your pal, Micah, then you'll get that through your thick skull." She paused and bore her eyes into the angered, pale-green depths of his, trying to ignore the warm tingles flowing through her veins. "And there won't be any more repeats of what happened today, nor will I tolerate you trying to humiliate me by toying with my emotions, so don't *ever* bring it up again. Do you understand?"

"Damn straight it won't happen again."

"Then we agree." A stab of disappointment pierced her heart as she took a step back and crossed her arms. "You and I don't have to like each other, Trace, but when it comes to these kids, nothing interferes. Asylum runs like a well-oiled machine because the children's needs come first, before all else. That includes our dislike for each other. When you're here, you leave your personal hatred of me at the door and I'll do likewise." She gave him a shove as she turned toward the sink again, when all she wanted was to keep touching him so she could feel something beyond her normal nothingness. "You do that," she said, picking up a dirty plate and rinsing it, "and give me more than your required two days a week, and I'll see what I can do about getting you back to work before your three months are up. Deal?" She glanced sideways at him. "I'll only make that offer once."

She wasn't sure why she had just offered to cut his sentence short, or even why she suggested he put in more days than what Bain had sentenced him to. Maybe a part of her just wanted to get him out of there as fast as possible. Then again, maybe she subconsciously wanted him to be around more, which was a scary thought.

Having Trace around more was dangerous, because despite her protests, she was drawn to him. He was magnetic. Even now, she yearned to touch him again. To stroke her fingers down the ridges in his abdomen, kiss him, press her body against his. Trace was excitement incarnate. What female wouldn't be drawn to him?

"Fine." Trace returned to scraping the dishes. "You've got a deal, because the sooner I get out of here, the better." He paused and poked her in the arm, making her suck in her breath as she jerked her head around to face him. "But let *me* make one thing clear." He drew closer, his voice deathly quiet. "You do *not* own me."

She forced herself to hold his gaze. "That's right. *Micah* owns you now, doesn't he? How *lucky* for you both."

Trace's eyes narrowed. A moment later, he went back to cleaning dishes. "Jealous much?"

"Don't flatter yourself."

For the next thirty minutes, the two worked in inharmonious silence. Cordray knew she had come off sounding like a jealous girlfriend with her Micah comment, but there wasn't anything she could do about it now. She really needed to be more careful what she said and how she said it from now on. The last thing she wanted was for Trace to pick up on her attraction to him.

Or maybe she was simply attracted to her ability to *feel* him when she couldn't feel a damn thing the rest of the time.

If only she could figure out why.

There had to be a logical explanation.

Maybe it had to do with that bizarre power of his? Maybe his energy existed at a different frequency from everyone else's or some shit, which made him more tactile. Or maybe it was something deeper, more meaningful. She didn't want to think about that possibility. The last thing she needed to consider was that he might be—however unlikely—her mate.

She just needed to stay away from him as much as possible. Letting him touch her in any way, shape, or form was to be avoided at all costs.

After setting the last dish in the rack and starting the dishwasher, she wiped down the counter then rinsed her hands.

"What now?" Trace said behind her.

She grabbed a kitchen towel and dried her hands. "You can do whatever you want. I'm going to spend time with Aiden and Null before I head out. This is their time."

Trace's strong brow wrinkled. "Head out?"

She tossed the towel on the counter. "Yes. I have work to do."

"But I thought . . ." He almost sounded disappointed.

"Unlike someone I know, I still have *my* job." She switched off the light and walked away, toward the large, open living room where Aiden and Null were sitting at the coffee table, coloring.

She assumed Trace would go upstairs to his room, but he surprised her by following her and taking a seat in one of the recliners as she settled on the couch and turned the volume up on the TV, hoping to send Trace the subliminal message that she was done talking.

"Coco, look!" Aiden held up a picture, all smiles. Angelic, blond ringlets made a halo around her face.

"Oh my goodness," she said, shoving her Trace-induced irritation aside and plastering a smile on her face. "Is that me?" She bent forward and pointed to one of the figures on the page, which was wearing a black shirt with what appeared to be a skull on it.

"Uh-huh." Aiden hopped up and climbed into her lap. "And that's Trace, and that's me, and that's Null." Her tiny finger, stained with black marker, pointed to each in turn.

Cordray grinned at the depiction of Trace, tall and hairless, until she saw that Aiden had drawn Trace holding her hand.

The little matchmaker.

"Can I see?" Trace said.

"Uh . . . sure." Cordray handed the picture back to Aiden. "Go show Trace."

The little girl took it, jumped down, and darted to him. "See. That's you and Coco. And this is me and Null." She shoved the picture at him as she pointed.

Trace's eyes scanned the drawing as he grinned, and then his gaze dropped to what Cordray imagined was their joined hands, because his grin faltered and his brow ticked. Then he recovered and handed the picture back. "Wow, that's some drawing, Aiden."

"Uh-huh!" Aiden spun and flew back into Cordray's lap.

Ignoring the matchmaking going on by the little girl, Cordray snuggled Aiden against her and, before she could stop herself, said to Trace, "Her gifts are artistic."

She hadn't wanted to talk to him, anymore, but sitting in the living room with him, with the TV on and the kids completing the family portrait she'd pondered earlier while watching Trace with the kids as he fixed the fence, felt comfortable. Despite their argument, there was a kind of simplicity and ease she felt around Trace when she wasn't consciously fending off the physical sensations he stirred to life within her.

Trace glanced from her to Aiden. "You mean . . . from her mixed blood?"

"Yes. She's already very talented with her hands." She'd never seen a mixed-blood display their talents at such a young age, but both Aiden and Null were already showing signs of how their gifts would manifest.

Trace bobbed his head in understanding. "I see." He looked down at Null and leaned toward him. "And what about you, little man? What gifts do you have?"

Null shrugged and set down his crayon. "I like to colow?" He offered his reply in a way that made it clear he had no idea what kind of gifts they were talking about and thought they were simply asking what he liked to do.

"I think his might have something to do with his eyes," Cordray said quietly. "He might be an empath."

Trace met her gaze. "Yeah, I was wondering about that."

"Are you referring to what happened at breakfast?" She had noticed something going on between him and Null this morning. Trace had seemed agitated, but when Null took his hand, it was as if he'd pulled all the anxiety out of Trace's heart.

A troubled frown furrowed his brow, as if he were remembering the incident. "Yeah. His eyes changed. What was that?"

"I'm not quite sure, but I've noticed it before. It's like he can absorb emotions or something, which is why I think he's empathic. He has a very calming influence, but I'm not sure exactly how this will manifest as he gets older."

Trace glanced down at Null. "Yeah, at one point he took my hand, and" — curious wonder fell over his face — "when he did, everything went calm." He met her gaze. "My heart stopped racing, and I felt like I could breathe again." He shrugged. "I'd been feeling a bit overwhelmed in front of everyone, and he shut off all that the moment he took my hand."

"I noticed."

He paused, eyeing her. "You know, only one other person has that effect on me."

"Micah?" She looked away and swallowed past the lump in her throat.

"No."

She turned back toward him and frowned. "No?"

He shook his head, his eyebrows scrunching over his nose as if were confused or in a state of dismay.

"Who then?"

"You." The single syllable unfurled quietly.

"Me?" That was the last thing she'd expected him to say.

But at least now she knew the bizarre metaphysical relationship they had with one another wasn't just one-sided. She affected him as much as he affected her, only differently. While she calmed him, he awakened her sensory response.

She would have been lying if she said this revelation didn't please her.

He scowled and shifted his gaze toward hers without quite meeting it. "Don't go getting all excited that you have all this influence over me. It doesn't mean anything."

She forced a tight smile at Aiden, who was absently tracing the tip of her finger around her drawing. "What about Brak?" She spoke gently so she didn't upset the kids. "I've seen inside your mind. I've seen what he is to you."

"He hasn't been around, though, has he?"

"No, but—"

"And even when we were kids, he wasn't around much." He sighed and turned away. "Nobody was."

This quiet resentment, tainted with what smacked of self-pity, didn't fit either the magnanimous male she'd come to know or what she'd seen inside his thoughts. Trace loved his brother, and he loved his parents. They'd been a tight family, even if an unconventional one.

Maybe his brooding contempt had more to do with the guilt he carried over what had happened to his mother. He did seem to shoulder a lot of blame where she was concerned, even though, from what she'd seen, he wasn't at fault for her death.

Whatever his reasons for saying what he had, she needed to tread softly so she didn't set him off. Maybe offering a lifeline could go a long way toward easing his mind and showing they weren't so different.

She offered a shallow smile and spoke softly. "You know, I know a thing or two about being alone." Understatement. Of. The. Millennium.

He frowned and snorted as he glanced at the kids then flicked his gaze in the direction of the dorm, where Brenna, Mya, and the other children were. "Doubtful."

"You might be surprised."

His frown deepened, but she saw the barest hint of understanding in his eyes. Still, he wasn't ready to let down his guard. "Maybe, but that doesn't mean you know me."

She sighed. This constant bickering, while entertaining at times, was exhausting. "Come on, Trace, how about a truce?" She needed a break from the constant mental vigilance.

His head swiveled toward her, his expression wary.

His dark eyebrows cut toward his nose as he seemed to take a moment to consider her suggestion, but he didn't say anything. Instead, he issued a shallow bob of his head, as if he, too, were weary of the fighting. He broke his gaze away from hers and peered over Null's shoulder at his crayon drawing, but when he spoke, it was to Cordray. "I simply can't understand how you could possibly feel alone here, C. You have all these kids. Mya. Brenna. The king."

Memories of Gideon filtered back into her mind. "I know more about being alone than you think I do, Trace. Trust me, I haven't always been surrounded by people I love who love me back."

His gaze flicked quickly to hers, and then he looked away as he nodded shallowly in understanding.

Given what she'd seen of Trace's past, he probably did understand. At least he would if she had the balls to fully share her own past with him. To tell him about Gideon. How Gideon had destroyed her, as well as how Trace was mending her.

Wait . . . what?

Mend her? Where had that thought come from? Trace wasn't mending her. Or was he?

Maybe her subconscious self was on to something her conscious self hadn't even considered, because Trace *had* awakened her sense of touch. He had made her feel things she hadn't felt in eight hundred years. Perhaps Trace really was repairing what Gideon had destroyed. And if he was, what did that mean?

Bewildered, she couldn't find the words to express how this new possibility affected her. All she could do was stare at him, study him, see him through a new filter the way a photographer did when changing lenses on his camera. Some of the mental mist she had programmed her mind's eye to see when she looked at Trace cleared, and for the first time since she laid eyes on him in Bain's court, she allowed herself to see him clearly. He was like a giant starburst of light, more awe inspiring than ever.

He bent forward and eyed Null's artwork and cleared the emotional turmoil from his throat. "What did you draw there, little man?"

Null's tiny finger pointed to a figure of a bald male with a gun. "That's you." Then he pointed to the blond male standing next to him, also holding a gun. "And that's me."

Trace picked up the picture. "You're all grown up," he said, examining the crayon and marker drawing.

Null nodded. "Uh-huh."

"And what are we doing in this picture?" Trace said.

Null got up off the floor and climbed onto Trace's lap as he sat back in the chair again, still looking at the picture.

"We'we killing bad guys." Null pointed briefly at the picture, and then settled against Trace's body.

"Bad guys?"

"Uh-huh." Null nodded and yawned. "I'm an enforcer like you." Enforcer came out sounding like enfowcew. Poor little Null. Someday his R's would sound like R's, but until they did, she would delight in how his little-boy voice mangled them into W's.

"You are, huh?"

"Uh-huh."

Trace wrapped a thick arm around Null's waist, holding his tiny body against his bigger, stronger one.

Cordray's heart melted just a little bit at the picture they created. So much like a father and son. Like a parent spending time with his child.

Normal.

Peaceful.

Simple.

All of which Cordray's life had never been.

Maybe Trace wasn't such a bad guy. After all, he was terrific with kids, which was something she never would have imagined two days ago. If someone had asked her then if she thought Trace would make a good father, she would have laughed in their face. Trace? A father? But now, seeing how he was with Null and Aiden, but especially Null, Cordray had to admit that she would have lost any bets where Trace's paternal instincts were concerned. The guy was big-time daddy material.

Cordray became faintly aware of Aiden quietly braiding her hair, her little fingers dancing with the sureness of an adult's as she absently and swiftly twisted strands of her hair into tiny braids.

If Aiden didn't grow up to be the world's most famous hairdresser, she would be surprised.

Null snuggled against Trace's body, his chubby cheeks rosy, his blue eyes twinkling.

"So, you like my pictuwe, Twace?"

Trace handed it back to him. "I think it's awesome."

Null's smile widened to show his perfect baby teeth. "I'm gonna be just like you when I gwow up. Big and stwong and cool . . ."

Trace chuckled. "I'm sure you will, little man." He met Cordray's gaze again. "Did you hear that? I'm cool."

"Poor kid just doesn't know you, yet." She couldn't keep from smiling, but she didn't care. Trace had earned a little kindness.

He smiled back at her, and for the moment, she and Trace found a middle ground . . . a field of grey between the black and white where they usually existed with one another.

"Oh, I think Null's assessment is pretty accurate." He hugged the little boy more tightly, squeezing the side of his tummy. "Isn't it, little man?"

Null giggled and nodded.

"See?" Trace said to her. "It's final. I'm cool."

She sighed and lost herself for several long moments in the idea that Trace might actually be a good guy. A great guy. The perfect guy.

"Thank you," she mouthed at him.

One of his eyebrows arched as a soft smile touched his lips, and he lifted his hand to his chest, gently jerked back, and made an expression as if she'd shot him.

With an exasperated roll of her eyes, she grinned and shook her head as she grabbed the remote off the coffee table and clicked through the channels, stopping when she found *The Lord of the Rings*.

Aiden and Null loved *The Lord of the Rings*, and they settled in, fascinated with the quest for the one true ring.

Aiden's fingers still worked through Cordray's hair, building a nice collection of braids, but before long, her hands grew limp and fell to Cordray's chest.

When Cordray looked down, Aiden's eyes were closed, her pink lips open, her body draped against the curves of Cordray's. She looked over to find Null passed out on Trace, face up, arms hanging at his sides. Trace had one arm still wrapped around Null's waist, and he was looking at the picture Null had drawn.

"He sees you as a father figure," Cordray said softly.

Trace looked up at her. "Huh?"

She gestured gently toward Null. "He never knew his father, so he sees you as a father figure."

Trace set the drawing on the table and glanced down at Null. "Oh." After a short hesitation, he said, "What happened to their parents?"

Cordray smoothed her palm over Aiden's golden, silky hair. "Their father was a full-blood who worked on the wrong side of the law more often than not. He was killed in a deal gone bad before they were born. Their mother was a human. She was diagnosed with breast cancer when they were only a few months old. She died six months later. I found them in an orphanage within a month of her death."

"Their father didn't turn their mother?"

She shook her head. "No. I don't know why, but he never made her his davala. Probably because of his illegal activities. My bet is that he didn't want to petition Bain for permission. That would have put him on Bain's radar." She shrugged one shoulder. "I would have just done it without getting permission, especially if I was already a criminal, anyway. Then again, this is all just speculation since I don't really know what his reasons were for not changing her."

Trace looked back down at Null. "He's a tough little guy."

"Yes, he is. They both are." She paused then added, "So are you." She nibbled the inside of her lip. "And I'm sorry for what I said to you in the kitchen. I was angry and out of line. I didn't mean it." As much as she hated having to apologize, something about apologizing to him was easier.

His face shaded red, and he lowered his head. "Yeah, me, too. What I said to you . . ."

"I know. It's okay."

"No, it's not okay. You didn't deserve that. I never should have done what I did this afternoon, and I never should have insulted you. I'm sorry, okay?"

They stared at each other for a drawn-out moment, and then she looked away and nodded tightly. "Okay."

For the next few minutes, they watched the movie in awkward silence. Then Trace cleared his throat as if putting the period at the end of one chapter and preparing to start a new one.

"So, what about the other kids?" he asked. "Where did they come from?"

She gently brushed her palm down Aiden's hair. "Various places. I find most of them lost inside the human foster care system."

Trace turned his attention back to the picture Null had drawn then set it down. He took a deep breath, blew it out, and fidgeted. "You, um . . ." He kept his gaze averted. "You're, uh . . . you're good with them." He coughed quietly and cleared his throat.

"Gee, Trace, you sound a little sick." She grinned. "That must have been hard for you to say."

His eyes met hers then instantly broke contact. "You have no idea."

She almost laughed but stopped herself so she didn't wake up Aiden. "I don't know, lice boy. I might have *some* idea."

He scowled at her. "I don't have lice."

This time she did laugh but abruptly caught herself as Aiden shifted against her. "I should pay Null for giving me that little nugget this morning."

"You're pushing your luck, *Coco.*" But his tone wasn't nearly as antagonistic as it had been earlier. Dare she say, he actually sounded playful, as if he were enjoying himself.

"Then I suppose I shouldn't dig for more information about Brak, huh?"

Trace bristled. "No. Definitely not."

"Okay." She held up her free hand. "You've earned a reprieve. No Brak talk tonight. I was only kidding, anyway."

"You? Kidding? Have I entered an alternate dimension?"

She sighed. "Is it so hard to believe I might not be the total bitch you think I am? Is it that hard to fathom I might actually be a nice person?"

He regarded her for a second. "I suppose it's possible. You *are* good with the kids. Maybe it's just your adult skills that lack."

"Or maybe I just don't like people who break the law?" Why, oh why, was she ruining a good thing? Bringing up what had brought them together in the first place was a surefire way to destroy the peace between them.

"And maybe I just don't like intrusive witches who can't keep their minds to themselves."

And there it went. The peace. Right out the door.

"And maybe I wouldn't have to be intrusive if more people didn't screw around with evidence."

"I only screwed with evidence because I was ordered to." Trace's face hardened.

Her blood began to boil. "You should have refused to follow those orders."

"And if I had, my pal would have been put to death to leave his pregnant mate inside a living hell."

Cordray huffed. "You don't know that."

"And you don't know that he wouldn't have been killed."

"You still shouldn't have broken the law."

Trace scowled at her. "I did, and I'd do it again to save an innocent male's life. It's called loyalty. It's called compassion. Maybe you should try it."

"You're a loose cannon."

"Only when provoked."

Cordray worked hard not to raise her voice, aware of the sleeping toddler in her arms. "Your actions could have started another war. They still could."

"How do you figure, sweetheart?"

They were back to sweetheart, were they?

"I told you not to call me that."

"Fine, whatever. How do you figure my actions could start another war, *Cordray*?"

She leaned toward him. "As an enforcer, you have rules to follow, *Traceon*. If you don't follow those rules and run off half-cocked, or if you follow the misguided orders of your commander without thinking of the consequences and end up fu—" She glanced down at Aiden. "I mean, *messing* with the wrong people, or even killing them with that out-of-control hand of yours, you could set off a chain reaction that could bring the races into a head-to-head confrontation."

"I don't see it that way."

"Of course not. You're too busy being a hotheaded ass."

"Hey, I could have killed you in Bain's dungeon, swee—Cordray. I could have easily snapped your neck, and we wouldn't even be having this discussion right now. But I didn't. I let you live when I was already compromised. Is that really how a hotheaded ass behaves?"

Actually, no it wasn't. The way he'd been in Bain's dungeon, holding her by the neck through the bars, his irises tinged yellow, she had seen inside his mind and known how close she'd come to death. But he'd held back. Something had reined him in and he'd let her live.

"Why didn't you just kill me, Trace? What stopped you?"

He obstinately sank back into the chair. His frown deepened as his jaw set in such a way that he looked like he refused to say another word.

"Tell me," she said, verbally pushing him. "Why *didn't* you kill me that day?"

His pale eyes flinched, and a quiet growl broke through his chest. "Because . . ."

"Because why?" Cordray glared at him.

For several seconds, silence stretched between them, and she began to think he wouldn't break.

"You might as well tell me or I'll just go in and see your thoughts for myself. You know I can."

That pissed him off even more, but he didn't respond to the threat. Just looked away as if he knew he was backed into a corner and hated how it felt.

He remained silent for several more seconds. Finally, he sneered and said, "Something told me killing you would be a mistake. That I would regret it if I did. Now, I'm kind of regretting that I didn't." He frowned and glanced away. A moment later, he exhaled a frustrated breath as his shoulders fell. "That's not true. I'm glad I didn't kill you that day, but I wish I could understand what made me stop."

Cordray studied him as he turned his attention back to Null, the wind suddenly gone from his sails.

Rigid stillness settled over them again. Peace wasn't re-emerging.

This feeling was too tense to be peace. But at least the aggression from a moment ago was gone.

"Why do you hate me so much?" she said quietly. "Is it because I had the unfortunate task of revealing what you and the others did to Bain's guards? I couldn't *not* tell Bain what you'd done, Trace. I work for him. I can't lie to him." When he didn't answer immediately, she said, "Or is there another reason?"

His gaze lifted to hers. "Why do *you* hate *me* so much?" He threw her own words back at her. "Is it because I had the misfortune of following orders to protect my comrade? Tristan is *my* boss. I work for him. When he gives me an order, I can't second-guess him. I have to trust that he knows the best course of action. It's why *your* boss made Tristan *my* boss. Because he had faith in his ability to lead and make the hard choices so I wouldn't have to." He stared at her.

Well, hell, she hadn't thought of the situation in those terms before. Trace made a good point. To disobey Tristan would be like her disobeying Bain. Not that she didn't disagree with her half-brother occasionally, but she didn't usually disobey him outright.

Her head began to ache. She didn't want to talk about this, anymore. Besides, she needed to get going. She had to get ready for Grudge Match and still wanted to investigate the pedway afterward if she had time.

"Look," she said, sighing, "I don't want to fight with you. Not tonight. Not when I've got to get ready for work." She already had enough on her mind. She didn't need to add yet another argument with Trace to the pile.

"Fine." He turned his attention to the movie.

Cordray stroked Aiden's hair. She didn't hate Trace. As much as she fought with him, called him names, and insulted him, she never once felt any hatred toward him. In fact, the exact opposite was true. She was fascinated by him. In awe of him. Jealous, even. Jealous because he had friends like Micah and Sam. And jealous because they had him.

She wanted what they all had with each other. What Micah and Sam got from Trace.

Him.

She wanted him.

She saw that now.

But damn it, it was so much easier to say she didn't. So much easier to push him away than to risk her heart.

As Frodo met the benevolent elves in the movie, she slid her gaze his direction.

Null had turned over and now lay on his stomach, with his head on Trace's shoulder. All the fresh air today had wiped the kids out.

"You're really good with him," she whispered.

Trace glanced down at the little boy then met her gaze.

She sighed as her heart opened, which was exactly what she'd been fighting so hard to prevent.

Too late.

It was done.

"Trace . . ." She briefly pursed her lips as she looked away. Being genuinely nice to him almost felt traitorous, but she was weary of fighting. Weary of pushing him away, when all she wanted was to pull him closer. Sighing again, she glanced back at him. When she spoke again, her voice was a gentle whisper. "Trace, I don't hate you. It would be easier if I did, but I don't."

God, hearing her own voice speak those words was both nauseating and exhilarating.

Blame it on the night. On the children's peaceful influence. On the full moon—was there a full moon tonight? The point was, whatever reason she had for warming to him and feeling the need to finally open up was not her own doing. Something else controlled her tonight. Something other than reality.

And the reality was that she was insanely crazy about the guy.

She was as hot on Trace as sizzle on bacon.

And all she wanted was to take a bite.

A long, luxurious, erotic bite.

TRACE COULD ONLY STARE.

Was Cordray coming on to him? Maybe their interlude earlier today had affected her more than she'd let on. It sure had with him, because he wouldn't have minded a replay of that action. But why now? He'd given her the opportunity to go there with him again when they'd been cleaning up the kitchen, and she'd slammed the door on the idea in glorious fashion, using the F-word on him. Freak. That had shut down all prospects of a rematch. So, her behavior now confused him.

Maybe he was reading more into the moment than there was. Her admission that she didn't hate him could just be a result of the truce she'd called.

He held her gaze for a long, drawn-out minute, just staring.

Finally, he admitted, "I don't hate you, either."

And, really, he didn't. She scared him, which was why he let loose on her all the time. She reminded him of those kids he'd grown up with. The ones who'd bullied him. The ones he'd never stood up to. She reminded him of Beth, the pretty girl he'd had a crush on who'd never given him the time of day.

Now, Cordray was the pretty girl he had a crush on. The beautiful female he couldn't wrest his eyes from. Covered in tattoos, with a ruby stud pierced through the side of her nose, a gold lip ring, and rings of silver and platinum covering every finger, she was an image of Gothic beauty. A vampire princess in modern times, clad in black, with raven hair streaked with turquoise and electric blue. Never had he seen a more striking female. Not even Sam, whom he adored.

Even so, she still reminded him of Beth. She teased and taunted him mercilessly, and all he wanted was to catch her eye.

And while he'd never stood up for himself when he was a child, he'd conditioned himself in the past two hundred years to do exactly that and protect his heart.

Even Micah had reminded him of his bullied childhood at first. But he'd forced himself to push through that barrier, because he'd known the rewards for befriending Micah would be worth the effort to overcome his resentment and feelings of isolation.

He just hadn't counted on Micah taking him in so wholly and unconditionally.

And Sam. He couldn't forget Sam in all this. She'd welcomed him in a way he'd never felt before. She and Micah loved him. And he loved them in return.

Wasn't it possible that if he dropped his guard a little, he'd find that he and Cordray could get along, too? That maybe a friendship with her would be just as rewarding as the one he'd discovered with Micah?

Maybe even more, because the feelings coursing through his blood felt stronger than mere friendship. These were lustful, dark, and heady emotions that awakened his anatomy and made his chest vibrate with needful warmth.

Her slender, black eyebrows drew in tight. "If neither of us hates the other, why do we fight so much?"

He shrugged. "I don't know, but I don't hate you. I'd like to say I do, but I don't."

They had definitely entered an alternate dimension. This was the most pleasant conversation they'd ever had with one another. And it came directly on the heels of another of their infamous fights.

She curled her legs under her as she shifted her hold on Aiden. "Tell me. If you could go back to that day at Io's house — the day when you altered those guards' memories — would you change anything? Would you do anything differently?"

She wasn't attacking him. She wasn't goading him. She genuinely sounded curious, as if his answer was the key to some personal mystery she was trying to figure out about herself.

He thought about it a few seconds. Shit had been fucked up in Io's basement that day, but his actions had kept Io alive.

He offered her a crooked, if not slightly guilty smile. "No."

"Why not?" Her tone wasn't accusatory, only curious.

"Because I know I did the right thing. I know I saved Io's life that day. I bought him and Miriam time to fully mate one another, and that's ultimately what brought King Bain around."

Aiden shifted against Cordray, snuggling closer and pulling Cordray's attention away for a moment. She wrapped her arms more tightly around the little girl and kissed the top of her head. Then she smiled sympathetically at Trace.

"You know, I was just doing my job when I fixed the guards' minds and discovered what you'd done. It wasn't personal. I wasn't intentionally trying to get you in trouble."

"I know." He glanced down at the top of Null's head. "And I was just doing my job. Keeping a friend safe." And he considered everyone on his team a friend even if they didn't feel the same way about him.

"I know that now." She rubbed her lips together and played her tongue against the metal ring through her bottom lip. "And I would have done the same thing in your shoes."

Trace narrowed his eyes on her. Then his lips turned up at the ends. "So the truth comes out. Why am I not surprised?"

"Now, don't go gettin' cocky on me." She rolled her eyes and let out an exasperated exhale. "I'm just saying that, on a personal level, I agree with what you did. It was ballsy, bold, and unusually selfless. Not many would put themselves at such risk to help someone else who was obviously doing something that would get him into serious trouble."

"And yet, you're telling me you would have." He tilted his head, enjoying this rare moment of humility from his nemesis. "What does that say about you, C?" He grinned. "Sounds like I'm not the only rebel in the king's employ."

Her mouth quirked on one side. "No, you're not. I'm the first to admit that I've gone against Bain a time or two."

"Or a hundred."

She threw him a kiss-my-ass glare that held zero bite. "I've never directly disobeyed him, but I'll admit, I do sometimes operate outside the law."

"Sometimes?" He grinned. "Why do I get the feeling that sometimes for you is more like the majority of the time."

"Because it takes one to know one, doesn't it? Isn't that how the saying goes?"

"Are you saying that you and I are alike?"

She lazily combed her fingers through Aiden's blond ringlets then twirled one around her thumb. "Maybe we are." She paused. "Who knows? Maybe that's why we fight so much."

He wasn't sure he wanted to think about the implications of that statement. On one hand, it was reassuring to think he'd found someone who understood him, at least on some level, because they were so much alike. On the other, if he and Cordray were similar creatures, did that mean he was like those kids who teased him growing up, because, at least until now, that's how he'd seen her.

It was enough to give him pause.

On the flipside, if they were so much alike, maybe she had endured the same kind of childhood he had. Or at least one that was similar.

"Earlier, when you said you understood what it was like to be alone. What did you mean by that?"

She looked away and bowed her head. "It's nothing."

From the way she said it, whatever she held back was definitely something, not nothing.

"The hell it is."

She tensed and cast a fearful, angry glance his way. "I'm not going to talk about it with you, so drop it."

He could almost see her walls shooting back up.

So much for finding their happy place.

He sighed. "And we were having such a pleasant conversation. I knew it couldn't last."

She sat forward and scooped Aiden into her arms. "Look, it's getting late, and I've got things to do, so — "

"What things?"

"*Things.* And they're none of your business." Yep, the walls were back in place.

It almost felt comfortable getting back to where they fought with one another all the time. Almost. Because he'd kind of enjoyed the softer side of Cordray and their attempt at getting along for a change.

"Fine. Whatever." He was beat, anyway. Working all day had worn him out, and he hadn't gotten as much sleep this afternoon as he'd wanted, thanks to their tryst.

He hefted Null in his arms, stood, and followed Cordray through the dining room, the kitchen, out the back door, across the lawn, and into the dorm. The older kids were still up in the rec room, watching a movie over a bowl of popcorn. Brenna was reading a book. Mya was in the kitchen preparing mugs of hot cocoa.

Upstairs, Cordray led him down the hall to a room at the end. Inside were two twin beds. She bent beside the far bed, pulled back the Barbie Doll cover and pink sheets, then set Aiden down.

Aiden squirmed and protested softly then quieted when Cordray placed her Pooh Bear in her arms.

Then Cordray turned toward him. In the dim light from the hall, her bright-blue eyes looked even more vivid, shining up at him as she reached for Null. The moment her hand touched his, electricity pulsed up his arm, sending warmth and a cascade of tingles down his spine to settle in his scrotum.

Well, not exactly settle. More like swim around like newborn tadpoles, circling, bumping against the sides of his balls, and making like a party in his sac.

She paused as if she'd felt the shockwave, too. Then she drew in a breath and shakily lifted Null out of his arms.

"Can you pull back the sheets?" she said, her voice airy and trembling.

He bent, dragging in her scent as he pulled the green and blue dinosaur-covered comforter back then did the same with the blue sheets.

Cordray leaned over and gingerly set Null on the bed.

God, she smelled good. Like midnight oranges covered in dew. Honey-scented, I-want-to-lick-it-off-her-skin dew.

She pulled the covers up and tucked Null in.

Then she turned her head toward Trace. They were still bent over Null's bed. Only inches separated them.

Her gaze fell to his mouth as her lips parted.

A force inside him urged him to close the distance. To taste her. To claim her.

He'd never felt such a magnetic attraction, not even to Micah or Sam.

"We should probably leave and let them sleep," she said without moving.

"Yeah." He didn't move, either. At least not at first. He stared at her in the darkness, enraptured by the magical hold she had on him. Then he forced himself to stand and moved toward the door, even though it felt like he was dragging his feet through quick-drying cement.

In the hall, he turned and watched her close the door. She was facing away from him as if she was purposely avoiding his eyes. All he wanted was for her to turn around and look at him again. To see her vibrant, blue eyes lock onto his.

The door snicked quietly closed. Cordray hesitated, her shoulders rising and falling heavily as she breathed. She seemed to be waiting for something.

Finally, she turned around.

Their gazes met.

And all the air whooshed out of Trace's lungs.

In an instant, he had her in his arms and swung her around, pinning her to the opposite wall as he claimed her mouth with the primal hunger of a lion devouring its prey. Heat whipped through his body, fire coursed through his veins. All he could see, hear, smell, feel, and taste was Cordray. Vivacious, untamed, tangy-sweetness-on-his-tongue, storm-in-his-blood Cordray.

And Jesus, she was kissing him back. Kissing him like her life depended on it. Clawing at his back through his shirt, biting his bottom lip, gasping and whimpering as though she had never felt anything so intense, so gratifying.

He certainly hadn't.

The way her breasts mashed against his chest felt more perfect than anything he'd ever known. The way her silken hair twisted around his fingers as he clutched her closer was a kind of shackling he'd never experienced as a submissive, but it bound him more tightly to her than any chain or thick leather cuff had ever bound him to a bench or cross.

She tethered him to her with her sighs, her rough tugs against his shirt, the on-the-edge-of-painful nips she gave his lips.

More. He needed more of this dazzling female he'd tried to hate but could no longer deny. More of her body. More of her skin.

In a flash of daring, he jerked the hem of her shirt away from her body and drove his hand underneath. She whimpered as his palm swept up her tight abdomen, driving toward her full breast.

God, he needed to feel her, hold her, rip her shirt and bra away and close his mouth over her nipple. He'd never caressed a female like this before. Had never felt a female's body without being strapped to a table or chair, or tied to a St. Andrew's Cross. Never of his own free will had he experienced such pleasure, but with Cordray, he reached new territory. He'd found a female who excited him without whipping him. A female who commanded his body simply by her presence. A female he wanted in every way imaginable and more.

His fingers pushed against the underwire of her bra.

But just as he began to cup her breast and feel its fleshy weight against his palm, Cordray jerked away and shoved his hand out from under her shirt.

"No!" She staggered sideways, pushing him away.

Her retreat was so abrupt that Trace fell forward, knocking his head against the wall where her face had been just a moment ago.

Struggling to right himself as intense heat continued coursing through his limbs, making them weak, he turned his head toward her and frowned. "What the—?"

"I don't want this." Cordray stared at him as if she couldn't believe what had just happened. As if she no longer knew who he was or even who she was. "I never wanted this. With you. Ever." She swallowed hard and urgently backed away, fear shining in her eyes.

Trace took a steadying breath, trying to cool the fire blasting through his veins, making his cock a rod of steel. He hadn't thought he wanted *this*, either, but now that *this* had happened, he wanted it back. He wanted more.

"Whether you wanted it or not, it happened. And you can't tell me you don't want it as much as I do." He started toward her, the need to close the distance between them stronger than blood thirst. He couldn't deny the magnetic pull she had on him, anymore. She belonged to him. She was his. And he would claim her. "You can't deny—"

"No." Cordray continued backing away, more quickly now. "Just stop. Don't you dare touch me again. Don't you dare . . ." Her pained expression gave away her confusion. Denial warred with desire, twisting her features into conflicted angles. Moisture welled in her eyes, her jaw clenched, her throat worked as if she were trying not to throw up, cry, or both, and she was practically panting as she reached the stairs. "Just stay away from me, Trace. It's better that way." With that, she darted down the stairs.

A moment later, the front door opened and slammed shut, and Trace was left standing in the hall, unsure what had just happened and what it meant, with a boner as hard as marble straining inside his jeans.

As he heard the whine of the Ducati tear down the driveway, a dull ache bloomed to life inside his chest, followed quickly by the thought that if anything happened to her out there—if anyone so much as harmed one hair on her beautiful head—he would rain death down like the apocalypse.

Painful, excruciating, bloody death.

Caused by him.

His hand.

His power.

Because, yeah, Cordray was his.

CHAPTER 17

As CORDRAY SPED AWAY FROM ASYLUM, her pulse raced as fast as the Ducati's engine. Her body still tingled from the explosive sensory overload Trace had awakened inside her, but with every moment she fled his presence, the sensations faded. Within seconds, the luscious feelings were nothing but a memory. Once more, she became a barren wasteland, her sense of touch dormant and absent.

How had she let him kiss her? And not just kiss her, but invade her? She'd told herself giving in to what she was feeling was a bad idea. She'd sworn to protect her heart and the fragile emotions that dwelled within it.

But in those all-too-short moments, she'd never wanted a male more. Never needed to feel touch as desperately as she needed to feel Trace's. He did things to her. He made her want. And wanting wasn't something she'd experienced in a long time.

Everything about him was perfection.

His body.

His face.

His powerful hand.

He was the most attractive male she had ever seen.

Even more attractive than—

She blinked and focused on the road as a sorrowful ache speared her heart. Trace had the same angular face as Gideon. The same seductively heavy eyelids and brooding sensuality.

But Trace's eyes were both kinder and more intense than Gideon's. And his lips were fuller, more sensuous. Gideon's mouth had always been set in a hard line, and his eyes had always held an almost palpable coldness, as if both were a shield to throw people off his benevolent nature and warm heart.

But her attraction to Trace went beyond his face. He held himself with an air of power and aloof confidence that beckoned her in the same way sunlight beckoned a flower to turn toward its warmth.

Not since Gideon had she felt such yearning. But as much as she had desired Gideon above all others, she wanted Trace more. And that terrified her.

That was why she needed to get as far away from Asylum as she could.

Good thing her Grudge Match audition was tonight, because if she stayed at the ranch one more second, she would lose the willpower to resist him.

God help her, but she was setting herself up to be hurt all over again. To feel heartache's traitorous stab.

Which meant Grudge Match was just what she needed. What better way to eradicate her fears than by beating somebody up?

She sped toward Chicago's South Side and the address she'd been given, ready to channel this heartache into beating the ever-living shit out of the unfortunate souls selected to face her in this thing called the gauntlet.

She had no doubt she would make it through. This was one time when her lack of feeling worked to her advantage. There wasn't a lot her combatants could do to stop her, and since guns and other piercing weapons weren't allowed in the gauntlet—according to the rules—she didn't have to worry about being shot or stabbed, which could actually do damage without her knowing it.

She rolled through a part of Chicago that law-abiding humans steered clear of. Human gangs ruled block-by-block here, dealing drugs, shooting up, pimping, and protecting their turf.

Fools. If only they knew how close they were to extinction, because if the drecks ever took over the world, the first thing they would do after eradicating vampires would be to enslave humanity.

Not that all drecks wore a shroud of villainy. Severin was half-dreck, and he was one of the good guys, and his dreck mother was as sweet as they came. But the majority of drecks followed Premier Royce, who had his corrupt hand in every evil undertaking Cordray had ever encountered. She just didn't have tangible proof, because while Bain knew of her gifts to see the truth inside people's thoughts, Royce would never honor her word against any member of his race. Which meant that until she found a smoking gun implicating Royce, there was nothing she could give Bain to throw in his face during one of their meetings.

As a CPD patrol car flew through an intersection up ahead, it's red and blue lights flashing and siren blaring, Cordray sighed at the folly of man.

The only things standing between total dreck domination and the annihilation of human civilization were vampires. Yep, that's right. A race of beings humans had glorified in their silly Hollywood horror movies — incorrectly, by the way — was what allowed gangbangers all over Chicago the freedom to kill each other over a stretch of turf three city blocks long.

In the heart of the South Side's warehouse district, she pulled up to the address she'd been given and hopped off her bike.

A hooded male who reminded her of the Grim Reaper approached. She couldn't see his face, but he was big, broad, and all business.

"Turn around," he said, swirling his index finger.

She did, and he began patting her down.

"You've read the rules?" he asked, his deep voice thickly accented, but she couldn't place his nationality.

"Yes."

His hands skimmed down both legs, back up to her hips, then down her arms. "Face me."

When she turned, she saw that he wore a white mask like the ones worn by the dance crew JabbaWockeeZ. Plain. No markings. Pure white, with holes for the eyes, nostrils, and mouth. Under his hood he wore a dark-grey skullcap with a red band around the hem.

Interesting. In only a few days she'd stumbled upon two males wearing masks. What were the odds?

"Nice mask," she said, as his palms began traveling over the front of her the way a police officer would search a suspect for weapons. At least he wasn't lewd and crude, stopping to fondle her breasts or grab her crotch. Jabba-man was all business.

He didn't reply to her compliment. Just finished frisking her. "She's clean," he said, speaking into a transmitter as he turned her toward a dark alley ten yards away.

"Then send her in." The leisurely male voice that came through the speaker was rich and elegant, the words flowing smoothly on a gentle lilt that sounded almost like amusement, yet not quite. More like curiosity.

"Go ahead." The man in the mask gestured for her to enter the alley.

"Don't I even get a good luck?" She arched one eyebrow at him.

He didn't move, not even a flinch. Just stood with his hands clasped in front of him military-style, feet shoulder-width apart. But she had a feeling that behind his mask, he was grinning.

When he didn't respond, she simply turned, slipped on the brass knuckles she'd brought with her, which were totally allowed in the gauntlet, and headed toward the mouth of the alley.

A few feet from the entrance, she stopped and surveyed the dark narrow gap between buildings, tilting her head as she studied the shadows. *This* was the gauntlet?

She'd expected it to be more ominous. More threatening. More this-could-end-your-life.

The alley looked more like the backdrop for a B-rated horror flick than a bone-crushing beat-down waiting to happen.

Whatev. If this pansy-assed stroll along the yellow brick road was what she needed to go through to find a connection between Premier Royce and Bishop's lab experiments, she would play Dorothy. Just as long as she didn't have to wear that disgustingly quaint powder-blue dress. But the ruby slippers were aces.

She would never turn down such a fine pair of footwear.

Let's do this.

The dull thud of her rubber soles on the wet concrete broke through the sounds of dripping water from the surrounding buildings as she entered the alley.

Fog turned what dim light there was into a milky haze, and condensation dribbled down the brick walls like alien secretions. Water *drip-dripped* somewhere in the darkness ahead.

Movement to her left!

She ducked as a thick arm swung at her head, wielding a length of heavy chain. Fast as lightning, she swept her leg out and knocked her attacker on his ass and jumped on him.

Crack! Crack!

Two hits and he was out cold. Probably with a broken jaw.

Easy enough. She drew a checkmark in the air with her finger then rose to her feet, standing over her unconscious assailant.

Then she eyed the chain. That pretty thing could come in handy.

She pried the chain from his muscled fingers and draped it around her neck before venturing farther in. *What was once yours is now mine, asshole.*

The gauntlet had to get harder than that guy. He'd just been bait, giving her a false sense of security.

Well, fuck that. She didn't do secure. And she didn't do false. Despite her sissy-faced footwork with Trace earlier, this Dorothy was a bazooka-toting badass compared to that bitch from Oz. If someone worse awaited her, he—or she—had better be prepared for an ass-whooping.

Her heavy combat boots thunked on the pavement as she marched onward. She didn't want these assholes to think she was afraid.

Because . . . well . . . she wasn't. Maybe she was scared of her body's response to Trace, but she'd be damned before she let something as trite as losing a little blood or breaking a bone stop her from doing her job.

Two vampires jumped out from the adjacent alleyway, one holding a bat and the other a whip.

Oh really now? A whip? So cliché. So unimaginative.

The one with the bat took a swing, and she dodged. He swung twice more, wielding the bat like it was a sickle and she was the field of wheat he was trying to cut down.

She heard the crack of the whip and felt a whisper of contact on her arm. Well, she didn't so much feel it as see her coat sleeve twitch against the bite of leather on leather.

She glanced at her arm to find he'd sliced a tear in her coat. Damn it! Enough of this shit!

Gripping the length of chain, she swung it over her head, and shot it toward whip boy as she double-dutched over another home-run swing. The chain whirled around her attacker's neck as she landed back on her feet.

"How do you like *my* whip, asshole?" She yanked, choking him, and spun around in time to clock bat boy in the nose with the sole of her boot before he could break her arm with another swing for the fences.

Seconds later, she dispatched them both to the wet pavement— alive but unconscious—then collected her chain and continued on. A glance at her forearm showed it was bleeding where the whip had sliced through her coat. What did that guy have on the tip of that thing? Razors?

As she walked, she yanked her sleeve up and licked the cut. Her venom healed it within seconds.

Too bad venom didn't heal leather coats. She let her torn sleeve fall back down her arm and scowled at the shadows, ready, waiting, torqued to get on with it and make it through to the inner circle. But no one erupted from the shadows to take her on. After another ten yards and no action, it felt like the onslaught was over.

No way. There had to be more to the gauntlet than that.

As if on cue, the alley became eerily quiet. *Too* quiet. Too dark. The shadowed exit was less than ten yards away, but she stopped, anyway. Something wasn't right. Call it instinct, but Cordray had learned to trust that deathly calm usually signaled a coming storm. Shifty, wary, and ready for anything, she took a cautious step forward.

Then another.

The scent of a dreck just beyond the exit touched her senses.

A dreck? It was one more clue to add to her growing list of things she hadn't expected about Grudge Match.

Was he watching? Waiting?

Despite taking a mental sweep, she got nothing.

Then she heard a low growl come from a dark corridor to her right. Then a snarl.

She took a defensive step to the left, preparing for whatever was coming for her.

"What are you afraid of, bitch?" A vampire taller and wider than any she had ever seen — even bigger than Bain — stepped out of the shadows.

Finally. An adversary worth fighting.

"Nothing," she said. "Just waiting for the show to start."

He took a lumbering step forward, all power and force. "You've got balls."

"You have no idea." She tightened her grip on the chain, although she doubted it would do much good against Sasquatch.

He cracked his knuckles then his neck with side to side snaps.

"Maybe I'll just knock you out and fuck you," he said with another steady step toward her. "Pretty little vampire like you. You'd be a nice fuck, wouldn't you?" His hands curled into fists.

"Only if you can get it up. But even if you could, you'd actually have to find your pecker to do something with it, and I doubt you'll be able to find something that small."

The beast's brow furrowed as if he didn't quite understand. Or maybe he hadn't expected her response and didn't know how to react now that she'd made it clear she wasn't going to shrivel up like a nancy and beg him not to hurt her.

"What's wrong?" she said. "Am I talking too fast for you?"

Sasquatch recovered and took an ominous step forward. "Bitch." Then he lunged and tackled her to the ground.

Since she didn't have to deal with the nuisance of pain, she throttled him two-fisted, slamming her brass-knuckled fists into either side of his neck right before his elbow crashed into her chest. She didn't feel it, but the shock to her lungs made her cough and gasp for air, anyway. But he was worse off than she was, clutching his neck as he rolled off her. She leaped behind him and swung the chain around his neck and pulled with everything she had.

But this fucker was a strong SOB. He grabbed the chain, pulled himself to a crouch, and then flung himself forward. She flew over his head and landed on her back. Pebbles of pocked pavement scuttled past her as he reached down and grabbed her by the hair. With a severe yank, he pulled her to her feet so she faced him.

"So you came to fight, huh?" he said, breathing in her face.

He needed a mint.

"You're about two IQ points shy of a genius, aren't you? Isn't it called the gauntlet? We are supposed to fight here, right?" She did *not* like this guy pulling on her braids one little bit. Little Aiden had worked hard on them tonight before falling asleep, and this asshole was messing up her mad styling skills.

"I think you want Old Navy or the GAP," he said. "This place isn't for dainty things and little women."

"Then what are *you* doing here, dick face?"

For a split second, she thought he might laugh, but instead he scowled and pulled her hair harder. "That's some mouth you've got there, pretty thing." He gave her braids a sharp tug.

She'd had just about enough with the hair. "Since you're so keen on thinking I'm too much of a sissy to be here, let me clue you in on a little something," she said.

"Oh? What's that?" He loomed over her, sneering.

She mustered the sweetest smile she could under the circumstances. "Never touch a lady's hair."

"Is that so?" His grip on her hair tightened. "And just what are you going to do about it?"

This motherfucker was so done. "I don't think you understood me."

He encroached farther into her personal space. "Then maybe you should spell it out for me, bitch."

Hell, no. Trace could get away with calling her a bitch. But this guy? Not happening.

"I said . . ." She made a fist, and the metal of the brass knuckles bit into her palm. "Don't!" *Punch!* "Fucking!" *Punch!* "Touch!" *Punch!* "My!" *Punch!* "HAIR!" *Punch!* With the last strike to his nose, his head bounced back and smacked the wet pavement, knocking him out cold.

But at least he no longer had a lock on her coveted braids.

She kicked his hand away, took a deep breath, and flipped her hair over her shoulder as she straightened. "I warned you."

Applause from behind made her spin around. The dreck she'd scented earlier stepped into the diffuse light at the end of the alley. "Well done," he said, clapping his hands. "I haven't been this amused by a run through our gauntlet in ages."

From his aristocratic tone, she knew he was the one who'd spoken through the speaker to Jabba-man a few minutes ago.

Even in his human form, she could tell he didn't mask much more than the color of his skin. He wore his black hair long, and he had a goatee. For a dreck, he wasn't half bad looking. Cordray bet the ladies fell over their panties for this guy.

He wore an unassuming, untucked white button-up with the top three buttons undone, which showed off a hairless but sculpted dip between his pecs. Dark denim trousers, a silver and black TAG Heuer watch, and black dress boots gave him a fashionable-bookie-with-sex-appeal look.

"Who are you?" She narrowed her eyes on him.

"I'm Digon." He smiled like the perfect host. "Welcome to Grudge Match, Miss Cordray. Come with me."

She followed him out the back of the alley into a dark hall and tried to get a peek inside his mind, but he stopped, turned, and wagged a finger at her. "No mind sweeping. I don't like it. And you already know I'm well-trained in my ability to block."

She recalled her earlier mind sweep and how it had turned up nothing even though she'd known he was standing in the shadows.

She sighed. "Can't blame a girl for trying, right?"

There was that crooked, amused smile again. "No. I can't. If I were in your shoes, I'd try to poke around in my head, too. But don't, or I'll kick you out." He issued her a dark, warning look that emphasized he meant what he said. Then he turned and continued to lead her through a maze of alleyways and halls. "As for the rest of the club's members, you can try to poke around in their heads if you want, but if they find out, you're on your own." Without slowing or turning around, he raised one hand and pointed his index finger straight up for emphasis. "But I can assure you, I'm not the only one who gets pissed off when someone tries to traipse through my thoughts uninvited. Remember that before you go peeking. We're a loyal bunch, but a private one."

If only she had Micah's power to dip in and out of others' heads without being detected. She considered herself lucky if she was able to pull off silent mind sweeps, but Micah was able to do it without even trying.

Looked like she would have to do recon on this band of merry underground scrappers the old-fashioned way. By observation and making friends with them. Going mind spelunking was too risky.

What good would it do if she got kicked out of the club before she could even find out if there was a connection between them and Premier Royce or Bishop—or both.

"I take it you're in charge?" she said, following him.

"I am."

They walked in silence for a few seconds.

"Where are you taking me, anyway?"

"To my office to sign some paperwork. Then I'll introduce you to the main floor." He paused, and Cordray could almost hear the smirk playing over his lips as he continued. "Then we'll see how well you do in the cage."

She noted that the dark, winding walkways were on a shallow decline and led below ground level. How low, she couldn't figure, though. "The cage?"

"Our version of the octagon."

Cordray's footsteps echoed up the high walls. "So, do I have to sign away my firstborn child or sign a contract with my own blood to make this official?"

Digon made a soft, amused sound. "We'll get to that when we reach my office, but we aren't *that* archaic." Silence stretched between them, and then he said, "So, Miss Cordray, how did you hear about Grudge Match?"

His long, dark hair billowed over his back as he led her down another passageway. He looked like a walking ad for hair care products.

"I was at Four Alarm the other night," she said, trying to sound nonchalant, "letting my fingers do the walking through the minds of some of the customers. A couple of your members were there and I saw Grudge Match in their thoughts." She was making this up on the fly, but the story was as plausible as any other she could think up, and while the story was almost true, she thought it better to leave out certain details. "It looked interesting, so . . . here I am."

Digon stopped and turned around. A frown creased his forehead as he stepped toward her and shifted into his dreck form. His blue skin shimmered for the split second it took to complete the transformation. "*Interesting*, you say? You thought Grudge Match sounded . . . *interesting*? We are not to be taken so lightly here. Do you know what you're about to walk into, Miss Cordray?"

"Just Cordray," she said. The formal address was for pussies and was starting to chafe her ass.

His spine straightened and he spurted an amused breath out his nose. "Well, do you know what goes on here, *Just Cordray*? *Exactly* what goes on here?"

"Drecks and vampires beat the shit out of each other?" She raised her eyebrows at him, daring him to deny what she'd read on their Dark Web site.

His eyes narrowed, and it looked as if he were contemplating how much to tell her. "We don't just beat the shit out of each other, *Just Cordray*. The things that go on here could start another war if King Bain or Premier Royce ever found out about them." He stepped closer and angled his handsome face, studying her. "Those that engage in our fights don't want another war. They want a safe place to act out their soldier fantasies, to expend their frustrations, to battle their natural-born enemy without repercussions. They are warriors without a war, *Just Cordray*. Grudge Match *is* their war, and what they do here is like Vegas. It stays here. Once they leave these halls" — he gestured elegantly at their surroundings — "once morning comes and they disperse back to their homes, their cubicles . . . their plain, ordinary, maple syrup lives . . . Grudge Match ceases to exist. But then they return, and the war begins again."

Digon inflected his speech as if he were a male of means from a bygone era. A cultured male familiar with the finer things in life, but in a way that bespoke ages-old discipline and moderation, not modernity's greed and gluttony. He came off as the kind of person who splurged on a twenty-eight-thousand-dollar bottle of Yamazaki single malt liquor then took a year to appreciate it before drinking it.

He stepped back. "There is a brotherhood here, *Just Cordray*. A sisterhood. A camaraderie. Despite the friction between our two races, members of Grudge Match have found a way to coexist in an environment where they can beat each other to within the brink of death and not feel the need to see through the urge to kill. Some even become friends, or as friendly as our two races can be. If nothing else, each member has come to respect the others, as well as what they've found here. So, while you find our little world *interesting*, it is not to be taken lightly."

"You make it sound like I'm going to find Jesus in there," she said.

He lifted his chin, studying her through narrowed eyes. "Maybe you will." His lips pressed into a thin line then relaxed. "You know, your flippant, lighthearted attitude could be grounds to ban you from the club, *Just Cordray*, but" — the corners of his mouth curled upward — "I like you. You made me smile back there." He gestured in the direction she assumed they'd come from. She was so turned around by all the twists and turns she wasn't sure which way was north. "You've got panache. Flair. And you passed our background check with impressive commendations. Our screener gave you high praise as a good fit."

Background check? She hadn't realized that was part of the application process. "Well then, my thanks to your screener. Maybe you'll introduce me so I can thank him personally."

The way Digon's blue eyes briefly dazzled made it clear he'd personally seen the results of her background check and had found something he liked. "Perhaps I'll introduce you next time. He was unable to join us this evening. However, all things considered, I think you'll fit in well here. But" — he raised one hand, his blue-tinted index finger extended in warning — "either you enter the world I created with the most serious of intent, or I escort you out now. It's your choice. Will you respect my rules and my arena, or are you trouble in the making?"

Digon made Grudge Match sound like some kind of cult. Like a nonfiction version of the fictional movie, *Fight Club*. The first rule of Fight Club is you don't talk about Fight Club. Insert Grudge Match for Fight Club, and it was the same goddamn thing, except without that hottie, Brad Pitt. Even Cordray could appreciate a handsome human like Brad.

All kidding aside, Cordray couldn't afford to lose this chance. Grudge Match was her way in. A way to obtain evidence against Royce. She could feel it.

Despite wanting to reply that she was, indeed, trouble in the making, she tilted her head in deference and said, "I promise to respect your rules and your arena. I'm here to participate, not stir up trouble."

What Digon didn't know wouldn't hurt him. After all, he was a dreck. All drecks were guilty until proven innocent, which gave her leeway to lie to him until she determined exactly whether he was friend or foe.

"Good." He uncrossed his arms and spun on his heel, once more leading her into the bowels of the building. "So, *Just Cordray,* the rules. If you still want to be a part of Grudge Match, you have to follow the rules." He began rattling them off as she fell in step beside him. "No knives. No blades of any kind. Nothing that will puncture or cut. No guns. Otherwise, you're free to use" — he nodded down at her hands — "brass knuckles, chains" — his gaze flicked to the chain still wrapped around her neck like a scarf — "as well as clubs, bats, or anything else you can hit your opponent with. Most prefer to use only their fists, and there are fights we call Raw Rage where no accoutrements are allowed. Raw Rage bouts are bodies only. None of this shit." He tapped her chain.

So, Digon *could* use unprovoked profanity. She had begun to wonder.

"Also," he said, "just in case I haven't already made this point clear, you're not to talk about what goes on here with anyone who's not already a member. The only exception is if you know someone you think would make a good candidate for membership. If you think someone would fit in well here, refer them to the application you filled out on our site. We'll process them and determine whether or not we'll issue them in invitation, but our decision is final. No second chances. But if anyone you refer to us sends up a red flag, you'll be placed on a six-month probation. If you do it twice, you'll go before our review board and face possible removal and could be banned from the club. So, choose those you refer to us wisely, *Just Cordray."*

Cordray nodded dramatically, saluting him. "Yes, oh mighty one. No loose lips about the secret club. And I will endeavor to send only the best cuts of meat to your cause."

Digon gave her a dubiously amused look as she pressed her lips together and pretended to turn a key and lock them. He stopped and spun toward her, looking her up and down. For several seconds, he said nothing, his expression unreadable. Cordray sighed and crossed her arms as she tilted her head with an air of annoyance. "Take a picture, Digon. Not only will it last longer, but it won't scratch your eyes out. I've been known to do that."

One side of his mouth lifted, and then he chuckled. It was a dark, majestic sound, as if Digon knew tremendous power above his current station. "I like you, *Just Cordray."* He shifted back into his human form, and his blue eyes turned dark brown. "You're not at all what I expected. You're full of verve. Quarrelsome even. But in a witty way that's a lovely change of pace among the females in the club, who more often than not are forcefully emphatic about how tough they are." He grinned and teased his goatee with his thumb and forefinger. "You're flippant . . . almost whimsical." He chuckled as he turned on the ball of his foot and started down the hall again "It's refreshing. Stimulating even."

Refreshing? No one had ever called her refreshing. Call the makers of Downy fabric softener, because Cordray Fresh was the new must-have scent.

"I like you, too, Digon," she said to his back as she fell in step behind him again. "You're stodgy. Like an English gentleman with a broomstick stuck up his ass, wanking off with one hand while holding a cup of tea in the other."

He broke into hardy laughter, pushing open the door to what was a surprisingly elegant office, gesturing for her to take a seat in a burgundy leather chair as he rounded the mahogany desk to what looked almost like a throne.

"Please, have a seat."

She parked her ass in the rich leather as he did the same behind the desk.

His dark eyes narrowed on her appreciatively. "I have a feeling you and I are going to get along splendidly, *Just Cordray*." He flipped open a slender, silver laptop.

She batted her lashes and forced a smile. "Just keep your hands to yourself, Diggy, and it'll be all good." After all, she didn't want to have to kill her best lead into Bishop's master plan just because he felt like taking a liberty or two.

"Diggy. Cute." He tapped a few keys, and the printer behind him stirred to life. "And there's no need to worry about my hands. I'm quite innocuous to the female membership, I can assure you."

"Why? Are you gay?"

His eyelids popped upward as his gaze dialed in on hers. Then his lips twisted into a subtle smile. "A valid question, given how I phrased my previous statement."

"And will I get a valid answer?"

He made a contemplative noise in his throat as he rotated his chair to snatch whatever he'd printed. Then he spun back around to face her.

"Perhaps I will rephrase my statement. I'm quite innocuous to *all* members, *Just Cordray*. I simply emphasized the female members because I am, in fact, unequivocally heterosexual." He leaned forward, sliding the piece of paper toward her. "I would prove it to you, but as I said, I don't pursue romantic entanglements with the members, even ones as strikingly beautiful as you." He bowed his head in dramatic deference. Clearly, he was making fun of her, but only because he knew she could take it.

"Ah, Diggy, you do say the sweetest things." She dismissed his flamboyantly insincere flirtation and perused the sheet of paper he'd just slid in front of her. "What's this?"

"Your contract." He folded his hands on his desk, back to all business. "It iterates what I've already told you about our rules. Read it thoroughly then sign it." He reached inside the top drawer and retrieved a pen, then placed it in front of her. Montblanc. Of course.

She reviewed all the points in detail then scribbled her John Hancock on the dotted line. Then she filled in a form with a few pertinent details, including her mobile number, as Digon explained that they don't use online files, which would be too easy to hack. And since secrecy and anonymity was of the utmost importance, he operated only out of hard files.

Smart, if not a bit antiquated.

"Now what?" She pushed the paper across the desk.

He tucked it into a leather folio, which he locked inside the top drawer.

He stood and gestured for her to join him. "Now I show you to the floor, *Just Cordray*."

She was in.

CHAPTER 18

RONAN PULLED HIS YAMAHA TO THE SIDE OF MONTROSE AVENUE behind Graceland Cemetery and shut off the engine. Once more, he checked his rearview mirror for a tail and found none. Looked like Micah and his buddies still hadn't caught his scent. Not that he expected they would or even could. He was too good at covering his tracks with the talents he'd learned from his father, which was about the only good thing he'd gotten from ol' dad other than the requisite sperm required to create him in the first place.

He was a ghost. A wraith passing through, nothing more. And he wanted to keep it that way.

But Cordray was getting close. She was cunning. More cunning than Micah. If anyone could find him, it was her, but tonight she was busy putzing around in Digon's world. Ronan had made sure of that so he could play with his new toy without worrying she might show up. Be that as it may, he still needed to pay her a visit to warn her away for good.

He had been pleasantly surprised to see her Grudge Match application hit his inbox this morning while they bantered back and forth. He wasn't sure if her interest in Grudge Match had to do with him or the work she did for her brother, but his inner thrill seeker hadn't been able to resist approving her for membership.

Oh sure, he'd had to doctor the background check to remove certain facts before showing it to Digon, but the potential payoff was worth it. He could use her preoccupation with the fight club to his advantage and slip out to do his extracurricular activities while Digon kept her entertained. Besides, taking such risks gave him a mental hard-on.

A Skeletor boner, as Cordray had put it. Yes, he'd been watching them as they floundered in that parking lot by the river. And listening. After all, that was part of the fun.

At any rate, it had been fortuitous that her application had cycled to him. Any of the others Digon had assigned to do background checks would have rejected it in a hot minute. All because she worked for the king. If only they knew her real relationship to King Bain. How would they feel if they knew they now had royal blood fighting in the cage?

As pleased as he was to have slipped her into the club, he'd stuck himself between a rock and a hard place and, in hindsight, might have been smarter to reject her application. With Cordray inside Grudge Match, she might eventually discover his identity. He used a lot of tricks and gadgets to hide his scent and keep his identity a secret, so it wasn't likely she would recognize him anytime soon, but he needed to be more careful, and not just on fight nights. He needed to be more careful, in general.

Today, for instance. He couldn't slip up like that again. He'd let his personal feelings get the better of him while exchanging messages with her. If he wanted to remain hidden, he needed to do a better job of staying inside his mind's neutral zone rather than diverting down the trail of personal resentment.

Unfortunately, the word careful wasn't part of his standard vocabulary. For him, the greater the risk, the greater the reward. He got off on taking chances, but with Cordray getting so close, either he needed to temper his daredevil ways, at least for a while, or he needed a contingency for when he got caught. Hope for the best, prepare for the worst. That was his motto. And if worse came to worst and the heat got too close, he could always quit the fight club. But that would be a shame.

Grudge Match was the first and only place where he felt like he actually fit in. It was his sanctuary. A place where he could publicly show off his physical talents without fear of condemnation for drawing attention to himself. In Grudge Match, he was treated like someone of importance. In only four months, Digon had made him one of his screeners, a job he shared with five others, including Rule, Digon's right-hand man who had taken a particular interest in mentoring him.

Rule must have seen something in him that his own father hadn't. So much the better. He could use a stronger father figure in his life.

As a screener, he was responsible for approving or rejecting applicants. Digon issued invitations to run the gauntlet based on *his* recommendations. No one had ever entrusted him with such an important task, and it gave him a sense of identity and purpose. He would hate to lose that, which meant he needed to figure out a way to keep Cordray from discovering who he was.

All the more reason to pay her a visit.

He dismounted the motorcycle and removed his helmet, which allowed his long bangs to fall over his eyes.

Flicking his head to the side, he pushed his hair off his forehead, looked up and down the street, then crossed.

It was a quarter till midnight, and the gate at the cemetery's entrance was closed, so he had to jump the wall and scale the fence. Fine by him. The mausoleum he was interested in sat two-thirds of the way through the cemetery, anyway. He could get to it faster by climbing the fence in back than he could by going through the front.

After securing the grip gloves on his hands and tugging the black ski mask with the skull face over his head, he leaped over the wall then pulled himself up the black, wrought iron fence with his special gloves and grip shoes then dropped to the ground on the other side.

Silent darkness and hundreds of light-grey tombstones stretched out in front of him.

Keeping off the roads that wound through the cemetery, he used the mature trees and their young, springtime foliage to stay hidden as he made his way toward the pyramid-shaped mausoleum where the lycans were rumored to have secretly created a gateway between dimensions.

He could have dematerialized and gotten there faster without risking being seen, but what fun would that be? Not only would that have been a safe move—a pussy move—but this way, if he got caught breaking and entering he could piss off his father. And other than stretching the limits of safety by risking his life, nothing thrilled him more than pissing off the old man and cementing his inferior status in Dad's eyes.

The pyramid silhouette of the mausoleum appeared about a hundred feet in front of him, and he slipped silently but swiftly toward it.

Less than a minute later he was standing in front of the light-green door with its snake handle. He had never broken into a mausoleum before, but surely one of his lock picks would do the trick.

Thirty seconds later, he was inside.

The space was compact. A stained-glass window, which probably made quite an impression with sunlight shining through it, took up the back wall. In the darkness, the window looked like nothing more than textured glass.

The energy contained within the four granite walls seemed vibrant and portentous, as if the structure had known he was coming and now rejoiced at his arrival.

He unzipped his jacket pocket and pulled out the ankh, which made the contained energy inside the tomb vibrate even harder. He could actually feel it pulse against his skin. Taking a Maglite Mini from his pocket, he began searching the closed-in space until he found the thin rectangular slot he was searching for along the back wall, near the corner.

That had to be it. He pulled his bottom lip between his teeth and stared in awe at the innocuous space between the frame of the stained-glass window and the granite surrounding it. The dark void couldn't have been more than a centimeter wide, but it was more than enough for the ankh to fit into.

His thumb caressed the rounded loop at the top of the ankh as hope rose within him. In theory, he knew how opening the gates worked, but in practicality he had no idea. Maybe some gates required certain keys, or maybe each gate had its own. He didn't know. Being that this gate had been created more recently, when the mausoleum was built in the late 1800s, attempting to open it with an ankh Micah had possessed for almost a thousand years seemed foolhardy, but he had to try.

What if this ankh *did* open the gate? The possibility was enough to spur him onward. Because if he could open this gate, maybe he could escape this godforsaken existence and go somewhere else. Somewhere he could make a difference. Where he didn't have to live in Micah Black's shadow.

But what if the gate didn't open? Then what? He supposed he would just have to try again somewhere else.

Refusing to wait a moment longer, he slipped the ankh inside the slot, held his breath, and waited.

Nothing.

He sent up a silent prayer. He wanted this to work so damn badly.

The ruby in the ankh began to glow.

A low hum vibrated the air, coalescing the coiling energy around him.

Holy shit, he'd done it! He'd opened a ga—

Abruptly, the hum stopped. The ruby's glow faded.

Almost forty years ago, when he'd still been just a kid, he'd awakened to a heavy, fresh snow. At least four inches had fallen overnight. He remembered standing just inside the garage of the home he'd shared with his father at the time, staring out at the pale-grey dawn as millions of fat, airy snowflakes floated lazily to the ground. The insulated silence had been deafening. Like he'd been inside a soundproof room.

That's how he felt now. Even the crickets had stopped chirping. His heart fell.

No gate had opened.

He was stuck here. There would be no magical journey to another dimension. No chance for a better life. No better future. No risk.

At least not tonight.

But there were other gates. He had the map. He couldn't decipher much of the writing on it, but he knew it was a map of the portals. Even if he had to travel around the world, he would find the gate this ankh worked in. And then he would be gone.

With a renewed sense of purpose, he pulled the ankh from the slot, tucked it in his pocket, and shut the mausoleum's door behind him as he slipped back into the shadows. A few minutes later, he was back on his motorcycle, speeding off into the night.

It was time to plan a visit with Cordray.

BEHIND THE MAUSOLEUM, the air shimmered as the portal ripped a seam through the fabric of space and time, opening a shadowy hole in midair. A flash of greenish-blue light lit the trees and tombstones. A moment later, a large male, clothed in a tattered shirt and pants, fell to the ground, landing on his side with a painful thud.

Hunter groaned and blinked, then squeezed his eyes shut and winced as his muscles protested the harsh impact.

What in Osiris's Netherworld had just happened? One second he was sleeping, and the next, he was falling then slamming into the ground.

Opening his eyes, he grimaced and rolled to his back. Then froze as he looked up through leafless branches at a starlit sky instead of the roof of the hut he'd called home for the last twenty years. Ever since Memnon had banished him to the moon of their home world for breaking the lycans' most coveted law.

But this wasn't their home world's moon.

This wasn't even their home world's star system.

This was Earth. He could tell by the map the stars created in the night sky. The only planet in the universe where you could find stars aligned this way was Earth.

Slowly pushing to his feet, he studied the constellations, scanning east to west. From the stars' positions, he was in the northern hemisphere—Chicago would be his guess, confirmed by the architecture he could make out in the distance—and it was spring. Most likely early to mid-May.

He glanced around, finding nothing but cold, grey tombstones and the pyramid mausoleum beside him. The portal.

Where were the others? Why weren't they here to greet him? More importantly, why had they brought him back? He'd been exiled. You didn't come back from exile.

Sniffing the air, he tried to identify who'd been there to open the gate, but he couldn't find a single familiar scent. What he did pick up was the essence of a vampire. A vampire who'd had *his* key, which he'd lost centuries ago. No wonder he'd fallen through this gate and not one of the others. He'd been drawn to his key.

But that was the least of his concerns right now. If Memnon didn't know he'd been pulled back to Earth, he would soon, which meant Hunter didn't have much time.

Not wasting another second, he took off at a full run, slicing through the shadows with an urgency fed by hope and desire. He needed to find Annalise. His beloved. His life. The very reason he'd been banished in the first place.

CHAPTER 19

MICAH SAT AT HIS DESK AT **AKM,** reviewing the Skeletor footage again, searching for anything he might have missed.

Sev had spent two hours combing the pedway today, only to turn up a lot of nothing. Stryker and his team had continued the hunt when the night shift went on duty, and Io was still trying to backtrace the hack into AKM's system. But with each minute that ticked by without news they'd found something, it became glaringly apparent they were back at square one, with nothing to go on. Which meant they were probably going to have to wait until Skeletor made his next move. Then they could get another shot.

But that didn't mean Micah was tucking his tail. He would continue to scour the evidence in hopes something would turn up.

A knock at the door pulled his attention from the video footage looping on his screen.

"Malek. What are you doing here?" He rounded the desk and pulled Malek into a heart-felt bear hug. Gina was with him and stood to the side, all smiles and gratitude. "I thought you were living the good life during your calling, buddy."

Malek clapped him on the back once then tightly embraced him. "I have been, believe me."

They separated, and Malek closed his hand over Gina's, pulling her against his side.

"You look good." Micah nodded, glancing from one to the other. "Both of you."

"Thanks to you," Malek said.

"And Brak," Gina added.

Malek nodded. "Yes, and Brak. Without him, neither of us would be here right now."

Gina had almost died less than two weeks ago. In fact, she *had* died. Her heart had stopped beating and everything. And Malek had lost his shit. But Brak had used his magic mojo and somehow revived Gina, bringing her back from the dead. Which saved Malek, who'd been seconds away from ending his own life.

Once more, they'd cheated death, beating the odds the way they always seemed to do. One day their luck was bound to run out, but Micah was happy to ride the wave as long as it lasted.

"So, what are you two doing here?" He leaned his hip against the side of his desk and crossed his arms. "You ready to come back to work?"

Malek and Gina exchanged secretive glances and Gina's cheeks colored as her smile widened.

"No, not quite yet." Malek cleared his throat. "Uh, we just came from seeing the doctor."

"Oh?" the bottom fell out of Micah's stomach. He knew what was coming. Taking a quick peek inside Malek's thoughts confirmed it a half-second before Malek said . . .

"Gina's pregnant."

He forced himself to smile. "Congratulations. I'm happy for you, my brother. I can't think of anyone who deserves a child more than you do."

The words felt like hollow-tipped bullets to his own heart, but he meant them. Malek had been through the worst kind of hell known to the universe. He truly deserved to find happiness. But being happy for someone else didn't mean he wasn't feeling a bit like a flat tire for himself.

Compassion filled Malek's eyes. He knew how long Micah had wanted a child and that hearing his own good news had to hurt. "Micah, I'm sorry. I—"

Micah held up his hand, cutting Malek off. He didn't need Malek's sympathy right now. This was his friend's moment, not his.

"Save that shit, Malek. I'm fine. I'll be okay. You just focus on making your female happy and seeing your child arrive safely into the world. Revel in this, Malek. And you . . ." He turned toward Gina and ruffled her short hair. "You let my brother from another mother dote on you all he wants." He faked an evil eye when Gina appeared ready to protest. "He's waited a long time for this, and I can already see how eager he is to take care of you, so you just sit back and enjoy being treated like the queen you are in his heart, you hear?" He lowered his chin and looked at her from the tops of his eyes for emphasis.

Gina sighed. "Males. You're all such hormone divas."

"Damn straight." Micah said, chucking Malek on the shoulder before turning and heading back behind the desk.

Malek stepped forward. "I heard someone broke into your apartment and you're having trouble tracking the guy down. Do you need me to stick around and lend a hand? I could — "

"Nope." Micah shook his head. "Get out of here. Take your female home and celebrate. We'll talk later."

"Well, if you need me, you know where I am."

Once he was alone again, Micah clasped his hands in front of him, elbows resting on the desk, and tilted his forehead against his thumbs.

Everyone was taking mates and getting pregnant.

Everyone except him and Sam. They'd mated, he'd experienced his first calling with her, but her body hadn't accepted his offering. Despite making love to her at least fifty times in less than two weeks, she hadn't gotten pregnant.

He rubbed his palms over his face and eyed the open door for less than a second before he got up and closed it. He didn't want to see anyone right now, and he didn't want anyone seeing him. Not like this. Not when he felt like a shark trapped in a net, on the verge of drowning.

Returning to his chair, he bowed his head into his hands as he spun around and faced the back of the office.

Josie was pregnant. Miriam was pregnant. Now, Gina was pregnant. If Sev and Ari had mated females instead of each other, they would likely be pregnant, too.

And yet, Sam remained barren.

Micah was happy for his friends. He knew how important having a young was for a male vampire.

God, did he ever know!

He lived it every day. Every time he made love to Sam, he hoped against hope he would be the exception to the rule. That he would be like Tristan or that sperm factory, Lakota, and somehow impregnate Sam without being in his calling.

But every day, every week, and every month passed without seeing Sam's belly swell.

It got so he no longer even checked for a baby's life signature inside her, a habit he had fought to get out of for weeks after coming out of his calling. One that had begun to cause him physical pain each time he placed his hand over her stomach as she slept, only to feel nothing but her presence. No stirring of a second life inside her. No cellular mitosis as new, microscopic life stirred into existence.

His fingers pushed into his hair and curled against his scalp as he slowly shook his head. He wanted to believe that Sam's body had just been too weak to get pregnant so soon after he'd changed her into his davala. But what if the truth was something else? What if, for all his efforts, he couldn't produce children? What if he was infertile?

It was possible. Centuries ago, when he'd been mated to Kat, they hadn't been able to have children, either. They'd assumed she was barren, but what if it had been him? Other male vampires had proven infertile. A rarity to be sure, but not an impossibility.

Micah sank his face into his hands again. What if he could never give Sam a child, no matter how hard he tried, how many callings he endured, or how badly he wanted kids? What if he was shooting blanks. Maybe a future with children of his own simply wasn't in his cards, and if it wasn't, would Sam be disappointed? Would she resent him?

"Please don't do that to me," he whispered into his hands, to God or whatever universal entity ruled over life on Earth. "Please don't be that cruel."

And there, in the silence of his office, with his face in his hands, Mighty Micah broke.

Not much got to a warrior like him. But when it came to his mate and having children, he could shed tears.

And shed them he did.

CHAPTER 20

NURSING A BUSTED LIP AND MULTIPLE CONTUSIONS she couldn't feel but knew covered her body, Cordray headed back to the ranch, racing along the highway. It was after one o'clock in the morning, and at least for a few hours, she had been able to push Trace from her thoughts. But she couldn't avoid him forever. After all, she was his boss.

Almost two hundred vampires and drecks had been at Grudge Match tonight. For her first fight, she had been paired with a dreck named Sonia. Red hair, green eyes, and one tough bitch. Cordray hadn't learned much about Sonia, but one thing was clear. Sonia was a master at Krav Maga. And Cordray's still-bloody lip proved it.

Speaking of which, her lip wasn't healing as fast as it should. Probably because the excitement of the last couple of days had depleted her energy and she was due for a feeding.

Later. Right now, she just wanted to get inside, shower, eat, go to bed, and avoid Trace as if he were a rabid piranha. Not necessarily in that order.

She slowed and turned onto Asylum's long, gravel driveway. Ghostly ribbons of fog hovered a few feet over the ground in front of her, breaking and churning like smoke as she sliced through them.

She parked the Ducati in the garage, shut off the engine, pulled off her helmet, and let her gaze fall to the dark oil stain that had soaked into the concrete years ago.

She was alone. With an oil stain. How symbolic was that? Because didn't she feel like a stain herself most of the time? A smear of living tissue that was only half alive, meandering through existence, her heart dead?

Well, not exactly dead. Because if it were really dead, she wouldn't have reacted to Trace the way she had earlier today, and she wouldn't be both dreading and looking forward to going inside, where she might run into him before she could escape to her bedroom and lock the door.

As if locking her door would keep a male like Trace out if he wanted to get to her.

The point was, the idea of never seeing Trace again was enough to spear dread into that four-chambered muscle that steadily thump-thumped inside her ribcage. So, yeah. Heart not dead. Got it.

With a frustrated sigh, she made her way out of the garage to the back door. She was in the habit of scanning the yard before going inside rather than entering the house through the garage. Call it an occupational hazard.

As she started up the steps to the back door, she glanced in the direction of the dorm and sensed the children sleeping inside. All except Leon and Riley.

Stopping, she scanned the yard, scowling as dread sank into the pit of her stomach. Those two had been steadily progressing toward taking their relationship to the next level for weeks. Had they finally gone there? Had they finally consummated their fledgling love to set certain tragedy into motion when—someday—Leon mated another or Riley's true mate found her and stole her away?

Stretching out her senses, she swept the property until . . .

There. In the barn. The scent of sex drifted into her nose a moment later. Then her sharpened hearing picked up a quiet moan.

What the hell? It was after one in the morning!

Those two would never learn. Did Riley want to end up like her when Leon mated someone else? She wouldn't be able to stop it. Leon might say he loved her now, and he might promise her the moon, the stars, and the entire universe, but when his biology stirred for another, he would leave her behind without a glance. She would be nothing. Nobody but a heartbroken female, left alone to suffer the emotional turmoil of being cast aside while Leon bonded to his mate and created a family.

Cordray rushed to the barn, desperate to stop what was happening. *Needing* to stop it. She couldn't let Riley end up like her.

She threw open the doors, making them rattle as they swung and cracked against the wall.

And there they were, on a stack of hay. Leon on top of Riley, his hands fisted around hers as he rocked into her, holding down her arms beside her head, her legs around his hips, her shirt pushed high to reveal her breasts.

Their heads shot up and around, fear catapulting into their expressions. In an instant, they scuttled away from each other, pulling their clothes back into place as they clambered to their feet. Leon's erection left nothing to the imagination. Riley's downturned face was shaded bright red.

"What are you two doing out here?" Cordray stormed toward Leon, seeing Gideon. "How could you do this to her? She's innocent. Only a child."

"It's not like that," Riley said, reaching for Leon.

Cordray batted her hand away. "Don't touch him."

"But I love him!" Riley's eyes filled with tears.

"And I love her!" Leon's hand shot out and grabbed Riley's before Cordray could prevent it.

Cordray saw red. How could they know what love was? Or how Riley's love for him would destroy her when they reached the end of their transformation into adult vampires?

"Love doesn't matter!" Her anger flared. "When you've grown up and come of age, you'll understand that whether or not you love one another won't make a damn bit of difference." She glared at Riley as she pointed at Leon. "How many times do I have to tell you this, Riley? He will take a mate, and the odds are stacked against you that you will be the one his body chooses. And where will that leave you?" Then she turned her ire on Leon. "And what if another mates Riley? What will you do then? Because King Bain's laws are explicit. A mated male's rights are sacrosanct. His rights to her body will trump your love for her, no matter how long you've been together, and you will be left out in the cold."

Leon's face warped into a mask of anger and refusal. "That won't happen."

She laughed bitterly. "Oh, really. And you know this how? From your vast experience as an adult vampire?"

Leon's face flushed, and he dropped his gaze to his feet.

"I thought so." Cordray paced away. "Do you really think you'll stand a chance if another male waltzes into Riley's life and mates her? You won't, Leon. She will be obligated to answer her mate's call. She won't be able to resist it. I've told both of you this time and again, and yet here I find you together, screwing one another as if you think you have forever in front of you. But you don't!" She slammed the side of her fist against the wall as she turned on Riley. "Is this really what you want? This pain? Because I can assure you, pain is all you'll have when one of you mates someone else."

Unless, like her, the agony ended up being so raw that it annihilated every nerve ending so that she never felt anything again.

"I don't care!" Riley's fierce grasp on Leon's hand turned her knuckles white. "I love him *now*. And he loves *me* now. I want him and he wants me. What's so wrong with that?"

"Everything!" Cordray clenched her fists. Couldn't they see? Couldn't they understand?

Leon wrapped his arm around Riley's shoulders and tucked her protectively against his body, the way a mate would. "We can't live for what tomorrow *might* bring, C," he said, his voice unusually calm. Remarkably confident. "Because tomorrow might not come. And if it doesn't, I don't want to waste even a moment I could have spent with her."

Cordray's eyes tightened as she studied Leon. He spoke beyond his years, his voice strong and sure despite his usually quiet demeanor. It was clear he had thought about this a lot, and when Cordray glanced at Riley, it was obvious she had, too.

Riley's gaze implored her. "C, we can't control what happens tomorrow, next week, or years from now. We can only control what we do today. And today, I love Leon. I want to be with him. I want to plan a life with him." She paused, looked at the dusty, straw-strewn floor, and said in a small voice, "If he ends up not being my mate, I'll cross that bridge when I have to. For now, can't you just let us be happy with one another? Can't you just let us enjoy what we have while we have it?"

Cordray rocked back. Riley knew the risks, as well as the unattractive odds that Leon might not end up being her mate. So did Leon. But they refused to let the possibility of a stark future affect them in the present. Like a cancer patient who knows he only has three months to live, Riley and Leon wanted to make the most of those three months, not live in fear of the end.

Because of her painful past, Cordray only saw the suffering Riley and Leon were destined for. When she'd been their age, she had only felt the thrill Gideon had given her, not the fear of their relationship's inevitable doom. Love and elation had ruled her decisions. Her awareness had been dominated by the way her heart skipped when she saw him ride around the bend in the lane, his gaze lifting to the window where he knew he would find her waiting and watching for him. In her youth, Cordray would have retaliated against anyone who tried to warn her away from Gideon the same way Riley and Leon resisted her now.

With the gift of hindsight, would she really have done anything differently? Would she have ended her relationship with Gideon knowing he would mate someone else? Knowing that she would lose her sense of touch because of it?

Honestly? No. Because despite the pain, those all-too-brief years with Gideon were some of the best memories of her life. How could she purposefully deny herself that?

"Go inside," she said quietly as an emotion she couldn't describe beat against her heart. "Both of you. We'll talk about this later."

"But—" Leon began to protest.

"Now!" Cordray pointed toward the door. "Go back to bed. Your *own* beds. You have to be up for school in a few hours." Leon was in college, but in vampire years he was still a juvenile, at least until he completed his transition. While Riley was old enough to be in college, she had fallen a couple of grades behind during the turmoil she'd endured before coming to Asylum, so she was still in her final year of high school.

They hung their heads, and Leon wrapped his hand securely around Riley's as he led her toward the open door.

After they were gone, Cordray slumped into a deck chair that would eventually find its way to the porch now that summer was upon them.

Yesterday, Mya had suggested that Trace might be the mate she'd thought she'd found in Gideon. Could that be true? Could she be pushing him away for fear he would make her feel the pain all over again when instead he was her true mate?

Was that why she could feel him?

Was that why she was so drawn to him?

She turned her head in the direction of the house. Trace was there. So close she could be in his room and against his body in less than two minutes. Feeling his lips against hers again.

Feeling!

That alone was enough to terrify her. What if something happened and her sense of touch shut off again after she allowed herself to get close to him? She wasn't sure she could take that. To be given the sun and stars only to have them all supernova at the same time would devastate her. The universe had a reputation for playing cruel tricks on her, so her trust in things working out this time wasn't exactly high.

And then there was Micah and Sam. Trace had a bizarre relationship with them. If he mated her, how would that pan out?

The mysterious heaviness in her chest spread. Her shoulders dragged forward, and she bowed her head. Her hands shook, and she raised her palm and pressed it over her heart, which felt like it was about to pound out of her chest. She could barely breathe. Tears broke in her eyes. A moment later, she squeezed her eyelids shut as a gut-wrenching sob ripped through her throat.

Fear.

She was afraid.

So much had been taken from her. But now, when everything she had always wanted might possibly be within reach, she was too scared to take a chance. Too afraid to risk it all again for fear the results would turn out the same.

Only a coward would resist taking a chance. Someone with courage would see the possibility for a very real, very tragic outcome but not let that stop her cold. Someone with courage would throw that potential future the proverbial middle finger and shout, "Fuck you! I'm doing this anyway!"

But for all her bravado, she couldn't muster even a single ounce of courage. Trace was right there. Within reach. And all she wanted to do was run away from him.

If only she had a friend. Someone she could confide in. Who could listen and offer advice. Trouble was, she didn't have a lot of friends. Mya. Brenna. That was about it. But they weren't who she needed. She needed someone who was both impartial and informed. Someone who could serve as a link between her and Trace. Someone vested in Trace's future.

Sam.

But was Sam really a friend? They'd share a couple of laughs, but that was about it.

Fuck it. Maybe she had wussed out on stealing into Trace's room and rubbing herself all over him like a cat in heat, but she still had enough lady balls to face Sam.

She was on her feet in an instant, out the door, and practically running to the garage.

Snagging her helmet, she shoved it over her head, swung her leg over the seat of her Ducati, and lit up the engine.

Seconds later, she gunned the gas and sped back toward the road.

By the time she arrived at Micah's home, desperation had her firmly in its grip.

She pounded on the door, her whole body clutched so tightly that if one muscle spasmed, she would fall over.

Sam opened the door and immediately frowned. "Cordray?"

Without waiting for an invitation, she rushed inside.

Sam shut the door. "What's wrong? What happened? Is it Trace?" Sam hurriedly followed her into the living room. "Is he okay?"

Of course Sam would worry that her visit was about Trace. She was practically mated to the guy, living with him, engaging in threesomes with him, even if she and Trace never touched each other. At least not in *that* way. Not in a way that would put his very worthy, very ample cock inside her.

She spun around. "Hit me."

Sam recoiled. "What? No!"

"Hit me!" She grabbed Sam's wrist and pulled her forward.

"Stop! I'm not going to hit you. Are you crazy?"

"Just do it, for God's sake! *Hit me!*"

Sam stiffened, and for a heartbeat, Cordray didn't think she'd do it. And then . . .

Smack!

Sam slapped her then immediately gasped as she pulled back, hand over her mouth, staring at her as if she were a freak.

Freak.

Just like Trace. Just like she'd seen in Trace's mind when those kids from his childhood had teased and bullied him, making his life hell.

She was a freak, too, because she couldn't feel a thing. She had seen Sam's hand shoot toward her face. She'd heard the harsh clap of flesh on flesh. Her head had even snapped to the side. She possessed all the sensory evidence necessary to prove Sam had hit her except for the sensation of feeling the contact.

"Harder, Sam. Hit me harder."

"Cordray . . .?"

"Just do it!"

SMACK!

This time, Sam struck her with enough force to knock her sideways. She stumbled then righted herself. Still nothing. No pain stung her cheek. No lingering echoes fired her nerve endings.

She was as unfeeling as one of Null's cold, heavy rocks. She was a jagged stone. Able to cause pain but not feel it.

"Harder!" she commanded.

"Cordray, I—what's going on?" Tears glistened Sam's eyes, and her face was contorted in horror mixed with disgust.

"Just hit me, goddammit!"

This time, Sam's fist shot out, clocking her on the chin.

Cordray staggered backward then tripped over her own feet, spinning and nose-diving to the floor.

"Cordray! Oh God! I'm sorry." In an instant, Sam was kneeling beside her, her hands gripping her arms as she tried to help her up.

But there was no helping her.

Not in the true sense of the word.

She was defunct. Damaged. Broken.

Gideon had broken her.

In one fateful moment, he'd shattered her heart and stolen her sense of touch. He'd destroyed her.

Tears welled in her eyes. Her throat tightened abruptly. A moment later, she sobbed, face in the carpet.

"Why can't I feel anything?" Until Trace, she had been able to live with her disability. But now that he'd reminded her of all she'd lost, she just wanted it back.

Sam stopped trying to help her. Instead, she brushed Cordray's hair off her face, sniffling. "What do you mean? Are you saying you can't feel?"

She shook her head.

"At all?"

Cordray shook her head again. "Nothing." She squeezed her eyes shut. "What's wrong with me?"

Sam sniffled again. "You're asking the wrong person, Cordray. I'm out of my depth here."

Cordray lifted her head and looked at her. Two wet trails extended down Sam's face, one on each cheek. A tear dripped off her chin.

"Why? Why me?" It was the self-pitying question she hadn't allowed herself to ask for eight centuries, but she was asking it now. For once, she wanted an answer.

Sam shook her head, and two more fat tears dropped from her eyes. "I'm sorry, Cordray. I don't know."

They stared at each other like that for a long time. Just the two of them. On the floor. Crying and staring.

Then Sam dabbed the skin over her upper lip with her fingers. When she spoke, her voice was gentle and persuasive. "Did something happen between you and Trace?"

That was the question of the hour, wasn't it?

"No. Yes." She sighed, wiping the humiliating tears from her face. "I mean, no."

But something *had* happened. Not just in her bedroom when she'd awakened to find him on top of her, but in the living room earlier in the evening, with Aiden and Null, when they'd looked like a family. When they'd talked to each other like two people who actually liked one another. And then something incredible had happened after they'd tucked the kids into bed. Something wondrous and fiery and all-absorbing.

"Cordray . . .?" Sam tugged on her arm again, goading her to sit up.

She did. "I don't know what's wrong with me, Sam."

Sam's wispy eyebrows crowded together as she slowly shook her head. "There's nothing wrong with you."

"Then you're obviously not paying attention."

Sam sighed and ass-parked on the couch. "Oh, I'm paying attention, Cordray. More than you know." She spoke as if she held a crystal ball that revealed all.

"What do you mean?"

Sam let out a breathy huff then pushed herself off the couch. "Do you want some tea? Coffee?" She hesitated and glanced toward the mini-bar. "Something harder? I could use something harder myself."

"Got any whiskey?"

Sam firmly nodded her head as if putting a period on a sentence. "Yep."

As Sam poured their drinks, Cordray pulled herself off the floor and took a seat in one of the club chairs, drying the rest of the tears from her cheeks. She hated crying in front of people. Hell, she hated crying period. She hadn't cried in forever, but just as with her sense of touch, Trace appeared to have awakened all sorts of long-forgotten emotions inside her.

Sam returned and handed her a double of Jack then set the bottle on the coffee table in front of her before taking the seat across from her, cradling her own glass.

"Smart woman." She nodded toward the bottle.

"Yeah, well, it feels like it's going to be that kind of conversation."

She took a hardy gulp of the burning liquid. "What kind of conversation is that?"

"The kind where you finally admit you're in love with Trace."

She pulled in an abrupt breath. "I'm not in love with him."

Sam rolled her eyes. "Like I said, it's going to be that kind of conversation." She sipped her drink. "Why don't you just start from the beginning."

The beginning. She scoffed. "You really want to know?"

Sam studied her for a long, pensive moment. "Yes."

"Fine." She sat back and gulped down the rest of the contents of her glass then held it out for more. If she was going to do this, she needed all the liquid fortification she could get.

Sam poured her another then set the bottle back down with a resounding thunk.

"Start talking, Cordray. I'm here as long as you need me."

"What about Micah?"

"He's working. And when he gets home, if you're still here, he'll just have to deal with it."

"Why? Because the two of you are so close he'll do anything for you?" She couldn't keep the resentful bite out of her tone.

Seeing what Sam had with Micah left a bittersweet taste in her mouth. They were so in tune with one another. So in love. Then again, they were mates. Wasn't that how mates were supposed to be? One mind, one heart, one body, more or less?

She wouldn't know. She'd never been mated. But she'd heard enough vampires speak of the mating phenomenon to understand how things worked.

Sam's green eyes softened, and she briefly glanced away before nodding. "Yes, Micah and I are close, but that doesn't mean we always see eye to eye. We just find a way to make our differences of opinion work. We're a lot alike, Micah and I." She paused. "You and Trace are a lot alike, too."

"No, we're not." But they were. They were both similar beasts. Both freaks.

Sam crossed her legs and sank more deeply into her chair. "Cordray, you and Trace are cut from the same cloth. You're both tough as iron on the outside but vulnerable inside. You're both extremely powerful and care more deeply than you let on. Don't try to deny it, because I can see it. You wouldn't have broken down the way you did just now if that weren't true."

"I didn't break down."

Sam held up her hand and bowed her head in surrender. "Okay, fine. Forget I said that, but it doesn't mean you don't care on a very deep level."

"So what if I do?"

"Then stop fighting it. Let go. If you want him, take him."

Cordray stared into her drink. She did want him. But taking him would mean she was allowing herself to be hurt again, maybe even killed this time around. Hadn't she learned her lesson? What kind of idiot would purposely allow herself to be put in harm's way when she knew the consequences.

"I was in love once," she said quietly.

A pulse of startled energy beat from Sam's body, but she didn't say anything.

Cordray sighed. "His name was Gideon, and we were in love."

She lowered her voice to a wistful whisper. "So in love." Then she pulled her gaze from her glass and met Sam's eyes.

Sam's mouth had fallen open, and her expression was one of surprised curiosity.

"Does that shock you? That I actually loved someone who loved me back? Me? Big, bad, scary Cordray?" She took a contemptuous gulp of whiskey.

"You're not scary — "

Cordray lifted her hand, palm out. "No, it's okay. I know what people say about me. I know what they think. I can see inside their heads, remember?" She tapped her temple then choked down another gulp. "I'm Cruella Deville. I steal puppies for their fur and drink the blood of babies. I'm Medusa incarnate, haven't you heard?"

"Cordray . . ."

All this woe-is-me bullshit rankled her blood, but she couldn't seem to pull her head out of the septic tank, thanks to the alcohol quickly pulling her into its grasp.

"Everyone avoids me." She laughed mockingly, raising her glass as if in a toast. "They cross busy streets just so they don't have to pass me on the sidewalk. They avert their gazes as if meeting mine will turn them to stone." She laughed at herself then drained her second glass. "I'm the boogey man, the thing that goes bump in the night, the monster hiding under your bed. I'm the stranger your parents warned you not to talk to when you were a little girl."

She glanced away, seeing the memories of her long-ago past as if only a few weeks had passed instead of eight hundred years. "But it wasn't always that way."

When she paused and said nothing for several seconds, Sam refilled her glass. God love her. Sam knew how to keep her talking.

She took a healthy swig of whiskey, her body growing warm and loose as she settled more comfortably into her chair.

"When I was young, I was innocent and sweet. Docile even, if you can believe that." Those days had been a lifetime ago. A hundred lifetimes ago. "I was as obedient and well-mannered as a princess."

And wasn't she? A princess? After all, her father had been the king. King Bain the First.

His affair with her mother, who had worked as a servant in her father's employ until he mated her, had been so scandalous, yet so perfect.

But Father already had a queen. She wasn't his biological mate, but she conceived a child, anyway. Cordray's half-brother and heir to the throne, Bain the Second.

Her brother's birth was practically a miracle. Unmated pairs struggled to bear young. That was the main reason why the vampire race hadn't proliferated much in the early times. Arranged pairings had been commonplace then, especially among the more affluent.

All that changed when her father mated her mother outside his union to the queen. That was when he began writing new laws protecting human mates. Until King Bain the First, for a vampire male to take a human mate was verboten. That didn't mean it didn't happen, but those vampires who did mate humans lived in secret. Others remained tied to their vampire spouses on paper but maintained their mated relationships on the down-low. Callings were horrific for a male mated to a human and sometimes resulted in death if he wasn't able to spend his fertile time with his true mate.

This was one reason why Cordray's father had changed the laws. He had refused to sit and watch their race die over archaic laws that had been written during a time before vampires had gained an understanding of how an existence shared with humans would pan out.

But his protection of mated males had also been about protecting his own mating. As the king, he couldn't just up and flee with his human mate. He had a job to do. He couldn't live a secret life with his mate and return home to his queen to make things look normal. He was, for all intents and purposes, a celebrity. Everything he did landed in the public eye. Legalizing vampire-human matings—as well as enforcing them—had been the only solution.

After his tragic death, her brother had continued their father's legacy. Protecting mated males and biological unions had become a priority. One that her brother understood better than most after watching his father live in torment every day he couldn't spend with Cordray's mother.

Certain circles in the vampire community still clung to those old laws, though. Namely the purists, many of which were the well-to-do. They still believed in arranged unions and insisted on pairing their daughters with those they felt were best suited to create a strong match, despite the challenges those unions faced.

One of those challenges was that having children would be nearly impossible. Secondly, if the male of such an arranged pairing mated someone else, or another male mated the female, Bain was forced to step in and nullify the arrangement and honor the mated male's rights. This didn't make him popular with the aristocratic families who'd coordinated arranged pairings, especially for those he had overturned. But as the king, popularity was the least of his concerns.

Cordray thought back on her parents' mating. It had been hard on her mother not to be with her father when he was away being the king. And the way her father swept her mother into his arms every time he visited, holding her close for so long Cordray sometimes wondered if he would ever let her go, proved how hard it was for him not to be with her, too. She and her mother had treasured those few-and-far-between visits. So had her father.

His visits were how she ultimately met Gideon. Beautiful and passionate, Gideon had been a young warrior in her father's court. A full-blood and fifteen years her senior, fully transitioned into an adult male. At the time, she had been a young, innocent, and impressionable nineteen-year-old, still in the early stages of her transition.

"I was a *fair maiden*," she said scornfully. "A maiden who caught the eye of the most handsome male in the king's guard." She blinked heavily, meeting Sam's gaze. "His name was Gideon."

Sam seemed to sense what Cordray was about to reveal was the key to everything, because she didn't say a word. She didn't even move. This was the reason for all the scary tattoos, the piercings, the attitude. Her inability to sense touch.

She gulped down the last of her third glass and set it on the arm of the chair. "Gideon and I embarked on a passionate, whirlwind love affair," she said, beginning the story.

Just as Leon and Riley vowed they would always be together, she and Gideon had vowed the same.

"We were so sure we'd be mates. So sure we were meant to be together forever. But week in and week out, year after year, his call to mate never fired. Despite how deeply we loved one another, Gideon never mated me." She let out a brittle laugh. "I wanted his child so badly. My father had conceived with another who wasn't his mate, and I thought the same thing could happen to me. That I would conceive a miracle child, too." She lifted her glass to her lips only to remember it was empty. She lowered it again. "But it never happened. I never conceived."

"How long were you together?" Sam asked quietly, as if she feared bursting the intimate bubble drawing them more tightly together.

"Six years. I met him as my transition to adulthood was just starting, and we were still together when it finished." She smiled sourly. "We'd hoped that the reason he hadn't mated me was because I wasn't yet an adult. But even afterward, he didn't mate me."

Her intoxicated mind jumped ahead, no longer functioning linearly, as often happens when alcohol's grip takes hold. Her thoughts fell to the night that changed everything. The night when she lost herself completely and life as she knew it shattered.

"He didn't come to me that night." Her body felt as flat and broken now as it had then. "He always came to me when the king visited, but that night, he didn't. So I stole away to the stable. His horse was gone." The memories were snap-shotting through her mind, the alcohol clouding the chronology. "I didn't understand. Why would his horse be gone? There was only one place where he could be. The cottage in the woods. It was where we went to be together. Our hideaway. I assumed he was there waiting for me."

The small one-room cottage in the woods, with its simple porch and small stone fireplace — paradise at the time — appeared in her mind.

"I darted into the woods, eager to see him. I couldn't understand why he hadn't come to tell me he'd be there, waiting for me. All I knew was that I had to see him. Feel his touch." Her gaze fell to the floor. She closed her eyes, remembering his touch. That night was the last time she'd felt it. The last time she'd felt anything until she met Trace.

Her vision blurred with tears.

"As the cabin came into view, I saw the glow of the fire through the window. He was there. I was so happy. So unbelievably happy. We were going to be together again. He was going to make love to me, and everything would be all right." She looked at Sam through a film of tears. Sam sat on the edge of her seat, eyes trained on her, her hands hugging her glass, which still had whiskey in it. "As I got closer, I heard muffled noises from inside. Gideon wasn't alone." Her heart ached all over again at the memory. "He was with a female. And they were making love."

Sam let out a tiny gasp and covered her mouth. "Oh, Cordray, I'm so sorry."

She held up her hand, already struggling to keep her shit together. She didn't need Sam's sympathy to send her totally over the edge. "Just wait, it gets better." She blinked against the tears clouding her vision. "I stood on my tiptoes and peered through the window. It was covered with a film of dirt and pollen, but I could still see them. On the bed we'd shared so many nights, he had another female beneath him. He was holding her down the way he'd held me so many times, his body surging against hers the way it had surged against mine. And wave after wave of hormonal heat pulsed through the walls, assaulting me like a bad punchline." She stilled and held her breath for a long moment. Then the air whooshed from her lungs. "He'd mated her. She was his mate, Sam. His goddamn mate."

"Omigod." The rushed exclamation breathed from Sam's mouth like a whispery curse. "I'm so sorry."

"What kind of cruel joke was that?" She slapped her palm on her chest. "He'd been mine for six years. I'd been his. I'd had a place in the world. With someone. An incredible, wonderful someone I'd given my heart to. But in the blink of an eye" — she snapped her fingers — "biology stole away the only male I'd ever loved. My first everything. He'd given me so much pleasure, made me feel desire, lifted me to rapturous heights with only the touch of his fingertips." She swiped a tear from her cheek as she met Sam's gaze. "Do you realize that I was so enthralled by him that he was able to send me into rapture with just a simple brush of his lips?"

Sam shook her head.

"It's true. He touched me, and it was euphoria. He kissed me, and it was pure bliss." Her gaze fell from Sam's. "And now I can't feel a thing."

Silence stretched for several seconds. Then Sam asked the inevitable.

"Why? What happened?"

The memories flew through her mind once more.

"Seeing him come inside her — his mate — was beyond excruciating. Pain shot through me with such force that I screamed. Physical pain, Sam. It felt like my heart exploded. Like my lungs closed in on themselves then ruptured.

"Gideon's head snapped around, and he saw me at the window. Guilt fell over his expression, but my heart was already shredding into pieces.

"I turned and ran. Just ran as fast as my legs could carry me. But he came after me. He was shouting my name. Telling me to stop. But I kept running. The only word I could say was no. Over and over, I just kept screaming no at him as branches sliced into my arms, my legs, my face." She lifted her hand to her cheek, remembering the lashes and the feel of sticky blood cooling on her skin. "He was faster than I was and caught up to me. He grabbed my wrist and spun me around, and I screamed, because it burned. It physically *burned* being touched by him after I'd just seen him with another female. I loved him. Seeing him with another destroyed me."

She sniffled, drawing in a trembling breath as the rest of the memory unfolded.

"He tried to calm me down. Tried to apologize. 'I had no choice,' he said. 'My body chose another. I'm sorry, but I've mated someone else.' I can still hear his voice as if he's right here and just spoke those words to me." She blinked heavily, and tears dropped from her eyes. "I fell to my knees, sobbing. Big tough Cordray, brought down by biology's brutal slap in the face." She uttered a bitter laugh. "But I was no match for life. It had played a cruel joke on me. It had given me a perfect male then ripped him away, and there was nothing I could do to stop it. Nothing I could do to get him back. Nothing. It was agony knowing I'd lost him and had no control." She shook her head. "Why couldn't he have mated *me*? What was wrong with *me*?"

"Nothing's wrong with you," Sam said. "He just wasn't the right man for you."

"Tell that to my body." She swallowed past the lump in her throat. "Something backfired in me that night, and I've never recovered."

Sam tilted her head and frowned. "Are you talking about losing your sense of touch?"

Cordray swiped at the traitorous tears that wouldn't stop leaking from her eyes. "He tried to comfort me. Tried to help me. But when he touched me, what felt like fire blasted through my body. The pain was indescribable. When I fell to the ground, screaming in agony, he tried to help me up. But as he gripped my arms, he only made the pain worse.

"I pushed him away, screaming at him not to touch me. 'Don't ever touch me again,' I said. Then I said — and I still remember the words as clearly as if they're seared into my brain — 'You've killed me. I'm dead now. Dead! *You're* dead to me!'"

Sam gasped.

Cordray pressed on. "He reared away from me. Pale. So pale. Terrified. *Of* me or *for* me, I don't know, but it didn't matter. The look on his face said it all. We were over, and he didn't know me, anymore. Seemingly overnight, we'd gone from being as close as two people could be to being total strangers." She let out a shaky sigh. "He apologized again, told me I'd never see him again, and left.

"I remained curled on the ground, knees to my chest, crying until I didn't think I could cry anymore. He had someone warm to return to. He had another's arms to console and comfort him, another's lips to kiss away his pain. I had nothing and no one. After years thinking I'd found the male I would spend the rest of my life with, he was lost to another, and I was all alone."

She sat quietly for a minute. Then she leaned forward, grabbed the bottle, and filled her glass to the brim before guzzling half of it down in one swallow.

"Hours later, I finally pushed myself up and headed back home. But as I trudged numbly along the path, I realized I couldn't feel the dewy, damp undergrowth beneath my slippers. Or the coldness of the cobbled path that led from the woods to the stable gate.

"Within hours, Gideon and his mate were gone, but so was my sense of touch. I couldn't feel anything. Nothing at all."

Silence stretched between her and Sam. Recalling her past had felt both like a purge and a reliving of events, leaving her mentally worn and bone weary.

"Years later, I heard that Gideon's mate and his young son were killed. I never learned what happened to Gideon, though. He disappeared, lost to his suffering, I'm sure. I don't envy him that. That's got to be a worse hell—or at least an equal one—than what I've gone through."

"But it doesn't mean you've been hurt any less," Sam said, her voice maternal.

"But it doesn't take away the hurt, either." She downed another swallow of whiskey. "But all this time, I've felt nothing. Nothing at all." Her eyes met Sam's. "Until now. Until Trace."

"What do you mean?"

Cordray chugged the remaining Jack in one swallow then clunked her glass on the table.

"I can feel him, Sam. He touches me, and I feel it. Everywhere, I feel it. What does that mean?" Her head buzzed thickly.

"I can tell you what *I* think it means, but I'm not sure you want to hear it."

She thought back to what she had said to Gideon the last time she saw him. That he had killed her. That she was dead without him.

She hadn't actually died, but in a manner of speaking, she had. Her desire had died. Her ability to feel had died. Her emotions and nervous system had died, making her an automaton. An unfeeling ghost.

Until now.

The more time she spent around Trace, the more her sense of touch revived, along with her emotions. He was pulling her back to the living. In his own way, he was resuscitating her. Resurrecting her heart. Isn't that what she'd thought a couple of days ago?

Earlier tonight, she'd wanted to be where Null was, pressed

against Trace's body, her cheek against his chest, his hands rubbing her back, his warmth pouring into her. Not since Gideon had desire so strong commanded her thoughts.

I don't hate you, Trace. Quite the opposite, in fact.

And then what she'd wanted actually happened. Trace had held her and pressed all that heat against her body. He'd kissed her. And it had felt so good. So incredibly perfect.

But then she had run away. As she had run from the cottage in the woods, so she had run from Trace. All because she feared he would do the same thing to her as Gideon had.

Even so, she couldn't resist his magnetism. Even now, she could barely keep herself from jumping on her Ducati and racing back to Asylum so she could see him, touch him, and be touched by him. To hear his voice and watch him while he slept. To share her dreams with him and awaken with him between her legs again, wanton, hungry, aching with need. To drink from him as he drank from her. To spend forever with.

Forever.

Had she really just thought that? Yes, she had. She wanted forever. With him. With Trace.

"Oh, God." She dropped her face into her palms.

"What? What's wrong?" The cushions rustled as Sam scooted forward.

She peeled her hands away and turned beseeching eyes on Sam. "You're right."

"What do you mean, I'm right? Right about what?"

This couldn't be happening. *Please don't let this be happening.*

"I'm in love with him. I've fallen in love with Trace."

CHAPTER 21

AT HALF PAST FIVE IN THE MORNING, Micah entered the house through the garage and stuffed his keys in his front pocket.

And immediately pulled up.

What the fuck?

The air smelled like the fresh scent of Jack Daniels-infused vomit. And Cordray.

Now there was a fragrance combination Glade should definitely look into. Not.

Just . . . blech.

He followed the wet, gagging sound of someone barfing and found Sam holding the hand-painted, metal waste can from the guest bathroom under Cordray's head.

Damn. He liked that trash can. What a waste of a fabulous floral paint job.

The offending empty Jack Daniels bottle sat on the coffee table.

"What's *it* doing here?" He dropped his duffel on the floor.

Sam gave him a scornful over-the-shoulder look. "Not now, Micah."

Cordray stopped puking long enough to say, "*It's* puking its guts out, asshole." To Sam, she said, "And here I thought your mate was the observant one."

He rounded the couch and picked up the bottle as Cordray retched again.

"Ol' Jack deserves better than this." He spun the empty bottle on his palm then caught it by the neck.

"Micah . . ." Sam's tone held an unspoken warning to be nice, something he emphatically didn't want to be to the female currently redecorating the inside of a perfectly good trash can.

Cordray dry-heaved so violently she fell to her knees and thrust her head deeper into the can. "Jesus!" She gagged again. "Fuck me, but this fucking sucks."

Micah almost laughed. Seeing Cordray so miserable was the best thing that had happened to him all week. "Look at the bright side.

You're getting a week's worth of ab workouts in two minutes."

Sam scowled at him.

"Fuck your bright side." Cordray flipped him off then heaved again.

Micah struggled not to chuckle. He really wanted to tell her she'd gotten what she deserved.

"Jesus," Cordray said, finally sitting back. Her face was covered with a sheen of sweat and was the color of dried concrete. "I can't feel when a bullet blasts through my shoulder, but I can feel this? How's that for irony?"

Was she talking to him, herself, or the great and powerful Oz?

"Excuse me?" What the hell did she mean, she couldn't feel a bullet?

She regarded him as if contemplating whether or not to explain herself. "Nothing. Never mind."

"Fine, whatever." He went to the kitchen sink, rinsed the bottle, then tossed it in the recycling bin.

Sam steamrolled into the kitchen behind him and slugged his shoulder.

"Ow." He rubbed his arm.

"You and I need to talk." She bobbed her head toward the back hallway.

Was she pissed at him? When had she become chummy enough with Satan's mistress to get all bent at him rather than her? Oh, that's right. Two nights ago. If only he could forget.

Once they were out of earshot, Sam spun around and shoved him hard enough to hurt. "Stop giving Cordray shit."

"What the hell? You know I don't like her."

"Not everything is about you, Micah."

"I don't like coming home to find her here. Throwing up our last bottle of Jack Daniels, no less. Why the hell is she here, anyway? Shouldn't she be lording over Trace? She barged in here for him the other night demanding we turn him over, and now that we have, she's back here again? What does she want this time? To borrow a cup of sugar?"

"Micah—"

"Jesus, I just want her out of our lives."

"Micah—"

"Can't she find someone else to torture?"

"MICAH!"

"What?"

"She's in love with him!"

The brakes engaged in his brain, and for a very long moment, his feet cemented themselves to the floor.

"What? What did you say?" Surely she didn't mean Cordray and Trace. No way. That was just absurd. This took the whole k-i-s-s-i-n-g song Sam teased him with the other day to a whole other level he'd never seen coming.

Sam sighed and took a step closer. "You heard me. Cordray is in love with Trace. *Our* Trace. She loves him."

He cringed. "Stop saying that." He glanced behind him as if he could go back to the kitchen, hit replay, and create a different outcome to this conversation. Then he turned back around and searched Sam's face, as well as her mind. "Does he . . .? Does Trace . . .?" He couldn't even finish that sentence for all the ramifications it held.

Sam finished for him. "Love her?"

A chill ran down his back, and he swallowed without nodding. But he could tell Sam knew she'd hit the monkey with the banana.

Sam's eyebrows rose, creating cute wrinkles in her forehead. "If you want to know what I think—"

"I'm not sure I do."

She crossed her arms and tilted her head. "Well, I'm going to tell you anyway, Mr. Grumpy. I personally think Trace has mated her and just doesn't know it, yet."

Micah sighed and closed his eyes. There went the last of his good mood. Just—*poof!*—right out the door.

"Now I think *I'm* going to be sick."

Sam smacked his shoulder again. "Would you grow up for five seconds and help me figure out how we're going to get those two to see what's going on between them?"

"I don't want them to see what's going on between them."

Sam huffed and adjusted her crossed arms as she cocked her head in a show of irritation.

"Fine," he surrendered, jacking his hands up on his hips. "What do you want me to do?"

He could think of about a hundred other things he'd rather be doing right now than discussing Trace and Cordray's romantic status. Furthermore, if Trace had mated that bitch, what would it mean for him and Sam? Would Trace up and leave?

He couldn't deny his mate anything she set her sights on, though. And right now it looked like Sam had taken the coupling of his dearest friend and his greatest nemesis as her latest project. Until he got on board, Sam would make his life hell.

Sam brushed her palm up and down his arm. "Why don't you

just . . . oh, I don't know . . . not interfere for once." She took his hand. "Do you think you can do that?"

He scowled, not liking the idea of standing by while Trace maybe, possibly, *probably* was moving to the dark side of the Force. He felt he needed to initiate a rescue mission and fight for Trace's soul.

Sam cocked her head to the side when he didn't answer. "Micah, we talked about this the other night. I thought you had already accepted this was a possibility."

Pulling pigtails.

That's how Sam had described it.

"Yeah, well, it was a possibility I'd hoped wouldn't come true."

"Then you weren't being realistic."

He nodded over his shoulder toward the living room. "I don't like her."

Sam let go of his hand and crossed her arms again. "Then I guess it's a good thing you're not the one she's in love with."

He actually cringed at the mental image. "But—"

"This isn't about you, Micah. This is about Trace. What's best for *Trace*. What *Trace* wants, not you. You're his best friend. Don't you want him to be happy?"

"How is Cordray going to make him happy? She's absolutely all wrong for him."

If only he could wave a magic wand and make all this nonsense go away.

Sam shifted her weight, the angle of her head deepening as her left eyebrow arched impatiently.

"That's not for you to decide, Micah. She might be *exactly* what he needs. Because let's face it, Trace isn't your typical male. He needs an atypical female. And how much more atypical can you get than Cordray?" She swung one arm in the direction of the living room. "If she's not the perfect match for Trace, then I don't know who is." She lowered her arm. "And, Jesus Christ, Micah! You don't need to be such a control freak about everything. Sometimes you just need to let go, sit back, and let nature take its course."

He sighed and took a step closer, resting his hands on her hips.

She recrossed her arms and angrily averted her gaze, chin high.

Sam. His little spitfire. It was why he'd fallen in love with her. Why his body had chosen her as his mate. Because few people, male or female, challenged him the way she did. Those who did normally felt his wrath. When she did it, it actually turned him on.

Like now.

"Are you finished?" he said.

Her gaze lanced his. "Are you?"

He sighed and pulled her closer. "Yes, dear. I'm finished. Just tell me what you'd like me to do."

"That's just it," she said. "I don't want you to do anything. Just let them figure this out on their own." She uncrossed her arms and played her fingers over the front of his shirt. "You meddle too much in other people's relationships, baby."

"Well, if I didn't, they'd never mate."

She offered him a crooked smile. "You don't know that."

He lifted his gaze to the ceiling. "Let's see, there's Sev and Ari, Io and Miriam . . ." He ticked them off on his fingers. "Malek and Gina." He met her gaze again. "If I hadn't gotten involved, Sev, Io, and Malek would probably be dead right now. And that's just since New Year's."

She patted his chest with her palms. "True, but Trace isn't in any danger. Let him figure this one out on his own."

"And what am I supposed to do in the meantime?"

Her grin turned into a playful smirk, and she wound her forearms around his neck. "Oh, I'm sure I can keep you busy." The way her gaze fell seductively to his mouth and her fingertips brushed the back of his neck gave him a clear idea of exactly how she planned to keep him busy.

"Now you're talking my language, female." He leaned in for a taste of her lips then bobbed his head in the direction of the living room. "Let's get her cleaned up and out the door, and then you and I can share some quality time downstairs."

She shook her head and rolled her eyes, biting back a grin. "Did you see the shape she was in? She can't go anywhere."

"She'll be fine."

"Uh, no. I may be in the land of the immortals here, but I'm pretty sure it's still not safe to drink and drive."

He could already see in her thoughts what was coming next.

"No," he said. "Absolutely not."

She gaped at him. "Micah, she can't leave when she's that drunk." She pointed toward the living room.

"So, you want her to stay here?"

"Of course. Isn't that the polite thing to do?"

When it came to Cordray, polite wasn't a word that came to mind.

"Micah, either she stays and sleeps this off or you're sleeping alone today."

"You're threatening to withhold sex to get your way?" Damn, but Sam knew how to negotiate.

"Whatever it takes," she said. "I learned to fight dirty from the best."

"Me?"

"Bingo."

"Fine. She can stay upstairs in one of the guest rooms. With a huge trash can beside the bed. I'm not having her ruin the carpet."

Sam let out an exasperated laugh as she began to lead him back through the kitchen. "She's not going to throw up everywhere. She's —" She pulled up and let out a breathy laugh.

"What?" He followed her gaze toward the living room.

Only to find Cordray passed out cold. She was facedown on the couch. One tattooed arm draped down to the floor, and one leg hung halfway off the cushions. Her long hair dangled in stringy ropes and haphazard braids over her face.

Sam nudged him toward the fridge. "Grab a bottle of water."

"Why?" He yanked open the refrigerator door. "Are you going to throw it on her?"

She rolled her eyes and quietly opened the cabinet. "No, I'm not going to throw it on her." She huffed and shook her head as she pulled the bottle of aspirin from the top shelf then reached for the water. "I'm making a care package."

He slapped the bottle in her palm and grinned. "I like my idea better."

"Of course you do," she whispered, practically tiptoeing toward the couch. She needn't have worried about being quiet. It didn't look like cannon fire could bring Cordray back to consciousness.

Sam set the aspirin and water on the coffee table beside Cordray's cell phone then rejoined him in the kitchen, taking his hand and tugging him toward the door leading to the basement. "Come on, baby, let's go play."

Play? Now they were getting somewhere.

With renewed interest, he turned his attention toward his mate and away from the monster sprawled in inebriated hibernation on his couch.

The idea that Cordray and Trace were on a collision course with one another didn't sit well with him, but there seemed to be little he could do to prevent it.

Maybe Sam was right. Maybe he just needed to stand back and let nature take its course. If Cordray was indeed Trace's mate, he wouldn't be whole until he let himself claim her.

And more than anything, Micah wanted his best friend to be happy. He just thought that happiness would come at his hands, not Cordray's.

CHAPTER 22

TRACE JOSTLED AWAKE to the uncontrollable giggles of two ornery toddlers jumping up and down on his bed.

"Wake up, Twace!" Null flopped himself over Trace's stomach then rolled all the way down to his ankles.

His laughter reminded him of bubbles popping.

Aiden dropped to her knees beside his head and pitter-pattered her palms on his cheeks.

"You're awake!"

Of course he was awake. A pint-sized earthquake was going down in his bedroom.

"No, I'm not." He closed his eyes as he reached around and tickled Aiden's tiny bare foot.

She squealed and fell backward then shot back to her feet. A moment later, she unexpectedly jumped on his torso, landing like a trick rider on a pony.

His eyes popped open as the air whooshed out of him. "Oomph!"

She laughed and straddled his stomach, kicking her legs as if she were trying to spur him on.

Null crawled back up the bed, his blond hair curled over his eyes. He grabbed Trace's hand and shoved it into the mattress. "Gotcha! Aidy, get his othew hand!"

She swooped to the side with a screech and landed on his arm.

Trace pretended he couldn't move. "Oh no. I'm trapped. You got me." Pretending to be their helpless captive was worth hearing their triumphant growls, which really sounded more like kittens purring, making them even more adorable.

He hadn't had this much fun in a long time. Pure, genuine fun. The kind he'd never had as a kid himself.

"What about food and water?" He feigned thirst, smacking his lips together. "What if I'm hungry and thirsty?" In fact, he was both right now. He always was upon waking. "You're not going to let me go hungry or die of thirst, are you?"

Aiden giggled. "You're silly."

"Am not."

Null tag-teamed into the conversation. "Yes you are." Are came out sounding more like awe.

"No fair. It's two against one." He began to pull his hands free.

Both of them doubled their efforts, trying to secure him. He let them think they had him for a few more seconds. Then he yanked his hands from their holds and scooped them up, one in each arm, laughing.

Their giggles were infectious. Innocent and cherubic. He had never heard anything sweeter and more heart-warming.

"You guys are trouble," he said, sitting up and swinging his legs off the bed.

"Nuh-uh!" They spoke in unison, slinging their arms around his neck, holding on like little crabs.

The cinnamon scent of french toast hit his nose, making his stomach growl.

"Mmmm, smells like breakfast is ready." He stood, his arms supporting their tiny rumps as they settled, one on each hip. "Are you two ready for breakfast?"

Eager, hungry nods and another round of giggles answered him.

"Then let's go downstairs and fill those tiny bellies so you can keep up your strength. That way, the next time you sneak attack me maybe I won't be able to escape your *iron holds of death*." He tickled them, making them break into fits of laughter as he stepped into the hall.

He glanced toward Cordray's closed bedroom door. His memory flashed back to last night and what they'd almost done to each other. Had she come home after he'd gone to bed? He vaguely remembered hearing her Ducati as he drifted in and out of sleep, but he couldn't smell her intoxicating scent, so maybe he'd been dreaming. Or maybe she had come home but wasn't in her room.

He felt little fingers scratching his stomach and looked down. Both Null and Aiden were laughing their bubbly laughter while trying to tickle him.

"Hey, what are you two trying to do? Make me pee my pants?"

They both threw back their heads, laughing so hard it was a wonder they could catch their breath.

"Coco won't like it if I do that." He set them down and took their hands. "Come on, let's go eat."

Once they reached the dining room, Null and Aiden let go of his hands and darted into the kitchen.

He followed, hoping to see Cordray.

Instead, Mya was the one preparing breakfast, with no sign of Cordray. Mya turned from the stove and a giant griddle steaming with slices of cinnamon-covered french toast and greeted him with a smile.

"Good morning." The front of her blue T-shirt read *My favorite number of the alphabet is blue.*

"Nice shirt," he said.

"Thanks." She glanced down at her shirt. "I'm into sarcastic humor."

"Obviously." He grinned at her then helped Null get the carton of milk from the fridge. "So, where's Cordray this morning?"

The look she gave him before turning back around to flip the toast was one that read all kinds of I-know-what's-going-on-between-you-two. "She's out."

"Out where?" Surely, she hadn't stayed out all night.

Mya shrugged. "Don't know. But this isn't unusual."

He grabbed two plastic sippy cups from the cabinet. "What do you mean?" He helped Null pour the milk. "She's not here every day?"

Mya used tongs to turn a battalion's worth of sausage links sizzling in a large iron skillet. This crew sure ate a lot of sausage. "Cordray comes and goes. She's always off working, doing something for King Bain, whatever. She'll come in for a few days then leave again. Could be gone a day or two. Could be gone a week . . . maybe longer. Just depends on what she's got going on."

Trace didn't like the sound of that. He'd fully expected Cordray to be there today. Dare he say he had *hoped* she would be there today, because part of him wanted what had happened in the hall outside the kids' room to happen again. Sooner rather than later. Only this time, he didn't want it to stop.

He rubbed his thumb up and down his sternum as something that felt like heartburn simmered inside his chest.

He was probably just overly hungry, except his stomach wasn't growling. There was a gnawing sensation in his belly, but it didn't feel like hunger. If he were a human, he would think he was coming down with a bug, but he wasn't human. He didn't get sick. Not like that, anyway.

He sighed and glanced out the window as a female he hadn't seen before — one with blond hair — crossed the backyard to the dorm.

"Who's that?" he said.

Mya followed his gaze. "That's Steffie."

"Steffie?"

"She's one of our volunteers. She comes in a couple of times a week to do laundry and clean. She brings in groceries, too."

He frowned. There was something he didn't like about Steffie, but he couldn't put a finger on what.

"How long has she been a volunteer?" He was still rubbing his knuckles over his chest but let his hand drop to his side when Mya turned a questioning glance toward him.

"A couple of months. Why?"

He tried to shake off the odd feeling Steffie gave him but couldn't. But he didn't want to worry Mya, either. "No reason. Just curious." He glanced around the kitchen. "So, can I help with breakfast?"

Mya set the platter of french toast in front of him. "You can if you're ready to eat?" She winked. "It'll be every man for himself once the kids pile in, so you'd better grab yours now so you can be out of the way when they get here. French toast is their favorite, and you could lose a hand in the feeding frenzy if you're not careful."

"Good to know."

She returned to the stove and took up the sausage while he stacked four pieces of french toast on a plate.

"Here." She dropped four sausage links next to the toast.

"Thanks."

He helped Aiden and Null build their own plates, and five minutes later, the back door flew open as the other five kids Cordray took care of flew in, flooding the dining room with chatter.

The girl named Panya blushed as she sat across from him, meeting his gaze for only a second before looking away. Leon and Riley were too absorbed in one another to pay him much attention, although both wore worried expressions and had dark circles under their eyes as if they hadn't slept. Riley's were rimmed in red, and it looked like she'd been crying. Between mouthfuls of french toast, Faith and Gavin quizzed each other on what sounded like tests they were taking later today.

The atmosphere was right in every way but one. Cordray wasn't there.

In only a few short days, he'd come to associate her with the kids. She was the lifeblood of Asylum. The heartbeat of the orphanage. Its soul.

Cordray made everything feel more alive — including him — with just her presence.

Ever since he'd met her, his heart beat a little harder whenever she was around. His blood heated, his skin sizzled. His entire body perked up. When she departed, she took all the light and spirit with her. Life just didn't feel as exciting when she wasn't there.

Cordray was as vital as oxygen to everyone she encountered. Vital to him. He *needed* her. Needed her as badly as he needed Micah. Maybe even more.

He'd been so committed to treating her like she was the enemy that the realization that she was important to him slammed into his soul with the force of a charging elephant. He actually dropped his fork and swayed backward in his seat.

Null's mysterious blue eyes twinkled as he giggled. Everybody quieted at the clang of metal on porcelain.

Straightening, he picked up his fork and spun the handle in his fingers. "Sorry." He cut off a bite of french toast and huddled over his plate.

What did these new feelings for Cordray mean for his relationship with Micah? He couldn't imagine his life without Micah or Sam, but it was rapidly becoming apparent he couldn't imagine his life without Cordray, either.

He'd just found order in his life, and now controlled chaos threatened to disrupt all the spiritual feng shui he'd fought so hard to put in place.

He was still struggling with his thoughts an hour later as he cleared the garden and prepared it for planting.

Gardening was a far cry from his job as an enforcer, but there was something oddly comforting in working the earth. It helped prevent the rampant thoughts whipping through his mind from spinning out of control. It also reminded him of when he was a kid, gathering herbs and roots for his mother's tinctures.

She'd been such a beautiful woman. Dark skin, green eyes, thick brown hair that she often had to wrap in a scarf, because she could never do anything with it. But he'd always loved how she looked when she let it down. By today's standards, Mother's hair had been a mess of tangles, but she owned it, carrying herself with grace and confidence.

And then she'd died.

All because of him.

He closed his eyes and lifted his head toward the sun's rays as a tremor of fear rippled through him.

He still hadn't faced Brak and his father.

What if Father blamed him? He'd never been close to anyone in his family. Not really. He'd been the black sheep. The one no one comforted. The one who had to fend for himself when he was being attacked by the other kids.

He blinked his eyes open behind his wraparound sunglasses and turned back to the garden.

A warm breeze blew in from the south, which probably meant a storm was coming. It was that time of year. Spring in Chicago always meant storms. So yeah, it would be nice to finish clearing the garden before the rain arrived.

The hours droned by. Lunch came and went. Riley and Leon returned home from school, and Null and Aiden came out to play at the edge of the garden while he finished up.

A little after four-thirty, he returned the tiller and shovels to the barn and went inside to retrieve his bag and dirty clothes before heading back to Micah's.

Hopefully, he would be allowed to borrow one of Asylum's SUVs. He would hate to call a cab, but since his custom chopper was still parked in Micah's garage, his travel choices were limited.

Other than Mya and Brenna preparing dinner in the kitchen, the house was quiet. Lonely even. Unlike this morning at breakfast.

He climbed the stairs, stuffed his dirty clothes into his duffel, then stepped back into the hall as he shut his bedroom door.

He felt like a gypsy. Bedroom here. Bedroom at Micah's. Dorm at AKM. He rarely went home anymore. To his true home, the little trailer that held almost all his worldly possessions. Not that there were many. He still had his old rock collection. That and a few clothes, some books, and that was about it. He'd learned to live simply, not leaving much of a footprint during his travels. Until joining AKM, he had wandered from place to place.

Story of his life. He'd never really felt at home anywhere.

Home. What did the word even mean to him? It was more than a place to lay his head. More than four walls, a bed, and a place to brush his teeth. Home was where the heart was. But where was his heart?

He loved Micah and Sam, but they had each other. With them, he would always be the thirteenth donut in a baker's dozen. And that was okay. He'd rather be that than nothing at all. But, ideally, one day he would be part of a pair. Not a spare tire but one that was necessary to get the car from *a* to *b*. Micah had Sam. Io had Miriam. Malek had Gina. Sev and Ari had each other. Even Tristan had someone, although Josie wasn't officially his mate. Trace wanted the same. He wanted a female who was all his own, who existed expressly for him. Someone he could build a life with. A home with. A family with.

As he passed Cordray's bedroom, his chest began to ache again. It had ached most of the day. A dull, nagging pain deep inside his rib cage. And it was getting worse.

He stopped and glanced at her door as he stroked the tips of his fingers down his sternum, remembering how she'd felt pressed against him. How her nails had dug into his shoulders as she pulled him closer. How her teeth had felt as they harshly nipped his bottom lip.

His cock thickened, and heat pulsed heavily throughout his body. Just the thought of her was enough to make him ravenous with arousal.

He set his hand on the doorknob.

She hadn't come home. He knew she hadn't. He couldn't stop himself from looking anyway.

It was like watching a movie you've seen fifty times. You know how it's going to end, but you still hope the characters will create a different ending. So, as the latch gave and he began pushing open the door, his heart skipped a hopeful beat as if he would find her lying on her red satin sheets, black hair spilling over her pillow, beckoning him to join her. All he found was a made bed, the lights off, and the windows shuttered.

His heart fell.

Her scent still hung in the air. It was stronger here, in her personal space. The subtle, musky, citrusy scent that was uniquely hers.

He drew in a long, deep inhale.

Cordray.

A few days ago he had hated her. Or at least he thought he did. Now? Hate wasn't the word for how he felt, but whatever mysterious emotion roiled in his blood was just as strong. He wanted to throw her off a cliff then rush to the bottom to catch her before she splattered into bloody pulp. All so he could be her savior, not that Cordray needed saving. But he wanted her to look at him as if he were the hero she'd never known she needed.

She was fire, but he still wanted to touch her. How twisted was that?

He shut the door then forced himself to walk away from her luscious scent, which—now that he thought about it—he'd become quite addicted to.

By the time he reached the stairs, the ache in his chest had intensified, as if retaliating against him for leaving her room. As he entered the kitchen, his chest was positively pounding.

He winced as he rubbed his knuckles against his left pec.

Mya glanced up from the stove and gave him a concerned frown. "Are you okay?"

He cleared his throat and nodded. "Yeah, um . . ." It hurt to breathe. "Can I borrow the keys to the Denali? I'll bring it back tomorrow morning." He raised his duffel of dirty clothes as if that was all the reason she needed to understand his request. Truth was, he was too busy trying to tame whatever this shit was ripping a chasm through his ribs to speak any more than he had to.

"Sure." She gestured toward the rack of keys hanging on the wall inside the mud room. "The keys are on the skull ring."

There were a dozen keyrings hanging on the rack. A dragon, a black widow spider, a snake. Cordray's Gothic influence was everywhere.

He lifted the skull ring off the rack, and the violent churning inside his chest diminished to a rough simmer. These were Cordray's keys. The chain was a part of her. He tucked the keys into his fist and inhaled easily for the first time since before he'd entered her bedroom a few minutes ago.

With a nod of farewell, he pushed through the door that led into the garage, opened the bay door, and hopped behind the wheel of the white Denali.

Destination, Micah's house.

Maybe after a session in Micah's dungeon he could get a grip on whatever voodoo spell Cordray had cast over him.

CHAPTER 23

CORDRAY STIRRED AWAKE in the late afternoon to the sound of her cell phone pinging with an incoming message.

She groaned as the residual effects of Jack Daniels filtered through her brain. Or maybe it was the remnants of her brain that were filtering through the residual Jack Daniels. She couldn't be sure, because, yeah, she'd shredded a few to a million brain cells with her frat-party drinking binge this morning.

Good thing her vampire genes could replace them as fast as she destroyed them or she would be nothing but an incoherent smudge of flesh and bone.

At least her head no longer felt like a hundred of those stubby, pellet-shaped Minions were inside her skull dancing to disco music, but her stomach still felt sour. Ironic that she couldn't feel anything that happened to the outside of her body, but everything going on inside felt magnified by the power of ten.

She rolled herself into a sitting position and rubbed her eyes before blindly reaching for her cell phone, which she vaguely remembered setting on the corner of the coffee table before passing out. Her hand landed on polished wood. Opening her eyes, she saw that her mobile wasn't there.

"Looking for this?"

She turned toward the sound of Micah's voice. He was standing in the doorway leading down the hall. He was holding her phone, and from the way his finger was slowly scrolling up the screen, he was reading her messages.

She lurched toward him. "What the hell—" A million ice picks dug into her brain, making her rethink movement, talking, and even breathing.

She clutched her head and sank back into the couch, propping her elbows on her knees as she cradled her forehead in her palms. She would have whimpered had Micah not been there.

"You've been a busy little bee." Micah's booted feet broke into her field of vision as he stopped in front of her.

She groaned when what she really wanted to do was snatch back her phone and punch him for violating her privacy.

"What are you doing with my phone? Why are you reading my messages?" Out of the corner of her eye, she spied the aspirin and bottled water sitting on the coffee table, just past Micah's left leg. Her mouth was as dry as scorched cotton, but she refused to show weakness in front of him, even if she was doubled over with the hangover headache of death.

Micah reached down, grabbed the bottle of water, and tossed it onto her lap before sidestepping away from her toward the chair she'd sat in last night as she'd expelled her past to Sam.

"Someone had to answer your phone," he said. "It's gone off three times in ten minutes." He dropped his ass into the chair. "What the fuck are you doing messing around with Grudge Match?"

Her head shot up. She instantly regretted it as pain speared her left eye from the inside out. "What do you know about Grudge Match?"

"I asked you first."

Really? He wanted to play that game?

Giving up all pretenses that she wasn't hurting as badly as she was, she picked up the bottle from her lap and twisted off the lid. Just feeling the cool water wash down her throat was enough to make her sigh in relief.

After guzzling half the bottle, she wiped the back of her hand over her mouth and glared at him as best as she could under the circumstances, which was to say she probably looked more like a blind Chinese crested than a pissed-off vampire with an attitude problem.

"Technically, I asked you first, asshole. If you recall, I asked why you're reading my messages?" She reached for the bottle of aspirin and popped off the cap.

"I told you—"

"You told me my phone was going off, not why you decided it was okay to read my messages." She tossed two tablets in her mouth and quickly washed them down before continuing. "You could easily have silenced my phone without violating my privacy."

Micah raised his hands, palms out. "You got me. I was spying. Sue me."

"Maybe I will."

"Fine. Now tell me what the hell you're doing messing around with Grudge Match."

"Sorry. No-can-do. Members only." She flashed him the sweetest smile she could muster with tiny trolls hammering at her brain with what felt like jagged pickaxes.

Micah blew out an abrupt huff and held up her phone. "Who's this Digon? And what's this about an audition and something called the gauntlet?"

Just how far back had he read in her texts? "Why the hell do you want to know so badly?"

"Because I've been hearing about Grudge Match for months and haven't figured out a way to infiltrate."

Cordray swallowed the last of her water. "That's because you don't know the secret handshake." She gave him a saccharine smile and batted her eyelashes, even though the slight movement played hell with her headache.

"Jesus, would you quit being so difficult for once in your goddamn life and tell me what you know?"

Wiping the smile off her face, she squared her shoulders. "Give me back my phone, and I'll think about it."

"Fine. Christ!" He tossed the phone at her.

She caught it and shot him a wicked scowl. "Are your only two decibel levels blaring and deafening, with a side of obnoxious? Or do you think you could manage something more — oh, I don't know — quiet and polite? And would it hurt you to say please and thank you once in a while . . . in a voice that isn't encroaching on space shuttle launch?"

"Would you just fucking spill . . . *please*?"

She tapped her screen and pulled up Digon's messages. "I said I'd *think* about it, not that I would."

Micah grumbled something unintelligible that sounded like a sentiment about how he felt sorry for Trace and couldn't understand why Sam liked her, but half the words came out sounding more like growls than decipherable English.

But she was too busy reading Digon's texts to pay him much mind. Grudge Match's next gathering was in two nights. He'd sent a separate message with a schedule for the next month, including dates and locations. The fight club apparently rotated venues to keep themselves as clandestine as possible, so a new schedule was sent out every month.

"What's going on up here, Micah?" Sam said, appearing in the kitchen, wearing jeans and a fitted T-shirt. "I could hear you all the way down in the basement."

Cordray lifted her head. "See?" She flung an I-told-you-so look at him and said, "Space shuttle launch."

Micah exhaled heavily, shook his head at her, and leaned back in his chair. Keeping his gaze locked on hers, he tilted his head back and said over his shoulder, "Sorry, babe. Just trying to figure out why I even bother trying to be nice to this witch."

"Micah . . ." Sam shook her head disapprovingly.

"You call that being nice?" Cordray said. "You read my messages without my permission and boss me around like I'm one of your personal informants, and you think that's nice?"

"Micah, you didn't . . .?"

He glowered across the coffee table at her, his jaw rigid, face shaded dark pink.

Sam poured a mug of coffee and brought it into the living room, extending it toward her.

Grateful for something stronger than water to help the aspirin kill her headache, Cordray took the mug. "Thank you."

Sam turned on Micah, her hands on her hips. "You need to apologize to our guest." Then she returned to the kitchen and started pulling out pans and skillets to make breakfast as if she expected Micah to do as she said without question.

Eyes narrow, his expression tight, Micah gritted his teeth as he stared at her.

"*Now*, Micah," Sam said as she pulled a carton of eggs from the fridge.

He frowned and glanced to the side. "I'm working on it, dear."

Cordray imagined that apologizing to her felt about as comforting to Micah as the asteroid crashing into the earth millions of years ago had felt to the dinosaurs.

He took a deep breath, held it for a moment, then blew it out. "I'm . . . sorry." He cleared his throat and shifted uneasily. "I'm sorry for reading your messages. And for bossing you around." His eyes narrowed as he glanced away. "And for yelling while you're obviously feeling like shit." The corner of his mouth quirked as if that secretly delighted him and he'd been talking loudly on purpose.

"You can be a real ass, you know that?" Cordray said, tucking her phone in her pocket."

"So they tell me."

Sam returned to the living room with another mug of coffee and handed it to Micah like it was a reward. "Thank you for apologizing," she said lovingly, bending down to kiss him.

He turned his face up to hers. Before their lips met, he said,

"Anything for you, baby."

She gave him a light pat on the cheek as her mouth lingered on his, and then she pulled away. "Yeah, well, it would be nice if I didn't have to remind you to be nice as often as I do."

"But then I'd miss out on these little rewards you give me when I apologize for being bad."

Sam rolled her eyes and grinned as she shook her head. "You're such a difficult man."

"Male."

"Whatever."

As they kissed again, Cordray dropped her gaze into her mug of coffee, feeling like an intruder. Watching Micah and Sam's dynamic as a mated couple reminded her of how alone she was.

Mates held a certain magic over one another. As soon as the mating bond connected them to each other, they ceased being separate entities, becoming one that dwelled within two bodies. Well, maybe not exactly like that, but close enough to generalize that that's what happened.

Mates could locate each other across vast distances as if guided by a homing beacon, as Io had with Miriam. They could feel when the other was in trouble, even if hundreds of miles separated them. A male's mate held incredible power over him, such as Sam did with Micah. She snapped her fingers, and he jumped. She told him to apologize, and he did. She was his conscience, and he was her champion.

Seeing how enchanting they were together made her angry. She wanted what they had, and — damn her traitorous heart — she wanted it with Trace.

But she was still too damn scared to open herself, especially to him. The way they lashed out at each other like two tomcats fighting over territorial boundaries warned of pending doom. What if she invited him into her bed? What if the sex was as epic as she suspected it would be? She had damn near detonated in the hallway as he kissed her last night, so sex would probably send her into a nuclear meltdown. What if that happened and she found the most unbelievable pleasure she'd ever known, allowed herself to fall in love with him, and then he realized she wasn't his cup of tea?

Or worse yet, what if he found his one true mate and left her? He'd made it no secret that he didn't like her, but sex was sex, and if it was one thing she had learned by penetrating Trace's thoughts, it was that he had never found arousal outside the playroom. But he found it with her. She had seen his erections straining his jeans. She'd felt his hard length against her when she awoke to find him on top of her, and again last night in the hallway as he pressed her against the wall. Of course he would entertain the possibility of having sex with her when she could arouse him in a way no one else could. Trace could choose to enjoy the benefits of their physical connection for as long as the whim carried him, and when the novelty wore off, he could walk away. Where would that leave her?

In a useless, unfeeling heap in the forest, that's where.

Been there, done that. Bought the T-shirt, wore it, burned it. Upgraded to body armor.

She had spent centuries erecting the walls protecting her, forging her prickly, aloof demeanor to keep everyone at arm's length. Now, she'd found someone she wanted to pull closer and didn't know how. She no longer possessed the social skills required to invite someone into her private space, even if her fear abated long enough to let her.

"If you guys are finished sucking on each other's faces . . ." she said pointedly.

Sam pulled away and smiled, her cheeks flushed. "Sorry." She straightened. "I'll let you two chat." She caressed Micah's shoulder as she turned and went back to the kitchen.

"So," Micah said, his tone milder, "*please* tell me what you know about Grudge Match."

Cordray hugged her coffee mug as if it were a lifeline. In a way, it was, because every sip made her head hurt a little bit less.

"Honestly, not much. Yet. But I've only been to one meeting."

"How did you get in?"

Cordray gave a halfhearted shrug. "They've got a website."

Micah's black eyebrows furrowed sharply as if he didn't believe her. "I haven't found one."

She would have laughed if she didn't think it would make her head blow up. "It's called the Dark Net, Micah." She snapped her fingers in hurry-up fashion. "See if you can keep up with technology, big guy."

"I know about the Dark Net." The hint of chagrin in his eat-shit expression told her he just hadn't thought to check it and felt like an idiot for not doing so.

"Yeah well, you should spend some time there. You'd be amazed what you can find out."

"I'll bet. Now, could you get on with it before you bore me to death?"

She rolled her eyes. Males could be so testy about bruising their egos. "I hit up their site, and lo and behold, they have an interest form to become a member, so I filled it out. Who knew it would be that easy?"

"They must be desperate if they accepted you."

"They just know talent when they see it."

"Whatever. So, then what?"

Talking to Micah was like talking to Trace, only not as fun. "After submitting my application, I waited a little while then got an invitation to run what they call the gauntlet. It's their initiation. If you make it through the gauntlet, you're in. If you don't" — she made a sad face and waved her fingers in a bye-bye motion — "too bad, so sad, sorry about your luck, but you're out."

Micah scoffed. "Well, if *you* made it through, so can I."

"Yes, but I had an advantage."

"Wait, let me guess. You really *are* able to turn men to stone with one look?"

"Micah . . ." Sam warned.

He threw his hands up in surrender. "Hey, she set herself up for that one."

Sam huffed and rolled her eyes before tossing poppy seeds into what looked like pancake batter. The scent of freshly grated lemon zest drifted on the air, and a bright-pink salmon fillet sat on a cutting board on the counter beside the batter bowl.

Was Sam trying to become the next Bobby Flay or what?

"Funny," Cordray said to Micah, "but no, I can't turn men to stone. Not anymore, anyway. Back in the day, though . . . that's quite another story." She winked at Sam, who lifted her gaze from the bowl of batter she was folding poppy seeds into and giggled.

Micah spun around. "I heard that."

Sam blew him a kiss as she scooted the bowl aside and went to work on the salmon. "I love you, baby, but you know I appreciate a good sense of humor."

Micah exhaled heavily as he faced Cordray again, one brow arched, his stare glassy and unimpressed. "Okay, fine. So what advantage did you have that I don't?"

"Ask Sam."

"Sam?" Micah glanced over his shoulder again.

Sam looked up from shaving paper-thin slices off the fish. "Me?"

"Yes." Cordray nodded once. "What I told you last night. You know, about what happened to me? How you were able to hit me without hurting me?"

"You hit her?" Micah asked, jacking his thumb in Cordray's direction.

"Uh . . ." Sam's face flushed, and she briefly glanced down. "I guess you could say that."

"And I missed it?" Micah looked back and forth between them. "Damn. I would have paid good money to see that." He smirked at Cordray.

"I bet you would," Cordray replied.

"Okay, so what does my mate punching you have to do with you having an advantage?"

"Sam?" Cordray raised her chin at her.

Sam met her gaze then looked at Micah. "She can't feel."

Micah's frown was almost comical. "You can't?"

"Nope. Not a thing." Cordray took another sip of coffee. "So, when some guy as big as a skyscraper punched me, I was able to keep on going. You, on the other hand, you'll feel it."

"Only if I let him hit me."

"Are you saying you're going to request an audition?"

"Maybe."

Sam didn't even blink. Apparently, she was already used to Micah putting himself in harm's way and coming out aces. Then again, the guy was pretty badass, as far as fighters went. And he had been for as long as Cordray could remember.

She'd never crossed paths with Micah in her youth, but she'd known of his reputation. Everyone had. She also knew that he'd been one of her father's most coveted warriors. He'd even had a hand in training her brother. If only he knew as much about her as she did about him, maybe he wouldn't be so quick to criticize and discredit her.

"I'm not sure what good it will do, since I'm such a new member, but I could e-mail Digon and vouch for you," she offered.

"Why would you do that?"

"Because it might make it easier for you to get an invite. Grudge Match has a thorough vetting process to screen candidates. Since you're a member of AKM, that might make them wary. And let's face it, your reputation does precede you, Micah." His shoulders lifted almost proudly, but before he could say anything, she quickly added, "Which could be to your detriment. You're a hothead, and you're also keenly devoted to King Bain and the vampire way. That could be enough to make them reject you." She paused, knowing on one hand that she shouldn't be telling Micah any of this, but knowing on the other that if Micah was allowed into Grudge Match, the two of them could work together to find the bad eggs in Digon's club. Bad eggs who were using Grudge Match to help supply Bishop with test subjects for his experiments. Members who could provide more direct clues to Royce's involvement. Maybe even Digon himself was guilty, but she doubted it. That wasn't the vibe she got from him. But if he was guilty, and the entire fight club was one huge sourcing pool, if she and Micah worked together, they could strike a major blow to Bishop, Royce, and whoever else was working to weaken the vampire race.

Micah studied her through narrowed eyes. "I'll ask again. Why would *you* want to help *me*? What's your angle?"

She had to appreciate his cunning and intellect. He knew she would never willingly lift a finger for him if she wasn't due to get something from the effort. They didn't have that kind of relationship. Not yet, anyway. Maybe they never would, but if they did this and found success, it would go a long way toward bridging the professional gap between them.

She leaned back and crossed one leg over the other, setting the base of the coffee cup in her lap. "Let's be honest, Micah. You can do things I can't. Things that could really come in handy inside Grudge Match."

Suspicion pinched the corners of Micah's eyes as he lowered his chin and angled his body away from her. "Like what?"

"Like, for instance, your annoying ability to see people's thoughts undetected." She shrugged. "I can't do that. Yeah, sure, maybe I can work through Trace's mental defenses when you can't, but he can feel me doing so if he pays attention. So can others." Which was the frustration where Grudge Match was concerned. "Digon has already warned me not to poke around in other members' thoughts."

"Really?"

"Don't look so smug." She drummed her fingers irritably on the side of her mug. "I tried to see inside his thoughts—he's the one who runs Grudge Match, by the way—and he got upset. Told me not to do it again, and not to do it to anyone else if I wanted to avoid unnecessary entanglements."

Micah smirked and let out an amused huff. "I think I like Digon already."

"Think again. He's a dreck."

"A dreck?"

"Yep, and my guess is that he comes from money. He holds himself almost regally and has an accent I can't quite place, but he sounds affluent. It's obvious he likes the finer things and has the resources to obtain them." She remembered Digon's TAG Heuer watch, the elegant accoutrements in his office, and the designer shoes. Even his denim trousers had been couture.

"Are you thinking what I'm thinking?" he said.

"That all depends on what you're thinking."

Micah shifted forward to sit on the edge of his chair, his hands linked between his knees. "What I'm thinking is that a dreck with that kind of money could be funding Bishop's experiments if Royce isn't."

Cordray bobbed her head to one side. "That thought *had* crossed my mind." She downed the last swallow of coffee. "But here's the problem. I can't see inside his thoughts to figure out just how deep he's in the shit, if he even is at all. That's where you come in. You can go where I can't, and no one will be the wiser." She held his gaze for a prolonged moment then said, "So . . .? What do you think? Can we put our differences aside long enough to work together on this? I'll do what I can to help you get an invitation. You do what you can to get through the gauntlet. Then we pool our resources to bring Royce and that fucker, Bishop, down."

Micah hesitated as if weighing the pros and cons of Cordray's plan. A moment later he stood and held out his right hand. "I'm not too proud to say I like how you're thinking on this, C. This could work, but it doesn't mean we're friends. Just business partners. Just so that's clear."

"Crystal clear, because I'm not particularly fond of you, either." She stood and clasped his hand.

"That's because the two of you are so alike it's scary," Sam said from the kitchen, flashing them both a playful glare.

"We are not." Micah swung his gaze around to eye his mate with an almost fearful expression on his face.

Sam laughed. "No one likes to see their faults reflected back at them from someone else, which is why people who are a lot alike sometimes don't get along."

Cordray pulled her hand from Micah's. "No. Absolutely not. I'm with Micah on this one."

Micah's gaze collided with hers. "At least we can agree on that."

"Besides" — Cordray sat back down — "I don't have any faults."

"Whoa, hello!" Micah ass-parked back in his chair. "Wrong answer."

"As if you're so perfect," Cordray shot back.

"Damn straight. I'm fucking awesome."

Cordray scoffed, shaking her head. "You wish."

Sam laughed even louder than before. "What did I tell you? You two are like mirrors for each other. No wonder I like you both so much."

Cordray eyed Micah out of the corner of her eye as he did the same to her. The realization that Sam might be right dawned on them both at the same time.

Micah's top lip curled. Cordray wrinkled her nose.

He swallowed thickly and looked like he might get sick as he stood. "I think I'm going to take a shower," he said dully, as if the thought that he and Cordray were alike tainted every inch of his skin like a layer of soot.

Cordray knew how he felt. As soon as she left, she would swing by her mansion on the North Shore for a shower and a change of clothes not only to wash off the stench of vomit but the feeling that she might have absorbed some of his aura. But first, she needed to tell him what she'd learned about the ankh, as well as the message from Skeletor.

"Wait, there's more." She sounded like one of those stupid commercials on TV.

Micah's shoulders wilted. "What?" Apparently, he was as ready to be rid of her as she was of him.

"Skeletor. He contacted me."

Micah's posture stiffened as he sat back down. "I'm listening."

"He hacked me yesterday while I was piggybacking off your system. We had a, um . . . shall we say it was an interesting exchange of messages?" Interesting because Skeletor knew who she really was, which was something Cordray would pointedly leave out of this discussion.

"Tell me."

"Let me tell you what I learned about the ankh first. Then I'll tell you what happened with Skeletor."

She proceeded to explain that the ankhs were really keys that opened portals between dimensions and that back before the time of the pharaohs, lycans and other mystical beings were using the ankhs to open those gateways.

"Why? What was their purpose?" Micah said.

"To bring in beings to help build the pyramids, work the land, perform rites" — she shrugged — "and do all kinds of things. According to the archives, lycans guarded the gates and possessed the only keys to open them, so I'm not sure how your father got his hands on one."

Micah shrugged. "Who knows?" He rubbed the scruff over his chin and jaw. "So where is this portal or gateway my ankh unlocks?"

"I was hoping you could tell me. Or whether or not you'd know if the ankh opened more than one, because some ankhs could open a group of gates."

Micah shook his head. "I've got nothin'. Like I said, my father died before he could tell me much about it. Did you learn anything about who would have knowledge about how the ankh works?"

"If I had about a decade to kill, I could probably find the answers in Bain's archives. Being that I don't, the next best place to find answers is from the lycans."

Micah nearly spit out a sip of coffee. "The lycans? You're kidding, right? You know they won't want to help us."

"I wish I were kidding, but no. I'm as serious as sin. And you don't know that they won't be willing to help. Maybe they're not big fans of our race, but we're not at war with them and never have been."

"Tell that to Memnon."

True, vampires and lycans had never engaged in outright war, but Memnon held little love for vampires, which was why he moved his family west and demanded that the rest of the packs living in the United States do the same. The eastern half of the country was dominated by vampires. The western half belonged to the lycans, and any vampires inside his territory had to operate by his rules. His code.

"Fine. Memnon's a dick. But" — Cordray held up her index finger — "from what I found, lycans are the key masters, and Memnon is at the top of the food chain. Lycans created the gates, coding each one to an ankh that would unlock it. They supposedly know where all the portals are, too. They're the ones who first mapped them. The first to use the ankhs to open the gates. The first, period. They were on this planet before we were, and from what I read, they weren't exactly excited when the first vampires slipped through one of their portals by accident."

"Accident? What kind of accident?"

"I don't know the details. All I could decipher from the archive was that it was some kind of accident and the vampires were never meant to come through, and the lycans couldn't reverse what happened and send the vampires back, so they were stuck here."

"Interesting."

"I know, right? My point is, if Memnon doesn't know how your ankh works to open a gate, or which gate it opens, no one will. Unless Skeletor has figured that shit out. In which case, the sooner we consult with Memnon, the better. Otherwise, who knows what Skeletor could unleash on the planet if he manages to open a portal and invite in an army of supernatural beasts to do his bidding."

Tension marked Micah's face. "Good point." He paused, and his eyebrows bunched together. "What doesn't make sense, though, is if the lycans are the key masters, how did my father obtain one of their keys?"

Cordray let out a long, heavy exhale. "I don't know. That's a question only your late father — and maybe Memnon — can answer." She set down her coffee cup and rubbed her temples. Her headache had receded to a dull throb, but it was still bad enough to bring mild waves of nausea every few minutes.

Micah scrutinized her in the silence that followed. "So, how is it you have access to King Bain's archives to research this stuff? AKM doesn't even have that kind of clearance, and we're supposed to be the ones guarding the kingdom."

She swiped her hand horizontally in front of her as if brushing away eraser shavings. "I do special work for Bain. That's all you need to know." Because she sure as hell wasn't going to tell Micah she was Bain's sister and could do pretty much whatever she wanted. "But I did find an ancient map in Bain's archives that seemed to illustrate where all the portals in the world were at that time. Unfortunately, I couldn't make heads or tails out of it. But I bet the lycans can."

"Great, so all I need to do is find a lycan."

Cordray shook her head. "Not just any lycan, Micah. If I were you, I'd grow a pair and take this straight to Memnon or Rameses. You know how riled up they get when someone circumvents their leadership."

Memnon and Rameses — but especially Memnon — weren't known for their benevolence.

A troubled shadow fell over Micah's face as he looked away.

"What?" she said. "What's wrong?"

His gaze darted to hers. "What do you mean?"

"You look uneasy. Don't tell me you're scared of them?"

"Hell no."

"Then why do you look so upset?"

He shifted and cleared his throat. "It's nothing."

She let out an exasperated sigh. "You know I'll just dip into your thoughts and see what you're hiding if you don't tell me. How about you save us both the trouble and just tell me what's on your mind."

"I said it's nothing."

Clearly, he still didn't trust her. But if what he refused to tell her could help their cause, she wanted to know what it was. Maybe by extending an olive branch, she could earn enough of his trust to open up.

"Whatever it is, I won't tell Bain, if that's what you're worried about. And I won't tell anyone else, either. You have my word."

"No offense, but your word is for shit with me right now."

The two of them had gone around and around since they'd met. She'd dropped the ball on him when she was supposed to be at the pickup facility at the time of Trace's release, and she'd gone at him and Trace as hard as they'd gone at her. This was the most civil conversation she'd ever had with Micah, so of course he would be wary.

"I know," she said, holding up her free hand, palm facing out as if she were trying to calm a snarling dog. "I know, Micah, but I'm trying to work with you here. We need to work together. At least for now. If you have knowledge that could help, I'd like to know what it is."

He leaned forward and scrubbed his palms up and down his face as he expelled a troubled breath. When he dropped his hands to his lap, his resigned gaze lifted warily to hers. "Fine, I'll tell you, although I don't think it has anything to do with the ankh or Skeletor. But . . . Jesus . . ." He wiped his palm over his face again then raked his fingers through his hair. "Who knows at this point."

It took all of Cordray's patience not to sneak into his thoughts and see what all the fuss was about, but she didn't want to do anything to violate the fledgling trust Micah seemed on the verge of bestowing upon her.

"There's a patient at AKM. A young male. He's"—Micah locked eyes with her—"half lycan."

Cordray's mental brakes engaged. "Wait . . . what?"

"You heard me. He's half vampire, half lycan. His name is Savill, and he was rescued from Bishop's lab. He'd been cut open as if they'd been about to dissect him. We didn't think he'd make it, but we've finally stabilized him, and it looks like he might actually pull through."

"Who are his parents?" She was sure that other half-vampire-half-lycan mixed-bloods had existed at some point in history, but this was the first she'd personally heard of one. An anomaly, to be sure.

Micah shrugged. "We don't know who his real parents are, but he somehow made it into the human adoption system when he was a baby, and he was adopted by a set of human parents. You run a shelter. Have you ever seen anything like this?"

She shook her head. "I've come across a lot of mixed-bloods who got lost in the human system, but never any with lycan blood in them."

Micah sighed and bowed his head. "I knew it was a long shot."

His body language was uncharacteristically compassionate. She'd previously seen inside Micah's thoughts that he wanted children of his own. That he longed for a family and had an enormous amount of love to give, and that as badly as he treated her, he was a kind, caring person. Almost overly caring. He'd stepped in to save the lives of his comrades on numerous occasions, both now and back when he'd been a member of her father's guard. Micah was a hero's hero. The kind of person who selflessly gave of himself so that others could be given a fighting chance.

No doubt Savill's predicament deeply troubled him. He knew just as she did that Memnon and Rameses, who were purists, wouldn't want anything to do with a damaged mixed-breed who carried vampire genes. Savill would never have a place within lycan society with those two at the helm. Not that Mem and Ram were bad guys. They weren't. They were just very strict about living by the lycan code. Cordray wouldn't be surprised if they'd banished the lycan responsible for conceiving Savill in the first place, because while mating with humans was acceptable under lycan law, mating with vampires was not. In fact, at one time mating with vampires was strictly forbidden and punishable by death. It might still be. Cordray didn't know. She didn't keep up with lycan law.

Cordray spoke quietly, treading softly on what she could tell was a sensitive subject. "Have his human parents been—"

"They've been handled."

Handled. Cordray was knowledgeable enough to know what that meant. "Good." She nodded. "That's good."

"It's not good, Cordray," Micah snapped. He stood and began pacing. "It's sad. It's tragic. The only parents he's ever known think he's dead. He'll never see them again." He stopped and flung his arm out to the side as if he were pointing in the direction of Savill's hospital bed. "And when he wakes up, he'll have no one. Absolutely fucking no one. He'll be caught up in a world he didn't know existed, with a body that will begin to transition into an adult any day now if it hasn't already." He grimaced. "A body with a big fucking scar from his neck to his groin.

"Can you imagine the fear he went through? The terror he must have endured inside Bishop's lab?" Micah paced back to his chair and dropped into it with the heaviness of a five-ton boulder. "He's going to need intense therapy. Constant supervision and reassurance. And even then it might not be enough to keep him from killing himself. There's no way to tell if his vampire side or his lycan side will dominate, or if he'll be an equal blend of both. So, yeah . . . fuck good. This is a fucking nightmare." He shoved his hand through his hair again then pushed forward, elbows on knees, head bowed so that his black mane fell forward, covering his face.

Cordray exchanged worried glances with Sam, who wore a mask of concern. Apparently, this was the first she'd heard of Savill, too.

"I just meant," Cordray said gently, "that it's good his human parents have been taken care of before the situation can become even worse."

Cordray dared to take a quick peek inside Micah's mind to see if there was anything else bothering him. What she found surprised her. Tonight, Micah had learned that Malek and Gina were expecting. By itself, Savill's situation was upsetting enough, but to find out that yet another of his teammates was expecting a baby when his own calling hadn't produced a child compounded his feelings of anger, heartbreak, and frustration that much more.

She quickly pulled out of his head before he could detect her and set her coffee cup on the table. "Maybe I should be going."

"No." Micah's head shot up. "We still have to talk about Skeletor."

"We don't have to do this now," she said.

Micah huffed and shook his head. "Don't you start acting nice, C. You've been a bitch up to this point. You don't get to act like you care about my feelings now, especially since you hacked into my system last night, which pisses me off and is grounds for royal punishment." He snapped his fingers as if commanding a dog to heel. "Start talking or I'll report your illegal activity to King Bain and see how *you* like being locked in his dungeon for a couple of weeks. What happened between you and Skeletor?"

She recognized Micah's abrupt aggression for what it was. A deflection. By attacking her, he could channel his stew of negative, resentful emotions on something tangible, thus finding an outlet to blow the steam out of his chimney.

Did that mean she liked being his punching bag? No. Did she understand where he was coming from? Absolutely. Could she take one for the team to keep the peace while they infiltrated Grudge Match? Yeah, sure. Just this once.

She told him about the exchange of messages between her and their mutual enemy, including Skeletor's last message, where he flew off the deep end. She was careful not to disclose the tidbit about how she and Bain were related. Maybe Skeletor knew that shit, and while she couldn't stop him from announcing the truth to the world, she certainly wouldn't help him by revealing it to Micah or anyone else.

"He talked about being forced to keep secrets and being shunned by those who worship your own flesh and blood but don't acknowledge your existence." She paused as an epiphany bloomed inside her mind. "He sounded resentful, Micah. I think this is personal for him.

Very personal. Do you have any living relatives?"

Micah shook his head. "No. My parents both died. I stopped hearing from my uncle about the same time my parents died, so I assume he's dead, too. And since I was an only child and Uncle Rory wasn't mated, there's no one else. I'm the last of my line."

"Nobody? You can't think of anyone else?"

He shook his head. "Not a one."

She scowled and nibbled her bottom lip, trying to figure out what Skeletor's angle was. It just didn't make sense that he would throw the sibling card at her the way he did without a reason. "Maybe he's the brother of someone you killed or someone who died, and now Skeletor blames you for the death. Maybe he's seeking vengeance."

"Then why would he steal my ankh rather than try and kill me?"

"Hey," Sam said from the kitchen, waving a knife back and forth, "no talking about anyone trying to kill you, baby. If that's what he wants to do, he'll have to go through me, and rest assured, he won't be getting through me to you."

"That's why I love you, baby," Micah said, flashing his first grin in over ten minutes. "You think you're a badass."

"I *am* a badass, thank you very much."

"Yes, you are, but I don't want you putting yourself in harm's way for me. That's my job." He faced Cordray again. "But if he was out for blood vengeance, don't you think he'd want to do a lot more to hurt me than steal an ancient key?"

Sam returned to preparing the oddest breakfast Cordray had ever seen. There was now a jar of green olives sitting open on the counter that Sam was eating directly out of.

Cordray peeled her gaze away from Sam's funky breakfast and shrugged at Micah's question. Perhaps she was overthinking Skeletor's intentions. "Maybe it's as simple as he wants to open a portal and knew you had a key?" Her intuition instantly refuted the possibility, and she shook her head as she furrowed her brow. "No, that's too random. Whatever is up Skeletor's ass is too personal for it to be just about the ankh. Maybe he wants to open a portal, but that's secondary to causing you pain. Hurting you is his primary objective. That's my gut feeling."

"I think you're right." He told her about the malicious poems Skeletor had written to him.

"Man, this guy really hates you." She rubbed her hand over her forehead. All this thinking wasn't good for her hangover. "Are you sure you can't think of anyone who wants to make you suffer?"

"Cordray, if I named everyone who fit that description, the list would be longer than my dick."

Her gaze dropped to his crotch before she blinked her gaze back up to his. "So you're saying the list would be a short one."

His eyes narrowed as his mouth pressed into a thin line. "It was a metaphor."

"A bad one." She held his stare. "Would you like to rephrase it?"

His jaw ticked as if he were clenching his teeth. "No, I'm good. I think my dick is sufficiently big enough to handle such a list."

Cordray let out an irritated sigh. "Males and their dicks." She shook her head. "I'll never understand the fascination."

Micah sprawled and slung his arm over the back of the chair. "That's because you don't have one."

"Thank God. It would suck never being able to use my brain."

He smirked, which was probably as close to laughing at one of her jokes as he would ever get. "Dick jokes aside," he said, "Is that it? Is there anything else you found out that I need to know?"

"No."

He stood again and headed toward the kitchen. "I assume you know our theory about the pedway since you were inside our system last night?"

"Yes. I wanted to go by the Heritage and see if I can find anything useful."

"Don't bother. Sev already looked, and Stryker's team is making a second go-round."

"But—" She preferred to do her own recon.

"You already have enough going on." Micah spoke with the confident, no-nonsense tone of a natural-born leader.

Too bad, because she didn't do subordination. She was her own boss and wasn't into taking someone else's orders.

"You're not my boss, Micah. If I want to investigate the pedway, I'll investigate the pedway."

He shrugged, turned, and snagged a piece of salmon from the platter Sam had set in the middle of the counter. "Suit yourself." He rounded the counter and kissed Sam's cheek before popping the salmon in his mouth. "I'm going to take a shower, and then I've got an application to fill out."

"Oh, about that . . ."

Micah held up and faced her. "Yeah?"

"Grudge Match is a secret. I could get kicked out just for talking to you about it."

One corner of Micah's mouth kicked upward. "In other words, if you piss me off, I can just tell this Digon guy that you told me all about the secret handshake and he'd boot you?"

"Something like that."

"Nice to know."

"Just wait until after we've finished our investigation to get pissed off at me. This is too important to blow. It could be our best chance of finding out who's kidnapping our people, as well as to take down Royce."

Micah lifted his hand as if telling her to hush. "Don't worry, C. I know how important this is. I'm not going to fuck it up."

"That sounds good, but let's face it, Micah. You're not known to be the most subtle or level-headed of Bain's enforcers. You could blow this whole operation just for sport."

He took a step closer and glanced toward his mate. "That was before I met Sam."

Cordray glanced at Sam, who blew Micah a demure kiss before turning her attention back to the cutting board in front of her. She was slicing grape tomatoes in half and tossing them in a large glass bowl.

Cordray turned back toward Micah. "You expect me to believe that just by taking a mate, you're a changed male? *Completely* changed." She knew that Sam had brought out a better version of Micah than had been there before, but surely remnants from his past still remained.

His dark eyes narrowed as he crossed his arms over his chest and leaned his hip against the side of the counter. "Oh, that's right, you're not mated."

"Micah . . ." Sam cast him a reproachful glance.

Micah lifted his fingers toward her. "No, Sam. I think Cordray needs a lesson in what happens when a male takes a mate."

Cordray crossed her arms and reclined defiantly in her seat. "I know enough." She exchanged glances with Sam, whose eyes filled with compassion. After last night's conversation, Sam knew exactly how up-close-and-personal she'd been with the mating phenomenon.

Micah cocked his head to one side. "What you know is the equivalent of book smarts. And book smarts don't mean shit on the streets." He let out a derisive puff. "Book smarts tell you that the lunar cycle impacts the tide and that changes in air pressure create wind, and all that shit. But until you walk along the beach, with the surf washing over your feet as the tide comes in and the wind is blowing through your hair, you have no idea how it actually feels.

"Same with mating. You know the semantics. You know the biological explanation. You know what you've heard from others. But you've never actually experienced it. You don't really know how it *feels*." His gaze pierced hers under black, furrowed eyebrows.

Sam shifted uncomfortably, her gaze troubled. "Micah, stop it."

But Micah wasn't ready to stop. Sam might hold sway over him, but not in this instance. "When you've experienced mating firsthand, Cordray, then you can talk to me about how I am or am not a changed person now that I've mated Sam."

Damn, Micah sure was ultrasensitive tonight.

"Fine. Whatever. You've changed. Blah, blah, blah." She flapped her hand like it was inside a hand puppet. "I'm sorry I brought it up. Just make sure you don't fuck up Operation Grudge Match, and I'll never have to say I told you so." She set down her half-empty coffee mug and stood.

"Aren't you staying for breakfast?" Sam said.

Cordray eyed the buffet of lemon poppy seed waffles, raspberry coulis, salmon on top of scrambled eggs, and tomatoes. But at least the jar of olives was gone. Still, her stomach did a little somersault.

She placed her palm on her belly. "I don't think my stomach could take food right now, but thanks anyway." Her headache was better, but she still felt like crap on top of shit. Her belly was in no mood for food, especially when what she really needed was blood. "And really," she added, gesturing toward the strange mix of foods, "I'm not sure if this is breakfast, dinner, or dessert." Sam sure had kooky tastes.

Sam stabbed a bite of waffle and smiled. "I was craving lemon waffles and salmon this evening. Go figure."

She shook her head, glanced toward Micah, who reached around and stole another piece of salmon, and then grabbed her jacket from the arm of the couch. "Well, enjoy your breakfast." To Micah, she said, "I'll e-mail Digon and let him know I can vouch for you." She shrugged into her coat.

He nodded once in acknowledgement as he dipped a segment of waffle in the raspberry coulis.

As Cordray started for the door, Sam said, "Stop by anytime, Cordray." The tone in her voice held a plethora of unspoken messages, all obviously aimed at what they'd discussed last night.

Cordray glanced over her shoulder. Sam was watching her with a mix of concern and hope, as if she were a mother watching her firstborn child take the car keys for the first time.

Cordray paused and dipped inside her thoughts.

Tell him. Please tell him. You need to tell him that you love him.

She squinted and bit her bottom lip as she averted her gaze. "I've gotta go."

She dashed toward the door, yanked it open, let it slam behind her as she descended the porch steps two at a time, and then hopped on her Ducati.

Within seconds, she was zooming away from Micah's home, vowing never to speak of her feelings for Trace again.

CHAPTER 24

THE FARTHER TRACE DROVE FROM ASYLUM, the more his chest ached. And the more his chest ached, the more pissed off his inner beast became. Which, in turn, pissed *him* off.

For God's sake, what the fuck was up with his goddamn power? He'd been worked over by Micah only a few days ago. *Hard.* Not spank-me-with-a-noodle hard, but rip-my-mind-from-my-body hard. The waxing session had been the most intense session he'd ever endured. But as puny as getting waxed sounded, his beast should have been sated ten times over, not clawing at him for another round.

By the time he reached Micah's house, he was almost doubled over and damn near ready to melt. His right hand trembled uncontrollably. His entire body hummed with mounting pressure. Fear replaced anger. Worry filled his heart.

His power had never claimed him so quickly before, but he felt as if he were on the verge of exploding like an overly inflated tire driving over jagged granite. There was only so much tension his body could take before it snapped and unleashed the full force of his power.

Wincing as a shard of agony ripped through his chest, he staggered up to the keypad for the garage, managed to punch in the security code, then ducked under the bay door as it slowly crept upward. At the inside door, he gasped and clutched his chest as he gripped the handle and twisted it.

Sam's laughter coming from the kitchen was music to his ears, as was Micah's deep voice, but neither calmed the strain compressing his lungs. It felt like a giant fist was wrapped around his torso, squeezing his rib cage, mashing his organs together.

He hesitated in the hallway and pressed his right palm against the wall to keep him upright. The plaster vibrated under his hand and cracked.

This was bad. If he didn't get to Micah soon . . . if he couldn't reach his master in time . . . he would mutate. That had to be what was happening to him. Never before had he felt such agony — such intense suffering.

Micah laughed from the kitchen. "No, baby, you put the banana liqueur in first, then the brandy."

"Like this?"

Trace could hear the smile in Sam's voice. He could practically see the shimmer in her clover-green eyes as she looked up at Micah with complete adoration filling every angle of her face.

How he wanted a female to look at him the way Sam looked at Micah.

"Whoa! That's enough," Micah said. "Are you trying to get me drunk?"

Sam giggled.

Trace pulled himself toward the kitchen, his hand dragging over the wall, leaving a hairline fracture in the paint as his power simmered just below the boiling point.

He turned the corner, saw Micah standing beside Sam at the stove.

"Now, stand back," Micah said. He was holding the handle of a sauté pan.

Sam leaned away just as Trace fell to his knees.

"Master . . ." The agony was so great he could only whisper. "I need you."

They couldn't hear him, too absorbed by whatever it was they were cooking.

Micah lifted the handle of the pan. "Let the edge of the liquid catch the flame," Micah said. "Like this."

"Master . . ." Trace clutched his chest.

A plume of blue-orange flames burst from the pan.

Fire!

Mother!

Oh God!

Trace shrieked as pain knifed his soul and memories of his mother burning to death blasted into his mind, almost blinding him with its ferocity.

Sam jumped and spun around. "Oh my God! Micah, help him!"

Micah dropped the pan back onto the burner, the flames stretching upward, and immediately lunged for him. "Trace! What's wrong?"

All Trace could see was fire. Maddening, life-taking fire.

His mother dying.

Because of him.

His power spiraled into a vortex. He was going to let loose. He could feel it. And there was nothing he could do to stop it.

"Sam!" Micah reached for her. "Help me!"

She started forward.

"No!" Trace lurched away from them both. "Stay away from me!" He didn't want to kill them. He didn't want to take yet another beautiful, innocent life the way he'd taken his mother's.

If only he'd been more disciplined. More responsible.

Micah grabbed his arm. "I'm here, buddy. I've got you. Stay with me."

Trace tried to pull away, feeling his power slither down his arm and coil in the palm of his hand. "Get away from me. You and Sam have to get away from me now. NOW!" He thrust his fist against the floor, forcing the leash to stay on his beast just a little bit longer even as a shockwave of energy pulsed down his arm. A dull boom sounded as the earth trembled.

He was losing the battle. Shit was going critical.

Sam froze, wide-eyed, terrified and unsure what she should do.

"Get away from me, Sam!"

Her panicked gaze flew to Micah, imploring him to do something.

Fear flickered over Micah's face, then determination hardened his features as he slowly rose to his feet. As he did, his master's persona fell into place until he stood tall and proud, confident, in total Domination mode. "Do you dare tell me what to do in my own home, slave? You dare to speak to my mate in such a way?"

Fast as lightning, Micah's hand shot out, striking him across the cheek.

Trace's head whipped to the side, but the wicked slap came just in time, seconds before his power would have burst from his hand and obliterated everything within a fifty-foot radius.

For the moment, he was saved. They all were, but the dull throbbing in his chest persisted, and his power remained poised to strike.

"Master . . ." He turned pleading eyes up at Micah. "What's wrong with me?"

MICAH WASN'T SURE IF THE QUESTION WAS LITERAL, figurative, or rhetorical, so he didn't know how to answer. There was nothing wrong with Trace in the figurative sense, but right now — at this very moment — it was obvious something was most definitely and gravely wrong with him in the literal.

"I don't know," he said a moment later.

He had never seen Trace in such awful shape. He was pale, and for a dark-skinned male, that was saying something. Sallow hollows filled the space under his eyes. Dots of perspiration sprinkled the skin above his upper lip. The guy looked shredded and completely strung out.

"Help me." Trace's pale eyes beseeched his, the pain he was experiencing evident in the twist of his lips and the way he grimaced as he clutched his chest.

He knelt in front of his best friend and placed his hand over his bald head. "Let me in, Trace," he coaxed gently. "Open up your mind and let me in. I can help you better if I can see what's going on inside here." He tapped his fingers on Trace's head.

Trace closed his eyes with an air of regret. "I can't."

"Can't? Or won't?"

"Does it matter? The result is the same."

Anger surged through Micah's blood, and he rose to his full height. Trace's refusal was unacceptable.

"Are you saying that you are willfully and intentionally keeping me out of your thoughts?"

Trace remained silent, head shamefully bowed, hands on his thighs.

Micah paced to the side and shot a look over his shoulder at Sam. "Turn that off." He pointed to the burner. "Make sure everything is shut down in here, and then go down to my dungeon and prepare the table."

He knew he wasn't Sam's Dom and that he shouldn't be bossing her around, but he was through being nice. He was going to deal with this shit with Trace today, and Sam was going to help him. Together, they were going to make Trace open up, even if it took all night, because this shit couldn't go on like this anymore. Trace had come within seconds of killing them all.

Anyone else would tell Trace to get lost and never come back, but that wasn't an option for Micah. No way would he lose his best friend when he had vowed to take care of him. And so help him God, he kept his promises.

Since banishing Trace was off the table, that left only one solution. Pry open the gridlock Trace had on his mind by force.

Sam disappeared down the stairs.

He paced back toward Trace and stood in front of him, feet solidly planted shoulder-width apart, arms crossed.

"Look at me," he commanded.

Trace flinched but kept his head down.

"I said *look at me!*"

Trace sighed in defeat then lifted his head. The misery and sorrow pulling on Trace's features nearly shattered Micah's heart. His friend was in hell. Despair and heartache had Trace fully in their grip.

What could be going on inside Trace's head to make him so miserable? So hopeless?

"I told you during our first session that you would let me in, Trace. Remember?"

"Yes."

"Yes what?"

"Yes, Master."

"And yet you tell me that you still refuse to open up to me. Not that you *can't*, but that you *won't*. There's a big difference between the two, slave. Can't is out of your control. Won't is within it. And yet you still won't let me in, knowing that I can't fully be your master until you do. Knowing I can't save you from yourself until I can see inside your mind."

"Master, I—"

"Do you need me, slave?"

Trace's chest rose and fell heavily. "Yes, Master. I need you."

"Will you open yourself to me if I service you?"

Silence.

Micah bent forward and grabbed Trace under his chin, cranking his head back so they were nose to nose. "Will you open yourself to me?"

Moisture glistened in Trace's eyes, but he held Micah's gaze like a champ.

Trace took a trembling breath. On the exhale, he said, "I'll try."

"Not good enough, Trace."

"Micah—"

Micah released Trace's chin and slapped him as he straightened. "I am not Micah to you, slave. I am Master. You call me Master until you either safeword out or I decide our session is over. Do you understand?"

"Yes . . . Master." Trace's voice was whisper quiet.

Micah hated seeing him so emotionally beaten down, but his instincts told him the only way to break through Trace's walls was to break him completely. That until Trace's spirit broke, Micah wouldn't be able to get inside. And until he got inside, he wouldn't be able to help him. And helping Trace was his number one priority, especially since Trace had almost suffered a nuclear meltdown in his kitchen less than five minutes ago.

"Get up, slave." He snapped his fingers and took a step back.

Trace did as commanded.

"We're going to my dungeon" — Micah clutched the back of Trace's neck and pulled him close until their foreheads touched — "and we're not coming back up until you let me in here." Micah tapped the side of Trace's head. "If I have to keep you down there for a week, I will, but you will let me in." He searched Trace's eyes. "Do you want to know why?"

"Why, Master?"

He squeezed the back of Trace's neck and drew Trace's head down to rest on his shoulder. He kissed Trace's scalp as he wrapped his other arm around him, hugging him hard. "Because I love you too much to let you suffer this alone any longer, Trace."

He would save Trace now or die trying.

CHAPTER 25

CORDRAY SWUNG BY HER MANSION IN THE CITY, showered, and then headed back out to feed. She needed blood. Not only had her lip still not healed, but her hangover was lingering longer than it should. She was totally depleted.

With the after-work crowd giving way to the dinner crowd, enough people milled around the Loop to provide plenty of options as she searched for a donor. Anyone in a group was out. No families or couples, either. She needed someone who was alone, which was a lot harder to find than it sounded. Not very many people ventured into downtown Chicago at night by themselves.

Turning into a parking garage, she circled through the levels. Parking garages were excellent places to find donors, especially at this time of day. The nine-to-fivers were already gone, leaving the structures with a lot less foot traffic, but she could usually find a healthy, overachieving CEO who had worked late.

And bingo. There was one now.

Her Ducati's engine purred as she rolled to a stop and removed her helmet.

"Excuse me," she said to the buff fortysomething strolling unaware toward her. He had his brown leather briefcase in one hand and his smartphone in the other as he used his thumb to scroll through his messages.

He looked up. The skin around his eyes pinched as he realized she was talking to him. He gave her the once-over and frowned. Without replying, he continued walking, lowering his gaze to his phone's screen again, pretending he hadn't heard her.

These hoity-toity types were all the same. They thought they were too good for people who had a little ink in their skin and streaks of blue in their hair.

She hopped off her Ducati, scanned the rest of the parking level to make sure no one was around, and started after him.

"You lookin' for a good time?" she said.

"No," he barked over his shoulder.

"Good. Neither am I." She gripped his arm and swung him into the shadows as her fangs distended.

He began to protest, but she pulled him into compulsion a split second before she sank her fangs into the side of his neck.

Aaaahhhh, blood. Sweet, life-giving blood. As it poured down her throat and broke into her system, she felt her body instantly brighten. The last of her hangover faded, and her energy spiked.

If only she were drinking from Trace.

What would his blood do to her? How would it taste? Like power and sex?

The muscles between her legs clenched greedily at the thought.

Every molecule in her body begged for her to return to the ranch so she could see him, and yet her brain still resisted.

This was what body-numbing heartbreak did to you. It clouded your emotions and instilled fear in your soul. It shattered the mechanism inside you that created hope, plunging you into hopelessness.

She wanted to believe she was tough enough to kick fear in the ass, but her fear was proving to be a powerful foe.

She finished feeding, sealed the bite mark, and wiped the encounter from the man's memory.

He robotically, if not a little unsteadily, walked away.

The man's blood had revived her body, but her emotions still felt like a carcass being fought over by two lions. Talk about your bloody games of tug-of-war. Her heart was smack in the middle of a titanic battle between rival gods.

As she settled on the seat of her Ducati and kicked up the kickstand with her left heel, a tremor broke inside her heart. A tiny jolt of fear.

Trace.

Another vibration of panic stirred inside her.

Something was wrong with Trace. He was hurting. He was in trouble.

Frowning, she tried to shake off the fear vibrating inside her. Could this just be an overactive imagination? A side effect of finally quenching her need for blood on the heels of telling Sam she was in love with Trace?

Whatever it was, her instincts told her she needed to get to him. Now.

And strangely enough, she could sense exactly where he was.

Revving the Ducati's engine, she leaned into the handlebars and lifted her feet off the ground as the motorcycle shot forward.

Back on the street, she blasted off in the direction of Micah's house.

CHAPTER 26

TRACE LAY ON A GIANT, NARROW SLAB OF CYPRESS. The wood was strong as stone, which was good, because if Trace lost his shit again — which was a distinct possibility — he needed to know the table wouldn't break.

The chains securing his wrists and ankles, on the other hand . . .? Yeah, those he would be able to snap as easily as chicken bones.

His chest still ached like a motherfucker, but at least he no longer felt like he was on a final countdown to detonation. The agony that had nearly cost him his dearest friends — and their neighborhood — a few minutes ago still simmered inside his soul, but, at least for the moment, they weren't in immediate danger.

Warm fingers caressed his palm, and he curled his hand around Sam's. She stood silently at his side, her gaze filled with concern and compassion as Micah busied himself somewhere out of his periphery.

Micah had made him take off his shirt, but he still wore pants. Not that it would have mattered if he'd been naked. Nudity wasn't something to be ashamed of in this house. Not with all the exhibitionist three-ways he'd had with them.

His mind flashed to Cordray.

The thought of her name alone made the pounding in his chest intensify.

He groaned, and Sam's hand tightened around his.

Being around Cordray was like being in the presence of an aphrodisiac. Just the sound of her voice was enough to make his pulse quicken. He longed to smell her dark scent. To touch her black, silky hair. To taste her skin the way he'd tasted her lips last night.

He closed his eyes and saw her face. She was a vision. Her body a temple. He wanted to outline every one of her tattoos with his tongue. Ink covered both of her arms, her hands, her neck. Did she have tattoos elsewhere? Did she have them on her stomach? Her hips? Her legs? Her breasts? He wanted to taste them all.

His breathing deepened. His cock stiffened. The ache in his chest ebbed.

Thinking about Cordray was a good thing. Very good. His body liked it. *He* liked it.

"Open your eyes." Micah's strong, commanding voice bit into his fantasy, and his eyelids flashed open.

Only to come face to face with his greatest fear.

Micah waved a flaming baton in front of him, it's blue flame deceptively serene. Trace knew the damage fire could do. He knew it all too well. Maybe it looked pretty — benign even — but that shit was just smoke and mirrors hiding the danger lurking in the shadows.

His heart hammered.

His body trembled.

Perspiration broke over his chest and stomach.

Micah wore a glove on his left hand and reached to the side to grab a second baton, but this one wasn't lit. He tucked it between the third and fourth fingers of the same hand holding the flaming baton, angling each away from the other the way an xylophone player holds a pair of mallets in one hand.

"What happened upstairs — the way you reacted to the flambé — gave me an idea." Micah eyed Trace's stomach as he smoothed his gloved hand over his skin.

Trace was practically panting now, his exhales coming in abrupt, urgent puffs. "M-master . . . please . . ."

"You're afraid of fire, aren't you, Trace?"

He gulped, and his dry tongue stuck to the roof of his mouth, almost making him gag.

"Answer me." Micah bobbed his head toward Sam, who drew her hand out of Trace's and took a step back.

"Y-yes, Master."

As long as the fire was small and contained or he was able to get away, it was all good. But chain him to a table so he had no control and couldn't flee, and then wave a burning cotton ball in front of him? Forget about it. Even the smallest, most innocuous flame became an inferno. One that made him feel like he was stuck inside a burning building with no way out.

As his agonizing past erupted inside his mind, an almost equally destructive detonation of emotional and sensual overload gripped him. Every sense was heightened. Every nervous response magnified. Things that would have been merely a nuisance a month ago were now either festering sores or cause for cosmic levels of rapture.

Cordray, for example. Less than three weeks ago, she'd been an annoyance. Now she was an addiction. Even now, with terror-inducing flames dancing in front of his face, the thought of her beneath him as he took pleasure from her body rocketed a sense of calm through his blood.

He was a study in extremes. While more fear than he'd ever known threatened to consume him, a pleasant calm more refreshing than anything he'd ever experienced coursed through his blood and maintained balance.

But as Micah brushed the unlit cotton ball over a patch of his bare skin, the scales tipped in favor of fear.

The unlit baton was wet, and it smelled of alcohol. Micah was rubbing alcohol on him. And now he was lowering the flaming ball of cotton toward his skin.

Surely, Micah didn't intend to light him on fire!

The chains securing his wrists and ankles rattled as he pulled on them, his body straining.

Must get away. Must . . . save . . . myself.

The flame tapped the wet spot on Trace's stomach, and Trace nearly wet himself as a blood-curdling scream launched out of his throat then went into lockdown as his esophagus constricted. Blue flames danced over his skin like ghostly tendrils. Just as he began to feel the heat, Micah swiped his gloved hand over the patch of skin, extinguishing the flame.

Trace let out a gasp of relief, his muscles briefly relaxing until Micah wiped another patch of skin with the alcohol swab. Before Trace knew what was happening, Micah lit him on fire again.

This time, the scream dislodged from his throat and shredded his vocal chords, his eyes wide with fear as the flames flickered like a fiery Grim Reaper over his abdomen.

But this Reaper was merely a puppet. A marionette controlled by a grand master. It rose to life at Micah's command, and it perished the same way.

Again, Micah brushed his gloved hand over the flames, putting them out just as the heat reached his skin through the vapor barrier.

Trace braced for the next hit, but Micah hesitated.

"Do you want me to stop?" Micah lifted his chin, his shoulders stiff. The black Under Armour shirt he was wearing stretched over his pecs and revealed the ridges in his abdomen. A sheen of perspiration covered his forehead.

"Y-yes, Master." He wanted more than anything for him to stop.

"Then open your mind to me. Let me in, and I'll stop. No more fire. No more fear."

Fear. The great motivator. And yet Trace couldn't loosen the hold on his thoughts. He still couldn't let Micah in. His hopes caved as Micah's back straightened, and he began rubbing the alcohol-soaked ball over his skin again, this time creating a larger patch to burn.

Panic surged through his blood once more. The lit baton lowered. The moment it contacted the vapor, flames erupted over his chest. He could feel its heat on his face. Could smell its acrid odor.

He abruptly cried out, and then his eyes rolled back as he sucked in his breath, seeing his mother in his mind's eye. The smell of burning skin filled his nose. The image of her tied to a stake, her skin blackened in patches, sprang to life. Memories flooded him. Painful memories of death and destruction.

He was no longer in Micah's dungeon. He was a young boy, watching from his hiding place in the bushes as the angry townspeople tied his mother to a cross then dragged her across the yard, shouting and chanting that she was a witch. A demon's mistress. Satan's spawn. They held torches and waved them at her, lighting her clothes and hair on fire.

Brak and his father were nowhere to be seen. Already dead? Had these people already killed them? His instincts told him he was in danger. That if they saw him, they would kill him, too.

This was all his fault. He'd hurt those kids by the pond when Mason threw his rock into the water. He had lost control of the power dwelling within him, and he'd hurt them all. Mother had warned him not to use his power in public. She had told him bad things would happen if he did.

And now bad things were happening. And it was all his fault. He'd caused this. His lack of discipline had caused the townspeople to kill his family.

And now he would kill *them*. He would kill them all!

CORDRAY PULLED INTO MICAH'S DRIVEWAY to find one of Asylum's SUVs parked to the side and the garage door open. Her heart skipped a beat as she realized Trace must have driven here this evening. She must have just missed him.

The urgent feeling that he was in trouble still hummed inside her chest, but if he was here, how could he be in trouble? He was with Micah the wonder stud. If Trace's power was getting the better of him, Micah should have been able to command it back into submission.

Even so, she couldn't shake the feeling that Trace was in bad shape. It felt like Trace—no, that couldn't be right. Cordray shook her head as she dismounted the Ducati, pulled off her helmet, and eyed the home's exterior as she reached out with her senses. Why would Trace need her? He loathed her. But that's exactly the message her heart was sending to her brain.

Unable to ignore his magnetic pull, she started up the driveway, glancing inside the SUV as she passed it. Trace's duffel bag sat on the front passenger seat. She opened the door, grabbed it, then entered the garage.

A black and copper custom chopper sat in the bay closest to the door leading into the house. As she passed, she glanced down at the gas tank. *Hand of God* was written in bold letters.

Trace sure had a sweet ride. She ran her fingers over the smooth leather seat, catching a thrill at touching something that his ass had been on.

She tried the doorknob on the door leading into the house. It turned.

Strange. Micah wasn't one to leave his house open like this, especially after what had happened with Apostle back in January. And since they'd learned Apostle was still alive, Micah surely kept his home more secure than this, just in case that asshole decided to finish what he'd failed to do the first time and make another attempt at killing Sam.

She poked her head inside. "Sam? Micah?" The place was much too quiet, and something smelled burned.

She set the duffel down, pushed the button to close the garage door, and then locked up behind her before she ventured into the kitchen.

Salmon shavings and lemon poppy seed waffles still sat on the counter, and something that resembled charred bananas but looked like a molten carcass rested in a skillet on the stove. Micah, Sam, and Trace were nowhere to be found. Looked like whatever had happened here had brought everything to an abrupt halt.

"Hello?" Her hackles went up. Something wasn't right. She could feel it.

A bloodcurdling shriek rang out from the basement, muted by the closed door to the stairs.

Without thinking, she raced through the kitchen, around the corner, yanked open the door, and took the stairs three at a time to reach the bottom in about two seconds.

Following her instincts, she blasted through an impressive bedroom, which housed an even more impressive bed with a hand-carved headboard, and nearly blew the arched, wooden doors off their hinges as she burst into what had to be the freakiest room she'd ever seen.

Terra-cotta walls held over a dozen gilded mirrors. A medieval, wrought iron bed sat along the far wall. It was covered by a blood-red satin comforter and gold-fringed pillows. All manner of contraptions made of leather and black wood sat around the room. There was even an iron maiden in the corner.

In the center of it all, Trace lay like a mocha-skinned god on a thick slab of dark wood. His skin glistened with sweat, and his wrists and ankles were bound by heavy chains to the four corners of the table. He looked like he was in agony.

"What the fuck are you doing to him?" She rushed forward.

Micah spun around. He was holding a pair of wands in his hand. One was on fire. The other wasn't. "What are you doing here?" Manic fear shone from Micah's eyes.

Sam stood over Trace, caressing his face, murmuring to him as if coaxing him. Tears streaked her cheeks.

A jolt of pain shot through Cordray's heart. "What's wrong with him?"

On the table, Trace snarled and hissed, pulling on his restraints, making the chains jangle like metallic rattlesnakes.

In an instant, Micah was in front of her. "Can you see inside his mind?"

She frowned. "Answer me first. What's wrong with him?"

"I don't have time to play these fucking games with you. Can you see inside his mind or not?"

Her mouth flapped open and shut as she glanced toward Trace. His muscles rippled like magnificent waves under his skin, contracting, swelling, then relaxing in turns.

Needling her way into his thoughts, she gasped at what she saw. "Yes. I can see inside his mind." She sucked in her breath and covered her mouth with her fingers.

The despair. The roiling anger. The desperate sorrow. It was almost too much to bear.

"What do you see?" he said urgently.

"I . . ."

"Tell me!" He shook her. "I need to know."

So much of what she saw was one gigantic, jumbled mess. His thoughts raced one into the other, knotting into a frenzy of rage and desperation, but a common theme connected each memory. Because that's what these were. Memories. Not thoughts. And his mother and her death dominated each one, as well as fury against those who had killed her, including himself.

"He's angry," she said. "Furious. He's seeing his mother's death, and . . ."

"What?"

"Fire is everywhere."

Micah snapped to attention and hurried back to Trace's side. He picked up the two wands he'd been using a moment ago and relit the one he'd extinguished before badgering her.

"What are you doing?" She rushed forward.

"Sam, step back." Micah applied a layer of alcohol to Trace's stomach. "Cordray, cut off his pants. I don't want to catch them on fire. And stay inside his head. I want to know what's going on in there. Tell me if anything new pops up."

Everything was happening so fast. Sam shoved a pair of scissors into her hand, and Micah touched the flaming wand to the alcohol on Trace's stomach.

Blue flames danced to life, making her suck in her breath as Trace's eyes blasted open, locking on hers.

But he wasn't seeing her. In his mind, he saw only his mother. He saw nothing of what was happening inside the dungeon. He was aware of Sam and Micah, she could sense that much, and he seemed vaguely aware that someone was inside his mind, but he was too wired to know it was her.

Micah brushed his hands over the flames, extinguishing them.

"Today, Cordray! Get those jeans off him."

She glanced down at the scissors, then at the cuffs of his jeans, and then at the impressive bulge straining the fabric at his crotch.

A series of rampant memories flung through Trace's gray matter in rapid-fire succession. Screaming. Taunts. He was racing through the woods, panicking, trying to escape. He was young. Not yet transitioned. Smoke. He smelled smoke. He broke into the clearing. His home. Fire. MOTHER!

Get out of my head, bitch!

Trace flung her from his mind with such force, she stumbled backward several feet and slammed into the wall, gulping to get oxygen past the painful lump in her throat. She'd felt everything the way Trace had that day. All of it. The excruciating sadness, the terror at seeing his home engulfed in flames, his mother being dragged by a rope knotted around her wrists toward a pyre.

"He threw me out," she said, righting herself, disoriented.

Micah turned his dark, domineering gaze on her. "Goddammit, Cordray, get those jeans off him!"

"I am NOT your submissive, motherfucker! Quit bossing me around! Jesus Christ!"

"Micah . . . stop," Sam said, still holding Trace's hand.

But Micah was a male on a mission. "Just do what I tell you, Medusa. This isn't about you or me right now. If we don't bring Trace down from whatever seizure or mindfuck he backed into, he's going over. Do you understand me? Do you feel where I'm going with this?"

Over? As in mutant?

Her knees wobbled. Trace? Mutant? Hell no. Without another word of protest, she sliced through the denim cuff at his ankle and began chewing the scissors up his pant leg. "What the fuck happened here after I left?"

"Shit went critical." Micah worked at the side table. A smattering of tools sat on a tray, and a towel soaking in a bowl of water sat at his right hand.

She cut through the last inch of denim at his waist then started on the other pant leg.

"He's terrified of fire, Micah."

"I know."

"Then why are you doing this to him? Why are you lighting him on fire when he's afraid of fire?"

"Because I need to break him."

"Why do you need to break him?"

"Because he needs to let me inside his mind." Micah leaned over Trace. "Do you hear me, Trace? You *will* let me in or we'll both die trying." He turned toward her. "Did he hear me?"

Cordray forced her way back into Trace's head. "Yes, but he's so far gone I'm not sure it registered that you were the one who said it. He's not even fully aware that I'm here."

"Damn you, Trace!" Micah slammed his palm on the table. "Let me in, goddammit!"

Trace's eyes blinked open. They glowed yellow. Like cat's eyes. Not good.

"Fuck!" He turned toward her, raking his fingers through his hair. "Are you finished?"

She sliced the scissors through the waist above his other leg. "Yeah. Done."

"Good. Pull them off."

She hesitated. The only thing standing between her and Trace's very erect, very imposing penis was a tenth of a centimeter of denim. "Uh . . ."

Micah spun and glared at her. "Pull. Them. Off."

"But . . ." Her mouth could have been one of those cotton balls Micah had dumped on the silver tray beside him. Every drop of saliva had dried up in an instant, and her salivary glands were in no hurry to replace them.

"Jesus, Cordray. It's a dick. Haven't you ever seen a stiff dick before?" He rolled his eyes. "Oh, that's right. It's you. You've probably scared off every poor fucker who ever imagined he had a chance to get with" — he gestured toward her — "*that.*"

Sam let out an exasperated sigh but didn't say anything. Probably because she knew it wouldn't quiet Micah down if she did.

Micah grabbed the denim and flung it away from Trace's body. "For God's sake, C, it's not like he's going to fuck you."

The stab of hurt and anger that ripped through her was diminished only by the awe of seeing no less than eight-and-a-half inches of turgid flesh pop to attention from a sparse thatch of dark hair at Trace's groin.

She *had* seen a stiff cock before. She'd even had one inside her. Back when she'd been normal. Centuries ago when she'd still been able to feel it . . . enjoy it . . . find pleasure in laying with a male. But what she remembered of Gideon's cock paled in comparison to the one standing proudly in front of her now.

Not only was Trace longer, but he was thicker, too. The rounded head was smooth and shaded dark pink compared to the shaft, which was the color of cappuccino laced with a shot of espresso.

Her salivary glands sprang back into action, making her mouth water at the thought of swallowing him down her throat. Of climbing on top of him and reminding herself what a stiff cock felt like. And with Trace, she would feel every glorious inch sink inside her, filling her, stretching her.

God, just the thought of fucking Trace was enough to get her wet.

Micah had turned his back on her, quickly finishing whatever preparations he was making.

Then his head snapped up. "What the fuck?" He turned halfway, lifted his nose, and sniffed. A moment later, his dark eyes slid toward hers as he slowly met her gaze over his shoulder. His top lip curled as if he'd gotten a whiff of putrid meat as he sniffed again.

"Fuck me." The words snapped from his mouth in a way that

made her envision a cobra whipping its hooded head up over its coiled body. Silent but deadly.

He'd obviously scented her arousal . . . and didn't like it.

She squared her shoulders and frowned, chin high. Fuck him. Maybe she'd laid out her cards like a virginal maiden at a Chippendales show, but to hell with showing him she was ashamed. Lots of women got turned on by naked men and stiff cocks. Like any hot-blooded female, she could attend an all-male review and mentally masturbate while watching the men strip and stick their barely concealed dicks in her face without feeling like it meant they had to get married. It was just a performance. It didn't mean she was emotionally connected to the material.

Except Trace wasn't performing.

And she did feel an emotional connection to him.

And the longer she was around him, the more she wanted—

Enough!

She didn't need to be thinking about Trace's stiff dick or him sticking it in her face . . . or anywhere else, for that matter.

And that cocky cuss Micah certainly didn't need to know how she *really* felt. Although Sam had probably already told him.

"Just . . ." Micah waggled his fingers as if he were shooing away a leper. "Just stand over there and get ready." He turned away, mumbling disgustedly under this breath.

"Get ready for what?" The harder she tried not to stare at Trace's erection, the more she couldn't look away.

She wanted to wrap her palm around it. Feel its warmth. It's hardness. How smooth it was. How virile. How powerful.

She had no reason to think his cock would be any different than the rest of him. He *was* power. Potent in every way. From the forces he wielded with his hand and his mind, to his magnanimous stature, Trace oozed intensity that beckoned every cell in her body to transform into mush.

He had commanded her desire from the first time she saw him in Bain's court. Even before that, if she was being honest with herself. Because when she saw him inside the minds of Bain's guards, coming down the stairs of Io's basement, matchstick loose between his lips, hand held in front of him like he was a great and almighty god come to bestow favor and punishment on his subjects, she'd been taken by him. His look. His devil-may-care attitude. Everything about Trace had beckoned every part of her.

Which was why she'd been adamant about slamming the door on

him right from the start, especially after she realized she could feel him. She didn't need a male in her life, stirring up trouble, stealing her heart so that she could be hurt again when he flung it back at her like discarded scraps after he was finished with her.

She'd gone down that road once before and found nothing but pain.

Damn her. Damn *him*. She loved him. She couldn't deny it. But she didn't want to love him. She didn't want to feel such emotion again. Love made females weak. It made them stupid. Made them behave like flighty butterflies tittering higher and higher with nowhere to go but down.

As much as her heart pulled her to take a chance, she refused to fall into that trap again, even if she had to force herself not to.

But that didn't mean she couldn't savor the delicious visual of his body. Even a blind woman could appreciate *that* generous rod of steel.

"Take a picture."

At the sound of Micah's voice, she tore her gaze from Trace's spank bait and met his gaze.

"What?" she said.

"Are you finished eye-fucking my friend, or should I wait? Because you smell like you're only a few mental thrusts away from creaming yourself."

"MICAH!" Sam glared at him from the other side of the table.

"Fuck you, Micah." Cordray scowled and looked away.

Trace laughed. A dark, malevolent, echoing laugh that sounded more like the devil corrupting God's angels than a vampire getting a good chuckle at her expense.

Micah's head snapped around. "What's going on?" His gaze shot back and forth between her and Trace. "What's happening?"

Cordray scanned his thoughts. "He hears us, but he's not fully aware it's us. He's trapped inside his own personal hell in there." She frowned at the repeating loop of his thoughts. "And he's getting worse." She eyed the wands and small bowl of alcohol on the table. "Whatever you're going to do, you'd better do it soon, or I'm not sure what's going to happen."

Micah grabbed the wet towel out of the bowl, briskly rung it out, and tossed it at her. "Here. Take this."

Wet towel slapped her in the face as she haphazardly caught it. "What do I do with it?"

"Stand over here. Sam, you'll need to move, baby." Micah worked quickly, pointing with one hand and gathering his equipment with the other. "Fuck, but I hope this works or we're all going to have to say quick good-byes to one another if it doesn't."

Sam let go of Trace's hand and shimmied to the side.

Cordray took up station across the table from Micah. "Now what?"

Micah lit another wand that had been soaking in alcohol. "Get ready."

"For what?"

"I'm going to try something, and I'll need you to be ready to cover him with that towel when I say so."

She nodded, but she wasn't sure she liked where Micah seemed to be going.

Trace pulled against his chains and strained his head back, clenching his teeth as he let out an angry, strangled cry.

Micah poised the flaming cotton ball over Trace's face. "Let me in, Trace," he said loudly. Trace stopped squirming as his eyes flashed open and followed the dot of blue-orange fire Micah waved in front of him like a hypnotist's watch. "Do you hear me? Open up your mind and allow me inside."

"He hears you," Cordray said softly. "But he's resisting."

Micah smoothed his free hand over Trace's sweat-streaked scalp. "No more resistance. I'm done playing, Trace. I told you that you were going to let me in." Micah spoke to him with deadly assertiveness. "And until you open your mind to me, this is how it's going to happen."

Trace rolled his head from side to side, eyes popping out of his sockets, clearly not down with this plan, even if he was only partially aware of his surroundings.

Micah tsked. "It's too late for that, slave. You had your chance. Now shit gets real."

Cordray held her breath as Micah drew a line of alcohol from his groin to his sternum.

Trace jerked, tugging on the chains as an alarmed grunt ripped from his throat.

Micah touched the flame to the bottom of the alcohol trail.

A terrified shriek exploded from Trace's throat as the fire shot up to his chest.

Tensing, Cordray prepared to throw the towel over Trace's stomach, but Micah chased the flame with his gloved hand, dousing it.

"Do it, Trace! Do it now! Open up to me so I can end this!" Micah slammed his gloved hand onto the table beside Trace's head, making the chains rattle.

Cordray gasped as a gust blew her hair away from her face. She exchanged glances with Micah.

"He's close," she said.

Micah turned urgent eyes toward her. "Close to breaking?"

She nodded then glanced at the fire. "Do it again."

The torrent of thoughts racing through Trace's head changed. He was thinking about his mother again, but this time, the thoughts didn't stop and loop back when he got to the point where she was being dragged toward the pyre. Now she was on the pyre. Screaming as fire overwhelmed her, licked her skin, vaporized her hair.

Cordray nearly dropped to her knees as Trace's agony and terror consumed her.

"Oh God . . . his mother." Her voice whispered from between her lips on an agonizing exhale. "They're burning her. Oh God, they're burning her! And the house . . . his father . . . his brother. They're inside. They're trapped." She began weeping and flung her forearm over her face, locked not just into Trace's memories, but his emotions, as well. "Make it stop! Please stop! I don't want to see this!"

MICAH SUCKED IN HIS BREATH. He needed inside Trace's thoughts before he destroyed not only himself but Cordray.

He grabbed Trace's chin and yanked his head around, latching onto Trace's eyes with his own. "Let me in, Trace. Now. I need inside."

Trace was panting, eyebrows scrunched, a film of perspiration beading on his face. His lips and chin trembled as tight exhales burst from his mouth. He shook his head, yellow eyes pleading.

"Now, Trace. Let me in there. I can help you if you just let me in."

A shiver raced through Trace's body.

"They're coming after him," Cordray said. She still had her face covered, so her voice came out muffled. "They want to burn him, too. They're going to set him on fire. Oh, God, no. No! Run, Trace! Run!" She blew out a relieved breath. "He's running . . . he's running . . . back into the woods. Blindly running. I can't see where we're going. They're running after him. It's all his fault. He did this. He killed his mother. It's all his fault . . . he thinks it's his fault."

Damn it, he needed to bring Trace back before he lost him.

"Cordray!" He smacked the table.

She snapped out of her daze and hurtled her pained, tear-filled gaze toward his.

"Help me!"

With a sharp nod, she took a tremulous step closer to the table.

"Hold up the towel. Get ready."

He was going to try something. Something dangerous. Something that could go very, very wrong. But his intuition told him it was the only thing that would provide the right impetus to unlock that goddamn stronghold Trace had on his mind.

Cordray held the towel in front of her.

"Are you ready?" he said.

She nodded shakily. Obviously, whatever she'd seen inside Trace's head had fucked her up, too.

"Can you do this, Cordray?"

She stared back at him, eyes wide, mouth open. He'd never seen her so shaken. If not for the seriousness of the situation, he would have laughed.

"I need to hear it! Tell me! Can you do this?"

She nodded, fighting back her emotions. "Y-yes. Yes, I can do this."

It felt like he was defusing a bomb. One that only had a few seconds left on the timer. If he failed, everything would explode and he'd lose his best friend, his home, Cordray, Sam, himself. His entire existence seemed to hinge on this one critical moment.

And time was running out.

He grabbed the small, folded towel he'd soaked in alcohol and rubbed it as carefully as possible over Trace's chest and stomach.

"Micah . . . no . . . what are you doing?" Sam gasped and covered her mouth.

"Trust me, baby." He took a deep breath and raised the flaming baton over Trace's body.

Trace growled. He sounded more like an animal than a vampire. He was one step away from going mutant. If this didn't work, Trace was a goner.

And it would be his responsibility to kill him.

He couldn't let that happen. He couldn't lose his best friend that way.

He nodded toward Cordray, who nodded back. He could feel her inside his head, so she knew his plan, as well as her part in it.

"Micah . . ." Trace's deep voice curdled his blood. His eyes blazed. His fangs dripped with venom as he snarled.

Fuck. Maybe it was already too late.

Now!

He pulled the folded towel away and tapped the flaming baton to the alcohol. Fire erupted over Trace's torso.

A monstrous screech split the air as Trace strained against the chains. Wind whipped through the dungeon. The sound of cracking and snapping wood took Micah's gaze to the table, but thankfully it held.

Then lightning bolts of Trace's thoughts fired inside Micah's mind, intensifying rapidly.

"Not yet!" he shouted at Cordray, who held the wet towel at the ready.

As the wind tossed the pillows from the bed and lifted his floggers from their hooks, more memories, detonating at supersonic speed, launched into Micah's mind, flying, streaming, discharging like a thousand nuclear bombs in less than a second.

Jesus! This was what Trace had been holding inside him?

"Micah!" Cordray's terrified eyes collided with his as she lifted the towel. "Now?" Her long hair whipped around her face.

"Not yet . . . hold on . . ."

Trace shrieked again—the sound an agonizing wail of torment— as a lifetime of pain rocketed from Trace's mind into Micah's.

"Now!" The fire had burned through the vapor barrier and was hitting Trace's skin.

Cordray threw the towel over Trace's body just as the swirling wind blasted into Micah with enough force to pick him up and hurtle him against the far wall. He bounced off, tossed like a ragdoll onto the floor.

"Micah!" Sam raced toward him, dropping to her knees beside him.

He shook out the cobwebs and grinned weakly up at her.

"Are you okay?" She brushed his hair off his face, desperate concern pouring from her gaze.

"Better than okay." His voice came out as a fractured whisper.

Her slanted brows bunched over her nose.

"I'm in," he said. Trace's mind was open. He was inside Trace's head. "I'm in, baby."

CHAPTER 27

Trace lay slack, his body warm, loose, and flying, even as the ghost of his childhood memories evaporated into ether.

He had finally opened up to Micah, and like a sinner confessing his crimes, a weight lifted off his soul. Guilt still resided in his heart, but the self-oppression no longer dragged him to the bottom of the ocean like a cinder block chained to his ankle, and the ache behind his sternum was gone.

Breathing more easily than he had in a long time, he became aware that something was lying on top of him. No, some*one*. A body draped crossways over his torso.

He peeled his eyelids open, lifted his head, and sucked in a pleasantly surprised inhale.

Cordray was slung over him like a blanket. Her long, partially braided hair lay like silken, ebony spider webs on his skin. Her full breasts pressed against his stomach.

She was the reason he was so calm. The reason his chest no longer ached. Not even a shadow of the pain he'd experienced for hours remained.

She'd taken his pain away.

Just by touching him.

His beast had completely receded . . . because of her.

He laid his head back on the wood between his arms, which were still stretched over his head. Quiet tranquility wrapped around him. He was a lily pad floating on a pond, the sun warming him from above, the water cooling him from below.

Totally Zen.

Micah was nearby. Trace could feel him. But wherever he was, it didn't feel like he had the energy to do much more than lay there. Kind of like him. Kind of like Cordray.

He grinned. It felt as though the three of them had experienced a giant, explosive three-way orgasm. One that had completely drained them, leaving them flaccid.

The fantasy would have been perfect had Cordray not twitched against him just then. A moment later, her shoulders shuddered, and she made a quiet, breathless noise that sounded like a sob.

Wait. What?

Was Cordray crying?

He had never seen Cordray cry.

"C?" he said quietly. "Are you okay?" A week ago, he wouldn't have cared. He would have been infuriated that her tears might be pity. Pity for him.

But something had changed between him and Cordray. He *did* care. And he could see that she did, too, even if she had an odd way of showing it.

At the sound of his voice, Cordray bolted upright, dashing her fingers under her eyes, collecting herself and looking away before turning back toward him, keeping her gaze averted. "I'm fine."

God, but she was more beautiful than usual with tears glistening in her eyes, making her irises shimmer like sapphires in the moonlight.

She was like the apple in the Garden of Eden, so tempting, yet so deadly. The combination made his balls tingle.

"Come here," he said, hardly daring to breathe for fear of scaring her away.

She hesitated then slowly glided up his body as if mesmerized.

If only he could touch her. He yearned to push his fingers into her hair and hold her against him.

Her tears glistened like diamonds. Like stars. He wanted to catch them in his palm and bring them to his lips. Taste them. Savor their salty essence.

She drew closer, her face only inches from his, her gaze locked on his mouth.

Yes, he wanted to kiss her. He wanted to feel her tongue slide over his. He had never wanted anything more.

He closed his eyes, lifted his head, held his breath.

And then Cordray jerked to a halt.

"What am I doing?" she said, as if to herself.

He opened his eyes to find her staring at him like she'd just caught herself buttering moldy bread.

She reared back. "I can't do this."

The about-face caught him off guard. It also pissed him off. "Why are you fighting this?" He tugged against the chains still securing him to the table. Anger at her rejection spiked in his blood.

She pushed off of him, leaving cold emptiness in her place. "I'm not fighting anything."

"The hell you aren't."

"Don't you dare presume to know me, Trace." She spun around, and all that glorious hair fanned out like silk on the wind.

"Where are you going?"

"Home." She stopped at the door and flashed him a pained glance over her shoulder. "I'll petition King Bain tomorrow to terminate your community service at Asylum. You're free, Trace."

With that, she blew out of the room like a sharp gust.

Free?

She was letting him go?

What the hell was this shit? She couldn't let him go.

Staring blindly up at the ceiling, his heart aching, he felt more like a prisoner now than ever. Because how could he be free when he wasn't with her?

CHAPTER 28

CORDRAY RACED AWAY FROM MICAH'S HOUSE, tears streaking her face.

She needed to go away for a while. The only way to recover from the hold Trace had on her was to put him in her rearview mirror and hope that time healed the ache in her heart.

At the ranch, she pulled into the garage, swept into the house, through the kitchen, and up the stairs to her bedroom, where she shut herself inside the bathroom and splashed water on her face for a good five minutes before lifting her head to look in the mirror.

The female staring back at her was a stranger. One who cried all the time like a pussy. One who'd been weakened by love. One who bore no resemblance to the tough-assed female she had become. For so long, she hadn't wanted or even needed a male. She had purged that need from her system the night Gideon betrayed her. Trace would just give her more of the same, so why did she care so much?

She'd almost lost him tonight. But instead of making her want to confess her feelings to him and let the cards fall where they may, she'd wanted nothing more than to get away. Seeing him almost die was a painful reminder of how precarious a relationship with him would be. Another reminder of how dangerous it would be to allow herself to love him. Because peril would always follow Trace around like a puppy. He would always be one breath away from turning mutant. And she refused to put herself into another situation where the male she loved could be taken away from her in a heartbeat, leaving her crushed and heartbroken.

Sighing, she shut off the faucet, dried her face, and turned off the light as she opened the door.

And came face to face with Skeletor.

"I NEED TO GO," TRACE SAID WEAKLY. His limbs, which were draped over the sides of the bathtub, were still as heavy as concrete from the working over Micah had given him, but he couldn't shake the feeling that Cordray needed him.

He hadn't been able to push her from his mind since she'd left an hour ago. It was like she was still there, inside his mind, even though she was gone.

Micah lifted his head from the edge of the oversized tub and gazed drowsily over the layer of lilac-scented bubbles at him. Sam was wrapped in his arms. Her head rested on his shoulder, and her nose was pressed against the side of his neck.

"You're not going anywhere right now, Trace." Micah's voice sounded as weary as he looked.

It had taken Micah ten minutes to recover enough from being thrown across the room to lift himself off the floor and release Trace from his bindings.

"But—"

"No. I can feel how tired you are. I can see it." Micah's eyebrows rose toward his hairline as he tapped his temple. "And God how I wish I couldn't."

"I warned you."

"Yeah, yeah." Micah laid his head back and groaned. "I'll get used to it, but right now, all your mental vomit is giving me one hell of a migraine." He lifted his hand out of the sudsy water and ran his palm down his face. "So much for aftercare. This isn't at all how I take care of my subs after a scene."

"I'll live." Trace's deep voice echoed from his chest. It was the voice of a male well-soothed. A male who had just unloaded a heavy burden and could no longer hold himself upright from the sheer exhaustion of letting go of so much mental waste. Waste that Micah now helped him carry.

"Want to talk about it?" Micah's eyelids cracked open.

"I thought you had a migraine."

"Yeah, well, this isn't about me right now, buddy. It's about you. I wouldn't be much of a master if I didn't put my own discomfort aside at least a little bit and tend to your needs first."

Trace studied the way Micah's eyelids drooped shut again. Clearly, he was exhausted. That had been some fucked-up shit back there. Connecting to Trace's mind and his past had to have been like an acid downpour, laden with sorrow and heartbreak.

Micah's eyes opened halfway again. They glistened with unshed tears. "At least you know now that your dad and brother didn't die."

"That doesn't bring my mother back, though, does it? She's still dead. I still killed her."

Micah's eyebrows ticked inward. "That wasn't your fault. I saw what happened, Trace. You didn't kill her."

"You saw what I did. You saw how I disobeyed my mother and let my power out in public. You saw how I lost control and hurt those kids. If I hadn't done that, their families wouldn't have learned what a freak I am. That I was the son of a witch." He curled his arms over his head and rocked forward, sending a gentle wave of water toward Micah and Sam's end of the tub. "They never would have come after her — after us — if I hadn't lost control of my power. They wouldn't have killed her." He splashed his arms back into the water as he dropped his head back.

Tears trailed out the corners of his eyes.

A moment later, Sam laid herself over his body, hugging him, kissing the side of his neck. "Ssshhh." She kissed him again, but it wasn't *her* lips he wanted comforting him. It wasn't *her* body he wanted to feel pressed against his. He wanted Cordray. He *needed* her. "It's okay. Everything's going to be okay now," she said.

No, everything wasn't going to be okay. Cordray had left. She had told him she was cutting him loose. Giving him his freedom. And yet, Trace didn't feel free. He felt more like a prisoner than ever.

"Why doesn't she want me?" he said softly, as if to himself.

"Hmm?" Sam lifted her head from his chest and frowned at him.

He stared back. "Why is Cordray releasing me from my community service?" Her behavior confused him. Less than two weeks ago, she had seemed so pleased with herself that she would be able to boss him around any time she wished, so why the sudden change of heart?

The moment Cordray left, an emptiness had opened inside him. That emptiness had spread inside his chest, to his stomach, out through his limbs, making him heavy all over. So heavy he could barely hold his head up.

Sam exchanged meaningful glances with Micah.

"What?" he said, perking up at their bloated silence. "What aren't the two of you telling me?" He rubbed his thumb up and down his sternum as that goddamn ache stirred back to life, along with another vibration that Cordray needed him, this one stronger than the last.

Micah groaned and scrubbed his face again. "Damn it."

"Tell me," Trace said pushing upright. "What are you keeping from me?"

Sam sighed, glanced sideways at Micah, then looked at him.

"She's in love with you."

"Who?"

"Cordray."

He shook his head. How could she love him when she pushed him away at every opportunity. He'd kissed her the other night, and she'd practically burned a path in the carpet to get away from him. He'd all but invited her to kiss him tonight, and what had she done instead? Told him she was terminating his community service.

"No, that can't be true."

Sam's eyes filled with sympathy. "Micah, tell him."

Trace looked from Sam to Micah, who breathed out a heavy, resigned exhale and nodded. "It's true, Trace. As much as I hate to admit it, it's true. Cordray has fallen in love with you."

"But it's more than that," Sam added. "Did you know she can't feel?"

Trace frowned. "What are you talking about?" From the way Cordray reacted to him, she could feel plenty.

"Until you came along," Sam said, "she couldn't feel a thing. Nothing. Not even a bullet."

"Did she tell you that?" If this were true, it shed a whole new light on Cordray.

"She told me last night."

He searched his memories of all the encounters he'd had with Cordray. Of how she'd sucked in her breath and stared at his hand on her arm the first time he touched her outside King Bain's courtroom. She had looked at him as if he were an alien. And every time he'd been around her since, she seemed to be on edge and intent on putting distance between them. He just assumed it was because he frightened her. And maybe she *was* frightened. Not of *him*, but of how he made her feel.

He looked from Sam to Micah, seeking confirmation even though he didn't need it.

Micah pulled Sam back into his embrace. "Sam's telling the truth, buddy. Cordray couldn't feel shit before. But now—and only with you—she can." His gaze fell to Trace's hand, which continued to rub his sternum as the ache in his chest deepened. Micah let out a soft, reluctant snort.

"What?" Trace frowned.

Micah jerked his head toward Trace's hand. "You've mated her."

Trace opened his mouth to protest, but no words came out as Sam sat up and let out a startled gasp and covered her mouth with her fingertips. He glanced down at his hand on his chest. No way. Sure, he thought Cordray's body was bangin' hot. Yes, he had fantasized about how it would feel to have sex with her. And absolutely, he missed her like crazy now that she was gone. He wanted nothing more than to go to her and . . .

He glanced back up as his mouth fell open. He dropped his hand into the water.

Holy fuck. He couldn't have. Had he . . .? Was Cordray . . .? She was his mate?

"Believe it, buddy." Micah sighed. "You're a mated male now." He shook his head. "Shit, there goes a perfectly good safeword."

His gaze collided with Micah's as disbelief tangled with shock. He was mated? Had he finally found his match?

A smile began to creep over his face, relief and joy swirling like fluttering butterflies in his stomach. He was mated. The search was over.

Then a bolt of panic rammed into him.

He ricocheted backward against the tub. Water sloshed over the sides as searing dread wrapped its heavy fist around him and squeezed. He arched against the pain, gripping the cold porcelain on either side of him, then splashed back into the water.

Micah lurched forward. "Trace! Are you okay? What's wrong?"

His gaze shot around the bathroom as he climbed out of the tub, flinging water everywhere as he stumbled on the bath rug then dashed toward his clothes. Fear cinched his heart. Cordray needed him. She needed him now.

"Cordray's in trouble. My mate's in trouble."

CHAPTER 29

AFTER A BRIEF BUT AGGRESSIVE CONFRONTATION, where a little blood might have been shed and furniture broken, Skeletor gained the upper hand and threw Cordray face-first to the floor. Stars and Tweety Birds broke free in her vision. Good thing she couldn't feel anything or this could be one fucking ugly sitch.

"Calm the fuck down," he barked, driving his knee into the center of her back as he yanked her arms behind her. "This is just a little courtesy call." He was using a modulator to disguise his voice.

"If this were a courtesy call, asshole, you could have simply picked up the phone. Or, better yet, hacked into my computer again."

He wrapped a pair of flex cuffs around her wrists and tugged the ends to tighten the bands before jerking her off the floor and shoving her into the club chair by the window.

She glared up at him as he paced to the side, head turned toward her. Today, he wore a grey and black mask that looked like something out of one of the war games her kids played on their PS4.

But she could still make out his eyes through the dark-grey screens of the eye holes. Those intense, grey-blue eyes that reminded her of slate were like beacons, even shielded as they were.

"Listen to me." He bent forward and pointed a finger at her.

She spat at him.

He pulled back, and an air of exasperation and frustration fell over him.

Trying to worm her way inside his head, she met with a wall of black. Nothing. He gave her nothing, his mind sealed more tightly than Area 51.

He chuckled. "Nope. You're not getting in there, sweetheart. Too many things I don't want you to see."

"I'll bet." She glared at him.

He glared back, unmoving and rigid.

"What do you want?" she bit out, pulling against her restraints.

"I want you to back off. Way off. My beef with *Micah Black*" — he said Micah's name as if it were a curse—"doesn't concern you."

"It concerns me *now*, dick face. You've broken into *my* home. You've endangered *my* kids. Don't expect me to let this go."

He blew out a derisive breath. "You've got bigger problems here than me."

Cold dread rained down her back. "What's that supposed to mean?"

He pulled a bundle of thin blue rope from one of the pockets in his cargo pants and began to uncoil it. "You're not the only one who knows how to do research." He knelt in front of her. "But if you want to know what I found out, stop helping Micah. Stop searching for me in that little computer of yours. And stop trying to track me. And then I'll tell you what's *really* endangering your kids. And trust me, honey, it's not me."

"It is if you don't tell me."

He stood, grabbed the front of her shirt, and yanked her out of the chair. "I'll tell you after you drop your manhunt. Then we'll both be happy."

"Then we're at a stalemate."

He remained motionless for what felt like an eternity. "So we are." He gruffly spun her around and lassoed her with the rope.

Ten minutes later, she lay on her bed, secured with a series of Shibari knots intricate enough to make Micah drool. It looked like Skeletor had gone to the same school of Domination and submission as Micah, but instead of fire and floggers, ol' Skellie got off on Japanese rope tying.

"Think about my offer, Cordray" he said, straightening and tilting his head to the side as if admiring his work. "I'll be in touch in a couple of days to see if you've changed your mind."

"Don't count on it."

"We'll see. Until next time . . ." He opened her bedroom door and disappeared like a wraith into the hall.

Cordray shouted after him. "Do you know which portal the ankh opens?" It was a desperate move to see if she could learn anything else about him, but seeing that she was tied up and all, she was in a desperate position.

A moment later, Skeletor took the bait and backed into the doorway. "You are a smart one, aren't you? I'm impressed."

"Do you?" She glared up at him, praying he would give her something. A clue. Anything that would help her find him once she got free of these fucking knots.

The way the outside corners of his eyes turned up behind the screens in the eye holes, she imagined he was grinning. He raised his index finger and waggled it back and forth. "Stop looking for me, Cordray. And stop working outside your pay grade."

"Or what? What will you do?"

His demeanor turned stony. "I'll tell the world who you really are." He paused as if he knew he'd gained the upper hand. "You wouldn't want that, would you? To ruin your *precious* brother and his *saintly* reputation."

What in the hell did this guy have against her brother?

It didn't really matter. The fact that he knew she and Bain were related was enough to catapult her pulse into the stratosphere. "How do you know that?"

He chuckled. With the modulator, it made him sound like a demon, which was perfect, given the mask he wore. "If I told you, I'd have to kill you." He winked at her. *Winked!* Then he was gone.

And all Cordray could do was lie there like a fucking human origami.

CHAPTER 30

TRACE REACHED ASYLUM IN LESS THAN THIRTY MINUTES and roared down her driveway on his chopper like a hundred fiery steeds breaking free from the gates of hell.

He killed the engine and burst through the garage door seconds later. It was after midnight, so the house was dark and quiet.

Too quiet.

"Cordray!"

He took the stairs three at a time, ran down the hall, and threw open her bedroom door.

Only to find her tied up on the bed, her arms and legs bent behind her, her wrists and ankles bound together.

"What are you doing here?" Her face blanched as she met his gaze.

"You were in danger." He leaped onto the bed, pulling out the knife he'd borrowed from Micah. Within seconds, he'd sliced through the knots. "What happened? Are you okay? Who did this to you?"

"I'm fine, and it doesn't matter who did this to me." Rolling away from him, she flung off the rope and planted her feet on the floor. "He's gone. I'm alive. Thank you for cutting me loose, but now you can leave."

She dusted her hands down her arms and darted past him into the hall.

Ah, hell no. She wasn't running away again. Not this time. Not now that he knew the truth that she was his mate and that she loved him.

He caught up to her in four strides and grabbed her arm. "Where are you going?"

"Anywhere you aren't." She tried to twist her arm from his grasp. "Let me go, damn it."

"No. Not until you tell me why you're fighting this."

"Fighting what?" She tried to turn away from him, but he grabbed her other arm and backed her into the wall.

"This."

His lips claimed hers with a fervor she'd never felt. And since this was Trace, she felt every ounce of the fervor he was channeling from his lips into hers as his hands traveled from her shoulders to her hands, which he slammed against the wall a moment later.

After a long, dizzying stretch in which she thought her lips might melt, he pulled back and searched her face, leaving her wide-eyed and breathless.

The power rolling off him set her senses on fire.

"Why are you fighting what's happening between us?" he said, breathing hard, gazing at her mouth. "Why are you always running away from me?"

Reclaiming her courage and her conviction, she freed her hands from his. "There is no *us*, hotshot. No matter how great a kisser you are." She shoved him away and turned to make her escape.

"Oh no you don't. Get back here." Trace tried to grab her arm, but she flung his hand away as his searing touch lit fiery excitement inside her muscles.

"Don't touch me!" She fled down the hall. If she didn't get away now, she wouldn't be able to.

"Don't you run away from me!" His body heat bled into her back as he followed.

Arousal blasted through the pit of her stomach, sending her thighs up in flames. The waves of power pulsing from his body beat the air around her like heavy bass from a high-def speaker. *Thump-thump-thump.* Only these hard palpitations hit her between the legs, each pulse like a heartbeat that throbbed deep inside her core.

She had to get away from him. She couldn't give in to whatever this was. If he was manifesting his power to get her in the sack, she couldn't let that happen.

With renewed effort, she hurried toward the stairs, trying to escape.

He raced ahead of her, blocking her way.

"Leave me alone, Trace!" She spun and darted back toward her bedroom.

But he was right behind her, assailing her body with wave after wave of sexual heat, weakening both her knees and her resolve.

"Tell me the truth!" He clutched her wrist and swung her back around to face him.

She staggered as her feet briefly went out from under her. "What truth?"

"That you love me!" His turbulent gaze searched hers. "You do, don't you? Don't lie and tell me you don't."

Damn Samantha. She'd told him.

"What does it matter?" she yelled at him as tears blurred her vision. "You don't want me! You hate me!"

"Just admit it, Cordray! Admit that you love me!"

"Why? Why should I? What fucking difference does it make?" She tried to break free, but he held her too tightly.

"Because—"

"Let me go, Trace. Just let me go so I can—"

"You're my mate, goddamn it!" He shook her then slammed her back against the wall.

Arousal exploded in her blood, and she sucked in her breath a split second before—

SMACK!

Her palm connected with his face. Hard.

His head whipped to the side, and he released her. The air thickened. When he brought his face back around, he was rocking the most intense set of fuck-me eyes she'd ever seen. As she slowly stepped to the side, he eased closer, and a blast of hormonal heat pulsed from his body like a sonic boom.

Warmth bloomed deep inside the heart of her and slicked her core.

She swayed as she cautiously circled him then took two backward steps toward her bedroom.

There was nowhere to hide, nowhere to run, no way of getting out of the coming storm as he bulldozed toward her, chest pumping, fangs extending, gaze locked on hers as if she were a pool of cold water in a desert and he'd been without water for weeks.

Retreating, she backpedaled over her own two feet until her back thudded against the wall again.

He was a predator, and she was his prey. In an instant, his arms caged her. The warmth of his body seeped into hers as another eruption of hormonal heat fired under his skin and sparked the air around them.

"Trace . . ." She broke eye contact and tried to duck under his arm, irrationally terrified of what was happening between them.

He blocked her and encroached even farther into her personal space.

"Hit me," he said, his voice a deep purr. "Hit me again."

God help her, but she actually *wanted* to hit him, and not because she wanted to hurt him, but because she knew—instinctively knew—that hitting him was the key to breaking his arousal wide open.

And damn her to hell, she wanted that. She wanted to feel him inside her, against her, touching her, kissing, sucking, biting.

Even so, she proudly jutted her chin. "No." But her body screamed YES!

The corner of his mouth curled upward as he pressed against her, setting off all kinds of alarms in her nervous system as her sense of touch accelerated to full throttle.

She gasped and instinctively thrust her arms out in front of her, only to meet with the brick wall of his body. The muscles of his torso felt like sculpted marble. Thank God for compression shirts that fit like a second skin, because she could glide her hands over this shit all day.

"Hit. Me." A low purr broke deep inside his chest.

She met his hooded gaze with as much audacity as she could muster. "No."

"Wicked female." The dark chuckle that broke from his throat like a spritz of tequila and honey made her knees tremble. "I know you want to. I can feel it."

The front of his body crushed hers, his chest mashing her breasts in such a delicious, erotic way. She drew in her breath and tilted her head back as his lips brushed up the slender column of her neck. His fists latched onto her hips. He grunted and yanked them forward, making her gasp again as his erection rubbed the juncture between her legs. Everywhere he touched burst with sexual awareness. Hot. Like someone had injected fire into her veins.

The sensory overload was almost too much, and she nearly came on the spot.

"Trace . . . I can't. I don't want . . ." Her voice trailed off, because what she'd been about to say was a bold-faced lie. Because she did want. She wanted everything he seemed ready to give her. If he stopped now, it would destroy her.

"Oh, but you do," he said, calling her bluff. "I know you want it." His warm breath flowed in staccato exhales against her neck, right below her ear.

She was so close. An orgasm sat just on the perimeter of her awareness, circling, closing in, almost there.

"Trace . . . please . . ." She didn't know what she was begging for. Her mind was a scrambled mess of desire and need.

He slid his nose up the side of her neck and into her hair, inhaling deeply as he continued rubbing his erection against her. His slow, insistent grinding was nice. Very nice. Take-her-breath-away nice.

"You're my mate, Cordray." His warm breath washed over her

skin. "Do you know what that means?"

She nodded then changed her mind and shook her head. Her fingers curled over his shoulders like hooks. He was so hard, so hot, so incredibly, insanely perfect.

"It means that this" — he thrust between her legs — "is mine."

She sucked in her breath and eagerly nodded. Okay, yes, that was his. It was so his.

"And it means that this" — he ran his tongue along her neck, right over her vein — "this is mine, too. Your blood is my blood." He nipped her flesh. "You will never feed from anyone other than me again, Cordray. Do you understand?"

No other. Her blood, his blood. Got it. She just didn't want him to stop.

Two weeks ago, she and Trace had been magnets that repelled each other, but that was only because they'd been facing each other with their north poles. But now . . . flip! North, meet South. They snapped together the way nature had always intended.

He pulled back and groaned lustfully as his eyes ranged her face.

"Hit. Me." The words rose like steam from his throat, his gaze sending all kinds of I'm-going-to-fuck-you-so-hard signals. "Please."

Well, since he'd said please.

HER HAND SHOT OUT, blistering his cheek with the delicious sting of pain.

Trace's head spun to the side, and lightning bolted down his spine to his dick. Five-alarm arousal burst to life inside his balls, and he suddenly wanted her more than he'd ever wanted anything, and not because his inner beast had been beaten into submission.

When he pivoted back around, she was staring at her hand as if she couldn't believe it was attached to her body but liked that it was.

"Again." Heat poured through him. He was panting hard, needing more. "Hit me again."

And God love her, she did. The hardest yet. He might melt he was so hot, and it was all because of her.

He closed his eyes and moaned, relishing the biting pain as it resonated briefly then faded.

He closed the short distance between them, hard as steel, aroused in a way he'd never been. The curves of her body welcomed his. Her heavy breasts rose and fell against his chest. Her hips cradled his as she locked her eyes to his and proudly lifted her chin.

347

She was as turned on as he was. Even more. He could smell her arousal. It smelled like orange blossoms at midnight.

He drew in a long, deep breath and let that tropically infused scent filter into his lungs and spread into his limbs.

"You're mine, Cordray. You belong to me now. Your body. Your heart. Your very breath. And tonight I'm going to claim what is rightfully mine." He didn't know where the words came from, but he felt the truth of them flowing through his blood. Blood that was hers now, as much as hers was his.

She started to resist, but he thrust his entire body against hers, snatching her hands in an instant and pinning her arms against the wall, extending them over her head.

Her staccato inhale and the drawn-out moan that followed were music in the silence of the house. A lusty serenade meant only for his ears.

Her eyelids drifted down, hooding her eyes. Her body undulated against his.

"Hit me again." He eased his hold on her hands, letting his palms slide down her arms to her breasts, where they paused before easing lower, to her flat stomach.

God, she felt good. Feminine yet strong. Like a female was supposed to feel. He dropped his nose to the side of her neck, where he dragged in another long, consuming inhale of her scent, musky and sweet. Sexy as hell.

"Trace . . ."

"Hit me, Cordray." He spoke against the expanse of skin at the base of her neck.

A wanton groan broke from her throat as she shuddered and tipped her head back. Her hands curled into fists against his chest.

"Trace . . . please . . ."

"Hit me." He pulled his face away from her neck and stared deep into her eyes. "One more time, and I'll give you what you want. What we both want." He licked his lips and gazed at her luscious mouth. "What we've both wanted since the moment we met but were too stubborn to see."

God, he needed the pain. Needed it to be free.

And then he could take what was his.

She took several quick breaths, fighting a final resurgence of resistance.

For one intense moment, she was trapped between fight or flight, acceptance or denial. Between consent and refusal. Her body ached for him in all the right places. For days, she had fought her attraction to him, struggling to keep him away when all she wanted was to draw him closer. And now he had forced the issue by announcing that she was his mate.

His mate!

Trace was the reason why Gideon had never mated her. Because she'd been meant for another. And nature had chosen well. Trace was perfect for her in every way, but remnants of fear still echoed in her heart. She couldn't expect them to cease altogether when she'd made fear a way of life for so long. After all, old habits were hard to break.

His strong hands held her hips against the wall, but even now their hold softened, his palms sliding higher and leaving a wake of sizzling fire.

His body pressed against hers, and she could feel how hard he was. Hard for her. His body heat churned the air around them into a feverish cauldron. All it would take to feel his hands on her bare skin, his lips against hers, his hardness inside her, and all that heat to wrap around them both, was one more slap. All she had to do was hit him, and fate would do the rest.

She had to decide. The time was now.

His face drew closer, consuming her field of vision with his hooded eyes. His pale-green, so-goddamn-sexy eyes.

"Hit. Me." He whispered the command against her mouth, so close that his breath washed over her lips.

She wanted that mouth on her. Everywhere. All over her body. Her lips, her breasts, her stomach, her sex.

Her hand whipped out.

SMACK!

Her palm connected with his cheek. Hard.

His eyes shut briefly then snapped opened as he let go of her and hastily shed his shirt.

"Again," he said urgently, gripping the sides of her body, slamming himself against her.

It didn't matter that he'd promised only once more. She would hit him as many times as he wanted. Whatever he asked, she would do. That's how far she'd fallen out of her own control in the last sixty seconds. It was as if something greater than herself controlled her actions, pouring through her blood, making her let go and embrace her instincts for the first time in her life.

She slapped him again, feeding the building frenzy spiraling around them.

"More." His hands drove under her shirt.

The moment his palms found bare skin, she nearly blacked out. She hadn't felt a male's intimate touch for so long she almost wept as his palms shot up her stomach to her breasts.

"No." But her mind screamed *yes* as she struck him twice more then clutched his shoulders. She tugged then pushed, both pulling him closer and pushing him away in a constant battle to resist and take all at once.

"Yes." Trace lifted her shirt, struggled against her uncooperative arms, and then fisted the material as he growled. He pulled, hoisting her away from the wall. The angry sound of ripping fabric was followed by the rush of cool air on her exposed skin.

"Stop," she said, but the single syllable sounded more like damp cheesecloth than the snap of a wet towel.

The only part of her that wanted Trace to stop was her fear. Fear that was dwindling and slipping toward surrender with each passing second.

Her body was in heaven. A torturous heaven that assaulted her senses and flooded her ability to cope. Every breath pulled more of Trace's earthy scent into her lungs and compelled her to touch him, to fall into the moment, to give him what he wanted and hit him again.

Trace shook his head, his gaze locked to hers as his fingers dove under her bra and grazed her nipples.

She sucked in a blast of air and gripped his shoulders to keep from falling as her knees buckled.

"You don't want me to stop." Trace was all male, virile and demanding, a tightly coiled bundle of need that commanded every cell in her body as he flicked his fingertips back and forth over her puckered skin. "I can feel how badly you want me. I can see it. You can't lie to me, anymore, Cordray. You can't lie to your mate."

"Bastard." She gasped the word then bit back a moan of approval as he nipped the side of her neck. Her knees quivered, and she clung to him for fear of tumbling to the floor.

He pulled back and grinned. "Sticks and stones, baby."

Flames erupted between them, and the air shifted as her fear vaporized. She would have Trace, and she would have him now.

With an aggressive surge, she shoved him against the opposite wall and drove her hands up his stomach to his chest. He willingly lifted his arms, exposing himself to her hungry gaze, staring at her with eager, fascinated eyes.

Then his hands found her skin once more as she shrugged out of what was left of her top. With the flick of his index finger, he snapped the tender lace in the center of her bra, and her breasts spilled into his palms. She let her head fall back, wound her fingers through the belt loops of his pants, and tugged him forward as she backed into the wall again. They were like two pinballs, magnetically connected, spinning and bouncing back and forth in the hallway.

Enchanted bewilderment filled Trace's gaze, which dropped to her chest. From his expression, it was obvious he'd never held a woman's breasts in his hands before. The way he stared gave her the impression he had never seen nipples, either. Surely, he had. He'd had plenty of mistresses who had taken pleasure from him. But never like this. Never when he wasn't under submission.

Something in his expression weakened Cordray's knees even further. Under his gaze, she felt like a rare artifact. Precious. A treasure to be admired and beheld with the utmost reverence. Then he dove down and claimed one of her nipples with his mouth.

Oh God!

She cried out and slapped one hand against the wall to support her as she clutched the back of his head with the other. Heat burned the insides of her thighs, and the muscles deep inside her clenched.

She was going to come. She couldn't breathe, couldn't find the ability to take in oxygen. Every muscle screamed, tightened, prepared to celebrate the rediscovery of her sexual response. For the first time in centuries, she was going to have a goddamn orgasm. Right here. Now. This . . . very . . . *second*!

"Holy shit! Trace!" Everything went black as the power of her long-suppressed sex drive blew her into the cosmos. A fraction of a second later, she gulped in air like she had just come up from being sucked into the ocean by a riptide.

On and on, the pleasure ricocheted throughout her body, rolling through her muscles. She couldn't speak, couldn't think, couldn't comprehend reality. All she was, was a mass of sensation, synapses firing, nerve endings reacting to stimuli. Trace's stimuli. With Trace, she was alive. Pleasure, pain, the warm wetness of his mouth. The sensations strangled her in such a beautiful, captivating way. And when he licked her skin, cool air washed over the moisture and sent a shiver through her body.

When her orgasm finally waned, she realized she was slung backward like a passed-out co-ed. The ends of her hair brushed the floor, and her arms were like slack rope. Trace's arms encircled her waist, and his lips were leaving a trail of tiny supernovas down the middle of her stomach.

"Oh . . . my . . . God."

As Trace continued his downward journey, she managed to pull herself back up and lean against the wall for support.

He unfastened her pants, pushed his thumbs into the waist, and shimmied them down her legs and off her feet.

When he lifted his gaze back up to hers, it was with a sense of wonder, as if he didn't understand what was happening to him, what drove him to continue, or why he was reacting to her the way he was.

Cordray could understand the feeling. Despite her attraction to him and the fact that he'd mated her, she'd gotten used to them hating one another. Or at least acting like they hated one another. Yet here he was, his large hands gripping her hips, the tips of his fingers playing over the elastic waistband of her panties, his gaze locked to hers, his face inches from where she wanted him the most. He had just given her the most incredible orgasm she had ever experienced, and it looked like he was nowhere near ready to be done with her.

And didn't that just make her day, because she wasn't ready for him to be done, either. Not even close.

She still had at least a dozen orgasms queueing up now that her libido was back online.

For another delirious moment, as her breath quickened to shallow pants of anticipation, they stared into each other's eyes. Then, as if his hardened will suddenly snapped, Trace dove his face into the apex of her body, burying his nose and mouth against the moistened heat of her core. Once more, her knees threatened to give as she cried out.

He breathed in, drawing cool air through the material of her panties, and then blew out, suffusing her skin with heat. When he exhaled again, his mouth opened. She felt it. Felt his lips part. Felt his tongue press against her through the satin. She looked down and moaned at the dreamy expression on his face. His eyes were closed, and he seemed to be savoring the moment, as if he didn't want it to end.

He was a slave to his sex drive, taking what rightfully belonged to him, granted to him through biology.

She writhed against the wall, caressing the top of his hairless head, wanting the moment to stretch on forever. Whisker-like stubble scraped her fingertips.

DONYA LYNNE

Somehow, she still managed to breathe, but each shallow inhale caught in her throat, held for a fraction of a second, and then burst out on a plaintive, staccato moan that made her sound like she was begging.

How long could she take this? Already, another orgasm was unfurling itself in her belly like a flower, stretching out its petals, growing, turning toward Trace's silent urging.

She was the flower. It was *her* petals uncurling from a tight bud. And he was the sun warming her, nourishing her, giving her life.

"More." Her whispered demand surprised her, because she hadn't intended to speak.

Trace hooked his fingers under the elastic waist of her panties and slid them down her legs, never removing his mouth from the heart of her. As the fabric skimmed past his chin, he burrowed deeper and laved her with his tongue. He licked her again, more insistently, drinking her in like he was sipping nectar from a honeysuckle blossom. His hands gripped her hips, pulled her against his face, lifted her legs over his shoulders one at a time. Her feet were no longer on the floor, and his mouth—God! His mouth! Teeth nipped her engorged flesh, his tongue dipped inside her, and he closed his lips around her clit—yes, she remembered her old friend Clitoris. How long it had been since they'd shared a moment like this?

"Don't stop. Please don't stop." She really was begging now, but she didn't care. All she cared about was the second orgasm rushing from the depths of her body, reaching for Trace's mouth and strangling her midsection.

For so long, she had lived without this. Lived without pleasure. And now, as her second orgasm crested and shattered her into a thousand pieces, she knew she never wanted to go back to that life of deadened reality again.

Her legs jerked against Trace's shoulders, clamping around his head as her fingers curled against his scalp. Her stomach quivered and convulsed. And she became aware that she was crying his name over and over with each pulse of rapture that broke through her body.

He remained as he was, his mouth pressed against her quivering core, riding her out. His warm, solid hands cradled her bottom as if she were a bowl, and he were drinking from her.

His eyelids lifted, and his eyes locked to hers, sending another shiver through her thighs as she clamped her palms around his head.

He took another long, luxurious draw with his tongue then withdrew his mouth from her core. His lips glistened with her release.

"I like how you taste," he said, slowly rising, lifting her legs from his shoulders and easily guiding them around his waist. He smiled and glanced down at them as if he'd never known the feel of a female's legs around him before.

"What's happening?" Even as she said it, her hands slid down between them and freed his leather belt.

Through half-closed eyes, he stared at her mouth. "I'm claiming my mate." The words fluttered from his lips as his hands joined hers, unfastening, unsnapping, unzipping. "And nothing will stop me until I do. Not even you."

It was as if she were watching from afar, like she was having an out of body experience. His pants dropped, he shoved down his briefs, and his erection was suddenly in her hands. The erection she'd seen barely two hours ago straining skyward as he writhed on Micah's table. And she was guiding him, positioning him, and then sinking down on his impressive, hard length.

His entire body jolted and shuddered as the connection was made. Strength and power poured out of him, and a chaotic surge of energy rocketed into her as he began pumping his hips.

He was like a virgin, out of control, at the whim of his body. He gasped with each haphazard thrust, his bewildered gaze crashing into hers as if he didn't understand what was happening but refused to stop.

He was strong. So incredibly powerful as he plowed her into the wall, thrusting hard and fast, pinning her hips with his hands. And yet his eyes pleaded with her, almost begging her for mercy.

"Oh God . . ." The skin on his face tightened. His eyes watered. His jaw clenched so tightly she thought it might break.

But she didn't have time to think about what was happening to him. Out of nowhere, a third orgasm rose inside her, fast, furious, unleashed as if the first two were nothing but child's play meant to pave the way for the real deal.

Her back knocked in rapid beats against the wall, her pleasure mounting. She tried to hold on to his shoulders, but perspiration slicked his skin, making it impossible to find traction. She dug her fingernails into his flesh like they were claws. She clamped her legs around his waist. Anything to find purchase before the deluge swept her away.

Trace was relentless. A fervent, sweat-covered mass of taut muscle driven by desire and biological need. A need that, until now, had only been fulfilled as a trade-off with pain.

Cordray had seen inside his mind. She knew that he'd never fucked like this. That he'd never taken a female without first being flogged into submission, humiliated, or bound to some apparatus. Or all of the above.

But now Trace was unbound, free, driven by his own demands, not someone else's.

As her third orgasm built to a fever pitch, a strong breeze blew her hair over her face. Then the picture hanging on the wall beside her popped off its fastening and plummeted to the floor.

Trace was breaking free, and his power was unleashing as he did.

But she couldn't stop. Whatever energy was breaking loose from Trace's body to redecorate her hallway would just have to wait, because she was close. So close.

"Don't stop!" She clung to his potent, virile body.

An onslaught of guttural growls rumbled from deep within his throat, one after the other, growing louder, beating in time with his thrusts.

A decorative porcelain bowl cracked and broke in half on the table at the end of the hall, and somewhere nearby, glass shattered.

She was only half aware of the destruction raining down around her as the wind increased in strength until it was whipping her hair around their joined bodies. Orgasm number three was about to go postal. And it sounded like he would join her.

From the well of her soul, a long, keening wail rose through her throat. Her vision blurred, her back curved into him, and her arms locked around his shoulders as the force of her orgasm threw her off the wall against his body.

Trace's legs buckled, and a thunderous roar tore from this throat as his thighs spasmed, rocked, and let go, dropping him to his knees. He took Cordray with him, locking her in his embrace. The muscles of his arms contracted and released in time with each pulse of his cock inside her. In a tumble, they rolled to the floor, Trace on top. His hips flexed as he continued pumping into her.

He was a hurricane making landfall against her body. Warmth spilled against her inner flesh, and she actually smiled as she fought back happy tears. She could feel it. She could feel every inch of him, every stroke, every spurt, every quiver of his stomach against hers, and every contraction of his biceps as he continued to rock himself against her.

Eventually, the euphoria subsided, and he gradually pushed himself up on his arms, breathless, glistening with sweat, gloriously virile and the damn sexiest thing Cordray had ever laid eyes on.

His tongue peeked out and slowly wet his lips. His full, luscious lips. His gaze searched her face, and she tried not to breathe, not to move. She feared that if she did, she would scare him away. He had that startled, what-did-we-just-do look on his face.

He blinked, frowned, then stared at her in wonder. "It's you." The words breathed out of him on a low, dazed whisper.

Cordray exhaled. "It's me."

It had actually happened.

The one thing she never thought would.

And it was Trace. It had always been Trace.

This time, when the tears stung her eyes, she allowed them to fall.

Because her true mate had finally found her.

CHAPTER 31

TRACE HAD SPENT HIS ENTIRE ADULT LIFE SEARCHING FOR HIS MATE. The one who would align his body and soul in perfect harmony, soothe what pained him, and fill the emptiness that only a mate could fill. And now he had found her.

He brushed his thumb over the apple of Cordray's cheek, smearing a tear over her skin.

"It's you?" he said again. The pitch in his voice sounded puzzled even to his own ears, lilting like a question. "It's really you."

From the moment he met Cordray, he knew she was different. She'd had a way of getting under his skin that no person, male or female, had ever been able to manage. She could do things to him no one else could, such as unlock the barriers around his thoughts. Not even Micah had been able to do that. Now he knew why. Because only a true mate could have such power.

She still lay beneath him, naked except for the collection of Gothic rings around her fingers, her lip ring, the ruby stud in her nose, and the magnificent array of colorful tattoos all over her body. She was a rainbow of color and metal even in the darkness.

He saw her in a new light now. She was no longer the wicked witch who could infiltrate his thoughts and mine out whatever she wanted. No longer did she set fear in his veins.

That had been the real problem before. She had scared him. She had been the first to peel back his protective shield and expose his vulnerability. And he had reacted the only way he knew how when he perceived a threat. He'd lashed out. He'd pushed and shoved, terrified of the way she stripped him so easily, when all along, she was his mate.

That was why she was able to do things to him no one else could, because she had been made expressly for him. Everything about her—her lustrous black hair with its dual-toned turquoise and aqua stripe, her sparkling blue eyes, the aristocratic slope of her nose, the subtle orange blossom scent that wafted from her body, even the silver lip ring and the miles of ink that decorated her skin—all of it was for him.

"It's been you all along." Could he really have had this weeks ago? Could he have really known this incredible sense of belonging and joy if only he hadn't been so locked inside his own self-imposed hell?

Holding his breath, he gazed in wonder as he gently, slowly, so very carefully ran the tips of his fingers through her hair. It felt like satin, smooth and silky soft. He trailed his fingers lower, to her shoulder, and outlined a tattooed tendril of dark ivy that curved and twisted across her collarbones, connecting her shoulders. Her skin was velvety soft, unbelievably smooth.

Her legs were still wrapped around his hips, locked at the ankles, but now they relaxed. Her feet slowly slide down the backs of his legs, her ankles finally unlocking mid-calf. She placed her feet on the floor, and he nestled more deeply into the cradle of her body, too comfortable to pull away as he continued discovering her.

"All this time . . ." He inhaled then closed his eyes for a moment in an effort to make sense of the past few weeks. Then he blinked his eyes open and continued his visual exploration of the last female he would ever love. "You were in front of me all this time." He spoke softly, his deep voice filled with awe.

Cordray didn't speak. Didn't even blink. Her eyes held his, and he saw the same fascination in her expression that he was feeling.

His thumb played over her lip ring. He brushed it with the pad of his thumb, marveling at how he could have had this all along had he not been so blindly stubborn.

"You're beautiful."

Her full, dark-pink lips curved into a smile. "So are you."

As her palms took an exploratory journey of their own over the expanse of his chest, across his shoulders, and up the sides of his neck before gently cradling his face, he got the sense that she was trying to determine if he was really there. Whether what they'd done had really happened or she'd only dreamed it.

His gaze dropped to her mouth.

He had never kissed a female. Never. His mistresses had never allowed it.

But tonight, he and Cordray had kissed. They had touched each other. He had felt her warmth. He'd experienced pleasure without first requiring pain. He had heard her moans, smelled the earthiness of her lust, feasted on her with his eyes, and tasted her musky flavor.

He wanted to kiss her again. To drink the flavor of her lips. Her full, rosy lips, which parted even now as if in anticipation.

As he slowly lowered himself, her fingers pulled at his cheeks.

He'd never seen Cordray like this. Pliant, almost docile. She had shed her prickly shield and replaced it with an inviting warmth he wanted to lose himself in for a lifetime.

He held his breath and paused less than an inch from her face.

Her eyelids flickered open. Her long, dark lashes softly framed her incredible, bright-blue eyes.

"What's wrong?" she said.

He gave a slow, subtle shake of his head. "Nothing. I just . . . I can't stop looking at you."

"Then don't close your eyes and kiss me, you big idiot." The outer corners of her eyes lifted as the apples of her cheeks plumped.

She thought that was funny, did she?

"We're going to have to do something about that mouth of yours." He was still inside her. Still hard. He rolled his hips forward and back.

Her smile evaporated as she closed her eyes and drew in a heady breath. As she exhaled, her eyelids peeled back open. This time her smile was one of lusty approval. One that expressed how much she liked what he was doing and didn't want him to stop.

"I can think of a few things you can do with my mouth." Her arms slithered down and around his shoulders.

He smirked, rolling his hips again. "Well, I think I *have* told you to suck my dick a time or two." He rotated his hips again and smirked at the way her eyelids fluttered.

"Yes, I do seem to" — she drew in her breath as he gently thrust into her — "oh, God, yes. I do remember you telling me that."

He'd never done this. Never engaged in sexual flirtation, dirty talk, or anything of the sort. But with Cordray, it felt as natural as breathing. Perhaps because verbal sparring seemed a way of life between them. Or maybe because she was his mate and everything would come easily between them now that he'd gotten out of his own way long enough to finally embrace her.

Her legs wrapped around his waist again. He loved how good they felt encircling him, locking him against her body.

"Remember how you once told me I couldn't boss your dick?" she said.

He grinned and pumped into her again. This was nice. Easy. So unlike anything he'd ever associated with her.

He lowered his mouth to her neck and suckled the skin right above her vein. "Mm-hm. I remember." He'd just been locked inside

King Bain's dungeon, and she'd paid him a visit to inform him she would be his boss after he was released, to which he told her she couldn't boss his dick.

Funny how that seemed like a lifetime ago even though it had only been a few weeks. So much had changed since then. He'd mated her, for God's sake.

She sighed and ran one hand over the back of his head as her other slid down his spine to his ass. Then she let out a short, quiet laugh. "Looks like I can boss your dick, after all."

He nibbled his way up her neck, along her jaw, to her chin. "You were born to, baby." Then he took her bottom lip between his teeth.

She moaned, her eyes drifting shut.

Releasing her lip, he pushed up on his arms and undulated his body over hers.

"You might be able to boss my dick, honey, but this" —He thrust into her. Hard. Making her cry out and dig her fingernails into his back—"This is mine. I own it. It belongs to me now." He pressed his pubic bone against her clit and ground his hips in a circle. He'd had enough experience in his mistress's dungeons to know how to please a female, and he would take great pleasure showing Cordray all that he'd learned. "I dare you to deny it."

She shook her head, breathing harder as he continued thrusting into her.

"Tell me you're mine," he said.

She nodded. "I'm yours."

"Tell me I own you."

Her legs squeezed his waist as she shuddered and bit back a throaty groan. "You own me."

"Your body is mine."

"My body is yours."

"And don't you ever forget it." He growled, and his hips took on a life of their own.

His arms strained as his own body fell into autopilot, claiming hers again, driving into her slick heat. He'd never experienced such raw need. The glorious intensity of making love. Truly making love. The complete submission of his inner beast so that all that remained was him. Trace. Only him. Stripped to his soul.

He crushed her mouth with his. Opened, tasted, swept his tongue over hers as she locked her forearm behind his neck and held him against her. She met him more than halfway, lifting her head off the floor, bruising his lips with her own, nipping his bottom lip, nibbling, biting, orally attacking him. And Jesus! He loved it. She was his kind of female. Strong, lusty, fearless, taking what she wanted and demanding more.

Breathless. She kissed him breathless, and his body responded, speeding into a higher gear he hadn't known he possessed.

Something cracked. Something wooden. Then it sounded like the legs of the table at the end of hall snapped in half. Glass shattered. Something heavy bounced down the stairs. But he was too enthralled with her body, her lips, her precious moans. Whatever destruction was happening elsewhere could wait. He was climbing toward orgasm number two, and nothing would stop his ascent.

She cried into his mouth, and he swallowed the sound as her entire body fell into violent tremors.

"Fuck!" He disengaged from her mouth, his fangs extending.

The beat of her heart echoed inside his mind. He could hear her blood surging in her veins, could smell its lustrous scent. His stomach clenched. His cock throbbed.

And God, he needed every part of her inside every part of him.

With a feral growl, he surged against her and sank his fangs into the side of her neck, latching on, taking heavy drags of her life-giving blood.

Mine, this is mine.

God help anyone who spilled a drop of her precious blood from this day forward, because they would have to answer to him. As her mate, he would protect her. It was his instinctual duty to take care of her. He would destroy anyone who tried to hurt her.

As his body let loose and spilled inside hers once more, he growled and sank his fangs even deeper as he rolled to his back, taking her with him. His arms shot around her and held her close, his hands buried in her hair as he took his fill and thrust his hips off the floor into her.

The venom euphoria sent her into another orgasm, and she murmured something he couldn't decipher as she trembled against him, her core pulsing hard on his cock.

He released her vein and dropped his head to the floor. His cock continued to empty inside her.

Once her euphoria wore off, she weakly crawled up his body, finding his mouth with hers, breathing him in, tasting her blood on his lips, connecting them in a complete circle.

"More, please more." She breathed the words against his mouth.

He had given her all he had. "You've taken it all from me."

She grinned and settled in a drained, panting heap against him, head on his chest. "Wimp." She chuckled weakly.

"Wimp?" Trace was too depleted to do much more than lazily slap her ass, but even that came off as more of a love tap than a slap.

She peeled her cheek off his slick skin and kissed his sternum. "Yes. Wimp." She grinned up at him. "I'm going to have to do something about this lack of stamina if you're going to satisfy the likes of me, Trace."

"Lack of stamina, my ass." He felt like he'd just faced a typhoon . . . and won.

"If the shoe fits."

Snorting derisively, he arched one eyebrow at her. "If you think you can build my stamina, *Coco*, then by all means, give it your best shot."

She mock-glared at him. "You are not allowed to call me Coco."

He grinned and glanced up at the ceiling. "Wicked witch?"

"Only in the bedroom."

That made him laugh. "Sweetheart?"

"Uh, hell no. As in, I'll withhold any and all sexual pleasure if you ever call me that."

This was nice. Bantering with her in the afterglow.

"Well, I give then. What am I allowed to call you?"

She settled her chin on his chest. "You can start with Cordray."

"Well, duh." He rolled his eyes at her as he absently began playing with her hair.

She caressed his chest with the tip of her index finger. "Okay then, how about Master of the Universe. That would be nice."

"Oh, yes. That's much better. Ego much?" He grinned at her. "Try again."

She smiled, and he liked the way it made her whole face light up. "Her Majesty?"

He shook his head and wrinkled his nose. "Ew."

"Fine. What do you suggest?"

He took a deep, cleansing breath. His body felt incredible. As good as it had after Micah worked him over, maybe better. No . . . not better. Just different. But good different. He lazily combed his fingers through her hair, still in awe of how she was able to send his power into the shadows like a punished child. But then, she was his mate. Of course she would hold sway over his inner demon. He grinned and twirled a strand of her hair around his fingers. "How about *She Who Tamed the Beast*?"

A sparkle lit in her eyes, and one eyebrow arched in amusement. "Beast master?"

He rolled the name around in his mind. "Yeah, beast master." He liked it. Then he chuckled. "Can I call you BM for short?"

She shook her head in exasperation. "You never turn off, do you?"

"Nope." He lifted his eyebrows questioningly. "So, can I?"

"That would be a no," she said, playfully slapping him and sitting up.

He hated the wash of cold air on his cock as she slid off of him. "Oh come on. Why not?" He pushed himself off the floor, which was easier said than done with muscles as pliant as raw cookie dough.

Cordray's gaze ranged up and down the hall then homed back in on him. "Because the last thing I want to be associated with is a bodily function that involves shit, *capiche*?" She stood. "Did you do this?" She gestured at the broken glass, smashed ceramic bowls, broken picture frames, and what was once a table but now resembled kindling.

He took in the disaster area. "Oops." One corner of his mouth slid upward as he drank in the splendor of her naked body. "I might have gotten a little carried away. But it's not entirely my fault." His eyes met hers again as she stood over him.

One of her eyebrows arched. "Oh? Are you saying that I'm somehow to blame for all this?" She gestured toward the wreckage, but he could tell she was fighting back a smile.

He sat forward and slowly ran his palms up her thighs. The muscles quivered against his touch, and she let out a shaky exhale as she slowly lowered back down to straddle his legs.

"If you weren't so fucking incredible, I might not have lost control of my power." He licked his lips. "Besides, I've never experienced anything like this before, so you're gonna have to cut me some slack."

"When have I ever cut you slack?" Her fingers skimmed up the back of his arms then lightly gripped his shoulders.

"Good point." He linked his fingers at the small of her back and pulled her forward, locking her against him. "So . . . what are we going to do about this?" He nodded over her shoulder at the mess.

They sat in silence for several seconds, their bodies drifting closer to one another, the vortex of desire beginning to spin again. Then Cordray let out an exaggerated, arousal-laced sigh. "If you ask me, it looks like we need to work on keeping your beast under control during extreme bouts of pleasure, and I think we need to work on it *a lot*."

His cock perked up at the suggestive glint in her eye. "I do like how you think, beast master."

She pulled away and pushed to her feet, lacing her fingers around his as he joined her. "No better time than the present?" She bobbed her head toward her bedroom.

He nodded then followed close behind as she led him to her room. "Only if you're not tired," he teased.

She stopped in the doorway and turned toward him, her face flushed as she shook her head. "Trace, I've waited for you a lot longer than you've waited for me. I can assure you, I'm not tired." She swallowed thickly as if forcing back her emotions. "And even if I were, I can sleep later. After I know for sure this isn't a dream I'm going to wake up from."

He stepped closer and cradled her cheek. "I can assure you, baby, this is no dream. You're my mate, and I think I'd like to stay buried inside you for at least a week. So . . . yeah. Not a dream. Not even close."

Her gaze fixed on his, and she took a deep breath and closed her eyes. "This is going to take some getting used to."

"What is?" He pulled her toward him.

She drew in a shaky breath, smiling and opening her eyes as she did. "All of it. You. This." She dragged her hands down his chest. "Seeing you as a friend and not a foe." She blinked her gaze to his.

He got what she was saying. He needed time to adjust, too. Treating Cordray like discarded rotten fruit had become a way of life.

He nodded toward the bed. "How about we spend the next couple of hours practicing being extra nice to each other then?"

She followed his gaze. "You won't break my bed?"

"I've got to learn sometime."

One corner of her mouth quirked upward as her lashes fell seductively. "Practice makes perfect?"

A lust-filled rumble broke inside his throat. "Hell yeah, and I believe in lots of practice."

She bit her bottom lip as he took her hand once more, tugged her into the bedroom, and closed the door.

CHAPTER 32

DIGON SAT ALONE IN HIS STUDY, staring at Micah Black's application, his fingers laced together under his chin. Rule had intercepted Micah's interest form personally and brought it to him. Now he had a decision to make.

He stood and paced toward the window facing the eastern horizon. A new day had come. A new era was dawning. One in which he would reveal his true identity. He couldn't remain hidden any longer. Micah and Cordray were getting too close. Not that he couldn't hold them off. He could. He just didn't want to anymore.

He'd always said he would know when the time was right to reveal himself. And the time was now. For so long, he had remained hidden behind his alter ego, but he could no longer stay silent. Too much was at stake, such as the survival of his race.

He closed his eyes, acknowledging the cold anguish in his heart.

If only he could go back in time, he never would have let the situation escalate the way it had. All that had happened in the past thirty-five hundred years was his fault. He alone had held the key to ensuring that events wouldn't unfold as they had, but he'd been too ill-equipped, too weak to do what had to be done. Of course, doing so would have resulted in civil war, but at least he would still have his daughter.

Now he would make those who had taken her from him pay. He would set right all he had allowed to go askew so long ago.

And Micah and Cordray would help him. He would make them understand, and they would have no choice but to join him. And with them would come King Bain's royal alliance. He would need that connection to make things right.

"Digon?"

A quiet tap on his door brought his gaze around.

Rule cautiously stepped into his office.

"Yes, what is it?"

Rule's gaze traveled to Micah's application. His shoulders lifted proudly. "What do you want me to tell him?"

Digon regarded the application then met the gaze of his closest confidante. No, Rule was more than that. He was family. Just like Sonia, who eased open the door and joined them a moment later, her red hair falling past her shoulders in waves. Eyes so like her father's expectantly met his and held. She and Rule were a testament to how much he'd grown since single-handedly lining up the greatest tragedy vampires and drecks had ever endured. He had succeeded with Rule and Sonia where he had failed before, and now the three of them faced the toughest test they would ever come up against.

Turning back toward the window, Digon breathed in the smell of freedom.

"Invite him. Tonight. I want him here tonight." He paused, and a faint smile touched his lips. "The time has come, my friends." He looked over his shoulder at them. "Time for us to step out from the shadows."

He could feel the hope and excitement bubble around them.

He returned to his desk and pushed Micah's application toward Rule. "Soon I will talk to King Bain. He needs to know about Micah, as well."

Rule rolled the application into a paper tube and held it in his loose fist. "What if he already does? After all, he is the king."

Digon arched an eyebrow at Rule. "Then we'll have a lot to talk about, now won't we?"

The time of Digon was at an end. It was time for his true self to reenter society.

Time for Argon to rise again.

CHAPTER 33

TRACE LAY ON HIS LEFT SIDE, facing Cordray, his head resting on his arm. She was on her back, arms stretched under the black, satin-covered pillow above her head. Her face was turned toward his.

Their gazes met in silent acceptance. It was as if they were locked inside a magical bubble, and Trace never wanted to leave. He wanted to stay right here, tucked away with her, where he could continue to discover every inch of her — everything she was — for the rest of his life.

No words could describe how he felt. Cordray was his other half, and now, with her lying quietly beside him, her eyes staring into his with the same sense of wonder he was feeling, he marveled for what felt like the tenth time that his search was finally over.

His gaze drifted to her bare breasts then to her flat stomach and the colorful dragon tattoo that wrapped around her torso. The dragon held a thorny rose in its claw. He understood the symbolism. The rose was considered the perfect flower. Beautiful in its perfection. But even perfection can cause pain. Get too close or hold on too tightly, and the thorns will prick you and draw blood.

With the fingertips of his right hand, he lightly traced a line up the subtle, shallow ridge that separated the two halves of her stomach. The firm muscles on either side quivered as a broken groan trembled from her throat, and he glanced up in time to see her eyes roll back as her eyelids fluttered closed.

She was so damn responsive. She mewled under his touch, submitting herself to him in a way that was fascinating to witness. Not only because — for once — he wasn't the one in submission, but because she wasn't normally so compliant. He was used to her sassy mouth and her feisty demeanor, but he liked this softer, milder Cordray. He liked touching her. Liked the way she responded.

Grinning almost proudly, he skimmed his palm up and around the orb of her left breast. He loved how the soft fullness gave and shifted against his hand. How her flesh molded to his gentle grip when he squeezed. What he loved even more was how Cordray moaned as she arched, pushing her breast more fully into his grasp.

He tickled his way to her right breast as she sank back against the mattress on a sigh. Using the tip of his index finger, he swirled circles around her rosy nipple. The center tightened, formed a soft nub, and then hardened as he continued coaxing it. What looked like gooseflesh prickled the areola.

Euphoria shone from her face. Erotic sighs drifted from between parted lips, and her thick black lashes framed hungry eyes as she met his gaze again. Her chest rose and fell heavily, and her legs scissored at the foot of the bed as she squirmed.

She was so fucking goddamn gorgeous.

With a hunger growing within his chest, he pinched her nipple between his thumb and index finger, and then watched in fascination as her body stiffened then fell into shudders as a ragged, choppy moan shivered from her throat. Her stomach muscles trembled, and her thighs pressed together and quivered violently as her hand shot between her legs and clamped down.

He smiled and shifted closer, releasing her nipple. "Did you just come again?"

A ripple raced through her body as she rolled toward him.

"Did you?" His arm wound around her and pulled her on top of him as he rolled to his back. Her hair spilled over his face, his chest, his shoulders. It was thick and soft. Heavenly.

Cordray's body continued to quake as her hips rocked against his cock, but she nodded as she licked her lips then laid her cheek on his chest. "Yes." She drew in a deep breath, blew it out, and relaxed against him.

How many times had Cordray come since they'd started their marathon in the hall? She seemed to have a never-ending supply of orgasms inside her. Every five or ten minutes, her body released another one, even when Trace wasn't trying to give her one. And how about that? For once, he was giving an orgasm to a female. Willingly. Of his own desire. Not because he had been beaten to do so. Not because he wanted to take advantage of a rare moment of peace from his beast. But because he was fully in the moment, lucid, and wanted to give pleasure for pleasure's sake.

"Sam told me you couldn't feel," he said quietly, playing with her hair, "but that you can feel me. Is that true?"

She sank more fully against him, almost as if her body were part of his. "Yes."

No wonder she couldn't stop coming. Her body had been starved of physical sensation and now had been presented a smorgasbord. It was feasting, and rightfully so.

He brushed his lips over her hair, truly content for the first time in his life. "I'm glad," he whispered.

His gaze remained on the ceiling, but every cell in his body was fully aware of the extraordinary female lying on top of him.

He didn't need to look at her to see her. He could feel her heart beating against his rib cage, hear the calmness of her thoughts in the way she breathed and pressed her cheek a little more firmly against his chest, taste her essence on the air and against his tongue, and smell the fragrance of her very soul as she infiltrated every molecule of his being. Looking at her with his eyes and taking in her magnificent beauty was simply the icing on the cake.

"Me, too," she said. "I can feel every part of you." As if to punctuate the point, she rubbed her cheek against his skin and caressed her palm down his arm, leaving a fiery trail in its wake. "For so long, I couldn't feel a thing, but when you touch me, I feel it."

"How?"

She lifted her head and looked at him as he brought his gaze down from the ceiling to hers. "I don't know." She shook her head in dismay. "All I know is that for the first time in a long time, I can feel something other than a vast, empty void. But only with you. No one else."

"So . . ." He licked his lips and gave her a playful smirk. "You're saying I'm special."

She rolled her eyes. "Oh God, you're going to make this a thing, aren't you?"

"You can't admit it, can you?" He grinned. "Come on. Say it. Say, 'Trace, you're one of a kind. You're special.'"

She bit back a smile. "You are. You're going to make this into a thing. Does everything have to be a competition with you?" A coquettish twinkle shone from her eyes, making it clear she hoped he would never change.

Trace chuckled. "If you don't say it, I win."

She flashed him a playfully dubious look. "You're special all right." She quickly leaned forward and nipped his bottom lip then started to push herself off.

Trace grabbed her around the waist. "Where are you going?"

"Can a girl pee?" She fought him off with a gentle smack on the cheek, which of course got his blood pumping even more than it already was. He liked when she smacked him around.

He let her go. "Hurry back. I'm not done with you." He watched her disappear into the bathroom then lay back on the bed, arms out to his sides, legs straight and open, cock hard against his stomach.

The smile on his face said it all. This had been the best night *ever*!

Visions of a teenage human virgin in his parents' basement, on a lumpy couch, fumbling with the clasp of his girlfriend's bra came to mind. No matter how shitty the surroundings, or how clumsy his fingers, or how he didn't know a damn thing about what in the hell he was doing took away from the fact that first-time sex was the best sex in the whole damn world. The kind of sex a guy never forgot.

Did it matter if it only lasted sixty seconds? Did it matter that he'd never properly held a female's breasts before? Or that he had no experience taking off a female's clothes?

Hell no. All that mattered was how damn good it felt, and that all he wanted was to do it for the next two weeks without stopping.

The bathroom door opened, and Cordray appeared, smiling at him like she was as happy as he was. Then she pulled up and frowned at the floor.

"What is it?" He propped himself on his elbow.

She bent down and picked something up. When she stood and held up her hand, she was holding a small, black button.

She set it on her nightstand and shimmied onto the bed. "Looks like I'll have to find out which pair of pants that came off of and sew it back on. Sometimes I feel like all I do is mend my clothes."

He lay back and moved his arm so she could lie down next to him on her stomach. She propped herself on her elbows.

"What's that cheesy grin for?" she said, snuggling closer.

He reached around with his other hand and brushed back her hair, tucking it behind her ear. "I've never felt this way before." He glanced down at her full lips. "I've never experienced anything like this."

It was an admission of vulnerability, but for the first time aside from Micah and Sam, he felt complete trust in someone. He instinctively knew that his heart and soul were safe with Cordray. He could open himself and show her his weakness, and she wouldn't abuse his trust.

Was this how it would always be with her? Was everything going to feel this safe from now on? After centuries of fear, loneliness, and despair, had he finally found the one person who could give him peace? Total, undeniable, blessedly granted peace in every way possible?

She smiled and nestled a little closer. "Neither have I." She bowed her head and kissed his shoulder. "I thought I had once, but . . ." She took a breath and looked deep into his eyes. "Never like this. It was never like this."

He searched her eyes. He was lost, yet found. Bewildered by how enraptured he was. "I don't know what to do. What you expect. What *I* expect . . ."

Biting her bottom lip, Cordray smiled like a shy but thrilled little girl. "Neither do I, but isn't that part of what makes this so exciting?"

Trace rolled toward her and settled his palm on the small of her back. Her perfect, round *derriere* was an inviting, curved bounty of flesh. "All I know right now is that I can't stop" — he ran his palm down one cheek — "touching you." Everything about Cordray drew him in. He never thought he'd like the smell of anything more than he liked the scent of lilacs, but Cordray's citrusy scent intoxicated him even more. Being with her was like walking through an orange grove in full blossom.

She sighed and sank into the mattress, letting her head drift downward as his hand explored first one full handful of flesh, and then the other. His fingertips ventured gently into the sexy crease that divided her bottom, and his heart skipped at her moan of approval and the way she parted her legs as his fingers slid lower and found her labia.

She was wet. He had never felt a woman's arousal like this before. Always, he had been bound, at the whim of his mistress, never able to indulge and enjoy. Now, like the proverbial kid in a candy store, he took advantage of his freedom, sliding his finger curiously up and down the slick opening between her legs, enthralled that he had done this to her.

Quiet, heated murmurs touched his ears, and he glanced at her face to find she had closed her eyes. The sounds emanating from between her luscious lips sounded both plaintive and surrendering, as if she were begging him and giving in to him all at once.

"You like this?" Did his inexperienced caresses on her most private, intimate flesh really turn her on? He felt more like a fumbling fool than a master of seduction.

She nodded and mumbled something he couldn't understand against the back of her hand, but which sounded like a plea for more.

His dick had been hard for the better part of the last four hours, but he'd been too enchanted with her — touching her, watching her, feeling her, listening to her — to do anything about his own needs. Right now, all he wanted was to memorize every inch of her skin, every curve, every dip and groove.

"Turn over for me," he said.

Without hesitation, she complied and laid her hand on his arm as he slid his palm between her legs, letting his fingers part her and return to the slick warmth that spilled from her like honey. Now that the fiery urgency they'd experienced in the hall had subsided, he relished the long, sweet exploration of her body.

"You're so wet." He gently swirled his fingertips in her nectar and felt the raised, firm nubbin beneath the pad of his middle finger. Her clitoris. Cordray sucked in her breath as he circled it.

The way her body writhed as he continued to tease her clit drove him crazy.

"I love how you move. How you use your body to show me what you like." He lowered his head and kissed the side of her breast as he urged his middle finger inside her.

She pressed her hand to the back of his head and moaned, her body twisting toward his.

"I love the noises you make." He laved his tongue over her rosy nipple, closed his lips over the puckered nub, and swirled his tongue as he did the same with the butt of his hand against her clit.

"Trace . . ." An urgent undercurrent simmered beneath her whisper. Her fingers curled on his skull, her nails digging into his skin.

"Mmmmm." He couldn't get enough of her. The way her body quivered, her taste, her heat. The bite of pain from her nails on the back of his head.

"Trace." Her hips ground against his hand, which he pressed more demandingly against her.

He was halfway on her body now, his leg slung over one of hers, his erection pressing against her hip. He feasted on her breast, stroked her inside and out with his right hand, which trembled against her from a new sense of power, one he had never felt before.

"Cordray . . ." His fangs extended, his hunger approaching insatiable levels. He needed her. All of her. Blood, body, and soul.

"Please, Trace. More. God, please."

Panting through his nose, Trace's eyes shot open and cast a yellow glow against her skin and the red-satin sheets, making them appear a deep shade of orange. His sight was hunter sharp. Was this normal?

Before he could conjure an answer, instinct took over. He growled and sank his fangs into her breast.

She gasped, spasmed, and the moment her blood touched his tongue, power surged down his arm. His hand clenched, and he drove his palm against her, curled his finger inside her, and felt power rocket from his palm. A split-second later, Cordray cried out and fell into ecstatic convulsions beneath him. Moisture flooded his palm, heated his skin, sent bolts of electricity through him. He ejaculated no more than a second later, spilling against her hip as he grunted and ground himself against her body.

For what felt like five minutes, wave after wave of orgasmic pleasure ebbed and flowed between them, sending them into shuddering aftershocks every few seconds. By the time Trace could actually move again to withdraw his fangs and his finger, the sheets were completely soiled. He had never come so hard or so much in his life. And from the slickness on his palm, neither had she.

"Fuck!" He lifted off of her. They were drenched in sweat. Cordray's body practically glowed. No. It *was* glowing. A dim, pulsing light emanated from under her skin then began to fade.

She uttered one last gasp, turned amazed, infatuated eyes on him, and then slapped him across the face.

Starbursts erupted down his spine. "What the hell?" Not that he was complaining. She'd just caught him off guard.

She swallowed, breathed, and then smiled. "I just wanted to say thank you."

Ignoring the mess he'd made on her, himself, and the bed, he snuggled closer. "And hitting me was your way of doing that?"

With a breathless nod, her gaze ranged up and down his body. "Slapping you was the first thing that came to mind."

"Of course." He grinned as their eyes met again. "But you should be more careful."

"Why's that?"

"Because I like when you slap me." They were practically nose to nose. "It turns me on."

"I know it does."

He raised one eyebrow. "Tease."

"You're amazing," she said. "Fucking amazing." Her head shook subtly from side to side as if in disbelief.

"Funny. I was just thinking the same thing about you. That was the hottest sex I've ever had."

A devilish grin crossed her face, and a frisky twinkle lit in her eyes as she bit her bottom lip then said, "Can you imagine how hot that would have been if you'd actually been inside me?"

He could almost read her mind, and his own evil smile spread over his face. "Are you thinking what I'm thinking?"

She grabbed his shoulders and pulled him on top of her then

wrapped her hand around his still-hard cock. "You know I am."

He felt the niggling sensation of her mind burrowing into his. He only smiled wider as she raised her hips and positioned the head of his cock at her silken entrance.

"We're going to have to work on your communication skills, female." He nudged forward an inch.

She moaned. "Shut up and fuck me, Trace. How's that?"

Oh, God. Dirty talk. His cock hiccupped in approval. "Perfect." He drove himself inside. "Now, keep talking, bitch."

She grinned, showing her fangs. "Oh, you are in *sooo* much trouble."

He shoved her legs farther apart with his knees, gripped her wrists, and slammed them against the mattress. "I certainly hope so."

CHAPTER 34

CORDRAY STIRRED AWAKE TO THE SENSATION of fingers caressing her face, from her temple, down her cheek, to her mouth. She sighed and burrowed closer to the solid, warm body she was tucked against. The thick arm wrapped around her coiled tighter, securing her inside its protective hold.

She blinked her eyes open to find Trace gazing at her from hooded eyes. Bedroom eyes. At once confident and seductive, like he was a male in total control. A male who knew what he was doing, even though he had admitted numerous times in the last few hours how inexperienced he was.

Then again, he was a strong, virile male. And he was her mate. Put all those qualities in a cauldron and stir, and abracadabra, you have one sexy-assed male on a fast-track learning curve.

"So, I wasn't dreaming." She swept her hand up his corded torso. "You really are here. This really is happening."

"Yep."

The sheets were draped haphazardly over their legs. She was surprised they were even still on the bed, given all she and Trace had done to one another since sequestering themselves in her bed hours ago.

"Did you sleep?" She stretched out alongside him. Her body ached in such a delicious way, especially between her legs.

"A little."

"Mmm." She snuggled against him. "What time is it?"

He lifted his head and looked over her at the clock on the nightstand. "Almost five thirty." He settled back down beside her.

Almost sunrise.

Mya and Brenna would be in the kitchen soon, preparing breakfast for the kids.

She really should get up. Take a shower. Get dressed. Clean up the disaster in the hallway.

Instead, she pulled the blankets over them and tucked herself more securely against him, his warmth, his strength. He was like meth. The more she got of him, the more she wanted.

Maybe in a few days, the fascination would wear off, but right now, she wanted to wrap him around her like a straitjacket and never take him off.

His chest rose and fell evenly as his fingers absently caressed up and down her arm, as if he, too, were blessedly content.

"Tell me about Brak and your family," she said softly. "What happened?"

The arm around her tensed, and his fingers stuttered over her elbow. Then he relaxed again. "Why don't you just go inside my head and see for yourself?" There was no animosity in his voice. No resentment. It was a simple statement of fact, as if he'd accepted her abilities to dip into his thoughts and no longer wished to keep them from her.

She rolled to her stomach and pushed herself up on her elbows. "I'd rather you tell me. That way, I can hear your voice." She smiled and briefly dipped her forehead against his shoulder. "I like your voice."

But her request was about more than hearing his voice. She also wanted him to talk about what had happened, because talking was active. Allowing her to see inside his thoughts was passive. And what he needed was to actively engage with his past rather than continue to dismiss it. That was the only way he would ever truly come to terms with what had happened.

"You like my voice, huh?" He reached across his body and brushed his fingers down her hair.

"Yes."

His eyes met hers and locked on, shining pure adoration upon her. But he said nothing further.

After several seconds, she shimmied closer. "Tell me, Trace. Tell me about them. Please."

He blinked, his gaze falling to her mouth momentarily before he turned away and stared off into space. But his arm wound more securely around her as if she were a buoy he refused to let go of for fear of being swept into the current. While his thoughts drifted back in time, the rest of him remained grounded by her side.

With a sigh, he said, "I was twelve when my mother died." His mouth curved into a wistful smile. "She was so beautiful." He turned his head on the pillow so he faced her. "She had mocha-colored skin and green eyes."

"Like yours."

"Yes, like mine. My father has pale-green eyes, too, but mine are more like my mother's." He looked away again, his gaze taking on a faraway appearance as he connected once more with the past. "She was a voodoo priestess, but my father called her an exotic island woman. She was human and refused my father's offer to change her into his davala. She said that her path was only meant to cross his, not run parallel with it for eternity. Of course, my father never stopped trying to change her, but she never relented. And he respected her decision, no matter how much he didn't like it."

"She sounds like a strong woman."

He smiled wistfully. "She was." After a brief pause, he continued. "She became pregnant with Brak and me during my father's first calling. And while we were in her womb, she conjured magic to protect us." He scoffed, shaking his head. "She gave Brak what she called the light, and she gave me the darkness. She never explained why. All she said was that Brak and I were two halves meant to balance each other, but it was clear Brak was the favored son. Both my parents treated him with so much love and affection. Me, on the other hand . . .?" Trace blinked several times and turned sharply away even as his arm tightened around her and pulled her closer. "Me they merely tolerated. I never received the attention Brak did. He was the good son. I was the anomaly."

Cordray frowned. "But they loved you. Surely, they did."

He expelled a burdensome breath. "In hindsight, I *felt* loved. But at the time, I was too young to recognize it. All I felt was distress. Like I was a scourge to the family. A disgrace. A freak." He nodded and met her gaze again. His eyes glistened. "Most of the time, I felt like a freak. An outcast. Brak fit in with everyone, and all I daydreamed about most days was being able to fit in like he did. That the other kids would want to play with me the way they did him. But that never happened. I was teased and made fun of all the time. Not a day went by that I wasn't reminded of how different I was from everyone else.

"I came to resent my mother for what she'd done to me. And I resented Brak, too. I resented his power. That he'd received the light instead of the darkness."

He stopped as if gathering his thoughts. Cordray remained quiet, waiting for him to get to the rest of his story in his own time.

Trace dragged in a heavy inhale.

"My power started manifesting when I was nine or ten. Small stuff at first. Pebbles, paper, things like that. It scared me, but it also fascinated me, and for the first time, I saw a way I could retaliate against those who made fun of me. I was able to move things with my mind, especially when I got upset. I would get angry, and then pebbles would skitter across the ground, or the pages in a book would begin turning as if by a strong breeze. Before long, the pebbles became tiny projectiles, and the books slammed shut and flew across the room.

"My mother told me not to show my power in public. That doing so would be dangerous, and that I needed to be disciplined and work at keeping it under control. That if I didn't work hard to keep my power under control, it would control me instead." He let out a bitter huff. "But her warnings didn't stop me. I was rebellious. I was angry that they didn't seem to love me as much as they loved Brak, and I was angry at the kids who teased me. So I let my power out around the other kids. Just little things . . . like the pebbles and the books. Enough to scare them without making them realize I was responsible. Watching them freak out over 'ghosts' was so fun, though, so I didn't see why I should try to rein in this magic Mother had given me.

"Then one day I was playing by myself by a pond when this group of kids came along. One of them, a boy named Mason, was my worst tormentor. He was a bully who took tremendous pleasure in making fun of me in front of the other kids. He began calling me names, taunting me."

Cordray had seen this in his mind the other night. She knew what came next. Still, she remained silent, letting Trace get everything off his chest.

"I remember this odd sensation coming over me." He frowned and used his free hand to make a fist. "Like I was being squeezed through a pipe. Like my muscles were being stretched to their limits. I'd never felt that before, and it terrified me. I began to panic. I struggled to breathe. I just wanted to get away from them. To get back to my mother so she could take away whatever was making me ill. I didn't understand at the time that it was my power unleashing at full capacity. That the very thing she'd warned me about was happening."

He paused and waved his free hand in the air over his stomach.

"I had this rock collection." He glanced at her. "I still do, actually. It's at my place, still in the leather pouch my father made for me." His face twisted as painful memories clawed at him. "I had this favorite. It was a shimmering white color, like fogged glass, with shiny black flecks all through it. Null has one similar to it in his own collection."

"I know the one you're talking about," she said. "I think it's quartz."

"Yeah, well, Mason picked up my favorite rock and threw it into the pond. The moment it hit the water, my right arm shot out"—he mimicked the motion, lifting his arm toward the ceiling—"and this blast of energy burst from my hand. It shook the ground like an earthquake, rattling the trees, and threw Mason and all the other kids away from me like ragdolls. Two were injured."

He paused and met her eyes. "I was terrified. I bolted. Ran all the way home. But I didn't tell anybody what had happened. Maybe if I had, things would have turned out differently, but I was too scared. I thought my family was already upset with me for all the other stuff that was going on around me, so I thought that if they learned about this, I'd be in grave trouble. I didn't want to be punished, so I kept quiet."

Cordray barely breathed, not wanting to disrupt him now that he was on a roll.

"A couple of nights later, I was out collecting herbs and roots for my mother's tinctures when I smelled smoke coming from the direction of my home. I ran as fast as I could, hearing the shouts of the townspeople. By the time I reached our cabin, it was engulfed in flames." Tears bloomed in his eyes. "My mother was being dragged by her hair toward a flaming pyre. All I could do was watch. I felt so helpless."

For a long moment, he said nothing. He didn't even breathe. Then he let go of her and sat up, burying his face in his hands, sobbing. She pushed herself up beside him and grabbed the throw blanket hanging off the corner of the bed. Wrapping it around him, she straddled his lap and pulled him into her arms. Right now, Trace was back inside his twelve-year-old mind, living those agonizing memories she'd seen thrash through his thoughts in Micah's dungeon. He needed to feel safe. Loved. Accepted.

"It's not your fault." She kissed his forehead.

"You don't understand." He buried his face against her breast, his arms holding her as if letting go would kill him. "I was careless. I never listened and didn't try to control my power the way she told me to. If I had, I might not have lost control of it that day, and if I hadn't lost control, the town wouldn't have come for her—for *us*. If I'd told my mother what I'd done, we could have fled before they came."

He turned his face toward hers. Tears streamed his cheeks. "I watched them tie her to a cross and toss her onto that pyre like she was nothing more than kindling. I heard her screams as she burned to death. I heard them calling her a demon. They were calling me that. And all I could do was stand there. And then . . ." He burrowed against her body like he could hide there forever. "I killed them. My power rose in a fury, and I killed those who were torturing her before I fled from the others, terrified of what I'd done and what I'd seen."

She caressed the back of his head, soothing him as best as she could.

"If you ask me," she said a few seconds later, keeping her voice soft, "they deserved it for what they did to your mother. To your entire family." She placed her hand under his chin and coaxed him to look at her. "For what they did to *you*."

For a prolonged, meaningful moment, she held his gaze.

He blinked and nodded curtly as more tears fell from his chin. Then he leaned forward and rested his forehead between her breasts, head bowed. "Maybe, but I was so ashamed of what I'd done." He paused. When he spoke again, his voice was softer. "That's why I chew on matchsticks. It reminds me of how my mother died. Of how dangerous fire is. Of how I always need to remain vigilant and not let my power take control of me like that again."

She pressed her cheek against the top of his head and hugged him close.

"I was so scared that night," he said. "I ran away as fast as my legs could carry me, until my legs gave out, afraid the others would catch me and kill me, too." His hold on her strengthened. "My mother was dead. I thought my father and Brak were, too. They'd been inside the house. No way could they have survived that fire."

"But they did," she said.

He nodded against her chest. "I had hoped they had, since I could still feel Brak's spirit, but I was never completely sure. And then I found my father in Bishop's lab . . . and then Brak came to me in the king's dungeon. Then it became real. They were still alive. But how could I face them after what I'd done? I couldn't." He pulled away and looked into her eyes. "That's why I haven't gone to see them. I don't know if I can face the guilt and shame that it was my actions that ultimately killed her. What if they haven't forgiven me?"

Cordray cupped his cheek. "First of all, your actions did not kill her. The actions of the townspeople did. Secondly, there's nothing to forgive, and even if there were, you're assuming your father and brother are so coldhearted that they would shun their own flesh and blood rather than offer forgiveness." She placed her hand on his cheek. "If they have even an inkling of compassion, they wouldn't want you to suffer like this. The three of you need to come together if for no other reason than to properly mourn your mother and put her to rest. Because I can't imagine her spirit is resting knowing that those she loved most—and she did love you, Trace—are suffering and haven't spoken to one another face to face since the day she died."

A week ago, Trace would have responded to her outpouring of concern with aggression. He would have told her to mind her own business, and he would have done so with language colorful enough to make a sailor take notes. But things were different now.

"I love you." Even though he whispered his declaration, his voice rang strong and clear.

And those three little words, said with raw sincerity and complete devotion, were a testament to just how different things between them had become in the past six hours.

"Is that your way of saying I'm right and you'll go see Brak and your father?"

He cupped her face in his large right hand. The hand that could strike death in an instant or infuse her with more pleasure than she'd ever felt.

"It's my way of saying that fate got this shit right." He pushed his fingers into her hair. "You and me? We're good together. Fate chose my mate well."

Cordray wasn't about all the girly shit. She wasn't into flowers, romantic shows of affection, or candlelit dinners on the beach, but something about hearing Trace proclaim that fate had gotten things right by making her his mate made her want to roll around in rose petals while snuggling with purring kittens.

After reeling in the smile that overtook her face, she said, "Yeah, well, you still haven't answered my question. Are you going to go see Brak and Maddox?"

The corners of his mouth turned up. "See? You're perfect. Always busting my balls."

"Two weeks ago, you would have sent me through the window for even bringing Brak up."

"That was two weeks ago. This is now." He reclined, dropping his head back to his pillow, taking her with him, pushing her hair away from her face. "My attitude has changed where you're concerned."

"Ditto, stud." She grinned down at him, supported by her arms outstretched on either side of his shoulders. "Now, are you going to go visit them or not?"

He searched her eyes then gently nodded. "Yes, beast master," he said mockingly. "On one condition."

"What's that?"

"You go with me so I can introduce you." He squeezed her rump.

"As my *mate*."

She smirked. "You're never going to get tired of calling me that, are you?"

"Nope."

She sighed then nestled herself against him, resting her head on his chest. "I guess I can live with that."

His fingertips traipsed up and down her back, sending pleasant shimmers through her nerve endings. "So, are you going to tell me what happened last night before I got here? And who I need to kill for putting you in danger?"

"I wasn't in danger."

"You were tied up."

"But I was never in danger."

"Still—"

"I'm fine, Trace."

"Just tell me what happened." He swatted her ass. Hard.

She shot up at the sharp contact and let out a startled squeak. She'd never been spanked, and she had to admit, she kind of liked it. Not being able to feel pain had its advantages, but some types of pain were obviously more pleasurable than others. "Did you just spank me?"

"Yes. And I will again if you don't tell me what happened here last night."

She briefly considered the idea, thinking it might be fun to experience a little painful pleasure at Trace's hand. Then she decided they could play later.

"Skeletor was here."

Trace shot up, gripping her around the waist so she didn't slide off is lap. "What?"

"Calm down, beast boy." She patted his cheek. "He wasn't here to hurt me."

"Like hell." Possessive, mated rage flashed over his expression. "He tied you up. He could have hurt you. He could have violated you."

Cordray had never even considered the possibility, because while Skeletor was a lot of things, rapist wasn't one of them. In the few encounters she'd had with him, not once had he put off the signal that he was capable of such an act. He seemed more noble than that.

"But he didn't." She took Trace's face in her hands and steadied him. "He didn't, okay? I'm fine. I'm safe. I'm untouched."

Trace's mated-male side wasn't ready to give up the chase. "I swear to God, when I catch him, he's going to wish he'd never—"

"Calm down, tiger." She had to admit, she liked seeing him so worked up over her safety. It was nice knowing she had a male like Trace — with a built-in nuclear device in his hand — catching her back.

His fury dialed back a notch, and he took a deep breath as if trying to force himself to relax. "What did he want?"

"To warn me." She averted her gaze, knowing she needed to tell Trace that she was Bain's sister.

She was between a rock and hard place. By keeping her relationship to Bain a secret, she would betray the trust that should exist between mates, but by revealing that relationship, she would betray her brother. Well, her half-brother, but what difference did that make? She was still going to betray someone in this scenario.

"Warn you about what?"

"He wants me to stop helping Micah track him down." She quickly told Trace about how Skeletor had hacked her. About how Micah had determined he'd used the underground pedway to escape. About what she'd learned about the stolen ankh.

She thought back over her encounter with Skeletor the night before. "You know, he said something strange to me last night. When I mentioned that he was endangering my kids, he said that I've got bigger problems here than him."

"What did he mean by that?"

"He wouldn't tell me. He said that if I wanted to know, I needed to stop helping Micah."

Trace scoffed. "And if we don't stop?"

"We?"

He grinned as his eyelids closed halfway, his expression dripping with possessive sexuality. "Oh yeah, baby. We're definitely a *we* now."

She rolled her eyes and sighed. "We are, huh?"

His arms encircled her more securely. "Definitely. So tell me, if *we* don't stop, what's Skeletor going to do?"

"Other than not tell me what my real problem is here?" She bit her lip and lowered her gaze, recalling Skeletor's words. *I'll tell everyone who you really are.*

Trace stiffened as if he'd picked up on her nervousness. "Cordray?"

She drew in a long, fortifying breath then blew it out as she lifted her gaze to his.

She had to make a choice. Either she was going to be faithful to her mate, or she was going to remain faithful to her brother. She couldn't have both.

"Cordray, what aren't you telling me?"

She bowed her head and sighed. "Trace, I need to tell you who I am. Who I *really* am."

CHAPTER 35

"You're King Bain's sister?" Now that Trace looked closely, he saw the family resemblance. The black hair. The blue eyes. The aristocratic nose and high cheekbones.

"Half-sister," she corrected, frowning. She nervously bit her lip.

It all made sense now. How she got away with addressing the king as Bain instead of King Bain. How she was able to speak to him so casually and disagree with him without suffering repercussions. Why she'd reacted with such disgust when he thought she and King Bain were lovers. How she had been able to persuade him to shorten Trace's prison sentence from a month to two weeks, as well as convince him to give Io a chance and not execute him.

Wait a second. Did this mean . . .?

"Are you saying I mated a princess?"

Her cheeks filled with color. "Technically yes. Officially? No. No one can know my true relationship to the royal family, or it will damage Bain's reign. People will see him differently. They'll judge him for the actions of our father."

Trace ran the backs of his fingers over her cheek. "I promise not to say anything. Not even to Micah."

"Yeah, but he can see inside your thoughts now. He'll find out eventually."

"And I'll swear him to secrecy when he does. Micah's tight. He won't reveal your secret if I tell him not to."

She swept her hands down his shoulders and over his biceps, letting them come to rest at his elbows. "If you haven't noticed, Micah doesn't exactly like me."

"Yeah, but you and I are mates now." He took her hands in his. "He'll honor that."

"Well, even if he does, Skeletor might not."

"What do you mean? Does he know?"

She bit her lip then nodded. "I don't know how, but he knows. And he says if I don't back off, he's going to tell everybody. I can't let that happen."

"Fuck him. We'll get to him before he can do any damage."

She nibbled the inside of her bottom lip, the skin around her eyes tight. "I want to believe you, but he's proving to be a worthy opponent. What if we can't stop him?"

He cradled her face in his hand and rubbed his thumb reassuringly over her cheek. "We will. He might have an advantage now, but the tables can turn in a blink. We'll get him."

She nodded tightly then let out an abrupt sigh as she shifted on his lap and forced a wary smile. "So, you're not mad?"

"About what?"

"That I'm Bain's sister."

He laughed and let go of her hands so he could wrap his arms around her hips and draw her closer. "Are you kidding? I mated a *princess*." He tilted his head to the side. "True, you're not the kind of princess who wears designer gowns and tiaras and paints her fingernails all day, but if you were, I'd probably curse God for pairing me up with you. I can't stand all that hoity-toity bullshit."

"Hey, I've been known to paint my fingernails."

"But I bet you paint them black or purple or dark blue. You know, some cool color. Something wicked. Just like you."

"You think I'm wicked?"

Trace arched one eyebrow. "Does Godzilla breathe fire?"

Her eyes danced upward as she rocked her head side to side. "Technically, it's not fire. It's nuclear fumes or some shit. Godzilla's a biological nuclear reactor." She leaned forward and nipped his upper lip. "Kind of like you."

Always the contrarian, but she was *his* contrarian. His feisty, frisky female. "Quit being cute. You know what I mean."

"Yeah, I know what you mean." She pushed away. "Come on, we should get cleaned up. Mya and Brenna will be in the kitchen getting ready for breakfast any minute."

"Not yet." He pulled her back down. His lips met hers in a blood-warming caress. He wasn't ready for the lust-inducing revelation of being mated to end just yet. "Five more minutes."

FIVE MINUTES TURNED INTO FIFTEEN, followed by a shared shower where, for the first time ever, Cordray actually felt the water rushing over her body as Trace pressed her face-first against the wall and fucked her from behind, sinking his fangs into the curve where her neck met her shoulder as he came.

He'd marked her with his bite at least half a dozen times. Her neck, her shoulder, her breast, even her inner thigh.

After the venom euphoria wore off, he shampooed her hair and lathered her body from head to toe, paying special attention between her legs, where he used his fingers to coax yet another orgasm from her.

By the time they finished, the water had begun to run cool.

Time to buy a bigger water heater.

While Trace cleaned up the mess in the hallway, she joined Mya and Brenna in the kitchen.

"Good morning." Even with only a couple hours of sleep, she was wide awake and alert.

Mya looked her up and down, holding a half-peeled orange, and flashed a knowing smile. "And good morning to you. What were you up to last night?" Today, Mya wore a light-blue T-shirt with a cartoon marshmallow, graham cracker, and slab of chocolate running away from a ball of fire. Where she found these funny shirts of hers, Cordray had no idea, but she seemed to have an endless supply of them.

Cordray poured herself a mug of coffee and leaned against the counter. "Nothing much." She blew over the hot liquid then sipped.

Mya leaned closer and sniffed. "Yeah, sure. That's why you smell like a sex marathon and have the remnants of a bite mark on your neck."

Her hand flew to her throat, and she quickly adjusted her collar to cover the evidence of what Trace had done to her.

Brenna glanced up long enough from cutting biscuits out of homemade dough to give her a wicked grin. "You wouldn't be taking advantage of the help now, would you, C?"

Both females giggled as Cordray found herself in unfamiliar territory. The I-just-got-fucked-silly-and-found-my-mate kind of territory.

Trace chose that moment to saunter into the kitchen like the sex god he was.

"Morning, ladies." He glanced from Mya to Brenna as he slid behind Cordray and purred, lowering his voice provocatively as he turned her around and brushed his lips over hers. "Beast master," he said in greeting.

Heat flooded her cheeks, as well as other parts of her body, as his arms slinked around her waist. He nuzzled her neck, that deep purr stabbing pleasure into the very heart of her.

After hours of enjoying each other, she would have thought they could go at least five minutes without getting hot for one another, but damn, this mated business wasn't having any of that. She wanted him now as badly as she'd wanted him in the hall last night.

"Don't you have someplace to be?" she said, gently nudging him, even though all she wanted was to take him back upstairs to bed. But he needed to go back for the SUV he'd left at Micah's house, and then she was planning on meeting him so they could visit his brother before she had to leave for Grudge Match. Hopefully, Micah had received his invite and would be there tonight so they could get started on figuring out the connection between the fight club and Bishop's lab.

Trace's lips brushed over her ear, and he whispered, "I'm *exactly* where I want to be." He placed a chaste kiss that was full of naughty intentions behind her ear.

Mya and Brenna giggled, knocking awareness back into her. Smiling, she eased out of his grasp and took his hand. "Um, yeah. Trace and I are sort of . . . well . . .we're—"

"We're mated." Trace proudly jutted his chin as his chest puffed out like a cocky rooster's.

Mya gasped. Brenna's mouth fell open a split second before she covered it with her hand.

Heat flooded Cordray's face as she first met Brenna's gaze then Mya's, who was smugly eyeing her. "Don't go looking at me like that, Mya."

"Like what?" Mya smirked, her eyes twinkling mischievously.

"Like you want to tell me you told me so."

Mya went back to peeling oranges. "Well, I did. I told you your biological clock was ticking."

Cordray lifted her abashed gaze to Trace's, only to find unadulterated reverence shining back at her. She nibbled her lip under his heated stare.

"My tough-as-nails mate." He flashed her a confident, crooked grin. His thumb rubbed back and forth on her knuckles. "But I don't care how tough you think you are, Cordray. It's my responsibility to take care of you. It's my duty from this day forward to see to your every need and protect you. Your breath is my breath now. Your blood, my blood. And I don't intend to take either for granted." He closed the short distance between them. "I've searched all my life for you. *You*, Cordray." He squeezed her fingers. "You were made expressly for me. You tame my beast and make me feel free for the first time in my life. Truly free. And in front of these witnesses" — he glanced toward Mya and Brenna — "I vow to have, keep, and nurture you for as long as I walk this earth — whether you like it or not — and rain hell down on anyone who tries to take you from me."

Damn. Now that was a declaration of love. Prince Valiant had nothing on Trace.

Girly shit be damned, if there had been a tub of pink candy hearts in her kitchen, she would have dived in and risked sugar shock. Bring this girl a bouquet of roses and a heart-shaped box filled with truffles, because Valentine's Day just became her favorite holiday.

"Um . . .wow?" They were the only words she could muster.

He smirked. "What's this? You're speechless? I actually rendered you speechless?"

"Don't get cocky, Trace. You caught me off guard, that's all."

He chuckled, and the sound reminded her of cherries covered in dark chocolate. Decadent and sweet, with a bit of tartness to make the tongue sing.

The back door flew open and Null dashed into the kitchen, little Aiden close behind.

"Twace! Twace! Make me fly!"

Trace leaned down, picked Null up, and spun him around before tossing him just high enough that he didn't hit the ceiling. Then he settled him on his hip and tapped his button nose with the tip of his index finger. "I've got to run into the city for a while, little man, but I'll be back later, okay? And then I'll really show you how to fly." He booped his nose again. "How's that sound?"

Null flung his arms around Trace's neck, squealing and kicking his little legs excitedly.

Trace caught Cordray's eye as he handed Null to her. "I'll see you later."

"I'll meet you at Micah's in an hour or so." She would dematerialize there rather than drive. Then they could take the Denali and ride together to where Brak was staying.

He leaned in, and as naturally as if she'd been doing it all her life, she lifted her face, meeting his mouth with hers in a tender kiss.

Null and Aiden giggled and slapped their hands over their eyes. "Ew, cooties."

Trace smiled against her mouth then kissed her again. "I like your cooties."

"You know, yours are kinda growing on me, too," she replied.

He gave her one last kiss then kissed Null on the cheek and bent to kiss the top of Aiden's head.

Then he headed out.

"Bye, Twace!" Null flapped his arm as he waved.

Mya eased up behind her while Null was distracted. "Hearts are flying out your ass, C," she whispered.

"Get used to it," she whispered back with a playful glare. "Because I'm crazy about that SOB."

Mya giggled and returned to making fruit salad.

Cordray bounced Null on her hip, patting his rump. A moment later, something fell off his back pocket, skidding across her palm, then flipped to the floor.

She set Null down, crouched, and picked up a button.

"Turn around, Null. Let me see your jeans."

He spun, and she inspected the tiny back pockets. One had a button and the other didn't. Great. Another button to mend.

She stood. "Good thing that fell off in my hand or we might never have found it, and you would have been all lopsided, little man."

He giggled and took off for the living room, where his coloring books waited for him on the coffee table.

Cordray frowned as a lightbulb flickered on over her head.

Wait a minute.

She glanced down at the button in her palm then up in the direction of her bedroom.

The button on her nightstand. That wasn't one of hers. It belonged to Skeletor. It must have fallen off his clothes during the struggle.

She gasped as she realized she had everything she needed to finally find that little prick.

Turning, she raced out of the kitchen toward the stairs.

"What's wrong?" Brenna called after her.

"Nothing. I'll tell you later," she called back.

By the end of the day, Skeletor would be hers.

CHAPTER 36

MICAH WAS SITTING QUIETLY IN THE LIVING ROOM when Trace arrived back at the house. He was reading. Classical music played softly from the Bluetooth speaker beside him.

"Hey," Trace said, disturbing the peace.

Micah looked up from his book. Their eyes met. "Hey."

"Where's Sam?"

"Sleeping."

Trace glanced toward the kitchen, which had been cleaned up since last night. "Why aren't you sleeping?"

Micah closed the book and set it on the table beside him. "I was waiting for you. I knew you'd come back." He regarded him for a moment. "Sam wanted to wait up with me, but she conked out about an hour ago, so I took her to bed."

Trace absently nodded and shuffled his feet.

Awkward silence stretched between them then Trace moved forward and sat down across from him.

How would his mating Cordray affect his relationship with Micah? He still wanted Micah. Still needed him. That hadn't changed. But the dynamic between them had.

"I'm mated." He worked his teeth over the inside of his lip.

"I know." Micah cleared his throat and crossed his ankle over his knee.

More silence.

"She's my mate." There was no need to explain who *she* was after the conversation they'd had in the bathtub less than twelve hours ago.

Micah uncrossed his legs and leaned forward, planting his elbows on his knees. "I know she is, buddy. I'm the one who told you she was."

The tension between them wasn't exactly thick, but it wasn't nonexistent, either. Trace drummed his fingers on his thighs. "I guess what I want to know is how this affects us."

Micah leaned back and placed his hands on the arms of the chair. "That's up to you, Trace. You tell me. As far as I'm concerned, I'm still your Dom. If you still need me in that way, I'm here for you." He placed his ankle over his knee again, watching Trace closely. After a bloated hesitation, he said, "Do you still want that?"

He would have to work out the details with Cordray, but yes, he did want that. He'd come to enjoy the submissive lifestyle. And even though he was now mated, he couldn't see his life without Micah as his master, especially now that he'd only just found him.

He bowed his head, nodding. "Yeah. Yeah, man, I do."

"So do I." Micah sat forward, elbows on his knees, his expression introspective. "By becoming my sub, Trace, you've given something back to me that I hadn't even realized I'd been missing. I don't want to lose it again."

He shook his head. "I've waited too long to find you, Micah. I'm not going anywhere." He pressed his lips together. "But if she wants to be in the dungeon with us, I want her there."

Micah stiffened. His nostrils flared as he inhaled long and deep. Then he exhaled and nodded once. "As long as she doesn't interfere, then . . . okay, I'm open to giving it a try. But she has to understand that's *my* dungeon down there, not hers. That she's your mate, but you're *my* submissive. Is that going to be a problem?"

Trace shook his head. "I'll talk to her."

Micah nodded thoughtfully, and they stared at each other for a long while, the air pregnant with anticipation. "Okay, good," he finally said, nodding again.

An undercurrent of rising excitement stirred around them. "It'll all work out," Trace said quietly, holding Micah's intense gaze. "I want this too much for it not to."

Micah's shrewd eyes regarded him for a long moment. Then he clapped his palms on his thighs as if slapping a period on the conversation, got up, and strolled to the liquor cabinet, where he poured two glasses of Lagavulin.

"What's this for?" Trace eyed the expensive scotch as Micah handed him a crystal tumbler.

Micah raised his own glass as Trace stood. "We're celebrating, Trace. It's not every day that you take a mate, and you've waited long enough to find yours, haven't you?"

Trace grinned. "Yeah, man. Too long."

"Well then, here's to you and your mate." Micah clinked Trace's glass with his. "Even if you did have to go and mate Medusa."

"Hey, that's my mate you're talking about, Mike." Trace pretended to be insulted, but he knew the score between Micah and Cordray.

He wasn't expecting them to be best friends or anything.

"Yeah well, don't go getting any ideas about mate-swapping. I might not have a problem with you getting handsy with Sam, but I am never going to want to reciprocate with Cordray, just so that's clear."

"More for me then."

Micah chuckled and lifted his glass to his lips.

As Trace was about to take a drink, the garage door banged open. Both he and Micah tensed and got ready to throw down against whatever idiot had decided to break into Micah's house in broad daylight. Then Cordray flew around the corner.

Trace's heart beat harder just seeing her.

She held something in her hand. Something small.

"I have his button!" She held it up and rushed forward.

Micah relaxed, downed his scotch, and shot Trace a glance out of the corner of his eye. "Speak of the devil." He set his empty glass down and said to Cordray, "Thanks for returning Trace's button and all, C, but you could have knocked on the front door like a normal person."

"No." She took another step forward and held the button higher. It was the one she'd found on her bedroom floor this morning. "It's his. Skeletor's." She looked from Trace to Micah. "He broke into my house last night. This fell off his clothes. It belongs to him." She raised her eyebrows, waiting, as if she expected them to do the math.

Micah plucked the small piece of plastic from her hand. "And this is good news why?"

Cordray shook her head. "It's a good thing I'm around to explain things to you, big guy." She turned toward Trace. "Your brother," she said to him. "Brak." Her gaze brightened. "He can use this to find him."

The realization hit Trace at the same time it hit Micah, both of them sucking in their breath in unison.

"Fuck me." Micah's fist closed around the button. "Of course. Brak. He can track him down, and then we'll know who he is."

"Exactly." Cordray's excitement was like soda pop fizz, bubbly and effervescent. She reached for the button. "Trace and I were going to see him today. We'll give it to him and see if he can help us."

Micah habitually checked the time then grumbled when he realized it was still morning. "Shit. I'm stuck here until nightfall." He huffed in frustrated resignation. "I want looped in on this. If Brak's able to find our guy, call me and tell me what he's got, but nobody move on him. No vigilantism. I don't want anyone blowing our chances by tipping our hand to this guy until we're ready to move. I don't care if Brak tracks him down and starts feeding us intel immediately. No one moves on this guy until I say we're set. I don't want this prick slipping away again. Got it?" The last he said to Cordray. "I'll contact the others and alert Stryker." He pulled his mobile from his pocket and tapped his screen.

Cordray rolled her eyes. "Jesus, you're bossy."

Trace took her hand as Micah ignored her and pressed his phone to his ear. "Mike" — he glanced over his shoulder — "we're out. Stay close to your phone. We'll call as soon as we know something."

Micah gave him a thumbs-up then turned his attention to his call. "Stryker, hey, it's Micah. I need your help."

Trace ushered Cordray through the garage to the Denali sitting in the driveway.

Cordray stepped toward the driver's side and held out her hand. "Keys."

He flipped the keys and caught them in his palm as he nudged her aside. "I'm driving. You ride shotgun."

She nudged him back. "Just because you're the big bad male in this relationship doesn't mean you get to drive. This is my vehicle. I'm driving."

He shook his head, his blood accelerating to a welcome simmer. Arguing with her was an aphrodisiac. One he hoped she never stopped indulging him with. "No. I'm driving." He pushed her aside and opened the door, letting his hand brush across her breast. He might even have given her a little grope.

She sucked in her breath and rocked backward.

"Trouble?" he said, smirking.

Her tongue peeked out and wet her lips as she smoothed her palms down her shirt. "No. No trouble." She narrowed her eyes at him but marched dutifully, if not a little haughtily, around to the passenger side. "Fine. You drive."

Less than twenty minutes later, they were parked in the driveway of a tan and brick cookie-cutter home in a neighborhood where all the houses looked more or less alike. It was a nice home — nicer than the small box Trace had called home for the last few years — with a two-car garage, a chimney, and a covered porch, but it paled in comparison to Micah's house.

But all this mental chatter was only procrastination. Brak was inside that house. The brother he hadn't seen in almost two hundred years was less than a ten-yard walk away.

"You okay?" Cordray touched his arm.

He startled to life and looked at her. "Yeah. I'm just . . ." He turned back toward the house as the door opened, and he was robbed of both words and breath.

Brak stood in the doorway. His long brown hair fell well past his shoulders and lifted on a breeze as he took a cautious step onto the porch, staring at the Denali. He was wearing a white linen pullover and tan drawstring pants. He wasn't wearing any shoes. Looked like some things never changed. Brak had hated wearing shoes when they were kids.

Trace opened the driver's side door and slowly got out, never taking his eyes off his brother, whose chest rose and fell heavily as a pained line pushed his heavy brow downward, pinching a tiny crease over the bridge of his nose.

Brak dropped his weight onto the first step of the porch.

Cordray came around the SUV and brushed her hand reassuringly down his arm.

"Trace?" Brak said, lowering himself another step.

A cinnamon-skinned female appeared in the doorway, her eyes pinched with emotion.

Trace's feet, which had briefly felt cemented to the driveway, began moving. Slowly at first, then more quickly. By the time he reached the walkway to the porch, he was practically running.

He met Brak at the bottom step in a crushing embrace as tears flooded his eyes. All the guilt he'd carried for so long vaporized the instant Brak's arms pulled him in. Love flooded him, chasing away his shame, filling him with unspoken understanding and forgiveness.

"It wasn't your fault," Brak said a moment later, gripping the back of Trace's head and pressing their cheeks together as he gave voice to the feelings flowing over him like a refreshing rainstorm. "I know you think Mother's death was your fault, but it wasn't. Father and I never blamed you." Brak's voice broke as his own emotions overcame him. "It was her choice to die. She always knew she would. She knew her fate, Trace, and she refused to stop it."

Trace's fingers curled against Brak's back as he squeezed his eyes shut. Tears soaked his lashes and fell to his cheeks. "I'm sorry." Even as Brak absolved him of guilt, he still felt the need to apologize.

Brak rocked him, crushing their bodies together. "It's. Not. Your. Fault. Father and I love you, Trace. We never stopped loving you." A harsh, raspy sob cut through Brak's vocal chords. "God, I've missed you."

And just like that, the fissure in Trace's heart healed. He'd spent almost two centuries carrying a mountain of guilt and remorse, and in less than sixty seconds, Brak had taken it from him. He actually felt the stigmatic weight lift off his shoulders, leaving him lighter than he'd felt in decades.

The final piece of his life fell into place. He'd found where he belonged as an enforcer for AKM. He'd found where he fit as a submissive with Micah. The lifelong search to find his mate was over. And now he'd come full circle with his brother, finding absolution at his hand.

Nodding against Brak's shoulder, he thumped his fist against his brother's back.

Yes. God yes. The suffering was finally over.

"I've missed you, too."

CHAPTER 37

AFTER INTRODUCTIONS, a quick lunch of chicken paninis and coleslaw, and a lot of awe-struck gawking between brothers who hadn't seen each other in almost three human lifetimes, Cynthia took Cordray out back so Trace and Brak could talk privately.

Trace had seen the love bites on Cynthia's neck and wondered just what the relationship was between her and his brother, especially given the platonic way Brak had introduced her.

"Is she your mate?" Trace bobbed his head toward Cynthia, who was showing Cordray around an array of potted flowers on the deck's banister.

Brak cleared his throat and sipped from the glass of water he was holding. "No."

Something about Brak's no-nonsense answer sent Trace's hackles up. "Does she know that?"

Brak shook his head and changed the subject as he gestured toward Cordray. "You're newly mated. Congratulations." He bobbed his head and briefly glanced down at his hands before squinting toward the sliding glass door again. "She seems like a strong female. Perfect for you. I always knew you'd mate someone strong."

Brak obviously didn't want to discuss his mated status or what was going on between him and Cynthia, so Trace wouldn't push it.

"She's tough as nails." His adoring gaze turned toward Cordray. Inked up, pierced, TNT-with-a-short-fuse, big-hearted Cordray. "Our bond became official just yesterday, but I think my body knew weeks ago." He smiled to himself as he recalled the way he'd gotten hard around Cordray right from the moment he met her. She had awakened him in every way imaginable, and now they were bound together for life.

"Why? What happened?" Curiosity—genuine and demanding—brightened Brak's face.

Trace preferred not to get too specific about the details. After all, he and Brak were still strangers in a lot of ways, so talking hard-ons and sex wasn't exactly comfortable. As they got to know one another again, maybe such conversations wouldn't be so hard.

"I just felt alive around her, that's all. My blood warmed." He placed his hand on his chest. "And my heart hurt when she wasn't around. It was like I was addicted to her." He glanced toward his striking mate again as she tucked her long hair behind her ear and bent to sniff a flower. Something in the gesture seemed so out of character for her, yet so perfect. He fell in love with her just a little bit more. "I still am." His heart skipped as she straightened and offered Cynthia a smile as pure as Rocky Mountain snow, completely transforming the character of her face. He hadn't seen Cordray smile half as much as she had in the last twelve hours, and never as genuine. It made him feel like a hero, because he knew he was the reason for her newfound happiness. She certainly was for his. "I think I'll always be addicted to her in one way or another."

Brak nodded and looked away. He seemed troubled, and Trace suspected Cynthia was the reason why.

"You sure everything's okay?" Trace said, frowning.

"Yeah." Brak fiddled with his glass then agitatedly set it on the coffee table. "I'm just trying to get acclimated to being back in the real world."

He'd mentioned he'd been held prisoner by a pair of unscrupulous vampires almost as long as Trace had carried around a lifetime of guilt, but he hadn't given him many details.

"What happened, anyway? How did they get to you?"

Brak sighed and rubbed his palms over his face. "After Mom died, Father began falling into a trance-like state. It began immediately, but the transition was gradual. He told me that our mother had cast a spell on him. One that would make him fall into hibernation when she died to keep him from succumbing to mated-male suffering."

Trace had never known. Then again, he had never fully learned the extent of his mother's voodoo powers. He'd missed out on so much.

Brak rubbed his palms over his thighs. "We didn't have long to find shelter before Dad fell completely unconscious, so we traveled to Louisiana, where Mother had family. The day after we arrived, Father fell asleep and never woke up. For all intents and purposes, he was in hibernation. Mom's relatives tucked him away in an underground room and tended to him every day. We were safe there for a while, but one of our cousins was an opportunist. He betrayed us, making a deal with a pair of vampires to get rid of us."

"Jacob and Haslet." Trace spoke quietly, nodding, putting the pieces together from what Brak had told him during lunch.

Brak's pale eyes somberly met his. "They killed everyone and took our father and me away." His eyes narrowed bitterly. "By then, my phantom abilities were no secret, and they saw an opportunity. They used me to do their dirty work. I had to kill for them. Over and over and over again. They threatened to kill our father if I didn't. They held his life over my head." He paused and glanced outside as if he were looking at some faraway place. "And I missed everything." His brow furrowed as a note of sadness and hidden pain fell over his face. "They made me use my power in a way it was never intended, and I missed the world growing up around me." He hung his head. "I missed it all. And maybe I missed my chance."

Trace didn't know what Brak meant by that, and he felt like he shouldn't ask. As if Brak had intended it as a rhetorical statement.

Moving slowly, Trace leaned forward and quietly propped his elbows on his knees and laced his fingers together. After giving Brak a few seconds to work through whatever was tugging at his mind, he said softly, "I found our dad in a dreck laboratory in Arizona. How did he get there if Jacob and Haslet were holding him prisoner?"

Brak took a fortifying breath and straightened, apparently pushing aside whatever was bothering him. "I guess Father had begun to awaken, and they didn't know what to do with him except drug him and keep him in an induced coma. Then Bishop came along, and they struck a deal with him and sold our dad to him. Like he was a piece of property that could be bartered away." He made a disgusted face then looked out the patio doors at Cynthia. His expression instantly softened. "Cyn took care of me while I was out of my body, as well as afterward, when I returned and couldn't function on my own. One day while I was out doing their bidding, she helped me find them." His gaze flicked to Trace's. "It was the same day I found you in that cell." Trace nodded in understanding. "Anyway, she helped me find them, and when she did, I ghosted into the home where they were holding me prisoner in the basement. That's how I learned what had happened — that they no longer had our father, which meant they no longer had leverage over me, either. So I killed them. And then I escaped to come and find you. Now, here I am."

"And our father? Have you seen him?"

"I've visited him once, but I've been too exhausted to go back. He's not very coherent, anyway. One minute he seemed to recognize me and the next he didn't."

"Is that normal?"

Brak shrugged. "I don't know how our mother's spell was supposed to work, except that he wasn't supposed to awaken until it was time for him to meet his next mate. I don't know how long the awakening process takes or what we can expect once he's fully lucid, but if he's waking up, I'd say he's going to meet his next mate any day if he hasn't already. Or, who knows, it could be another year. Like I said, I don't know exactly how the spell was supposed to work."

Trace rubbed his hands up and down his face then over his scalp as he settled back in the chair again. "Jesus, everything's happening at once."

"What do you mean?"

It seemed like Trace's life had been a whirlwind for weeks. Up, down, around. He'd been tossed more than a salad and longed for a reprieve so he could enjoy being newly mated for a few days.

"There's just a lot going on. I'll tell you about it later, when we have more time." He thought about Skeletor and the button Cordray had brought with her. "Right now, I'm hoping you can help us."

"Sure. How?"

Trace went to the patio door and tapped on it to get Cordray's attention. Then he motioned for her to join them. Cynthia trailed behind as they re-entered the house.

"Everything good in here?" Cordray glanced from Brak to him.

"Yeah, it's all good." He held out his hand. "I want to show Brak the button."

Her eyes lit hopefully as she pulled the button from her pocket and set it in his palm.

Trace handed it to Brak. "We need to find the person who belongs to this button. Can you help us?"

Brak wrapped his large hand around the small piece of round plastic and exchanged glances with Cynthia. Then he nodded as he lifted his eyes toward Trace again. "Trace, my brother, my gift is your gift. I was born to help you."

CHAPTER 38

CORDRAY PULLED HER GAZE AWAY FROM THE FIGHT in the center of the crowd and checked her watch. Heavy metal roared through the small but powerful speakers set up inside the South Side parking garage playing host to Grudge Match for the night. There was just something about head-banging music and fighting that went together like chocolate and peanut better. Thrash metal brought out the primal in a person.

As one bout ended, and the battered and bruised opponents hobbled into the crowd to nurse their well-earned wounds, another pair of fighters—a scrappy little vampire who looked like he couldn't lift a potato and a scrawny dreck with spaghetti arms—made their way to the center of the fray. They looked more like pencil pushing accountants than brawlers, but maybe that was why they were there. Maybe they had gotten tired of people underestimating them. Grudge Match was their ticket to glory, at least for one or two nights a week.

Whether they actually possessed fighting skills or Digon simply respected their courage for facing the gauntlet and surviving, the fact they were there was a bit heart-warming. Everyone deserved to feel like somebody once in a while, and even the most innocuous of geek wannabes deserved to feel like a hero . . . like he mattered in the big picture and made a difference.

Cordray could get down with that.

Despite the cage, as the fight got underway everyone pushed back from the center action like dancers at a disco giving John Travolta room to go all Night Fever.

Blood splattered from the dreck's nose as he took a fist to the face, which sent up a roar from the crowd. Cordray was quickly learning this bunch liked seeing blood. As if drawing blood stamped a badge of honor on the person who drew it and proved that the one whose blood was drawn had just completed a rite of passage.

Cordray stood in the shadows, behind the surging, fist-pumping mass, and checked her phone.

Not only was she waiting for more intel on Skeletor, but Micah had texted her as she and Trace had been leaving Brak's place to let her know he'd been invited to run the gauntlet tonight. According to the time, he should have been finished by now. So where was he?

She scanned the area beyond the cage again, but there was still no sign of him.

Brak had found Skeletor easily enough by using the button to track him down, and from the description he provided after coming back into his body, the guy sounded like a New York fashion model. Lean build, black hair, Grecian nose, strong jaw, nicely trimmed beard and mustache. His hair was longer on top and shaved in a tight fade on the sides. Brak said the bangs hung in a loose arc around his eyes, and that while he didn't part it, it swept from right to left. He also had a small scar above his right eyebrow.

Vampires and scars didn't usually go hand in hand, so this tidbit was helpful.

They still didn't have a name, but at least Cordray had more of a description to go with those bluish, slate-grey eyes. They also had an address, which was the pot of gold at the end of the rainbow, as far as Micah was concerned. With an address, not only could they get to him, but Io could track down Skeletor's real name, which he was supposedly doing this very minute.

She checked her phone again. Still no messages.

A cheer roared up from the crowd as the skinny dreck landed a brutal punch on the side of the scrawny vampire's face. He flew sideways and landed on the oil-stained, concrete floor and raised his hand in Grudge Match's sign of surrender.

Fight over.

The group cheered again, thumping their fists over their heads. The music changed to a song rich in heavy drum and bass. It was like a modern-day Woodstock for supernatural UFC fighters. All they needed was some Jimi Hendrix, a few peace signs, and a whole lot of flowers, and they'd be back in the Age of Aquarius. Peace, love, and happiness, man. And a good-spirited fight.

The dreck helped the vampire up, and they locked hands and bumped shoulders like bros, man-hugging it out. Then they made their way back into the crowd, gesturing in such a way that made it obvious the dreck was explaining how he'd taken the vampire down. Now, that was sportsmanship, telling your opponent how you beat him.

Cordray grinned as she watched them limp away from the crowd, talking animatedly, replaying their fight, the vampire hanging on every word like an eager student trying to learn how to be as good as his mentor. And maybe that's what they were to one another. Mentor and student.

She'd gotten the impression that several of the members mentored some of the others. In both meetings she'd attended, smaller groups had broken out like they were teaching workshops, and from bits of conversations she had picked up from the others, Digon held teaching sessions where he illustrated fighting techniques from different disciplines about once a month.

Which meant Grudge Match wasn't just a place to fight, but a place to learn *how* to fight. Kind of like a self-defense class with a twist.

She checked her watch again then glanced around the large, open space as another fight got underway.

Except for Micah getting his ass there, everyone was ready to fulfill their role in the great Skeletor hunt. Trace was at AKM with Brak. While Brak ghosted after Skeletor, Trace would connect with his mind and relay everything in real time to dispatch, who was in constant contact with the teams in the field. Cynthia was at AKM, too, and as Trace revealed where Skeletor was, she would text Cordray and Micah to keep them in the loop. Everything was set. They just needed Skeletor to make the first move, and it was game on.

Cordray's phone vibrated at the same moment she saw Micah round the corner with Digon. Another male Cordray hadn't seen before strolled behind them. This new guy was tall and angular, confidently powerful, with dark eyes and dark-brown hair that hung almost to his shoulders. He was built similarly to Micah. Hell, except for the difference in hair color, they could have been brothers.

The threesome stopped on the other side of room, and Digon leaned toward Micah and said something. Then he and the mysterious newcomer slipped away as Micah entered the crowd. His gaze met Cordray's almost immediately.

While Micah made his way toward her, she read her text, which was from Cynthia.

Brak has Skeletor. He's on the move. South Side.

"Did you see the message?" Cordray said when Micah joined her.

"Mm-hm." Micah pretended to be interested in the fight going on in the cage, but Cordray sensed he was strung tighter than a power line in a hurricane.

"Who was that with you and Digon?" She glanced toward the opposite side of the garage, where Digon stood with the other male and that female with the long red hair she'd fought on her first night. Sonia, she thought her name was.

"Some guy named Rule," Micah said. "Real asshole. He wouldn't stop staring at me the entire time I was in Digon's office signing my life away to the club."

Digon, Sonia, and Rule turned in unison and glanced at her and Micah.

"Do you think they're on to us?"

"Who the fuck knows?" Micah crossed his arms and glared back at them as if laying down a challenge.

"Calm down. You don't want to get yourself kicked out in the first five minutes." Jesus, but Micah could be a hothead.

"I don't like him." Micah tugged his gaze away and glanced down at his phone. "Something about him rubs me the wrong fucking way."

"Everybody rubs you the wrong fucking way," she said dismissively.

"Some more than others." He scowled pointedly at her.

"Well, look inside his head," she hissed quietly. "See if you can figure out what his issue is."

"I can't."

"What do you mean, you can't?" She glared at him.

"Do I need to spell it out for you?" He huffed. "I can't see his thoughts. His *or* Digon's."

"You can't be serious." The whole point of bringing Micah into Grudge Match was so he could see inside Digon's head without being detected. Now Micah was telling her he couldn't see his thoughts? Talk about a major fail. This op had just become a way for them to spend more time with one another. As if either of them wanted or needed that.

"Digon and Rule are like you." Micah shot her an angry look. "Well, not exactly like you. With you, I feel your mental block. With them, I see nothing but black. Just"—his gaze slid toward the trio on the other side of the room—"empty darkness."

"Well, great. Now what do we do?"

"Hey, this is your party, sweetheart. I'm just a guest."

Cordray huffed and glanced again toward the threesome against the opposite wall. "What about her? Can you see inside her thoughts?"

"Who? The red-headed bitch? Yeah, but I doubt the image of an Italian beach is going to help us much."

"An Italian beach?" She turned toward him.

He lifted his shoulders as his eyebrows shot upward. "Yep. That's all I've gotten from her in the last five minutes. She popped into

Digon's office while I was getting the rundown. She's been nothing but sunshine and sand ever since."

Their brilliant coup was turning into a brilliant disaster.

"She's blocking you."

"Yep. Probably because she knows what I'm capable of."

"As in . . .?"

He frowned as if the answer should be obvious. "As in, she probably knows I'm able get into her thoughts without her feeling me, so she's put up a wall just in case I try."

Before Cordray could reply, her phone buzzed again at the same time Micah looked at his.

Cynthia's text read, *Skeletor has stopped. Here's the address.*

Cordray typed the address into her GPS app.

Wait a minute. This couldn't be right.

She checked the address again then looked up at Micah just as he turned amazed eyes toward her.

"He's here," they said at the same time.

CHAPTER 39

"Tell the teams to hold," Cordray told Micah, scanning over the heads of the crowd to see if she could see anyone who fit Skeletor's description coming or going.

The place was packed. There had to be five hundred in attendance tonight, not that everyone would fight. Some seemed to enjoy the camaraderie more than the fighting, while others seemed more intent on getting in the cage than being social. But the sheer volume of members made finding one specific person nearly impossible, especially when she wasn't exactly sure what he looked like. She only had a general idea.

She received another text.

Trace said he hears a lot of shouting. Like fighting.

Yeah, because Skeletor was here. He was a member of Grudge Match. While Micah texted Stryker to hold, she texted Cynthia that Skeletor was where they were.

"I'm going to head to the other side." Micah pointed. "If he tries to leave, I might be able to corner him."

Another message vibrated her phone.

Brak sees the fighting cage. Skeletor is close to the wall. The number 3 is right behind him.

Cordray's head shot up, and she looked toward the wall, found the 3, and began searching the faces. Out of her peripheral, she saw Micah closing in, as well, having received the same message.

There were so many people packed into the small, shadowy space around the cage. Even if she found him, she wasn't sure she'd be able to get to him without climbing over the tops of people's heads. The place was a mosh pit.

Micah stopped, his eyes fixed dead ahead as if he'd found their guy. Cordray followed his gaze, zeroing in on a head of shiny black hair hanging in a sweeping arc around a pair of seductive, slate-grey eyes.

Skeletor.

Those intense eyes lifted and met hers then widened when he

realized she was looking at him. Like a startled deer, his body twitched to high alert. He spun, preparing to flee, only to run smack into Micah.

For a second, it looked like they had him, but Skeletor was much too wily. In a flash of movement, his fist shot up and connected with Micah's jaw. Micah staggered backward but quickly fell into a defensive stance.

Cordray fought through the thick, cheering crowd as the fight inside the cage reached a bloody conclusion. Meanwhile, the fight outside the cage was just getting started. Micah landed a clean backhand that threw Skeletor sideways, but he quickly righted himself and deflected a volley of punches before gripping the front of Micah's shirt and rolling backward to the cement floor.

She knew that move all too well, remembering their fight in the alleyway the other night.

Cordray briefly lost sight of them, and then Micah flew through the air. A moment later, Skeletor was back on his feet, swiping blood from under his nose with the back of his wrist. His gaze met hers. He smirked, glanced quickly over his shoulder, and then took off before Cordray could reach him.

By the time she made it into the small clearing, Micah was on his feet, sprinting after him.

She gave chase, less than a hundred feet behind.

By the time she caught up on the street, Micah had slowed to a jog.

After a few more seconds, he stopped altogether as the sound of a motorcycle whined into the distance.

They were both breathing heavily, trying to catch their breath.

"Why did you stop?" She stood akimbo, giving her lungs more room to expand so she could take deeper breaths. "He's getting away."

He looked at her and shook his head, grinning like a demon who'd latched onto a soul. "He didn't get away."

"Okay, you've lost me. You could have dematerialized and chased him."

He leaned in close enough for Cordray to smell his sweat. "We know where he lives, remember?" He glanced down at this phone and smirked. "And thanks to Io, we now have a name."

He held his phone up so she could read Io's text message. Ronan. Skeletor's name was Ronan.

Micah tucked his phone back into his pocket, unusually calm. "Besides, I hate dematerializing. It makes me dizzy." He spun on his heel and headed back into the parking garage.

Cordray followed. "You still could have gone after him."

He kept on marching. "No . . ." He kept his gaze to the front, but a wry smile curved his mouth. "I want *Ronan* to get nice and relaxed. I want him to think he's safe." He sneered and gave her a wicked side-eye. "And then I'm going to fuck. His. World. Up."

CHAPTER 40

CORDRAY STARED OUT THE PASSENGER WINDOW of the Denali at the dark houses and fields as she and Trace returned to Asylum.

It was almost three in the morning.

She'd wanted to stay and help Micah go after Ronan, but, after thanking everyone for their hard work, Micah had insisted they go home. He said he would take care of Ronan on his own. Which meant Ronan had maybe forty-eight hours left to live, tops.

But if Micah wanted to take Ronan down himself, Cordray would let him. Her list of priorities had shifted sharply in the past twenty-four hours, and kicking Ronan's ass wasn't as high on that list as it was a couple of days ago. Taking a contented breath, she turned and gazed at Trace's strong profile. He had become her number one priority and had just jumped to the top of her to-do list, thanks to Micah's independent streak.

The corner of his mouth lifted as his eyes flicked toward her. Then he took his right hand off the steering wheel and held it over the center console. She slid her fingers between his and smiled as warmth seeped into her palm. It felt good to feel again, even if she still couldn't feel anything when he wasn't around. Trace was her lightning rod. Her lighthouse in the fog. He grounded her and made her feel safe. Something she never thought would be the case a few weeks ago.

Squeezing his hand, she finally broke the comfortable silence. "How did it feel working with your brother tonight?"

"It felt good." He grinned and glanced at her. "Real good." He faced the road again. "Everything is finally starting to feel like it's going to be okay."

"Of course it is. Why wouldn't it be?" She knew his life had been filled with heartache, and that he'd been barely inches from going mutant a couple of days ago, but that was then. This was now. And now they were together. No more resistance. No more fighting fate. All she wanted was to get home and feel him inside her until sunrise.

"What about your father? Are you going to see him?"

Trace gave her hand a squeeze. "Brak and I are going to visit him in a couple of days, after he's recovered and I've gotten some rest." He cast her a sideways glance. "Someone's been preventing me from getting any sleep."

"And I'll be preventing you from getting even more once we get home, so don't get any ideas about wimping out on me."

"I wouldn't dream of it."

They drove in contented silence for a few minutes. Then Cordray noticed an orange glow in the distance. In the area of the ranch.

"Trace . . .?" she straightened, her instincts spiking to high alert as the glow got bigger.

"What is that?" Trace leaned forward and squinted.

"I don't know." Her heart began to race as a sinking feeling dove into her gut. "Hurry. Hit the gas." She planted her hands on the dashboard and strained forward. "Faster, Trace!"

The glow grew larger, flickering. Smoke billowed into the air.

"Oh my God! It's a fire. The ranch is on fire!"

She glanced across the seat to find that the color had drained from Trace's face. He pressed harder on the accelerator.

When they reached the ranch, he slammed on the brakes, jacked the steering wheel to the right, and fishtailed onto the gravel driveway. Rocks spit up under the Denali, clanking against the undercarriage as they raced toward the fire, bouncing over the pair of potholes that still hadn't been filled.

Several of the children were in the yard, hugging themselves, staring at the blazing dorm. Mya and Brenna were there, too. Mya was holding Faith. Brenna was on the phone. She spun around as the Denali skidded to a halt on the rocks.

She and Trace were out of the cab before the engine could even shut off.

"What happened? Is everyone okay?" She ran a circle around the shivering, crying kids in the yard. "Where are Null and Aiden?" Her pleading eyes jumped to Mya's. "Please tell me they got out."

The expression on Mya's face said it all. Her two youngest were still inside the dorm.

"No!" Without thinking, she raced toward the open front door.

She had to save her kids.

"CORDRAY!" TRACE STARTED AFTER HER, but his legs gave out, and he fell to his knees.

Fire. Why did it have to be fire? Give him an ocean to swim across, a mile-wide chasm to leap over, or a hurricane to fly through, but not fire.

As he stared up at the blazing dormitory, it seemed to stretch skyward, growing ten stories tall instead of just two. One of the windows shattered, and he threw his arms in front of his face as glass and flames shot out.

Cordray was in there. His *mate*! It was his job to protect her. He had to do something. He couldn't lose her now that he'd just found her. And what about Null and Aiden? He'd only known them a few days, but he already thought of them as his own. Would a father allow his children to die? All because he was a little scared?

Okay, make that a lot scared.

Terrified.

Just hearing the crackle of the flames was enough to send his pulse into orbit.

"Trace!" Brenna knelt beside him and shook his shoulder. "Do something. Please!" Horrified panic filled her bloodshot eyes.

He faced the fire. Saw his mother as she burned. Smelled her charred flesh.

He'd let his mother die. He hadn't been strong enough to save her. But he was strong enough now. He had to be. He refused to let another female he loved perish.

In his mind, he saw his mother's eyes open on her charred face and look right at him.

Go, Trace! You can save them. You were made to save them.

Her voice touched his mind so powerfully it felt like she was really there. As if she had never died and was still with him.

Now, Trace!

Pulling courage into his gut and strength into his legs, he rose and staggered toward the burning building. Smoke flooded the doorway, and he could see flames shooting across the ceiling in the rec room.

On the verge of hyperventilating, he forced his feet to move, then run, and then he was inside, surrounded by fire. The rail of the staircase smoldered. Flames licked up the slender posts.

"Cordray!"

Something crashed upstairs as the ceiling caved. He heard a scream. A child's scream. Aiden's.

"TRACE!" Cordray shouted from the second floor. "Help us!"

Heedless of his fear, he raced up the stairs and into the hall, which was filled with smoke and flames. Burning beams hung from the ceiling, blocking the way to the kids' room at the end of the hall.

The sound of breathless coughing reached his ears.

"Cordray!" He pushed forward, oblivious to the intense heat.

"We're in here!" Cordray yelled from beyond the blockade of fire-consumed wood. "Back here!"

Oh God, they were trapped.

You can do it, Trace. Use your power.

His power?

How?

Just do it!

Desperate and terrified, he thrust his hand out in front of him, letting loose an explosion of energy unlike any before. It was so powerful that it couldn't possibly have come from him, but it had.

A boom sounded, and the fiery blockade vaporized into ash, cutting a path to the children's bedroom. He rushed forward.

Cordray was huddled with the kids on the floor. They were covered in soot. Aiden clutched her Pooh Bear with one hand and held a small blanket over her mouth with the other, as if she were using it as an air filter.

Cordray's fearful gaze met his and instantly transformed into one of relief and hope. And love.

"Can you dematerialize?" he said. He wasn't able to. That was one vampire gift he'd been born without. His mixed blood allowed him to hide in the shadows, but not poof out of a burning building. Lucky him.

She shook her head. "I'm too torqued. I won't risk it. Not with the kids." Dematerializing could go very wrong if she was too jacked up emotionally to keep herself separate from the kids while she ghosted.

"Then give them to me. I'll get them out. You go."

"No. I'm not leaving you in here."

"Cordray, don't argue with me! Get out of here!"

"No! We go together, Trace! I will *not* go without you!"

He wanted her safe, but he could tell she wouldn't leave him and the kids behind to take herself to safety. Her gaze penetrated his as if it were a dagger, her resolve set.

"Fine." He reached for her as the ceiling groaned. The heat was almost unbearable. "Let's move. We don't have much time."

She lifted Null toward him. "Take him. I'll get Aiden."

"Hold on, little man." He tucked Null against his body. "Hide your eyes, okay?"

Null flung his tiny arms around Trace's neck and thrust his face against his shoulder.

"You ready?" he said to Cordray, helping her up.

She nodded as another beam broke through the ceiling over Null's bed and crashed down in a shower of sparks and fire.

Aiden screamed and put Pooh in a choke hold as she burrowed against Cordray's body.

"Follow me and stay close." He raised his right arm in front of him, palm outward.

The smoke was getting thicker.

He sure hoped this worked.

CORDRAY COUGHED AND TRIED TO COVER HER MOUTH so she could breathe, but that made it hard to hold on to Aiden. Screw it. She would just have to deal with the smoke, because she couldn't let anything happen to Aiden. She hugged the little girl more tightly. Hot tears stung her eyes. She blinked several times, trying to clear her vision.

A beam crashed down behind her, and she jumped forward. "Trace, hurry!"

"We're moving. Now!" A blast of energy burst from his hand. In an instant, anything blocking their path vaporized into ash.

"Go!" Trace rushed forward, arm held out in front of him.

Flames shot out from the bathroom, obscured by smoke, which clouded the way.

For a moment, she couldn't see.

"Trace!"

His hand wrapped around her wrist and pulled her forward.

They reached the stairs, but they were totally engulfed. Even if Trace could vapor the flames and embers into ash, the stairs wouldn't hold their weight.

"Back here!" She tugged Trace into the back bedroom, where Riley slept. The flames weren't quite as bad in here, which meant the fire had probably been started on the other end of the dorm.

Had Gavin been playing with matches again? So help her, if he didn't learn his lesson from this, she didn't know what she was going to do with that boy.

She opened the window. Probably not the best thing to do for a fire, but what choice did they have?

She knelt and set Aiden on the floor. "I'm going to jump down to the ground, and then you're going to jump down so I can catch you, okay?"

Aiden shrunk backward and shook her head.

"Aiden, please. I promise I'll catch you. I won't let you get hurt."

She cringed, hugging her Pooh Bear close. Tears streamed from her eyes. "I'm scared."

"I'm scared, too, honey. But we don't have much time. We have to jump."

Flames were already snaking into the room.

Trace knelt and pulled her into his free arm then stood and nodded toward the window. "You go first," he said to her. "I'll take care of the kids."

"But—"

"Go, baby. Jump. We'll be right behind you." He nodded encouragement as the fire spread farther into the room.

She placed her hand on the open windowsill, her eyes locked on Trace's.

A meaningful look passed between them for what felt like an eternity. When a loud groan echoed through the attic, she glanced to the ground then turned back toward Trace.

"Don't you dare leave me, Trace. I've waited too long to find you."

HE KNEW WITHOUT HER HAVING TO SAY IT that her fear was that he could die. And here they'd just found each other. They'd been mated only twenty-four hours. What a bitch it would be for either one of them not to make it out of this alive, because the bond he had with her was already strong enough that if she didn't survive the fire, he wouldn't survive losing her.

"I know the feeling, baby. Now jump."

I love you, she mouthed. The ends of her hair were smoking as if they'd been singed.

I love you, too, he mouthed back.

She turned and leaped. He peered down to see her land on her feet then turn and raise her gaze to the window.

"Okay," he said to Null and Aiden, taking a step forward, "our turn."

They both cried out and grabbed on as tightly as they could, hiding their faces against his chest. "No! No! Don't jump! I'm scared!"

"It'll be okay. I promise. I'll never drop you." As another groan rippled through the ceiling and down the walls, he sensed they were quickly running out of time.

Jump, Trace. Now!

His mother's voice burst into his mind. He climbed onto the windowsill as best as he could with two squirming bundles tucked inside his arms.

A split second before he leaped, he heard a loud click, a fizzing sound, and then . . .

THE BLAST THREW CORDRAY BACK A GOOD TEN FEET. She landed on her ass and rolled feet-over-head once before spinning to a dizzying stop just in time to see Trace and the two children somersaulting away from the dorm. They landed several feet away, Trace taking the worst of the fall as his knees slammed into the earth. He tossed forward, but not before he ensured Null and Aiden made a soft landing, which had to have taken a miraculous work of physics, and then slammed face-first into the ground before tumbling over himself.

Cordray heard a dull pop, like bone breaking, and then Trace landed on his back and stopped moving.

"TRACE!" She was on her feet in an instant, gobbling up the distance between them in a blink.

Falling to her knees, she pressed her fingers to the side of his neck, searching for a pulse. She couldn't find one. Blood spilled out of his nose and over his mouth

"TRACE! No! Don't you leave me here alone, you asshole!"

This couldn't be happening. Not again. How many times did she have to lose someone she loved before the universe cut her a break?

Well, no more. She wouldn't suffer through this again. Either Trace lived or they both died.

"Don't you fucking leave me!" She thumped her joined fists on his chest hard enough to awaken the devil.

"Oomph!" Trace jackknifed off the ground then fell back. "Jesus, baby!" He coughed and rubbed his chest, wincing. "What'd you do that for?"

She gasped and froze, her mouth flapping open. "I thought . . . you weren't . . . I thought you were dead."

He coughed and rolled to his side. "I just got Bruce Willis'd from an exploding building. Can't I get a second to get my bearings?"

He groaned and sat up, dabbing his fingers against his nose. That's when she realized it was broken. That had been the pop she'd heard.

"Here, let me set that for you." She pushed him onto his back, grabbed his nose, and snapped it back in place before he could stop her.

He let out a bloodcurdling cry and cupped his hands over his face. "What the fuck?"

"That'll teach you to play dead on me, asshole."

"I wasn't playing dead! I was catching my breath. Holy Christ, C." He wiped the blood off his lips then turned merciful, adoring eyes on her. "Do you really think I would leave you?" He reached for her hand then gave her a weak smirk. "I mean, wouldn't you just hunt me down in hell and beat the shit out of me if I did?"

She frowned, confused. "I . . ."

"Baby . . ." He pushed himself into a sitting position and cradled her face in his palm. "I would never leave you. Now that I've found you, not even Satan could keep me from you."

Her heart shattered open as the weight of all that had happened in the last ten minutes barreled down on her and knocked her soul to its knees. Before she could stop them, convulsive sobs ripped through her body, and tears gushed from her eyes. She thought she'd lost him. She'd seen her life flash before her eyes without him in it and thought it was all over.

"Damn you!" She slapped his shoulder. "Don't you ever scare me like that again!"

"I guess this means you're keeping me, huh?" He winked at her.

She let out what sounded like a half sob, half laugh as relief washed through her. She wiped the tears from her face and nodded. "Yeah, asshole, I'm keeping you." Pushing forward, she kissed him. Hard. Like her life depended on it.

And it did.

Because he *was* her life. From this day forward, there was no her without him.

CHAPTER 41

FIRE TRUCKS FILLED THE LAWN.

Trace sat on the deck beside Brenna, who was wrapping a bandage around a burn on his forearm. Bruises were forming around his eyes from his broken nose, and he'd sprained his right knee jumping out of the window, otherwise he was in good spirits. Cordray had retrieved a set of crutches Leon had used last year after twisting his ankle playing soccer, and they leaned against the wall beside him. Trace would need them to get around for a day or two, at least until he got in a few good feedings, the first of which Cordray planned on giving him later when all the excitement was finally over.

As for her, she'd escaped the fire relatively unscathed. The ends of her hair had been burned, so she'd need to get a haircut, and her right hand was bandaged from a small burn she'd gotten during their retreat in the hall, but that was about it.

She'd been lucky. Luckier than some of her kids. Riley had suffered the worst. She'd tried to get to Aiden and Null and had been badly burned. After applying as much first aid as they had access to at the ranch, Mya rushed her to the AKM medical center. That had been about forty-five minutes ago. Leon had gone with them. That left Null, Aiden, Panya, Faith, and Gavin, who sat by himself on the corner of the deck, his legs crossed, head down.

She might as well get this conversation over with.

Sighing, she joined Gavin and took a seat beside him. "Gavin, honey, did you do this?"

He looked up. There were tears in his eyes. "No." His tone was defensive.

She pointed toward the pile of smoldering rubble that had once been the dorm. "That's what fire does, Gavin. This is why I tell you over and over not to play with matches. Just a tiny spark is enough to do this kind of damage."

"I didn't do it!" He slammed his hands on the deck. "Just because I like playing with fire doesn't mean I burned down our home." He crossed his arms and lowered his head in a pout. It was obvious he didn't think she believed him.

But he seemed so sincere.

"Then who did it, honey? Tell me."

He hid his face, hunching forward as if he feared saying anything further. "I can't."

Can't? She frowned, growing worried. If Gavin hadn't done this, who had?

"Gavin, do you know who did this?" If he didn't tell her, she would have to go inside his mind and find out for herself.

He looked away, rocking forward and back. A moment later, he broke into tears. "Steffie did it! She set the fire!"

"Steffie?" Cordray scanned the faces of the others then turned her focus on the yard as if she might be able to find Steffie hovering in the early morning shadows. "Are you sure?"

"I saw her." Gavin sniffled. "I got up to go to the bathroom, and I heard something downstairs. I went down to the living room and saw her. She said she would make it look like I did it if I told on her. That no one would believe me if I told the truth."

Cordray shot into Gavin's mind and saw the truth of what he said. Steffie was hunched over in the front room downstairs, lighting the curtains on fire.

Her blood boiled as she quickly pulled out of his thoughts. When she got through with that bitch, there wouldn't be enough left of her for a DNA test.

"I believe you," she said, trying her best to keep her voice under control. "Did she tell you why?"

Gavin wiped his hands over his soot-covered face, smearing streaks of black over his skin with his tears. "She said we were evil. She said we were all freaks and deserved to die."

Oh, did she now? Well, Steffie didn't know evil. Cordray would be sure to give her a proper definition — with examples — the next time she saw her.

She didn't know what Steffie's primary malfunction was, or why she thought the kids at the ranch were evil, but as soon as she recovered from the day's events and got her brain screwed back on straight, she was going to find out. Like Ronan, Steffie wasn't going anywhere Cordray couldn't get to her. Right now, she needed to tend to her family. In time, she would deal with Steffie.

"You're not evil or a freak, Gavin." She wrapped her arm around his shoulders and ruffled his hair. "You're special. A very special boy. You're like Trace, and one day you'll grow up to be strong and powerful. The kind of male everyone looks up to."

He blinked away his tears then turned his gaze toward Trace as if he looked up to him. "You think so?"

She kissed his smoke-scented hair. "No, I know so."

She turned toward Trace and met his gaze. He'd been listening, and a tender smile touched his lips. She smiled back, feeling the truth in her words. One day Gavin would mature into his gifts, and everything would make sense. Until then, she and the others needed to help him along and support him.

She took Gavin's hand and stood. "Come over here with the rest of us, okay?"

He reluctantly stood and shuffled his feet as he followed her to the group congregated near the door. The children looked exhausted. Faith could barely keep her eyes open and was nestled against Trace's side. He had his arm around her.

"Brenna, why don't you take the kids inside and set them up in the spare bedrooms? I'll be in in a minute to help you get them cleaned up." Everyone was covered with ash and soot and needed baths.

"Sure." Brenna stood and held out her arm in round-up fashion. "Come on, kids. Let's go inside."

After everyone got some sleep, they would pack up what they could and move into her mansion in the city for a few days until the rubble could be cleaned up. Or at least until the kids didn't feel so traumatized about what had happened.

As soon as the door closed, leaving her alone with Trace, she sat down next to him and nudged his arm. "You're special, too, you know."

"Aw, you do care." He nudged her arm, flashing a crooked smile. "I heard what you said to Gavin. Thank you."

She frowned. "Why are you thanking me?"

"Because that's exactly what he needed to hear. Remember, I've been in his shoes. I know."

She wrapped her forearm around his and scooted closer. "Yes, you do, don't you?"

He placed his hand over her arm, and then they watched the water arc from the hose on the latest pumper truck to arrive on the scene, splashing over the smoldering embers of what was left of the dorm. Luckily, the fire department arrived and got to work on the fire before it spread to the barn and the main house, but the scent of smoke hung in the air and probably would for days.

"I knew something wasn't right about Steffie," he said after a few seconds had passed.

"Yeah, well something's definitely going to be wrong with her when I find her."

"I'm surprised you haven't taken off after her already."

She squeezed his arm. "A few days ago, I probably would have, but now . . .?" She pressed against him. "Some things are more important than retribution."

He reached around with his free hand and pressed his palm against her forehead. "Are you sure you're feeling okay?"

She pushed his hand away with a huff. "Don't get me wrong, I'm mad as fuck. But right now I can think of someone" — she glanced over her shoulder at the door her kids had disappeared through — "well, a lot of someones who need me more than I need to punish her." She eyed the dried blood on his face. "How's your nose?"

"I'll live." He wrapped his hand around hers. "What about you? You've been putting on a strong front, but I can feel your exhaustion. Are you okay?"

She gave him a tired smile and allowed her shoulders to relax. "It's been a long couple of days, but" — she winked at him — "I'll live."

He grinned at the way she tossed his words back at him.

The trucks finally pulled out a few minutes after sunrise, leaving nothing but the sound of early morning birdsong as nature greeted another day, oblivious to the tragedy that had unfolded over the last several hours.

Nature had a short memory when it came to disaster. Within months after a forest fire, new trees began to grow. After forty years, no one even knew a fire had taken place. All they saw along their hiking trail was lush vegetation.

Fire was a natural part of life. It was a symbol of regeneration. Didn't the mythical phoenix rise reborn from its own deathly ashes?

She rested her head on Trace's shoulder, bone weary and so tired even her teeth hurt, but she didn't want to move. She just wanted to sit there, listening to the birds, more alive than she'd ever been. How perfect that she could feel the beautiful ache of exhaustion. The sting of the burn on her hand.

Trace had given her that. Feeling. Sensation.

Life.

Because the pains of life proved a person was, in fact, alive, while granting a greater appreciation for more pleasant sensations, such as the wash of cool morning air over her skin, the kiss of the sun's warmth as it broke the horizon.

The soft caress of lips on her forehead as Trace kissed her.

For eight centuries, she'd been dead. Unfeeling and existing, but not living. Now she'd been reborn, and Trace was the spark that had burned her old self away to give rise to the new.

He was her hero. He'd faced his greatest fear and charged into the fire to get to her and the kids . . . to save them. He'd walked through fire and came out a changed male.

She smiled. "You're like the phoenix," she said softly.

He tilted his head against hers. "Hmm? What's that you said?"

She lifted her head from his shoulder. "You know. The phoenix. The mythical bird that dies in a shower of flames, only to rise reborn from the ashes to live again."

A slow smile spread over his face as he turned toward the blackened remains of the dorm. "I feel reborn." He squeezed her hand.

"So do I, thanks to you." An amused huff broke past her lips. "A few weeks ago, I thought I hated you. I *wanted* to hate you. Hating you was easy, because it meant I didn't have to face the fears I'd carried around like a security blanket for centuries. Facing my fears was hard. It was painful. It was work. But" — she pressed against him and tightened her hold on his arm as he wrapped his hand around the inside of her thigh and pulled her closer, watching her intently — "anything worth having in life is worth working for."

Love and understanding seeped into the lines of his face, along with a hint of amusement. "Are you saying I'm worth working for?"

She sighed and tipped her forehead against his cheek. "Don't make this a thing, baby. I'm not used to being all girly and sentimental like this. Don't get used to it."

"Ah, so this is a rare moment I should mark on my calendar."

She rocked her head side to side. "You're going to make this a thing. You are, aren't you?"

He turned and kissed the top of her head. "I wouldn't dream of it, baby. You're tough enough to kick my ass if I do. And then I'd have to kick your ass. And then shit would just get ugly." Playful bravado laced his words.

She liked knowing the banter that had defined their relationship since its inception still held a place between them. Only now it was playful and endearing, not hurtful and degrading.

"Damn straight I'd kick your ass."

He chuckled. "Well, you know that shit turns me on, so kick away, princess."

"Don't call me princess."

He bit back a smile. "Oh, that's right. Beast master. I forgot."

She shook her head. "Even after you walk into a fire and get blown out a window, you still never turn off, do you?"

"Nope."

She let out an exasperated exhale. "Well, do you think you can turn off long enough to go upstairs with me and get a few hours of sleep before we have to pack up and head to my place in the city?"

Humility and something else—something mysteriously private—passed over his face as he glanced toward the yard. His gaze seemed to stretch farther away than her property extended, to some faraway place she couldn't see.

"Trace?" She touched his arm.

He smiled at her. "Yeah, I'll join you in a minute. You go on up."

She didn't know what he saw, but she nodded. "Okay, I'll meet you inside."

She got up, frowned curiously toward the yard, and then left him alone.

Whatever he saw, he wanted to face it alone.

And she was okay with that.

TRACE PUSHED TO HIS FEET and grabbed the crutches Cordray had given him. Tucking them under his arms, he hobbled down the steps and across the yard to the enclosed fire pit.

Behind the wall of shrubs, his mother, ghostly yet beautiful, waited for him.

"Mother?" Peacefulness washed over him.

"Trace . . ."

He stared at her, unable to speak.

"You're free now," she said.

Part of him wanted to be angry that she was only just now showing herself, after all this time, but he simply couldn't find the emotion. All he felt was love.

She shimmered and touched his face. "Now you understand."

And he did. The answers flashed inside his head like lightbulbs turning on. About his childhood. His power. Her magic. Her death.

She'd died because that was how it had to be. In death, she was more powerful than she ever could have been in life. All this time, she'd been watching over him, guiding him, protecting him. And she'd protected Brak and his father, too. But she'd never let her presence be known, because he needed to find his way without her. What he thought had been a lack of affection turned out to be a lesson he'd had to learn to survive.

The years of guilt, the struggle to control his power, the search for a mate and a place where he fit in. All of it had been about learning how to rein in the magic she'd given him so he could forge his own way into the future.

"You see?" she said. "You were always the stronger one. Your power was always stronger than Brak's. It's why your father and I were so hard on you. It's why we treated you the way we did. Because we loved you enough to put our selfish needs aside. Every time you fell, we wanted to pick you up, hold you, and take away your pain. But we knew if we did that, we'd be destroying you. We had to be harder on you than we wanted to be so you grew up strong enough to control your power." She touched his hand. The sensation felt like ice but calmed him anyway. "You're strong enough now."

He'd thought his parents hadn't loved him as much as they'd loved Brak, but that wasn't the case at all. They'd loved him tremendously. Enough to put aside their own desire to protect him. To ensure he grew up with the abilities to cope with the power she'd gifted him inside her womb.

"I think I finally understand." Tears balanced on the rims of his eyes as he nodded. "I love you, Mom."

"I love you, Trace. Tell your father and your brother I love them, too. That I'm always with them . . . and you."

He inhaled deeply, drawing in the scent of jasmine he'd always associated with her. "I will."

She took a step back as if preparing to leave.

"Wait. Will I see you again?"

She shook her head. "No."

"But—"

Her fading image smiled. "You'll be fine. You'll all be fine, and I'll always be nearby. Now, forge your path, Trace. Forge it with your mate . . . with your family . . . and be happy. That's everything I ever wanted for you."

He watched her disappear, knowing that even though he would never see her again, she would always be with him in his heart. In his mind, she would be there. But no longer would he see her as she'd been burning on the pyre outside their home when he was a child. Instead, he remembered her for the amazingly strong woman she'd been. Strong and fearless, facing death like a warrior.

He grinned, recognizing in himself all the qualities he now saw in his mother.

Just as Cordray had said, he was the phoenix risen from the ashes of his troubled youth. No more was he the terrified, victimized child burdened with guilt. He was a mature male. A male who'd found his purpose, his path, and his mate. He owned his power, not the other way around.

Glancing toward the fire pit, he pulled the box of matches from his back pocket and tossed them into the grey, powdery coals that had once been logs of wood. As he did, a weight lifted off his soul. He'd faced his past, his fears, and his demons. He no longer needed the matches to remind him of where he'd come from and the dangers his power presented.

Feeling lighter than he ever had, he turned and hobbled back to the house.

Cordray met him at the door. "Everything okay?" Her inquisitive gaze explored his face.

He wrapped his arm around her waist and guided her inside, where he pressed her against the wall and kissed her. When he broke away, he stared deep into her sapphire eyes, drinking in her soul. "Everything's perfect. Just perfect."

CHAPTER 42

TRACE LAY PROPPED ON HIS ELBOW, WATCHING CORDRAY SLEEP. It had been two days since the fire. Two days since he'd said good-bye to his mother. It seemed like a lifetime.

Then again, every minute spent with Cordray felt like a lifetime, but in the most glorious way.

Micah and Sam had agreed to take the kids for the day, allowing him and Cordray much-needed alone time with one another, especially since it felt like his calling was on the verge of blowing wide open any moment. They hadn't had ten minutes to themselves since moving the kids, Mya, and Brenna into Cordray's North Shore mansion, and Trace had been nearly volcanic in his need to claim her before Mya and Brenna had left with the kids this morning.

They'd spent all day in bed. First they'd fucked. Then made love. Then fucked some more. Until finally they'd fallen into an exhausted, sated sleep.

Now Trace was awake, needing her again, but wanting to watch her sleep even more. She was so beautiful as she slept. Peaceful. Angelic. Her black and blue hair tousled and strewn like silky tendrils over the pillow.

She lay on her back, angled toward him, with her forearm over her stomach.

He leaned in and kissed the expanse of skin along her collarbones, leaving a soft, tender trail from right to left. Then pulled back and waited, smiling as she inhaled deeply.

Her eyes fluttered open a couple of seconds later, and she smiled when her gaze met his.

"Do you mind?" She stretched out beside him like a giant cat, lithe and sleek, rolling to face him. "How many times are you going to do that while I'm sleeping?"

He lowered himself, folding his arm under his head so he could lay eye-to-eye with her. "I like waking you up like that. It means I've still got it."

She blinked sleepily and grinned. "Baby, I'll let you in on a little secret. You're always gonna have it."

"Yeah, well, I enjoy reminding myself."

"At the expense of my REM sleep."

"Okay, go back to sleep then." He shifted closer.

"Why? You'll just wake me up again."

He smiled and skimmed his palm over the slope and fall of her hip. "Only because I love the color of your eyes."

She closed them for several seconds then popped them open again. "How's that?"

He shook his head. "It's just not the same. It's kind of fun watching the sleep drain out of them."

She shimmied closer and pressed her palm to his chest. "You know, they say that lack of sleep leads to hallucinations and even psychosis."

"Yeah, well, you're already crazy."

She let out a soft laugh. "Crazy for you, asshole."

"You're such a romantic."

"Not even close."

He rolled her to her back, needing to feel her come again. Every time she came, her body shuddered like she was having an internal earthquake, and something about knowing he did that to her made his chest swell with pride. He gave her pleasure, and, in return, that pleasured him.

"What do you think you're doing?" Despite her contrary words, she wrapped her arms and legs around him, holding him place.

"Claiming my female."

"You enjoy claiming her, don't you?"

He eased inside her, and nearly came at the way her fingernails bit into his back as she closed her eyes and moaned.

"I can't resist." He thrust his pubic bone against her mound, making her gasp and shiver. "She's just so" — he pumped into her again, and her entire body fell into an orgasmic spasm — "fucking responsive."

"You b-bastard." Her thighs shuddered against his hips as she whimpered through an aftershock. "You shouldn't be taking advantage of my centuries-old sensory deprivation like that." It was obvious she loved that he took advantage of it as much as he did.

"Not so big and tough now, are you, sweetheart." He pumped into her and moaned at the way her inner muscles contracted and quivered around his cock.

Her eyes flared as they met his. "You talk too much." She linked her hands at the back of his neck and pulled him down so her lips pressed against his. "Now, shut up and fuck me."

He grinned. "You tryin' to boss my dick, baby?"

She smiled and nipped his bottom lip. "Every day."

That was exactly what he wanted to hear.

He began pumping in earnest. "Don't you ever stop, either."

"I won't if you won't."

"Never."

LATE IN THE AFTERNOON, Cordray trailed behind Trace as he led her into the living room of Micah's home. He still had a slight limp but no longer needed the crutches, thanks to feeding from her several times in the last couple of days.

Toys, crayons, and coloring books were strewn everywhere, and it looked like Micah and Sam had purchased a gaming unit and every video game known to man to play on it, which Gavin and Faith were taking full advantage of while Null colored.

Panya was in the kitchen with Sam, baking what smelled like chocolate chip cookies.

Micah had grown particularly fond of Aiden, who was now, this very moment, perched beside him on the couch, braiding his shoulder-length hair in dozens of skinny braids.

"Look at you," Cordray said to Micah, taking a seat across from him. "If you were in a beige bathing suit running along the beach in slow motion to Ravel's 'Boléro,' I'd think you were Bo Derek from the movie, *Ten*."

"Yeah," Trace added, "looks good, Mike."

Micah surreptitiously flipped them both off.

She smiled and said to Aiden, "You're doing such a good job, honey. I can't wait to see his hair when you're all finished." To Micah, she asked, "Where are Mya and Brenna?"

"Shopping for more clothes."

They were still replacing everything they'd lost in the fire.

"You have soft hair," Aiden said, twisting and tying off another braid before starting another, her fingers working with the confident sureness of someone ten times her age.

"Well, I condition every day," Micah said, lightly tapping her nose.

"Don't let him fool you, Aiden," Sam called from the kitchen. "His hair is naturally soft like that."

"Hey now," Micah said over his shoulder, "I condition . . . occasionally."

Aiden giggled.

Cordray glanced at Null. "Hey, little man, are you about ready to leave so you can show Trace whatever it is you want to show him?"

"Where are you guys going?" Micah said.

"Null said he wanted to take Trace somewhere."

Null hopped up and thrust a picture toward Trace.

Trace took it and held it out where Cordray could see it.

The picture showed a burning building in the background and a dark-skinned male in the foreground. He was wearing a blue and red cape and held hands with two little kids with blond hair and blue eyes.

Cordray smiled and nudged Trace's arm. "I think he's trying to tell you you're his hero."

Humility crossed Trace's face as his eyes softened. He nodded. "I get that." He smiled proudly at her.

Null grabbed Trace's hand. "Come on, Twace. I wanna show you something." He tugged Trace off the couch and started for the front door.

Cordray stood at the same time Micah did, hoisting Aiden up with him and resting her on his hip.

"Looks like Null is eager to get going," she said.

"Yeah, me, too," Micah said. "I've got to work tonight." He looked at Aiden. "So you'll have to finish my hair later, okay?"

She giggled and swiped her fingers left to right over the ends of his braids, making them sway side to side like strands of beads. "Okay."

"Are you paying our friend a visit tonight?" Cordray knew Micah had been watching Ronan for the last forty-eight hours, making sure he fell back into his complacent routine before striking.

Micah's eyes narrowed mischievously as one corner of his mouth lifted in a lopsided smile. It was all the confirmation she needed.

"Thought so." She ruffled Aiden's hair then said to Micah, "Good luck. Not that you'll need it."

"I don't." He held her gaze for a long moment. "But thanks." He set Aiden down and joined Trace by the door, locking forearms with him in a bro hug. "I'll see you later. You gonna be around?"

"We'll probably stick around for a while." Trace met her eyes. "But we'll be spending the night at Cordray's place again."

Micah rolled his eyes and turned as he dashed his hand in a downward motion at them. "You two are like rabbits."

Trace chuckled. "Takes one to know one."

"Come on, Twace." Null tugged Trace toward the door. "Let's go."

Cordray waved to Sam over her shoulder as Micah disappeared around the corner. "Save us some cookies. We'll be back later."

Sam looked up from helping Panya stir another batch of cookie dough and waved. "We'll have plenty. I think we're going to make snickerdoodles after this."

What was up with that female? She'd become an eating machine. There were already platters of chocolate chip cookies, brownies, and something that looked like deconstructed s'mores, and now it looked like she was making some kind of peanut butter cookie.

"Is Sam okay?" Cordray said to Trace as they closed the door and followed Null to the Denali.

He helped secure Null in his car seat. "She's just feeling maternal with a household of kids is all."

Cordray's instincts told her that wasn't it, but for lack of a better explanation, Trace's would have to do.

FORTY MINUTES LATER, Trace followed Null into the woods behind Asylum. The remains of the dorm had already been cleared, leaving only a charred rectangle of dirt, but construction on the new dorm was to begin in a few days. King Bain had already assigned a team of architects to design a new one. A larger one.

The kids would be back at the ranch before they knew it, and they would live in style.

"Over here, Twace." Null motioned him toward a stream.

With the sun dragging toward the horizon, the afternoon light was quickly fading into evening, but it was still light enough to see where he was going.

He sidestepped down a steep embankment and knelt beside Null at the edge of a sandbar.

Cordray waited quietly behind them.

Null squatted and inspected the earth then began digging his tiny fingers into the wet soil.

"What are we looking for, little man?" Trace asked, unsure what he should be doing to help.

"Just wait. I'll find it." The little boy continued digging, getting his shoes wet. Mud turned the hem of his jeans brown.

Five minutes passed.

Ten.

Fifteen.

The sun was beginning to set.

"A-ha!" Null yanked his hand out of the stream, showering them with water.

Trace shielded himself then lowered his arms.

"What's that you've got there?" He peered closer at the rock Null held in his hand. It was whitish in color, speckled with black.

"It's a wock. Like the one in my collection. You said you had one like it when you wewe my age."

Trace gingerly took the rock from Null's tiny hand and let it rest in his palm as he slowly lowered himself to a crouch.

It wasn't just a similar rock to the one from his childhood collection. It was the same rock. The same exact one.

Mother.

She'd brought it to him. Somehow, she'd found it and brought it here so he could find it. Tears stung the backs of his eyes.

Null dropped to his knees in front of Trace and patted his little hand over the rock as he turned up his chipmunk-cheeked face and smiled so brightly it was a wonder the sun didn't get jealous. "This is a hewo's rock." *Pat-pat-pat.* "You'we my hewo, and one day, I'll be a hewo, too."

Cordray placed her hand on his shoulder and squeezed.

He didn't have to look at her to know she had a smile on her face.

"I told you you're his hero," she said.

He shook his head and ruffled Null's hair. "Naw, little man. I'm not a hero." He winked and glanced skyward. "I'm a guardian angel. Just like my mother." He turned his gaze toward Cordray as he stood, holding her eyes with his. "I'm a guardian angel, bound to protect those I love and care about with the power my mother gave me." His heart swelled with happiness and pride as he gazed at her. "Until now, I thought my power was a curse, but now I see it was really a gift." He wrapped his hand around hers. "A gift meant to lead me to you, and I swear on my every heartbeat that I will protect you, your children—and ours—for as long as I live. You are my family now, and I will destroy anyone who tries to harm my family."

He'd come full circle, closing the last remaining door on his past.

He wasn't a freak. He was a protector. He'd been created to protect, not destroy.

As he turned and led Cordray and Null up the embankment, he swore he heard his mother's contented sigh on the breeze and felt her smile at his back.

But he knew if he looked, he would find nothing but burnished sunlight, shimmering water, and shadows.

I love you, Mother.

A refreshing breeze scented of jasmine was his only reply.

But it was enough.

Enough to know she was with him and always would be, in death as she had been in life.

Forever.

EPILOGUE

THE MOMENT HE HEARD THE KEY SLIP INTO THE LOCK, Micah raised his Sig and pointed it at the door. He'd been waiting in the shadows inside Ronan's rental home for nearly an hour. Silent. Deadly. Ready for answers and retribution, not necessarily in that order.

Ronan's silhouette slipped inside. He shut the door then fell still as he peered into the darkness, as if he knew he wasn't alone. Micah actually felt the air prickle with Ronan's sudden awareness.

Perceptive little fucker. Micah couldn't deny that a part of him was impressed with the little shit. He was resourceful and cunning, with strong instincts and keen senses. He reminded Micah of how he'd been when he was younger, and in any other circumstance, he would have considered recruiting Ronan. AKM needed talented enforcers, and Ronan clearly had talent. But this shit was personal, so yeah, there would be no sales pitch about how Ronan needed AKM as much as AKM needed him.

Without turning on the light, Ronan pulled a gun from the back waist of his pants and swung it around, prepared to fire.

Micah fired first, catching him in the shoulder.

Ronan staggered backward and slammed into the door.

"Welcome home, asshole." Micah rose from the chair he'd been sitting in and trained the gun's sight on the center of Ronan's forehead. This fucker had broken into his apartment, stolen his property, and toyed with him. Now he would pay the piper.

Ronan regrouped and started to bring his gun back around to attempt another shot.

"Don't even think about it" — Micah kicked the gun out of his hand — "or I'll blast a hole in your other shoulder so you won't even be able to hold your dick to take a piss. Because one way or another, asshole, you're going to answer my questions, return what belongs to me, and then — if you're lucky — I *might* let you live." He took a menacing step forward, gun trained between Ronan's eyes. "*If* you're lucky."

From the angry sneer that overtook Ronan's full lips and the way his thick, black eyebrows bunched over his nose, he didn't seem willing to cooperate. "Fuck you. I don't owe you *shit*."

"Wrong answer." Micah surged forward, fisted the collar of Ronan's shirt, hoisted him away from the door, and pressed the Sig's muzzle against the underside of his chin.

Contempt fumed from Ronan's gaze. "Go ahead. Kill me. Then you'll never know the truth."

"Oh yeah? And what truth is that? That your pecker is the size of a thumb drive?" Micah tried to burrow inside Ronan's head but saw nothing but black. A vast, empty darkness like what he'd come up against with Digon and that odd fucker, Rule. The black hole felt more like a vacuum of sight and sound than a wall. Ronan wasn't blocking Micah. Micah simply couldn't see inside his mind.

Ronan sneered then let out a mocking chuckle. "You still haven't figured it out, have you?"

Micah's hold cranked more tightly on Ronan's shirt. "You're really starting to piss me off, you little prick. Maybe I should just kill you now and count my losses." He applied pressure to the trigger.

"Go ahead then. What's stopping you?" Ronan's breath hissed through his teeth. "Kill me."

Micah had never seen such intense resentment and animosity in someone's eyes, not to mention indifference for one's own life.

"Do it! Kill me!" Ronan's jaw clenched as his breath came in tight, urgent bursts. "Your own *family*! Your own *brother*!"

Micah's finger abruptly released the trigger. What the fuck? Was he serious?

"You're lying."

"Am I?" The skin around Ronan's eyes pinched. "Then why can't you see inside my thoughts? You can't, can you? I know you can't. You know why? Because I'm your blood." He barked out a derisive laugh. "Big bad Micah Black." Sarcasm snapped over every syllable. "Mighty Micah, right? You, who can *do no wrong*. You can't see my thoughts because you're my godforsaken flesh and blood." He spat in Micah's face. "Lucky fucking me."

Micah let go of Ronan's shirt and wiped the spittle from his cheek then glared back at him. "No." The single syllable burned his throat like betrayal. "I'm the last. There are no others in my line."

But Ronan's declaration was enough to give him pause. Could it be true? The family resemblance was there. The black hair. The angular jaw. The lean, powerful build. Could he be . . .? No. Ronan couldn't be Micah's brother. That would mean . . .

Doubt sliced through his confidence. Maybe he had been wrong about his parents' deaths.

Ronan's mocking laughter rankled Micah's last nerve, and, in a rush of aggression, he swept forward and clocked him hard across the chin, tossing Ronan sideways.

"I don't believe you!"

Ronan recovered quickly and spun back around to face him, clutching his wounded shoulder. "Then kill me. What's stopping you?" His eyebrows dug a malicious trench over his eyes, casting a shadow over the bitterness burning from his blue-grey irises. "If you don't believe me, then kill me and end this."

Micah lifted the Sig, lined up the sight with Ronan's forehead, applied pressure to the trigger . . .

And froze.

He couldn't do it.

If there was even a chance Ronan was of his blood, he couldn't kill him.

He had to know the truth.

"How . . .?" He uttered the question more to himself than to Ronan. "How could this even be possible?" No scenario he came up with provided an answer.

Ronan let out a disgusted exhale. "All these years I've had to listen to stories about *Micah*" — he did his best to straighten his shoulders, given his injury — "the *greatest warrior* in the king's guard. The *prodigal son*! He who could *do no wrong*!" Ronan spat at his feet again then uttered a brittle laugh. "Why can't you be more like Micah?" he said mockingly, as if quoting someone. "Do you know how many times I heard that growing up? Do you? I half expected you to be a god when I came face to face with you, given all the buildup. But you're not a god. You're nothing special. You're — "

"That's enough, Ronan!" A shadow moved to Micah's right.

He whipped toward the movement, training his gun on the backlit silhouette that entered the room. A cold pit opened inside his stomach. He knew that shape. He knew that voice. He knew the energy coming off that male's body.

Micah's voice quivered with forced denial when he spoke. "Who are you?" But he already knew. With the certainty of the setting sun, he knew.

The tall male flicked on the light switch.

Micah blinked against the instant brightness then gasped as he laid eyes on a face he hadn't seen in over nine hundred years. Hair as black as coal. Eyes the color of midnight. It was like seeing a ghost. He staggered backward until the backs of his legs hit the couch, and he dropped onto it, unable to tear his gaze away.

This couldn't be happening. That male couldn't be his . . .

"Father?"

DID YOU ENJOY READING THIS BOOK?

If you did, please help others enjoy it, too:

Recommend it.

Review it at Amazon, iBooks, or Goodreads

If you leave a review, please send me an email at donya@donyalynne.com or message me on Facebook so that I can thank you with a personal e-mail.

Find out what happens next in BLACK, the next book in the AKM Worlds saga, available now for preorder on iBooks. Follow Donya on Facebook or **www.donyalynne.com** *for updates.*

BOUND GUARDIAN ANGEL
READER GROUP GUIDE

1. During Sam and Cordray's first conversation, Sam calls Trace a gentle soul. Why do you think she said that about him? Would you agree? What have you seen of Trace in this and previous books that causes you to think the way you do?

2. A lot was made of fear as being "the great motivator" in this book. Sam even says that fear makes a treacherous ally. What do you think she meant by that? Where and how did you see fear influencing the characters' decisions. Are there situations in your own life where you've allowed fear to dictate your decisions? What ways do you think someone can overcome their fear?

3. Trace, Cordray, Micah, and Sam are all alike in many ways. Sometimes, these similarities allow them to understand one another and find common ground, such as how Sam did with Cordray when they first meet. At other times, these similarities create friction and prevent the characters from getting along, such as between Micah and Cordray. Sam even says she thinks she likes them both so much because they are so alike and that they don't like each other because no one likes seeing their faults reflected back to them from others. What do you think she meant by that? What types of similarities do you think draw people to one another? What types push people apart? In the case of Sam, Micah, Trace, and Cordray, what characteristics and traits create bonds between 1) Sam & Micah, 2) Sam & Trace, 3) Micah & Trace, 4) Trace & Cordray, and 5) Sam & Cordray. What similar characteristics and traits create discord between 1) Micah & Cordray, and 2) Trace & Cordray?

4. Trace mentions he lives in a small trailer. Why do you think he hasn't shown his home to Micah and Sam? What about living in a trailer suits his personality? What about it doesn't suit his personality? Now that he's mated, what do you think will become of his trailer? Why did he even live there in the first place?

5. Speaking of Trace's home, Cordray tells Sam at the end of chapter

five that Trace's home is there, in the home she shares with Micah. What do you think she meant by that? What does home mean to you?

6. What do you make of Micah and Trace's relationship? Micah tells Trace he will never fuck him, and yet he gave him an orgasm. He kissed him. He behaved toward Trace as though they were lovers. And yet he took his physical needs to Sam rather than expended them with Trace. Do you think this will be enough for them both, especially now that Trace has mated Cordray? How do you think their D/s relationship will affect their relationships with Sam and Cordray? How do you think Sam and Cordray will react to Micah and Trace's ongoing need to spend time together in Micah's dungeon? What would you like to see happen for these four as their relationships with one another grow and evolve?

7. There are a lot of "awakenings" in this book. Cordray awakens from her past. Brak awakens from his imprisonment. Trace awakens from his guilt. Even Micah awakens as he learns that he's not the last of his bloodline. Can you draw parallels from the characters to the real world? How do we close our eyes to the magic and wonders of the world around us? What do you think causes us to "fall asleep" to life and not see its wonders? Going back to the question about fear, how do we let our fears keep us from experiencing life?

8. Brak was imprisoned for almost 200 years and missed out on so much. Now he's beginning to understand just how much. What would you miss the most if you weren't able to live freely, anymore? If you were immortal, how would you feel after being freed a hundred years later? How do you think the world will have changed? Would you be scared of what faced you or excited about the possibilities?

9. When Trace and Cordray finally consummate their relationship, Cordray acknowledges that Trace has brought her back to life. She says, "With Trace, she was alive." Beyond the loss of her sense of touch, in what ways was she dead before? Do you think we rely too much on others for our lives to be complete? Do you think we put too much weight on others' influence on our lives? Can such influence be healthy as well as crippling? Why or why not?

10. Cordray has a tattoo of a dragon holding a rose on her torso. Trace immediately understands the symbolism of the rose: Beauty and perfection come with the threat of pain. How do you equate this idea to Cordray? How do you think we embody this idea in the real world?

ABOUT THE AUTHOR

Donya Lynne is the bestselling author of the award winning All the King's Men Series and a member of Romance Writers of America. Making her home in a wooded suburb north of Indianapolis with her husband, Donya has lived in Indiana most of her life and knew at a young age that she was destined to be a writer. She started writing poetry in grade school and won her first short story contest in fourth grade. In junior high, she began writing romantic stories for her friends, and by her sophomore year, she'd been dubbed *Most Likely to Become a Romance Novelist.* In 2012, she made that dream come true by publishing her first two novels and a novella. Her work has earned her two IPPYs (one gold, one silver) and two eLit Awards (one gold, one silver) as well as numerous accolades. When she's not writing, she can be found cheering on the Indianapolis Colts or doing her cats' bidding.

For more information on Donya's books or just to say hello, visit her on Facebook or swing by her website.

www.facebook.com/DonyaLynne

www.donyalynne.com